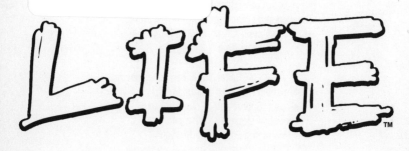

Volume 8

Created by
Keiko Suenobu

TOKYOPOP®

HAMBURG // LONDON // LOS ANGELES // TOKYO

LIFE Volume 8
Created by Keiko Suenobu

Translation - Michelle Kobayashi
English Adaptation - Darcy Lockman
Copy Editor - Shannon Watters
Retouch and Lettering - Star Print Brokers
Production Artist - Lauren O'Connell
Graphic Designer - James Lee

Editor - Stephanie Duchin
Digital Imaging Manager - Chris Buford
Pre-Production Supervisor - Erika Terriquez
Production Manager - Elisabeth Brizzi
Managing Editor - Vy Nguyen
Creative Director - Anne Marie Horne
Editor-in-Chief - Rob Tokar
Publisher - Mike Kiley
President and C.O.O. - John Parker
C.E.O. and Chief Creative Officer - Stuart Levy

A  Manga

TOKYOPOP Inc.
5900 Wilshire Blvd. Suite 2000
Los Angeles, CA 90036

E-mail: info@TOKYOPOP.com
Come visit us online at www.TOKYOPOP.com

ISBN: 978-1-59816-195-3

First TOKYOPOP printing: March 2008

10 9 8 7 6 5 4 3 2 1

Printed in the USA

ライフ

8

Life

CONTENTS

8

Life

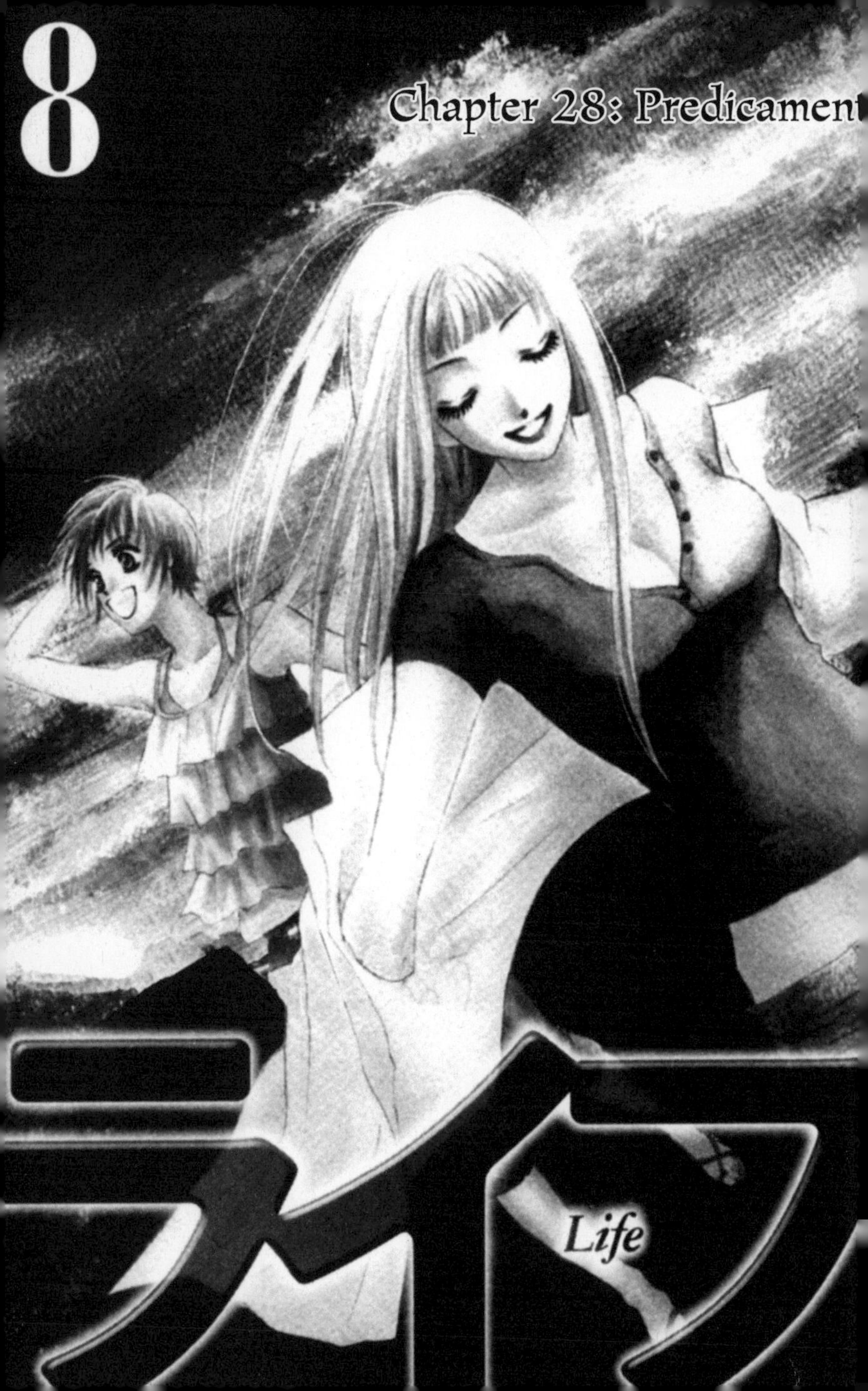
8
Chapter 28: Predicament
ライフ
Life

ライフ
Life

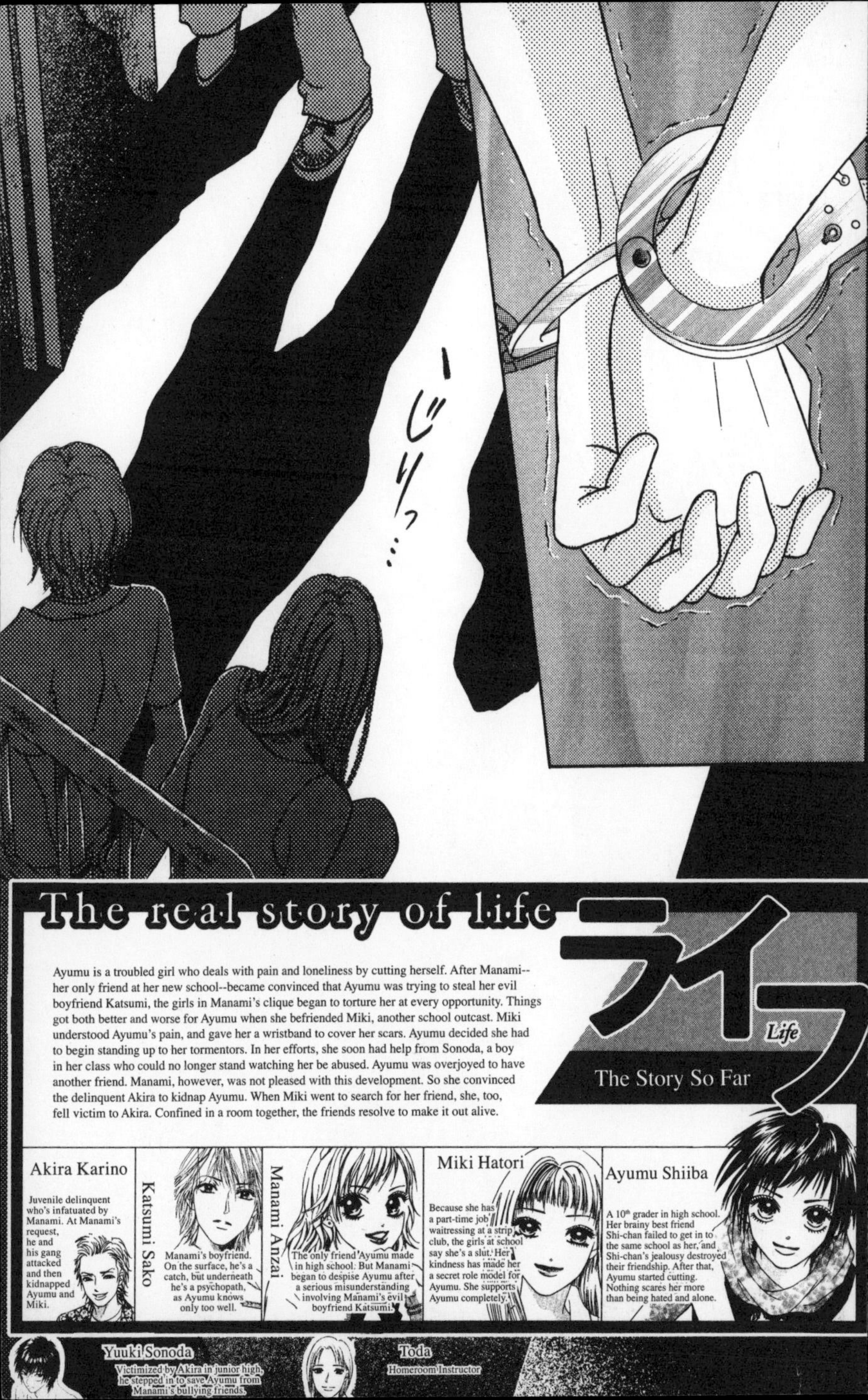
じりっ…

The real story of life

ライフ Life

The Story So Far

Ayumu is a troubled girl who deals with pain and loneliness by cutting herself. After Manami--her only friend at her new school--became convinced that Ayumu was trying to steal her evil boyfriend Katsumi, the girls in Manami's clique began to torture her at every opportunity. Things got both better and worse for Ayumu when she befriended Miki, another school outcast. Miki understood Ayumu's pain, and gave her a wristband to cover her scars. Ayumu decided she had to begin standing up to her tormentors. In her efforts, she soon had help from Sonoda, a boy in her class who could no longer stand watching her be abused. Ayumu was overjoyed to have another friend. Manami, however, was not pleased with this development. So she convinced the delinquent Akira to kidnap Ayumu. When Miki went to search for her friend, she, too, fell victim to Akira. Confined in a room together, the friends resolve to make it out alive.

Ayumu Shiiba
A 10th grader in high school. Her brainy best friend Shi-chan failed to get in to the same school as her, and Shi-chan's jealousy destroyed their friendship. After that, Ayumu started cutting. Nothing scares her more than being hated and alone.

Miki Hatori
Because she has a part-time job waitressing at a strip club, the girls at school say she's a slut. Her kindness has made her a secret role model for Ayumu. She supports Ayumu completely.

Manami Anzai
The only friend Ayumu made in high school. But Manami began to despise Ayumu after a serious misunderstanding involving Manami's evil boyfriend Katsumi.

Katsumi Sako
Manami's boyfriend. On the surface, he's a catch, but underneath he's a psychopath, as Ayumu knows only too well.

Akira Karino
Juvenile delinquent who's infatuated by Manami. At Manami's request, he and his gang attacked and then kidnapped Ayumu and Miki.

Yuuki Sonoda
Victimized by Akira in junior high, he stepped in to save Ayumu from Manami's bullying friends.

Toda
Homeroom Instructor

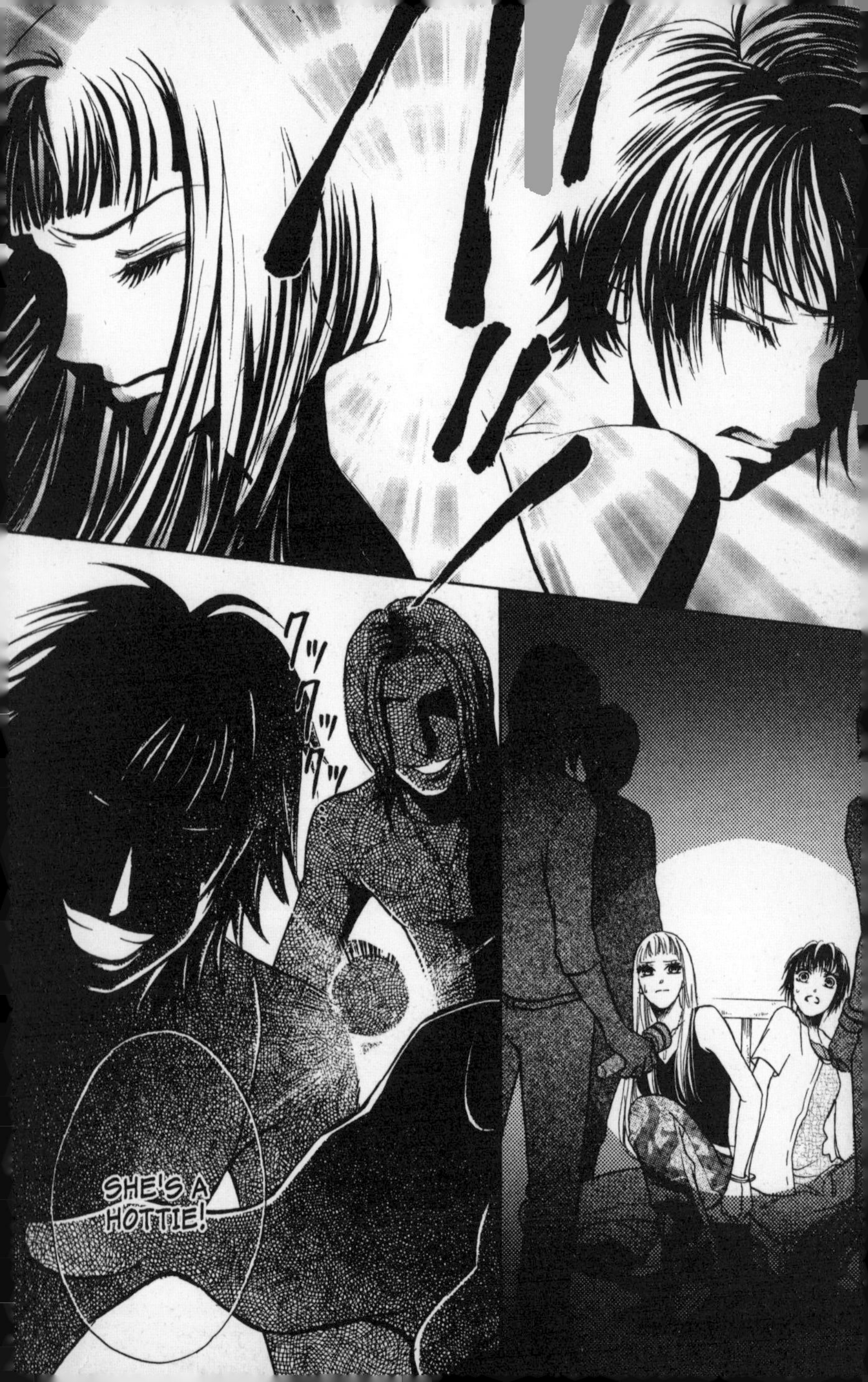
SHE'S A HOTTIE!

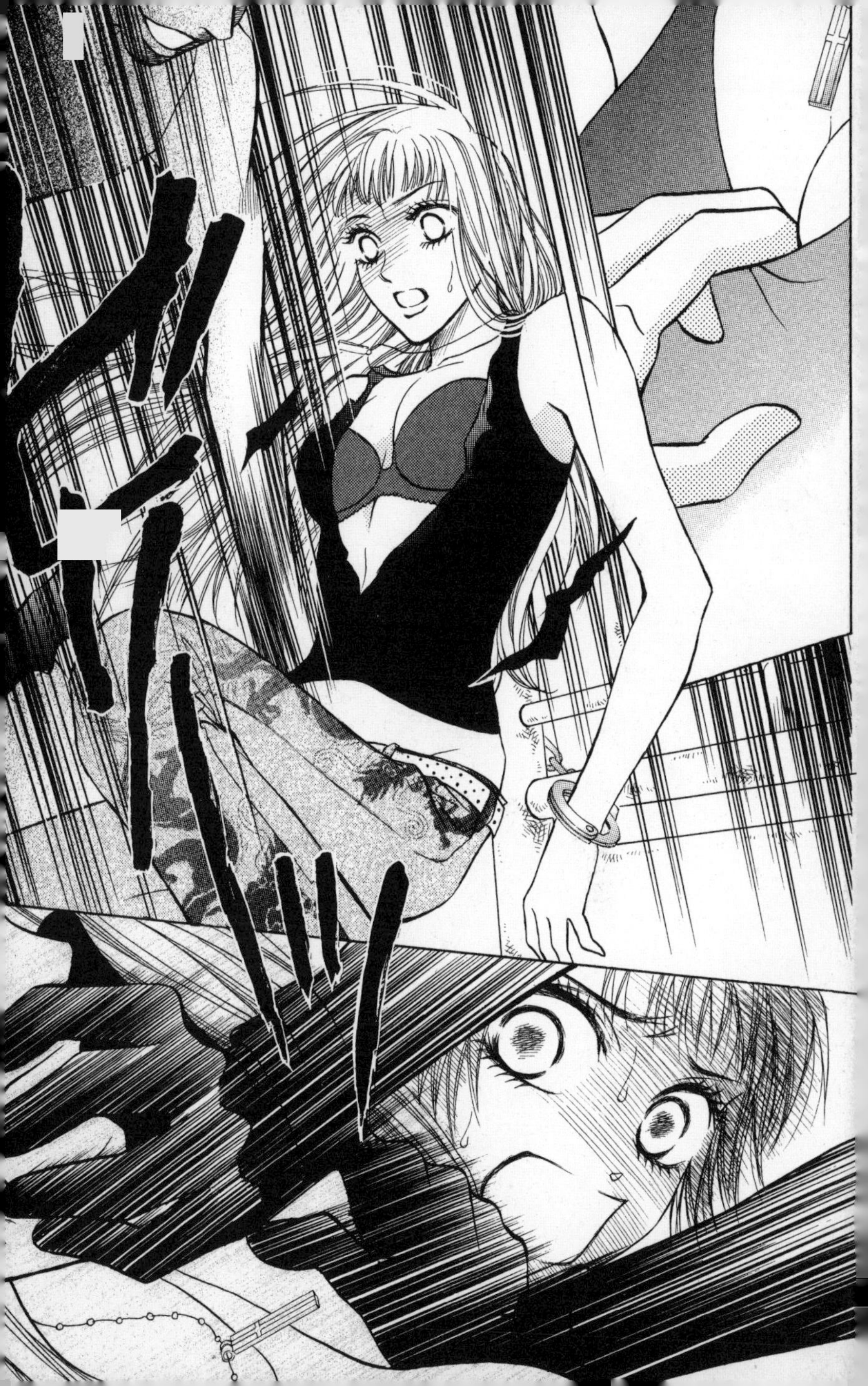

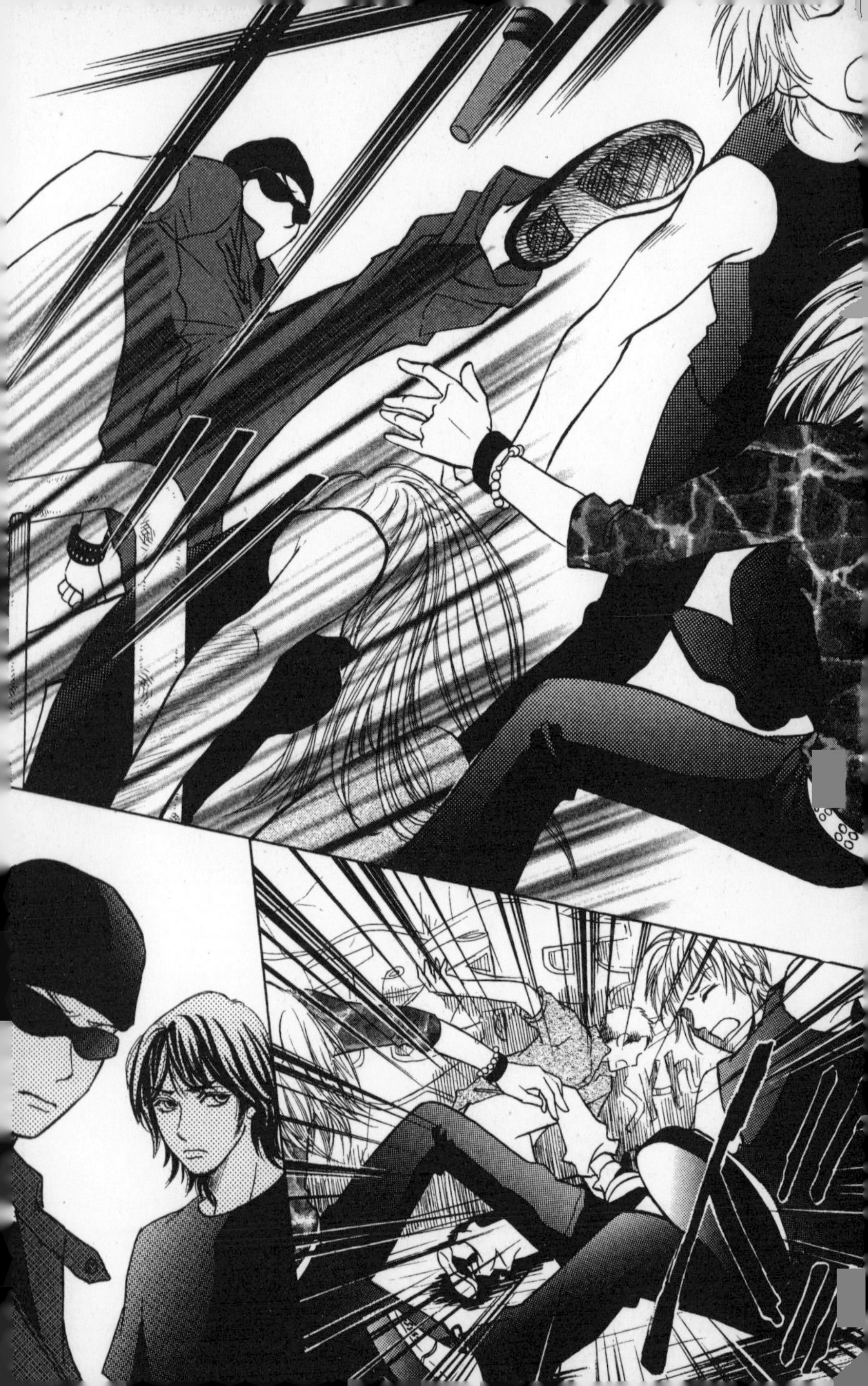

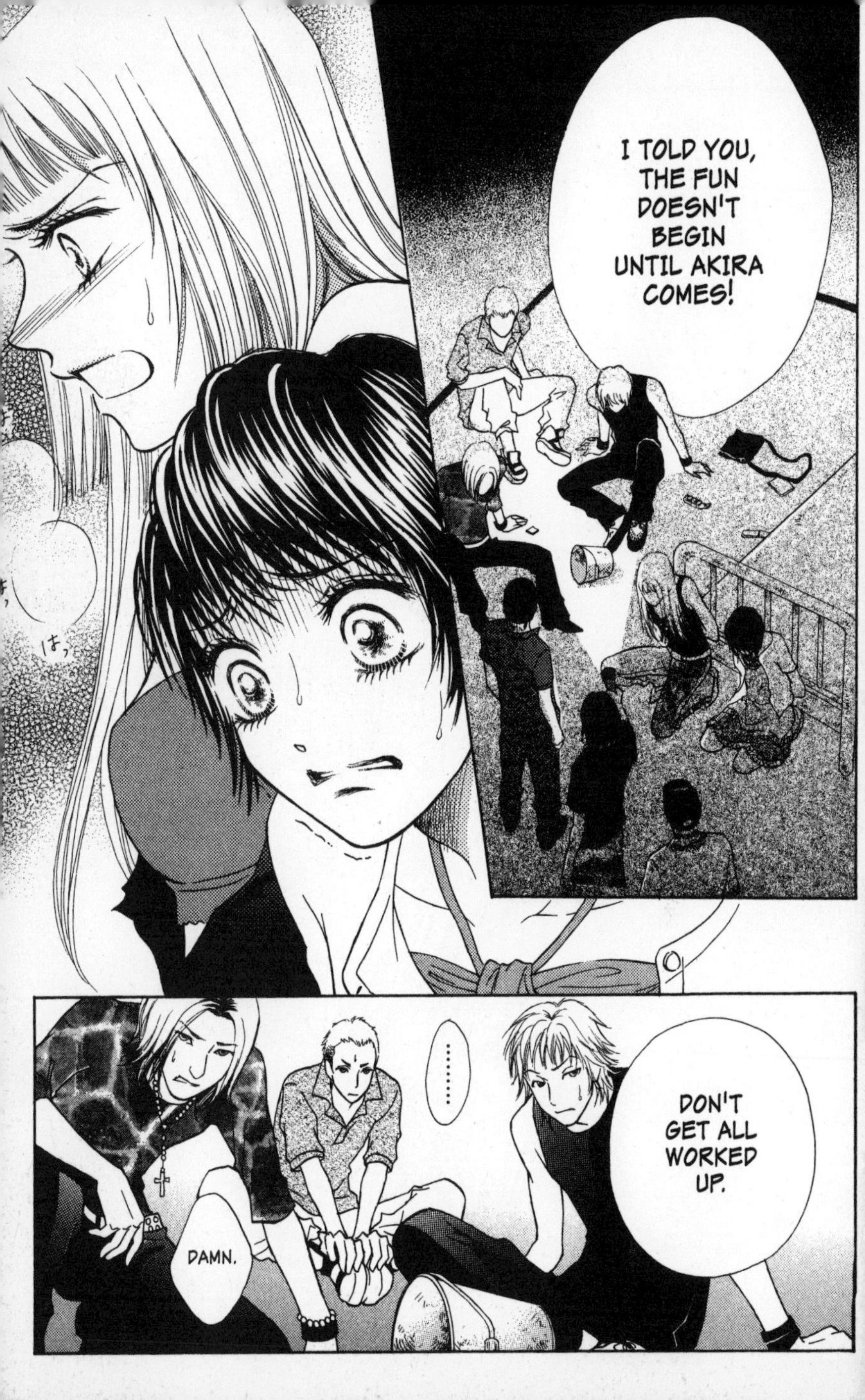
I TOLD YOU, THE FUN DOESN'T BEGIN UNTIL AKIRA COMES!
DON'T GET ALL WORKED UP.
......
DAMN.

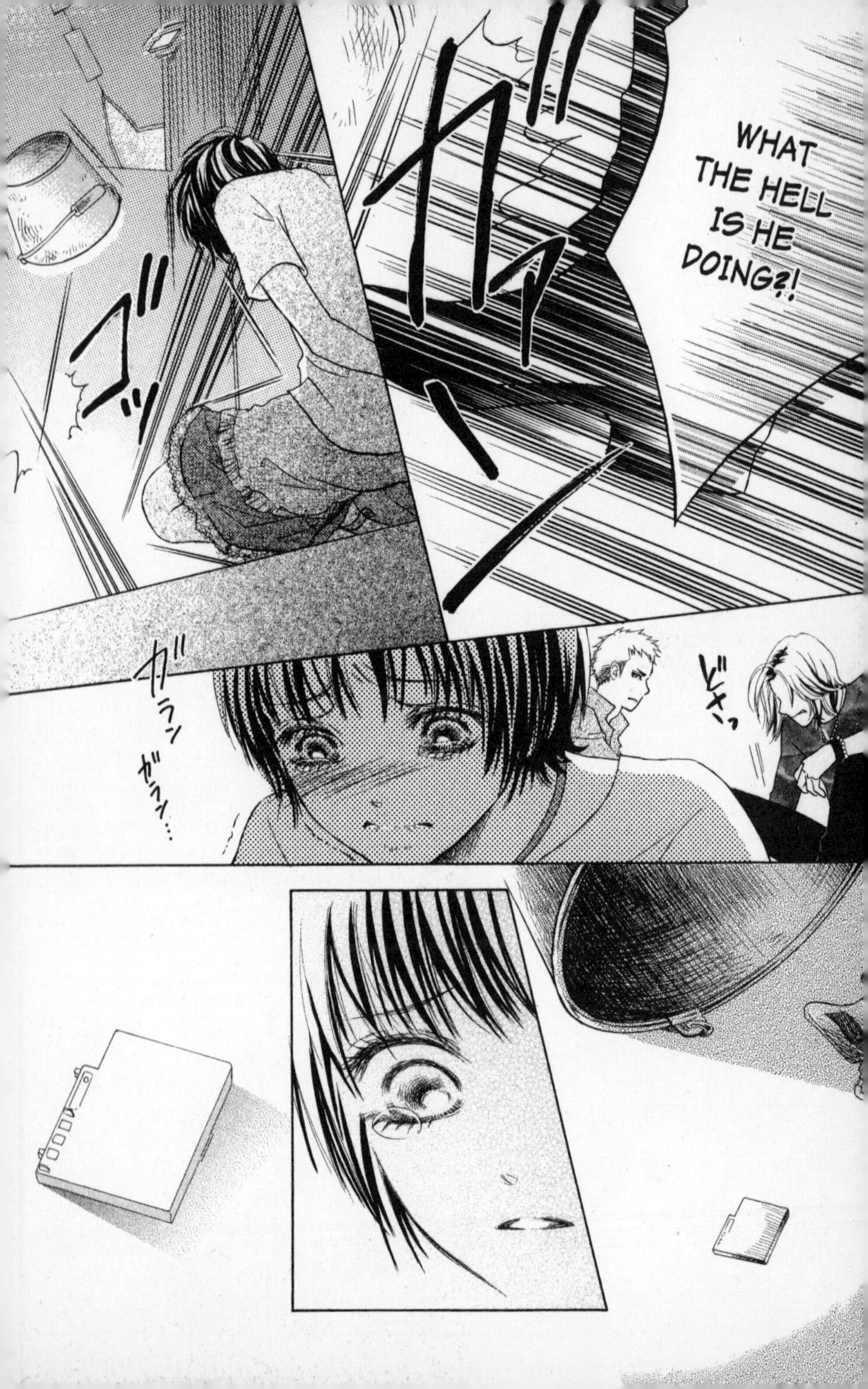
WHAT THE HELL IS HE DOING?!

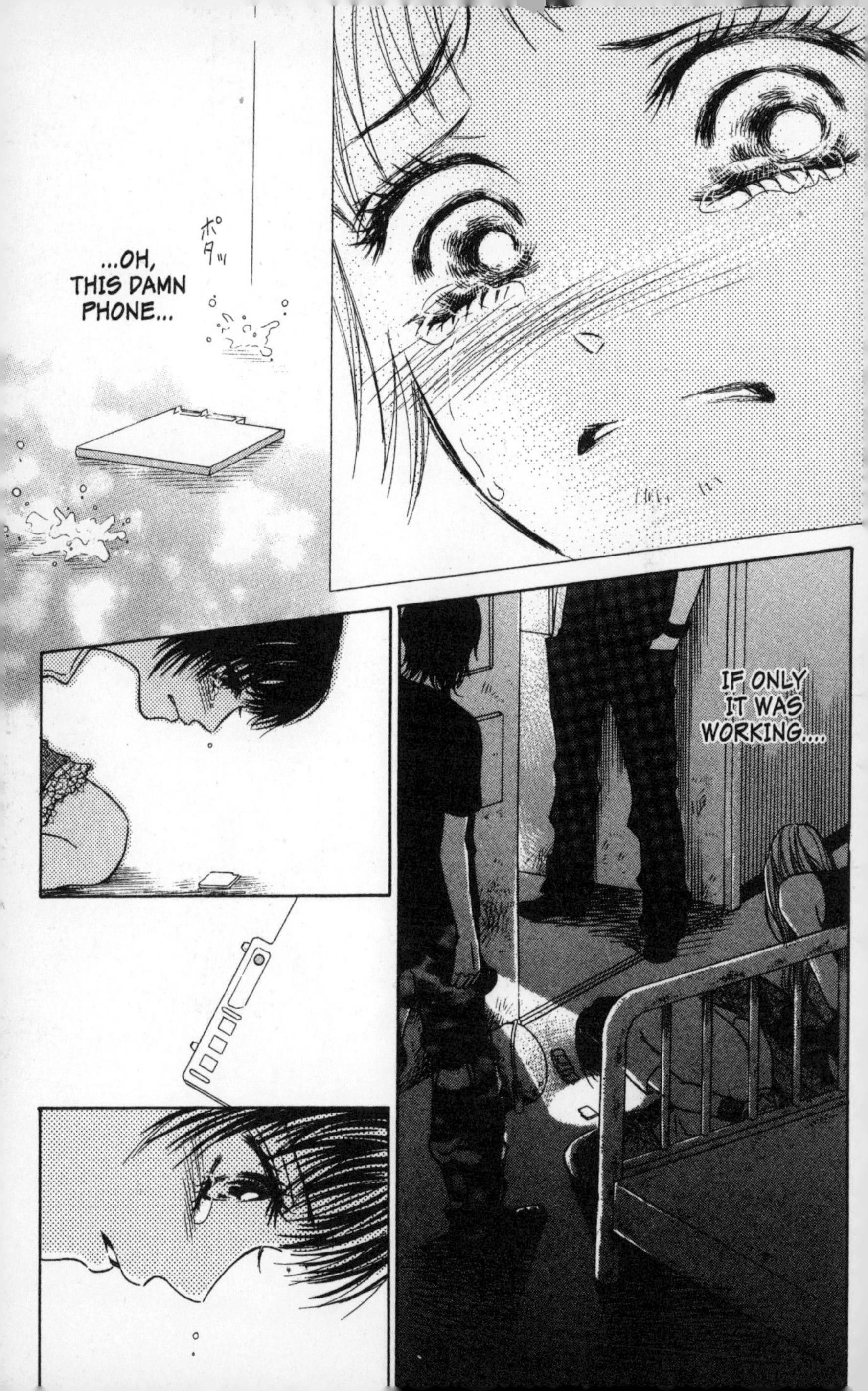
ポタッ
...OH, THIS DAMN PHONE...
IF ONLY IT WAS WORKING....

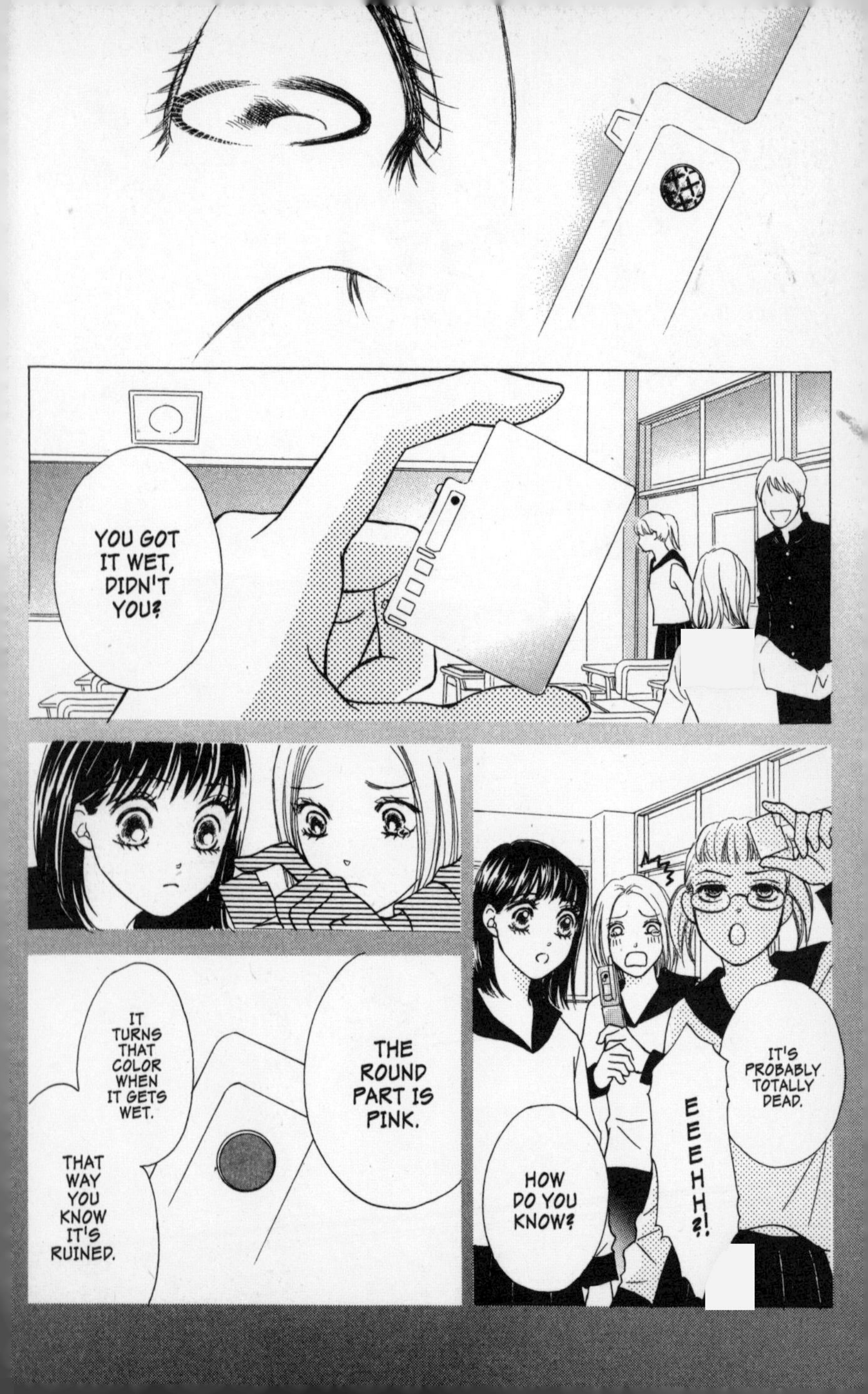
YOU GOT IT WET, DIDN'T YOU?
IT'S PROBABLY TOTALLY DEAD.
EEEHH?!
HOW DO YOU KNOW?
THE ROUND PART IS PINK.
IT TURNS THAT COLOR WHEN IT GETS WET.
THAT WAY YOU KNOW IT'S RUINED.

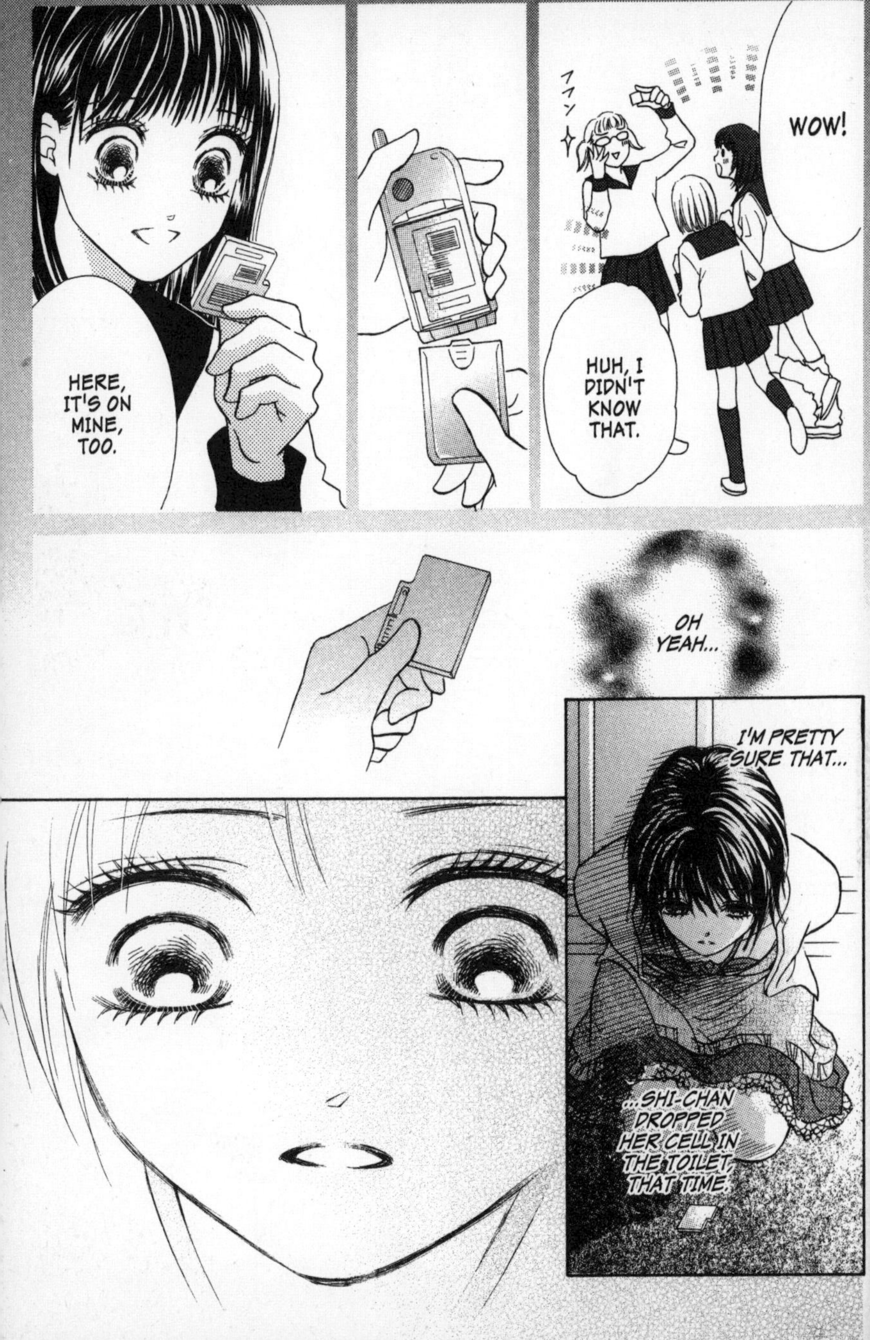
WOW!
HUH, I DIDN'T KNOW THAT.
HERE, IT'S ON MINE, TOO.
OH YEAH...
I'M PRETTY SURE THAT...
...SHI-CHAN DROPPED HER CELL IN THE TOILET THAT TIME.

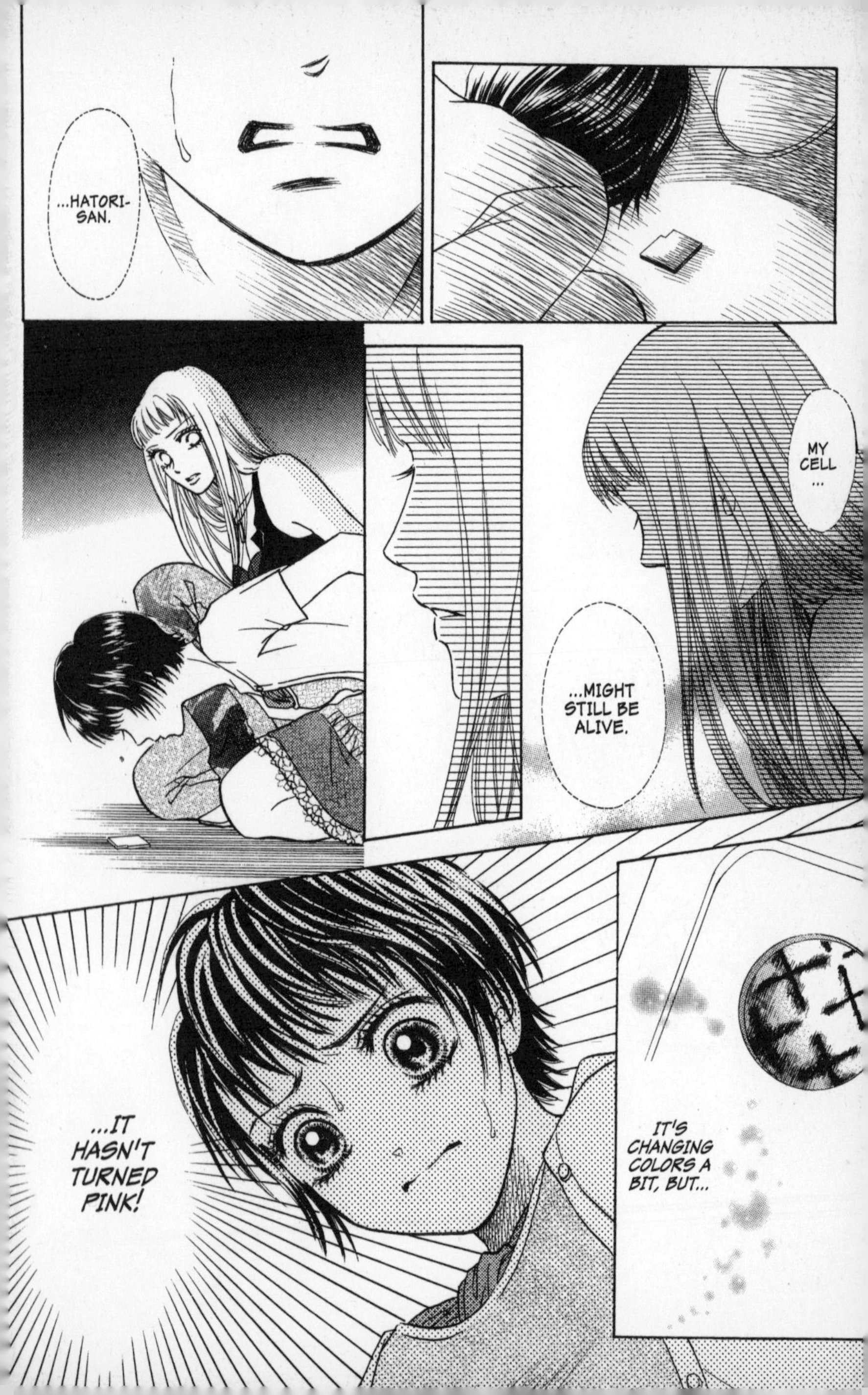
...HATORI-SAN.
MY CELL ...
...MIGHT STILL BE ALIVE.
IT'S CHANGING COLORS A BIT, BUT...
...IT HASN'T TURNED PINK!

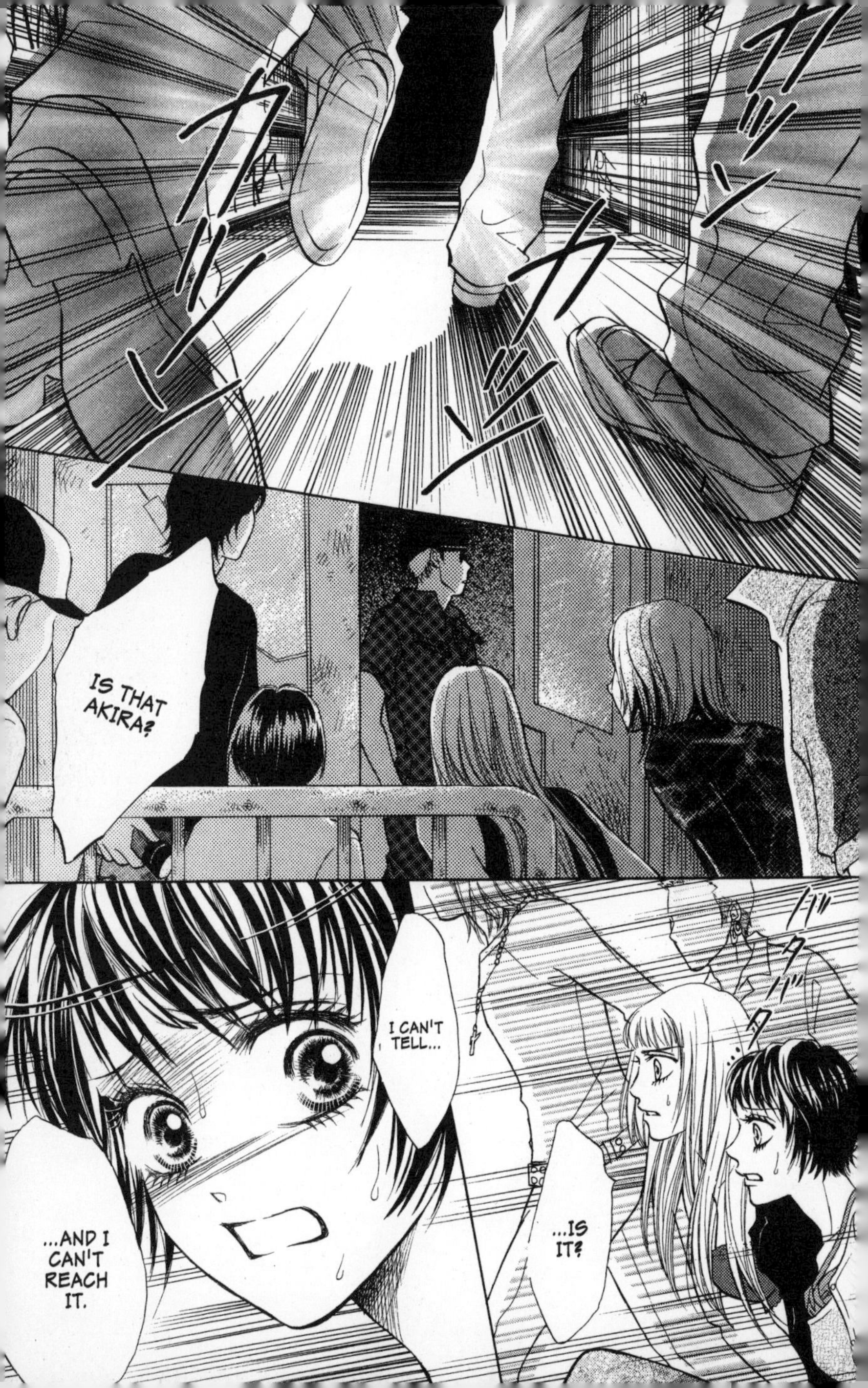
IS THAT AKIRA?
I CAN'T TELL...
...IS IT?
...AND I CAN'T REACH IT.

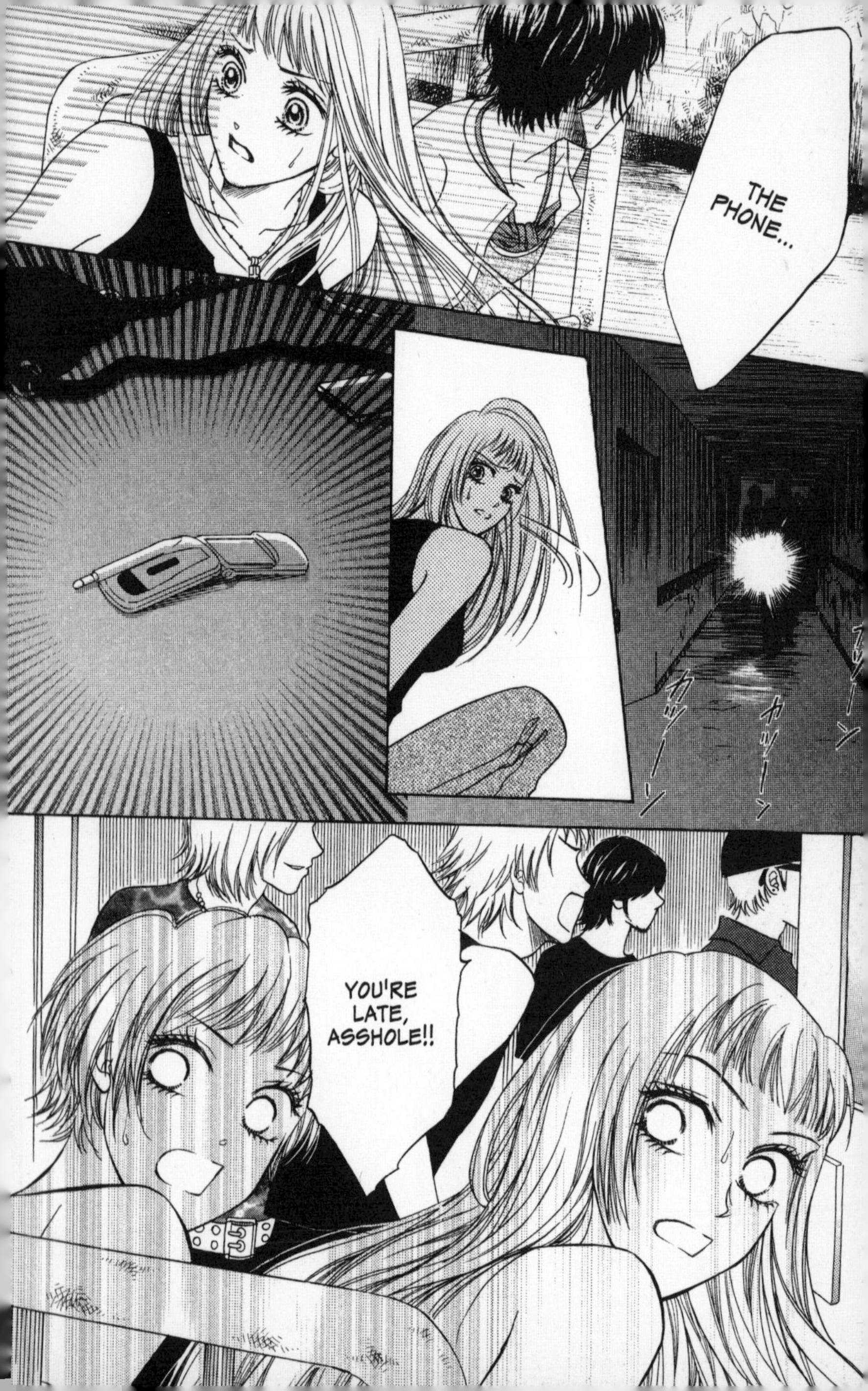
THE PHONE...
YOU'RE LATE, ASSHOLE!!

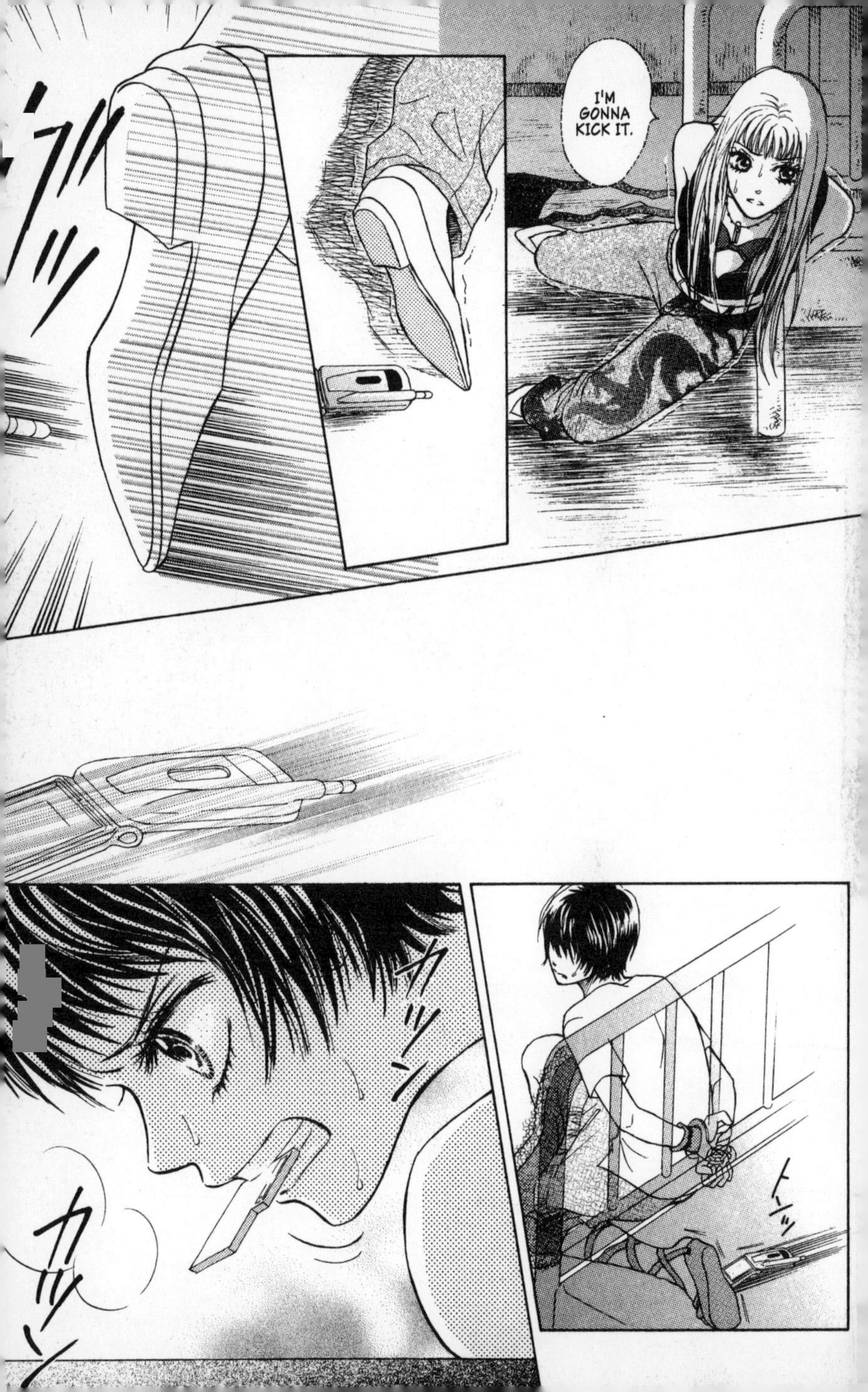
I'M GONNA KICK IT.

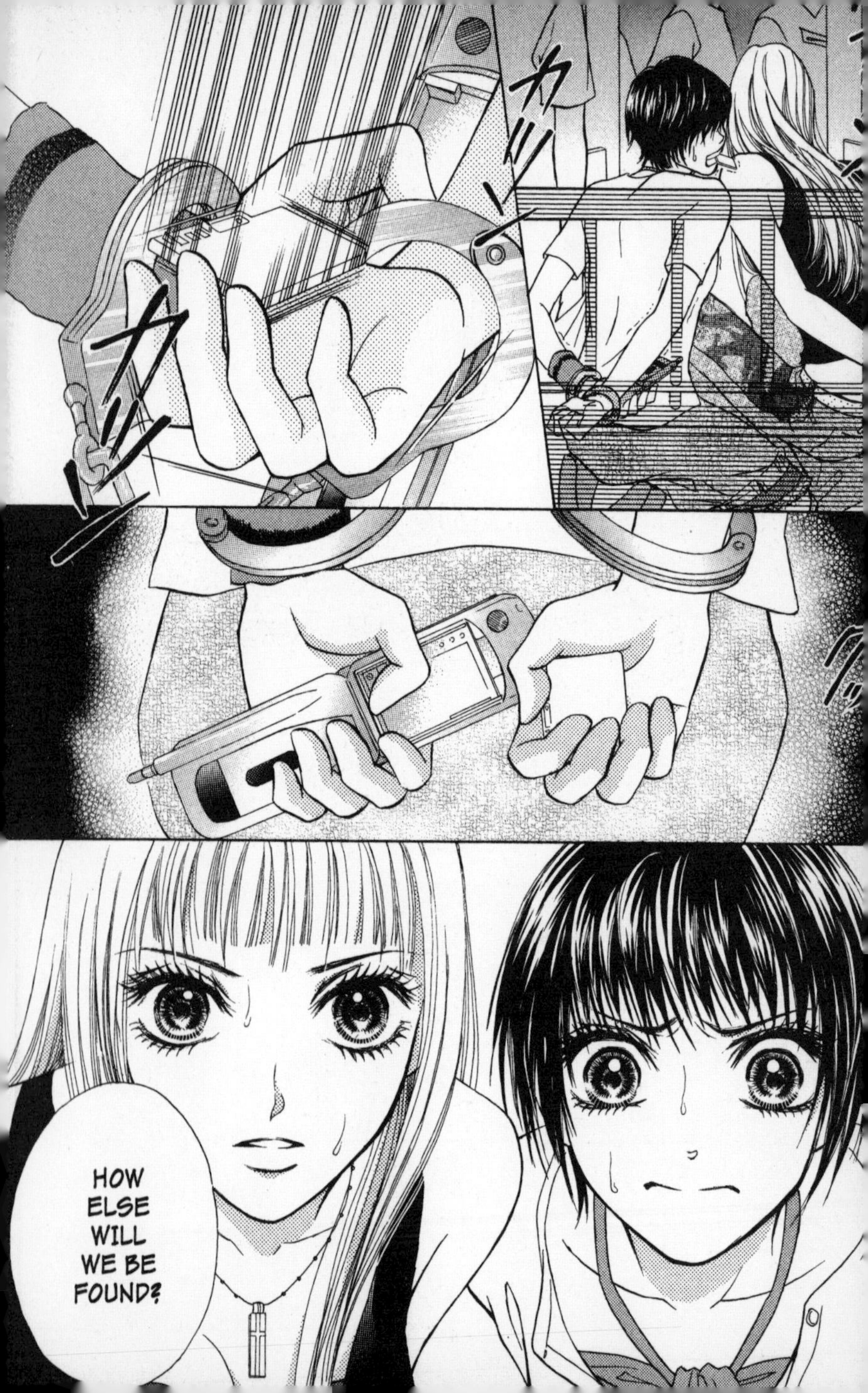
HOW ELSE WILL WE BE FOUND?

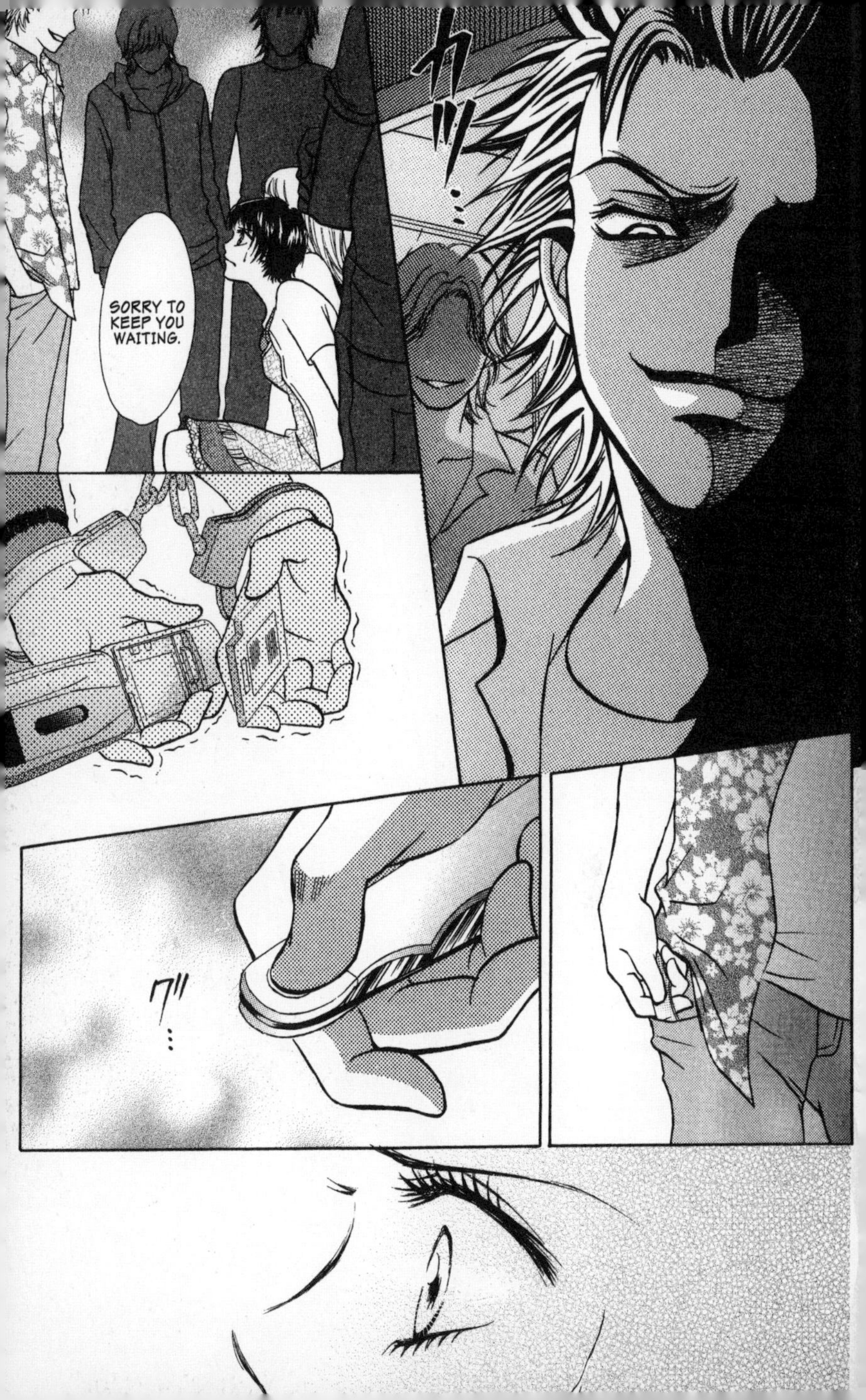
SORRY TO KEEP YOU WAITING.

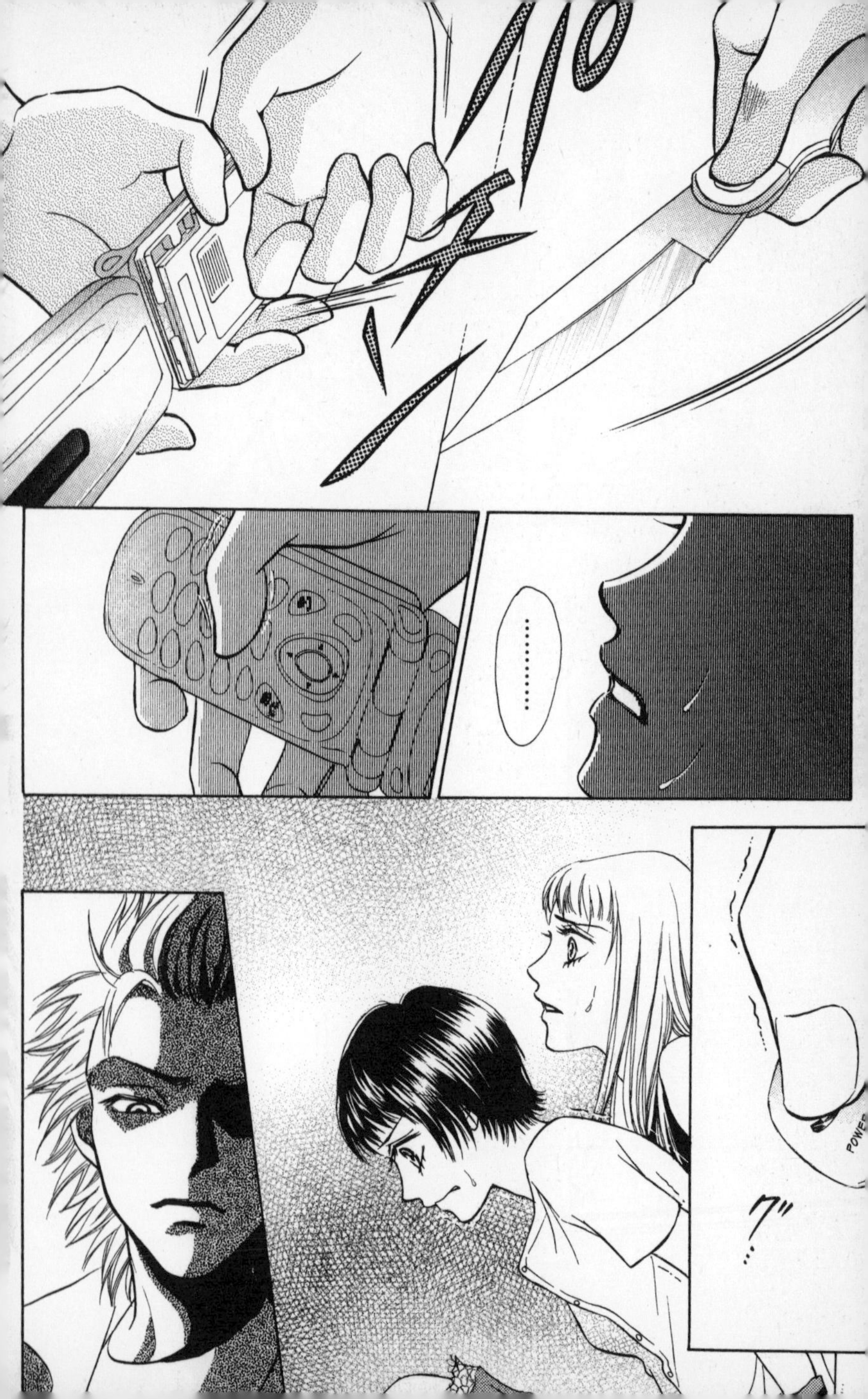
……
POWER

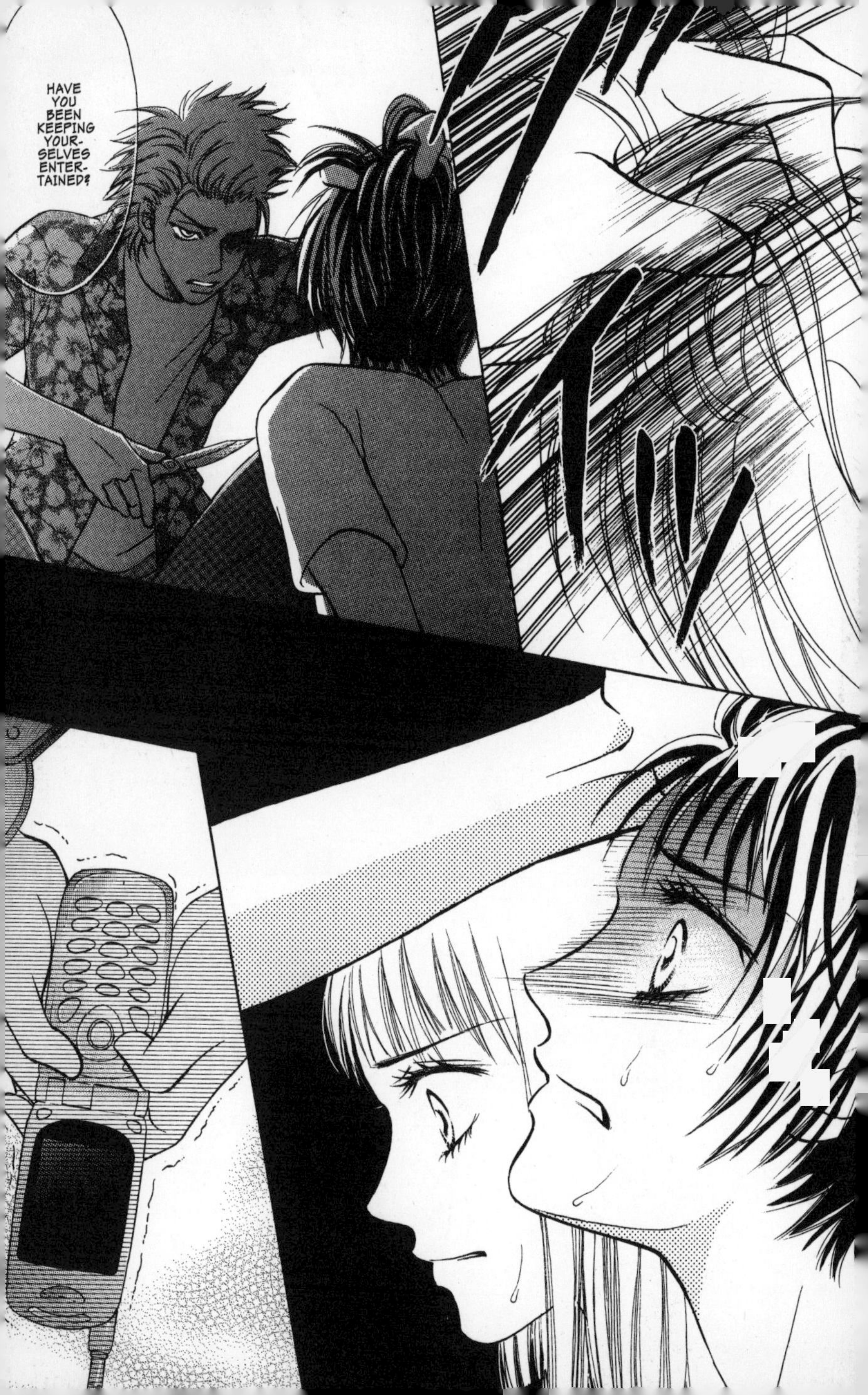
HAVE YOU BEEN KEEPING YOUR-SELVES ENTER-TAINED?

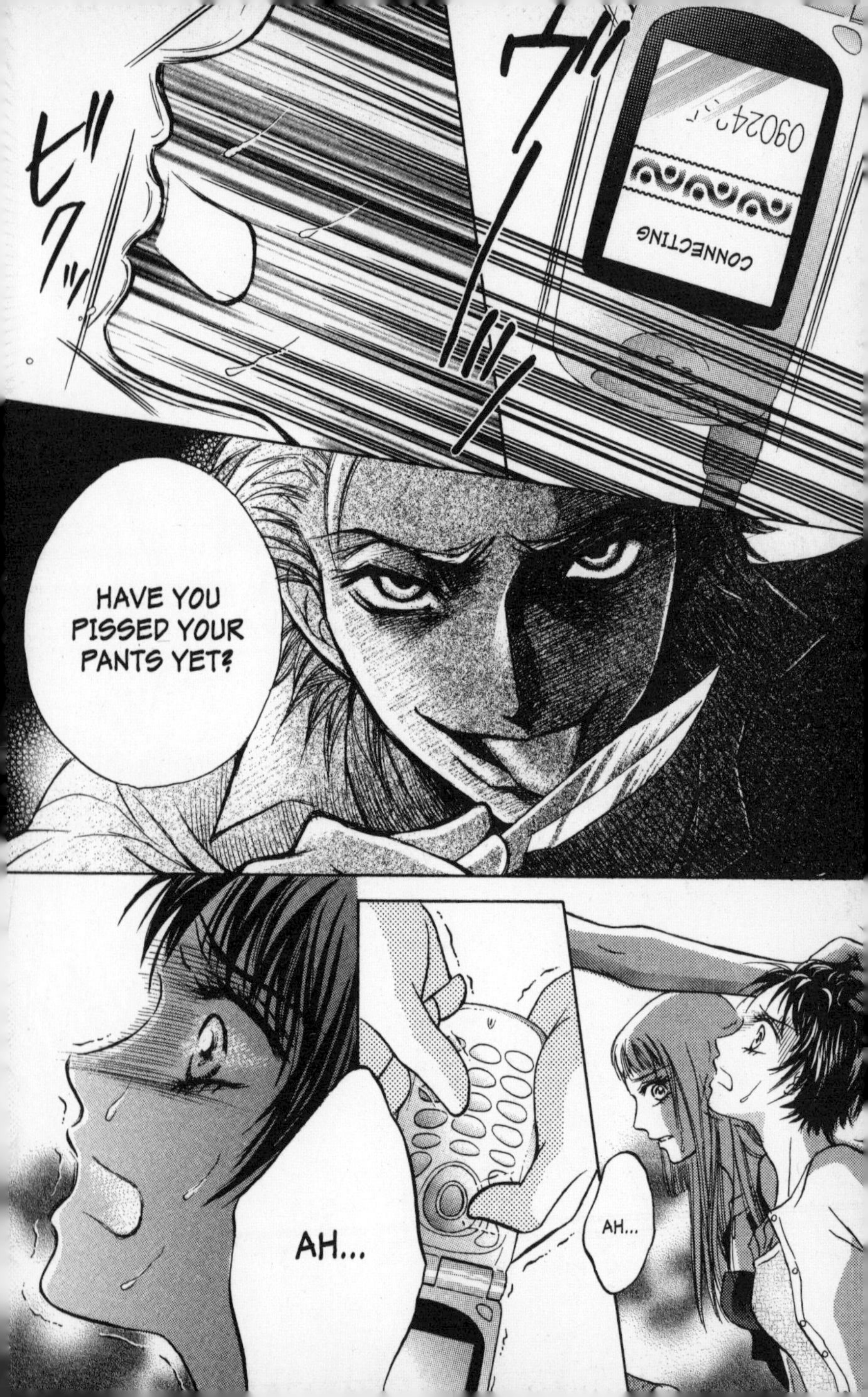
CONNECTING
09024
HAVE YOU PISSED YOUR PANTS YET?
AH...
AH...

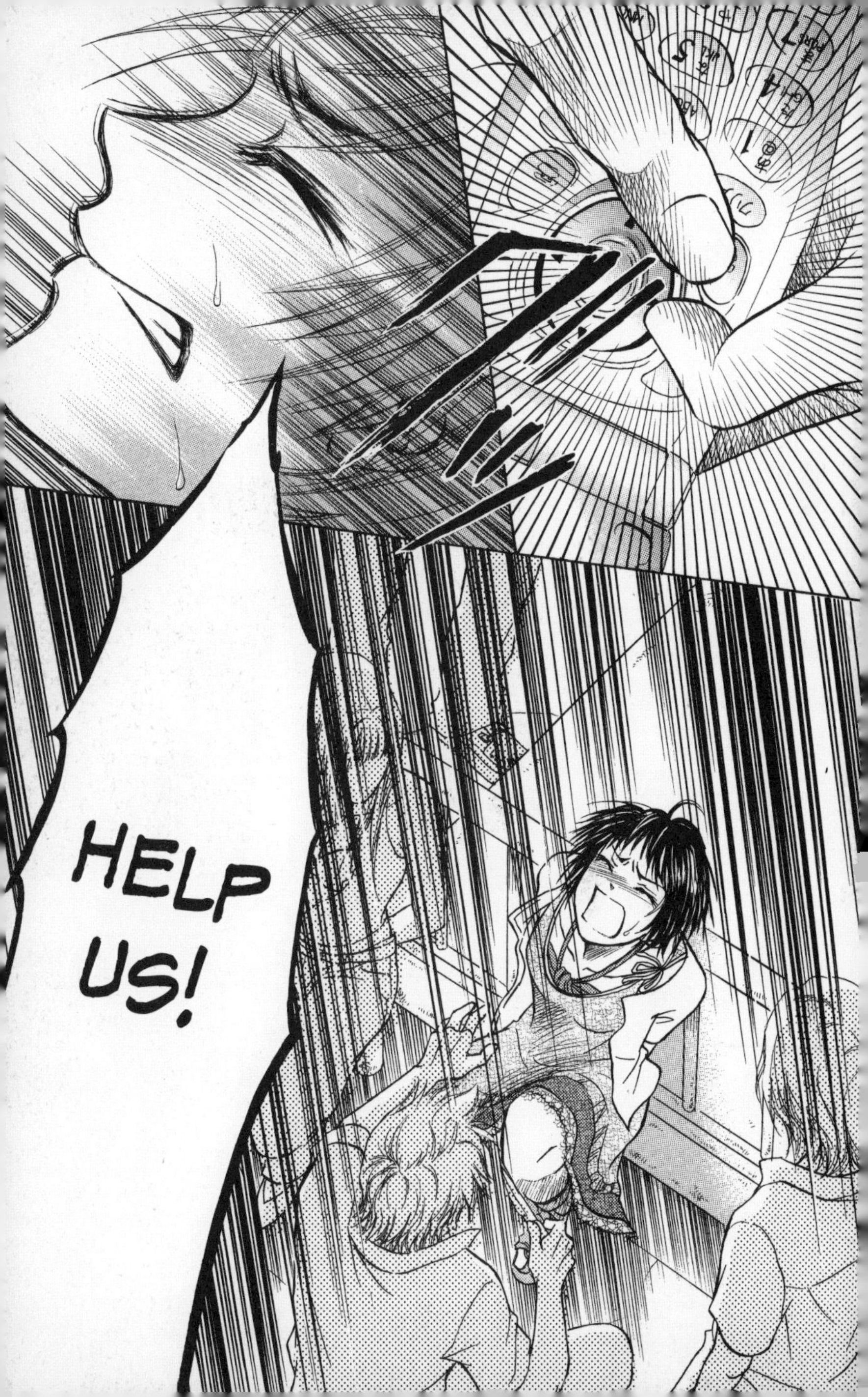
HELP US!

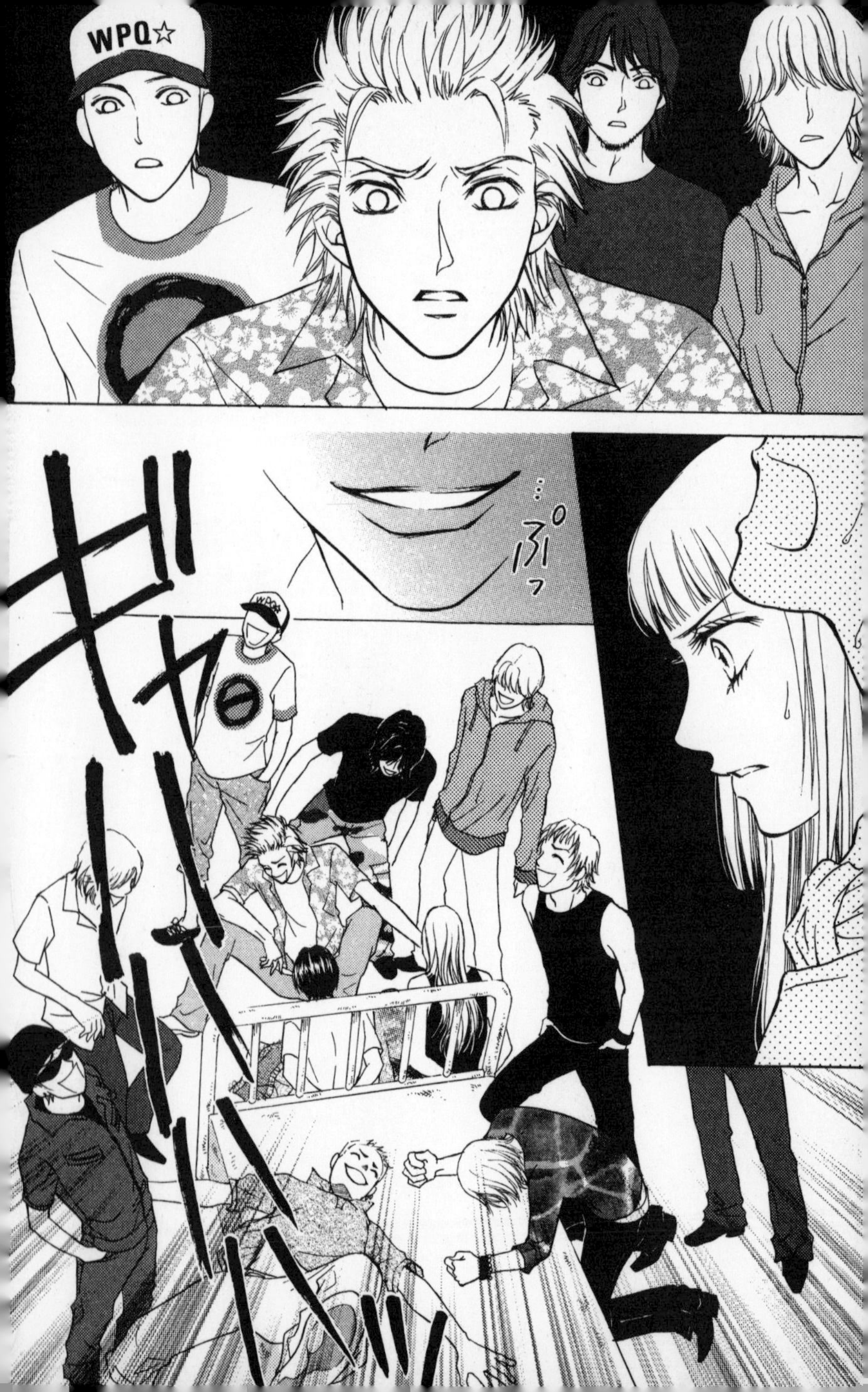
WPQ☆
…ぷっ
ギャ

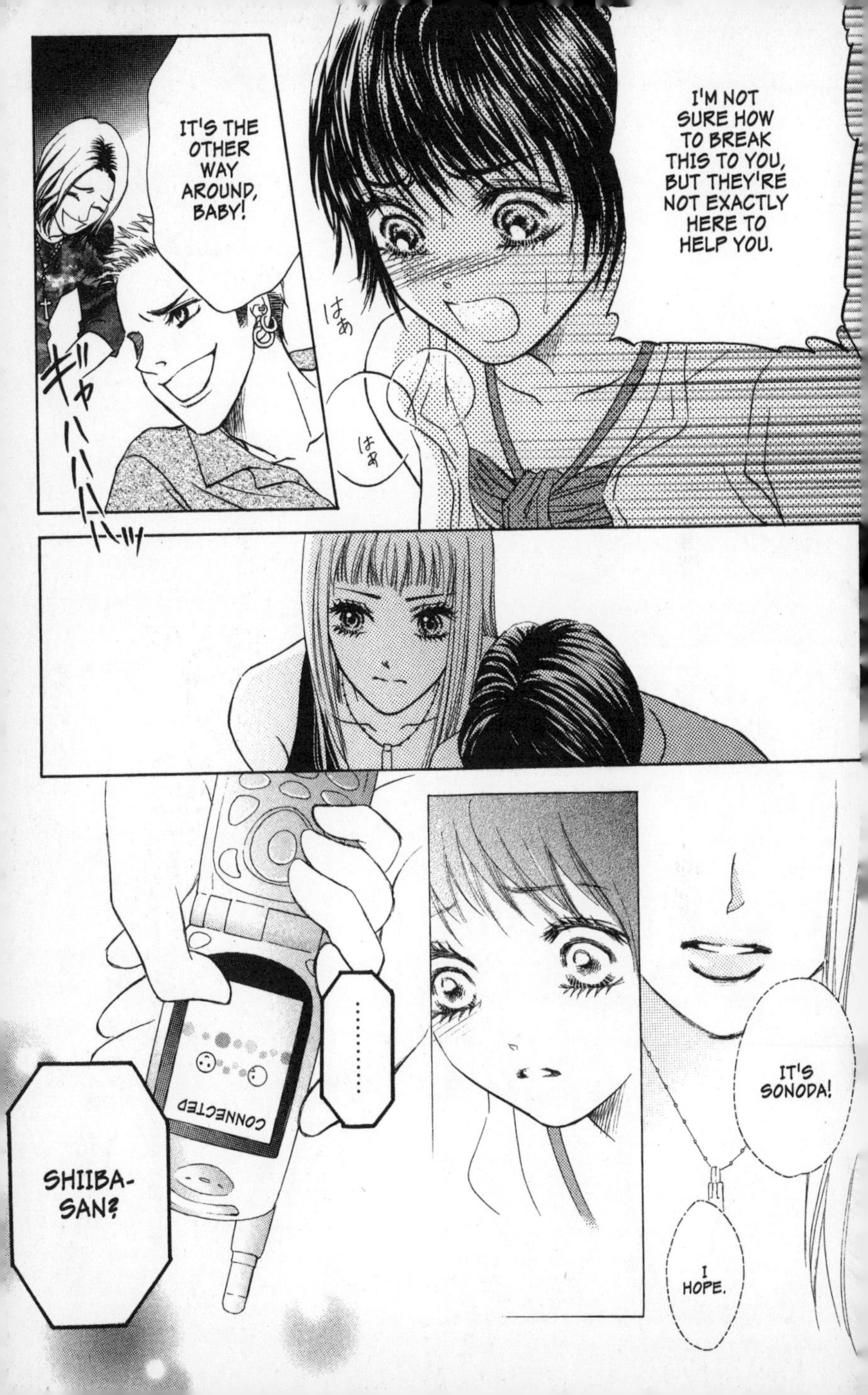
I'M NOT SURE HOW TO BREAK THIS TO YOU, BUT THEY'RE NOT EXACTLY HERE TO HELP YOU.
はぁ
はぁ
IT'S THE OTHER WAY AROUND, BABY!
ギャハハハハーッ
IT'S SONODA!
I HOPE.
......
CONNECTED
SHIIBA-SAN?

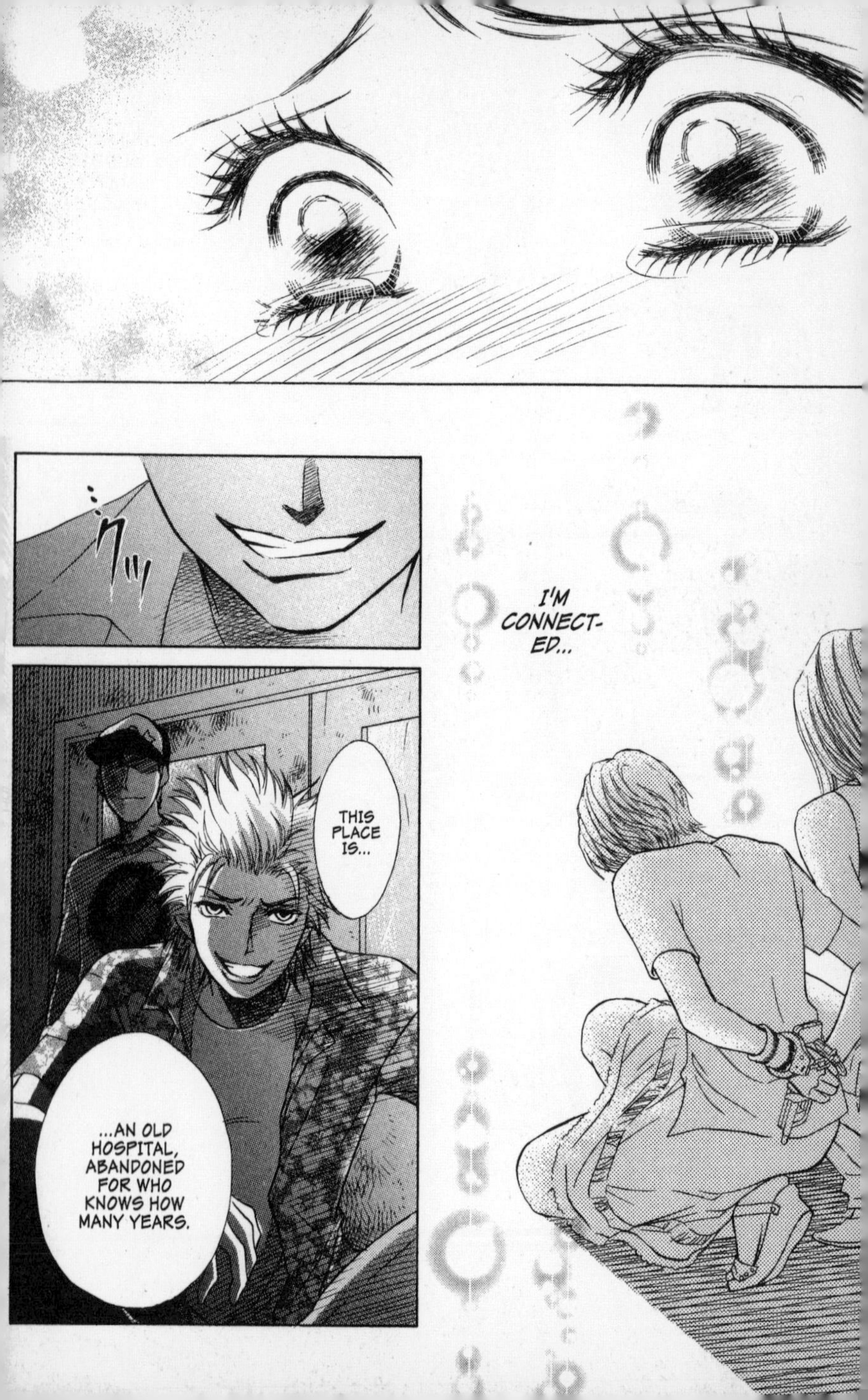
I'M CONNECT-ED...
クッ
THIS PLACE IS...
...AN OLD HOSPITAL, ABANDONED FOR WHO KNOWS HOW MANY YEARS.

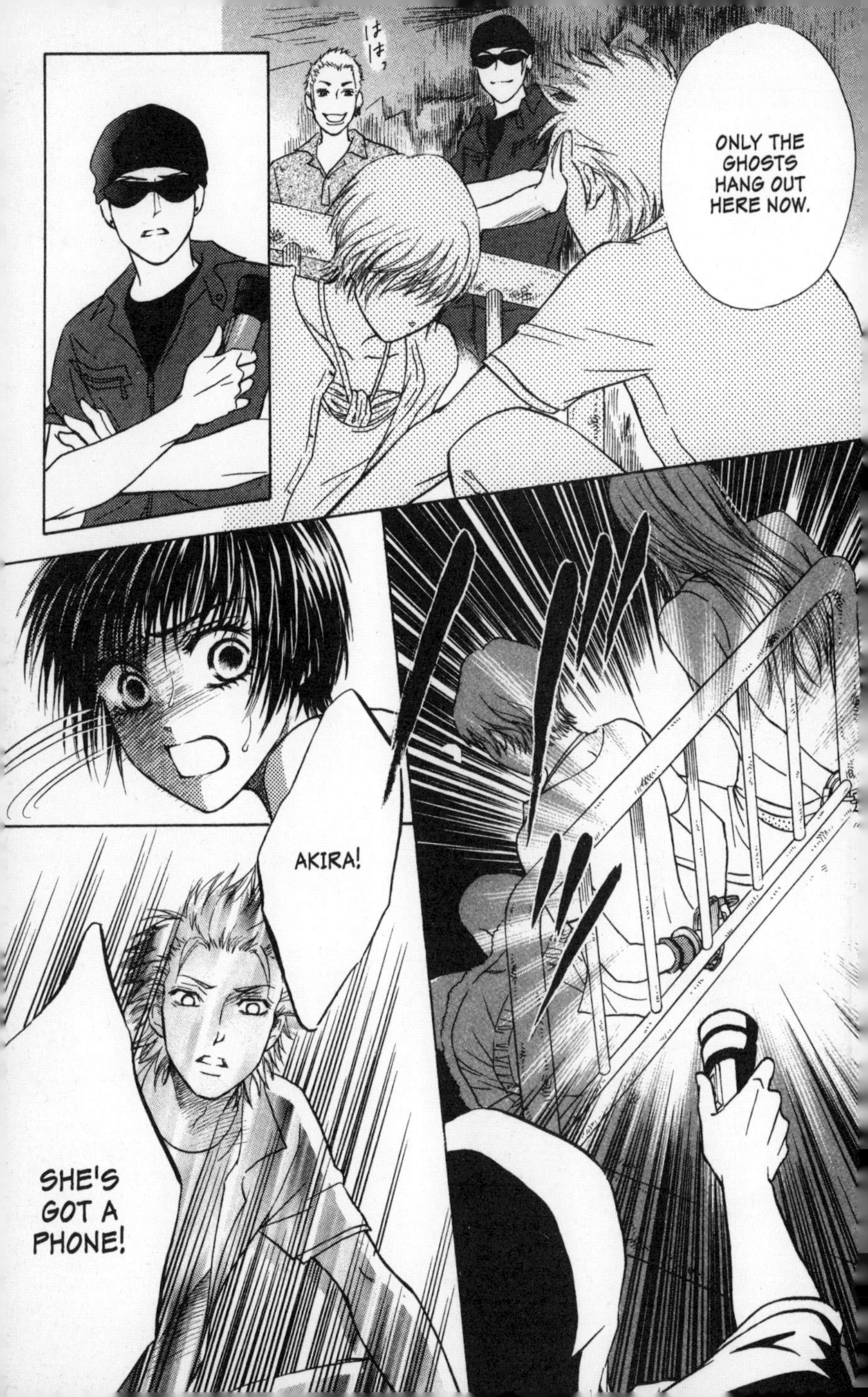

ONLY THE GHOSTS HANG OUT HERE NOW.
ははっ
AKIRA!
SHE'S GOT A PHONE!

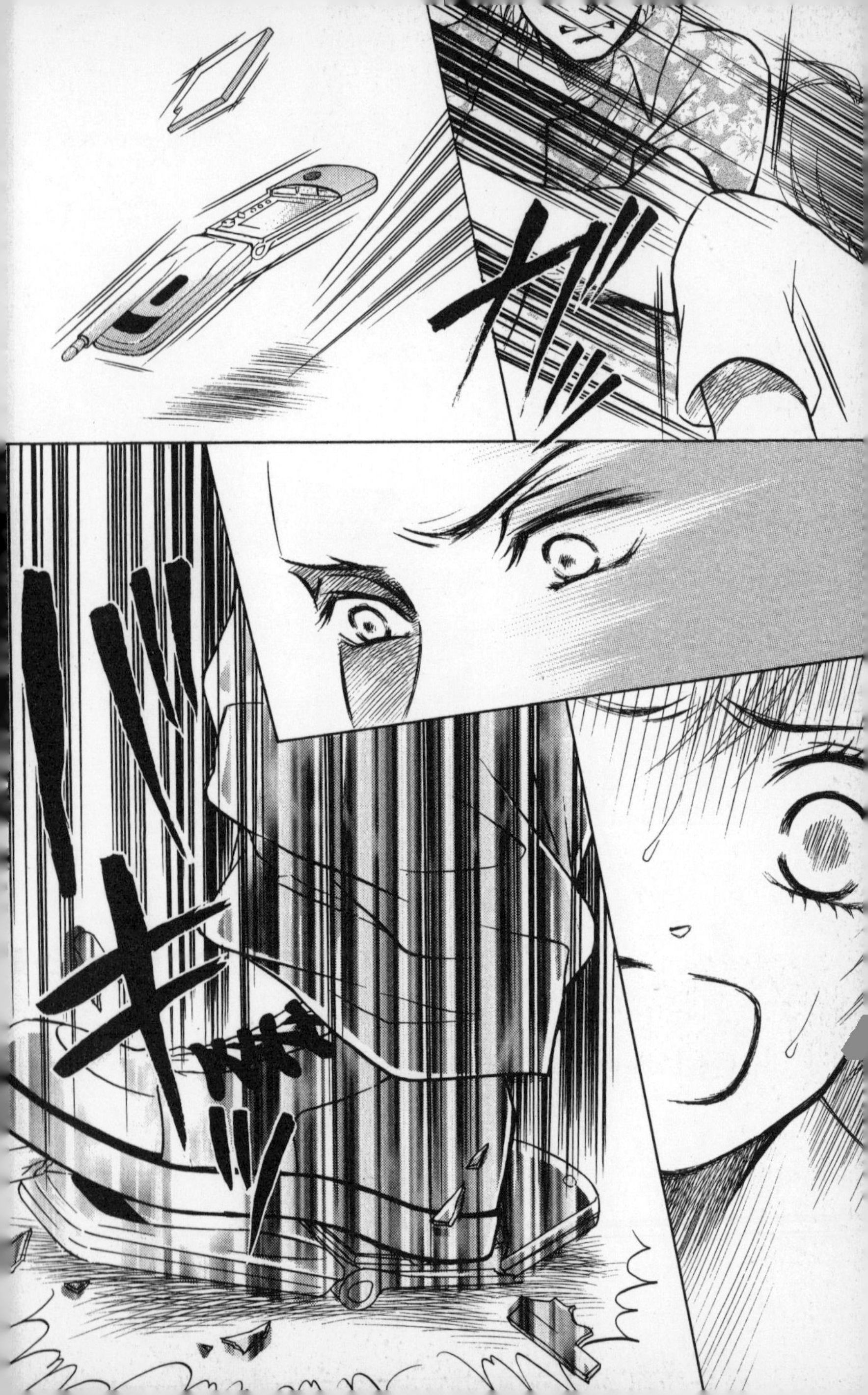

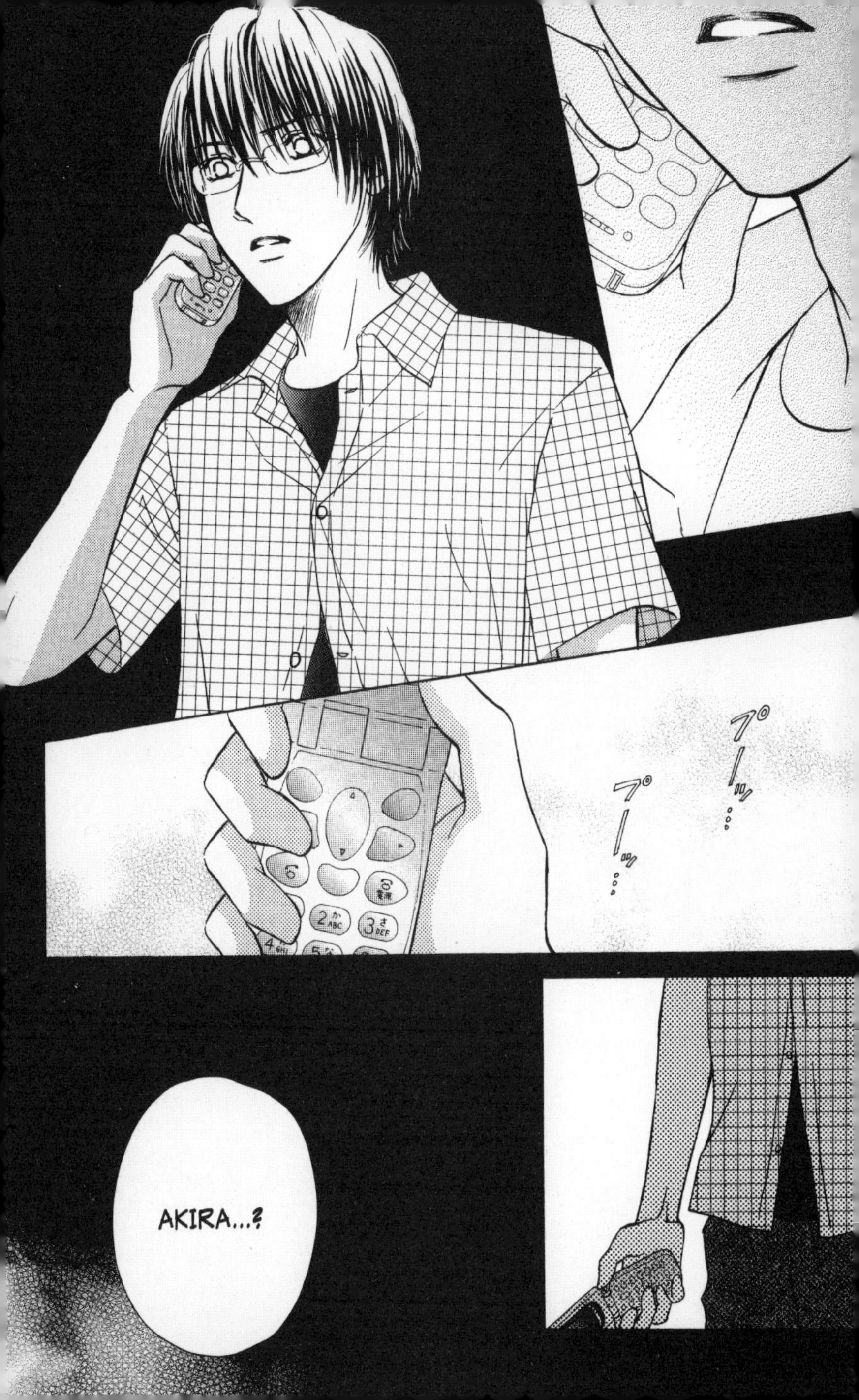
プーッ…
プーッ…
AKIRA...?

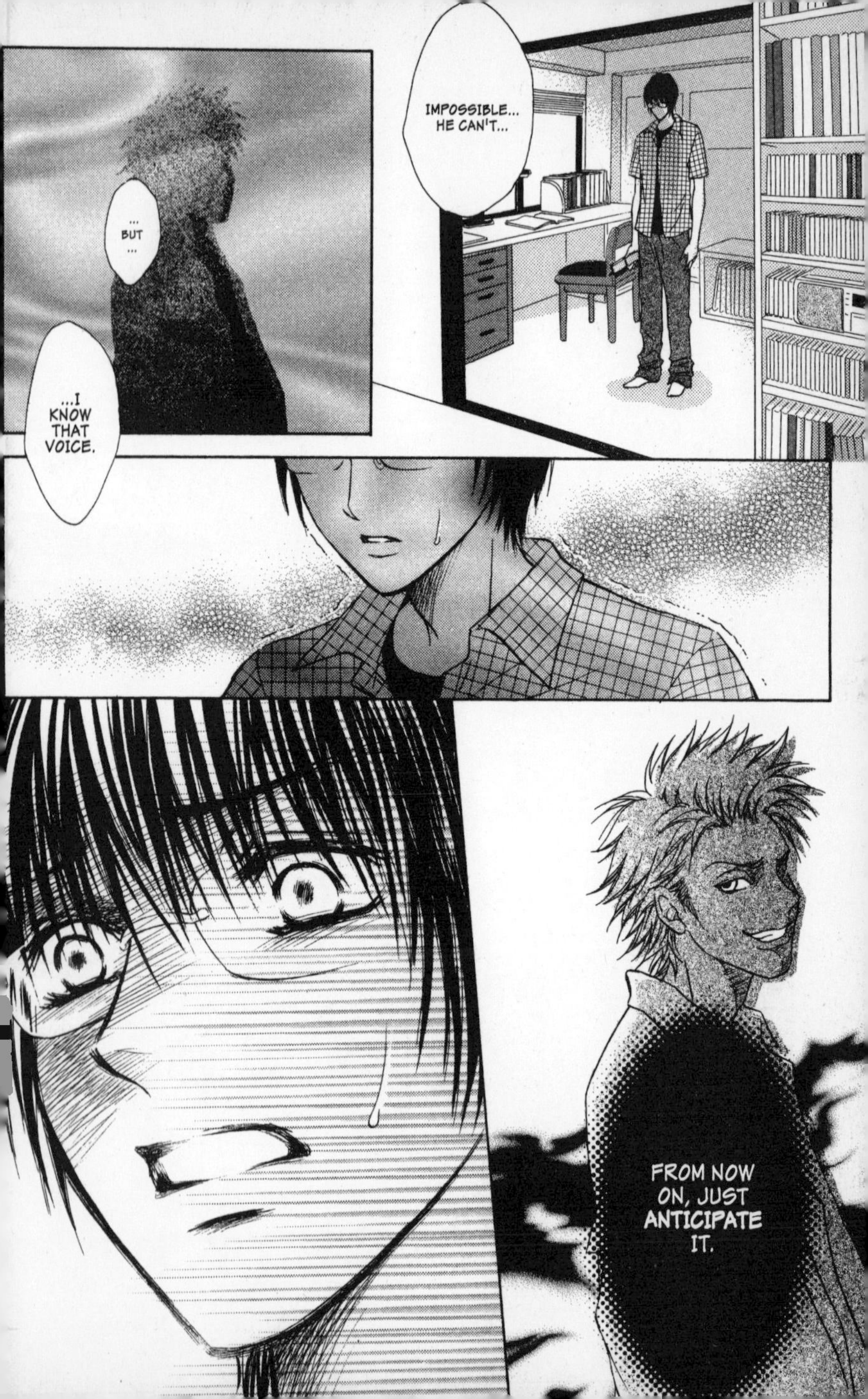
IMPOSSIBLE... HE CAN'T...
... BUT ...
...I KNOW THAT VOICE.
FROM NOW ON, JUST ANTICIPATE IT.

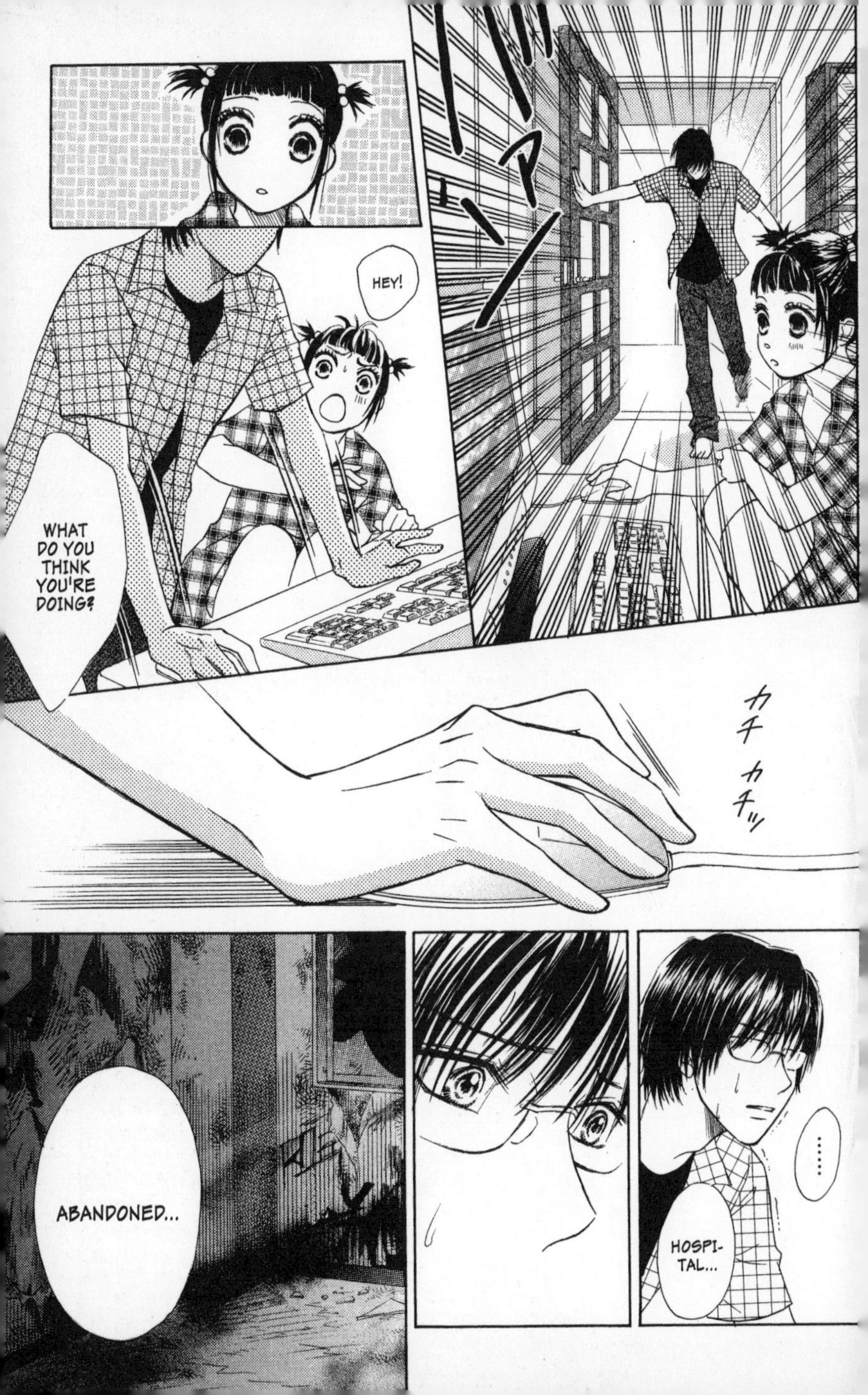

バアーン
HEY!
WHAT DO YOU THINK YOU'RE DOING?
カチ カチッ
......
HOSPI-TAL...
ABANDONED...

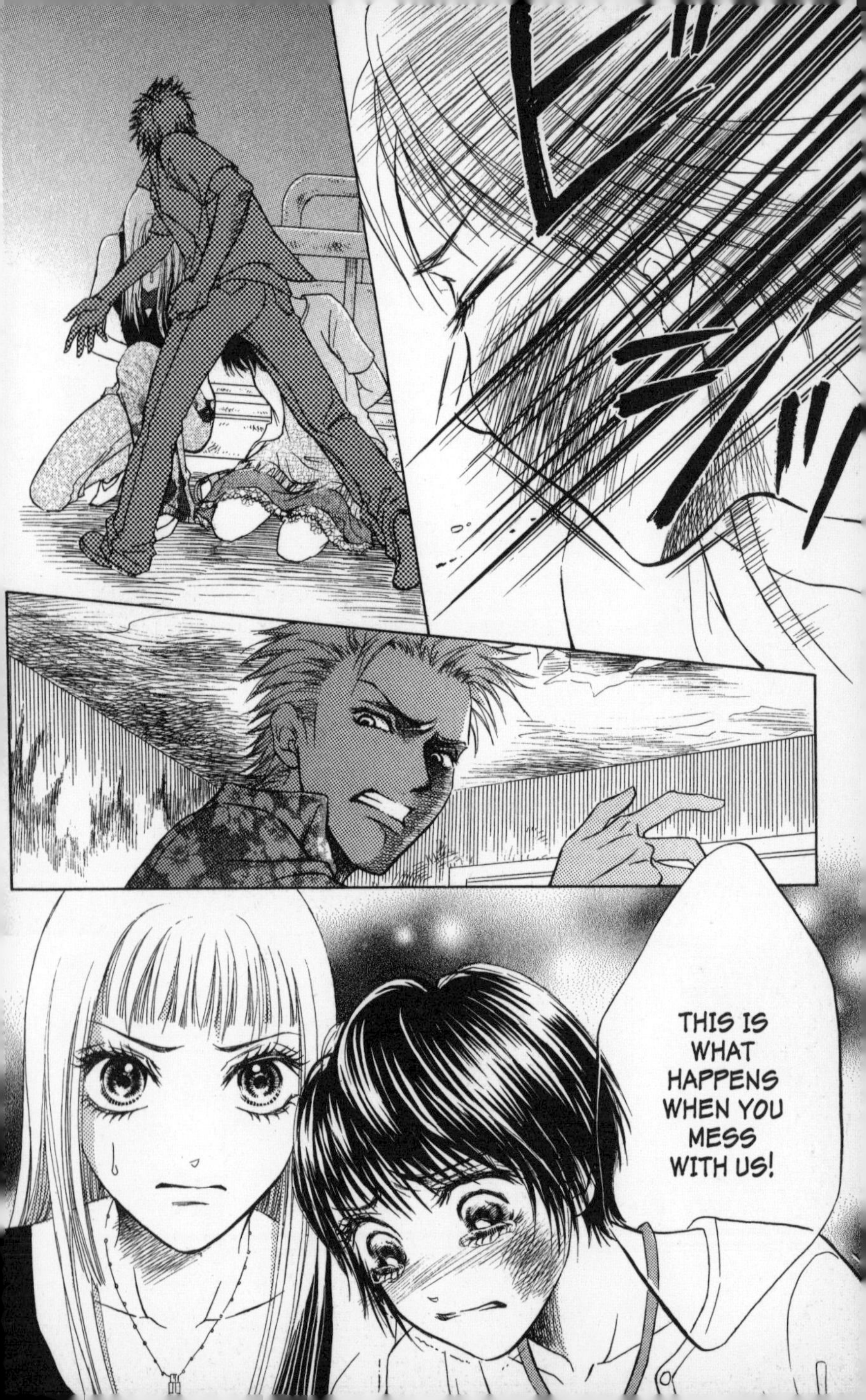
THIS IS WHAT HAPPENS WHEN YOU MESS WITH US!

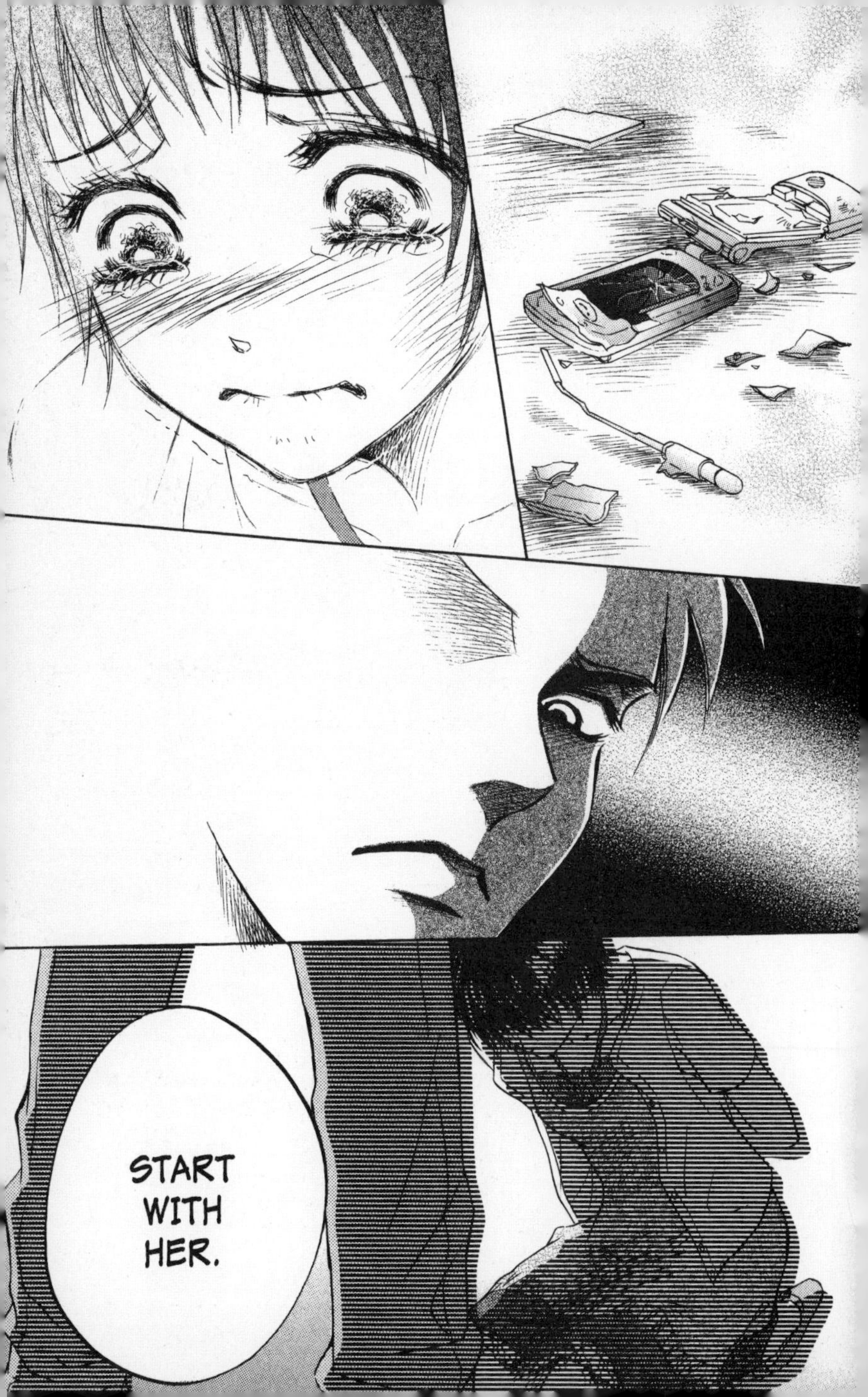
START WITH HER.

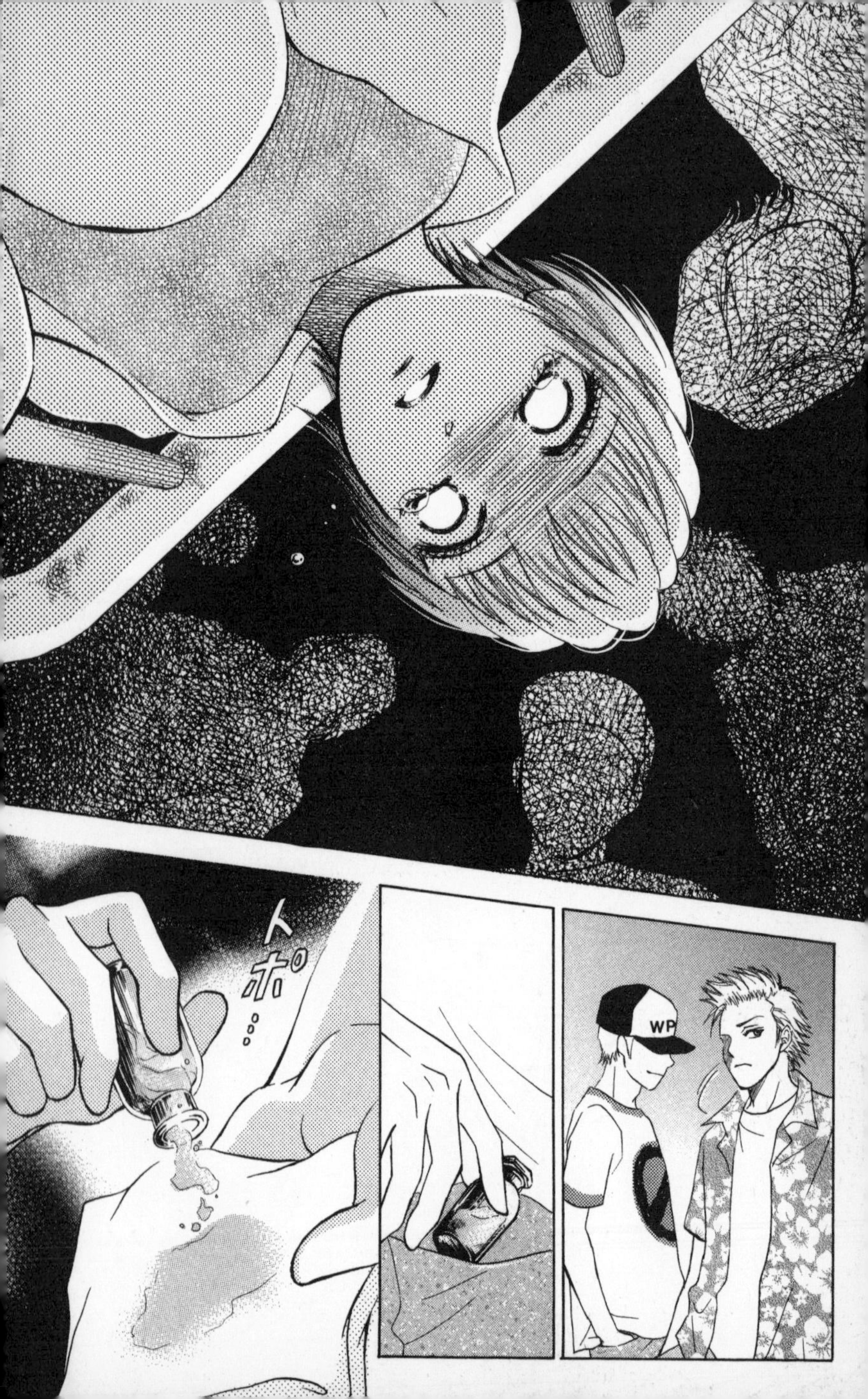
トポ…

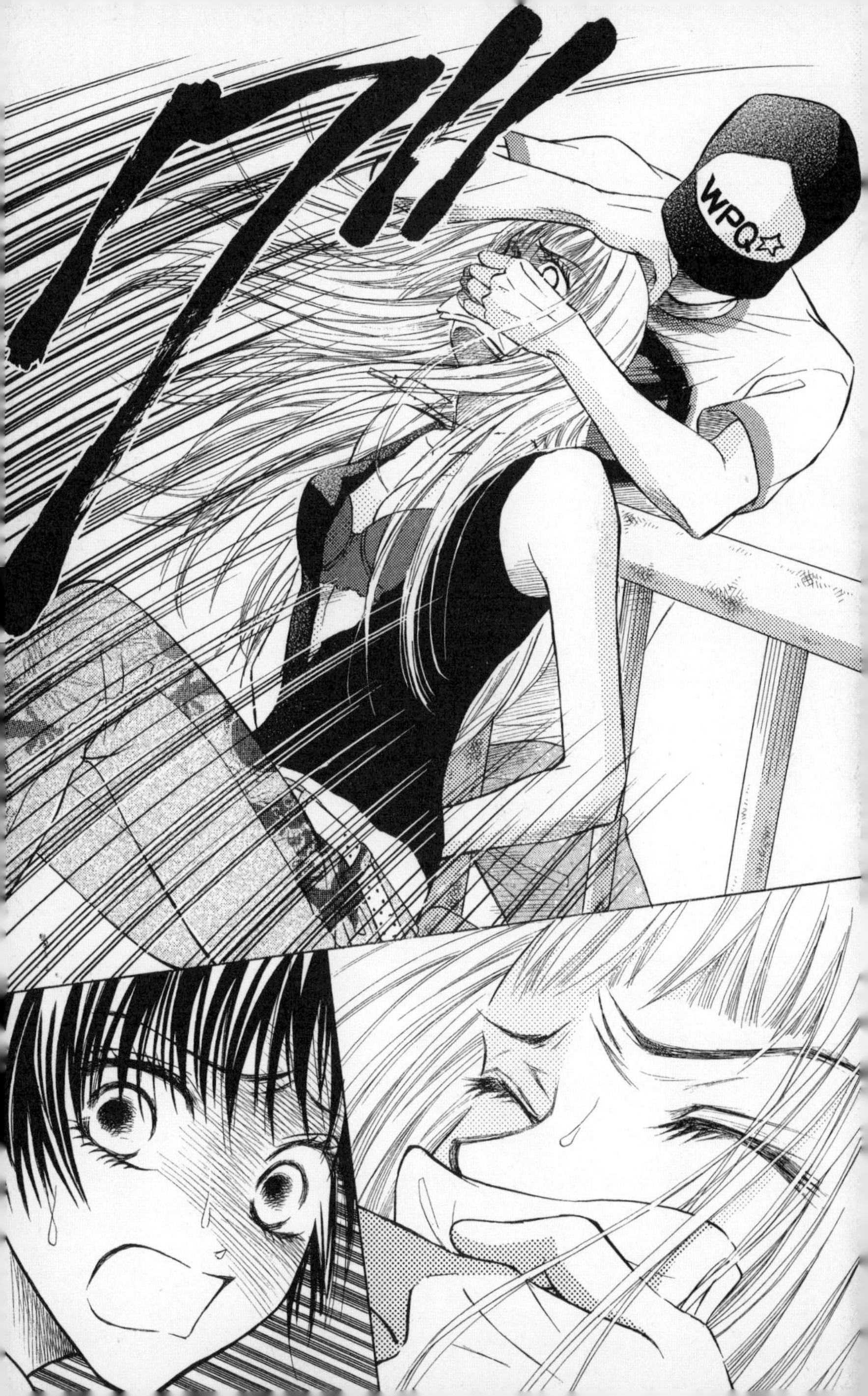
WPQ☆

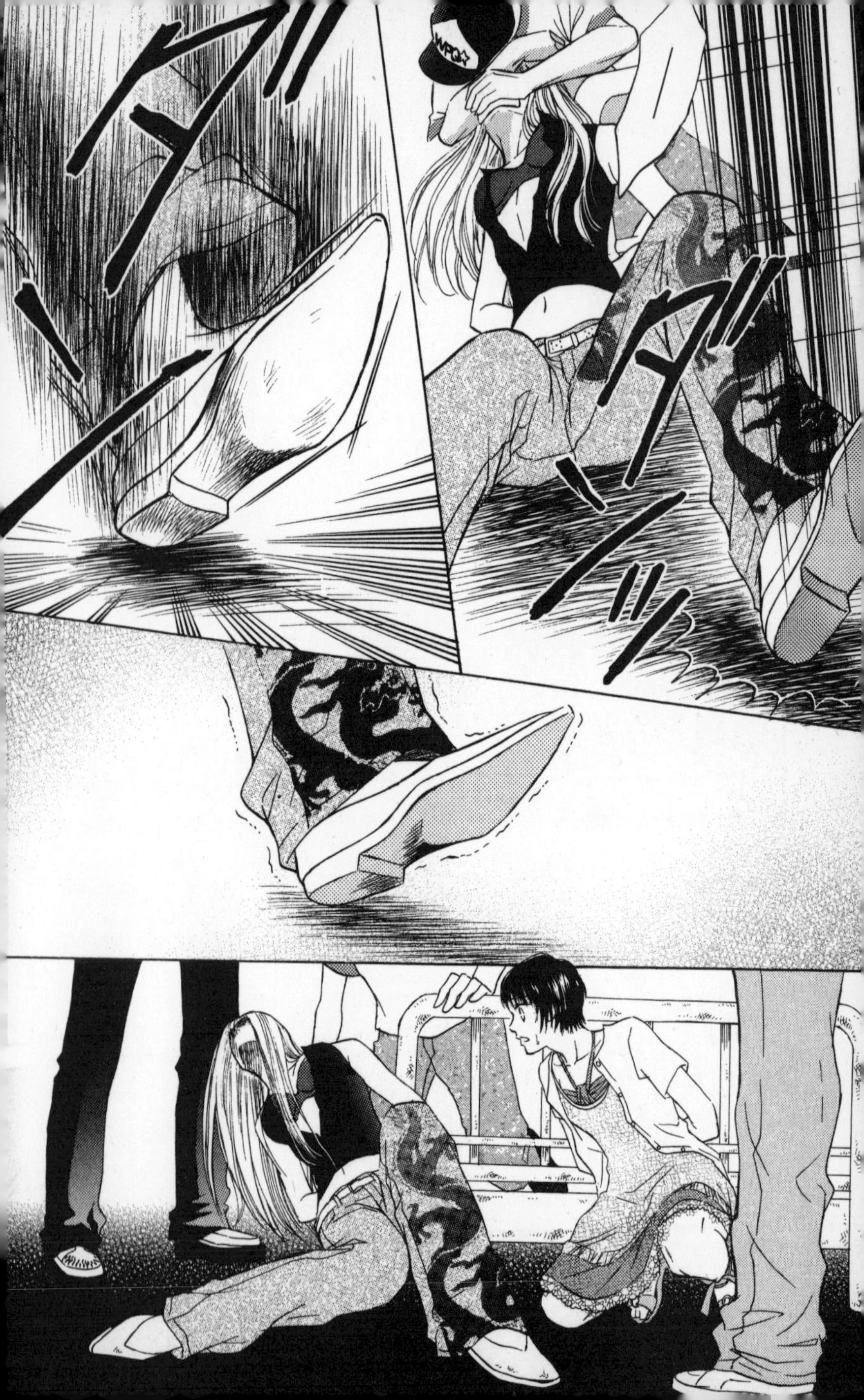

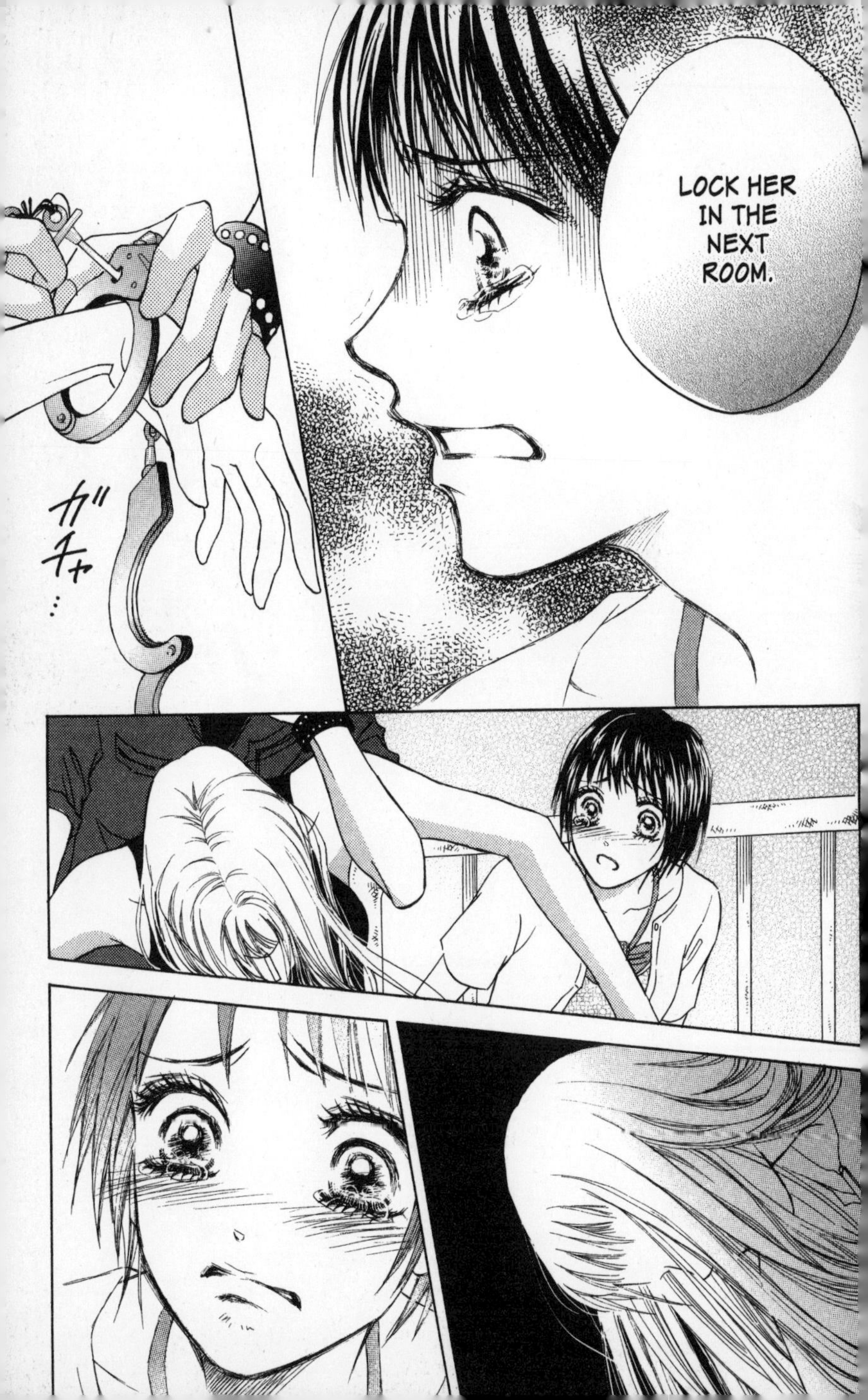
LOCK HER IN THE NEXT ROOM.
ガチャ…

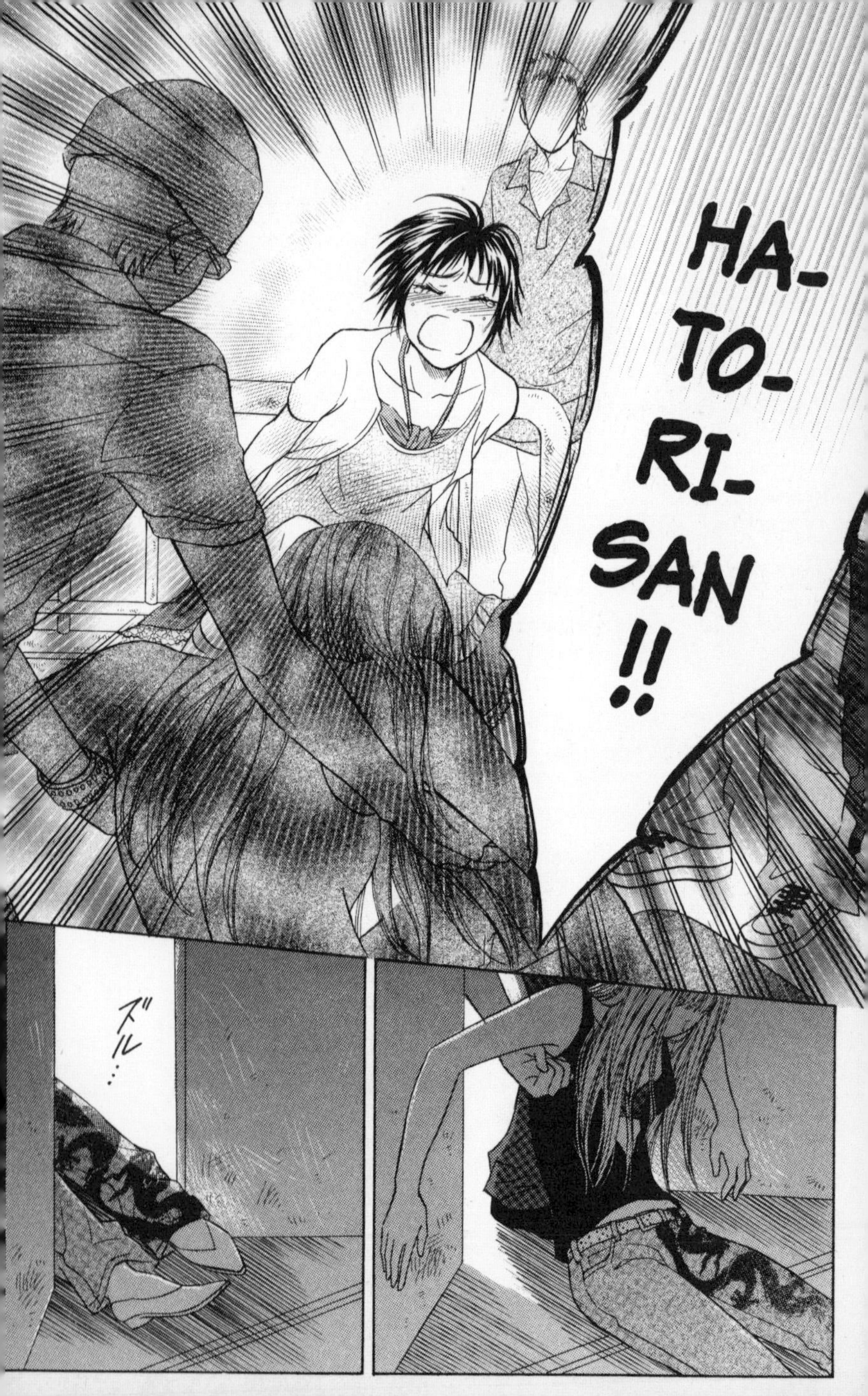
HA-
TO-
RI-
SAN
!!
ズル…

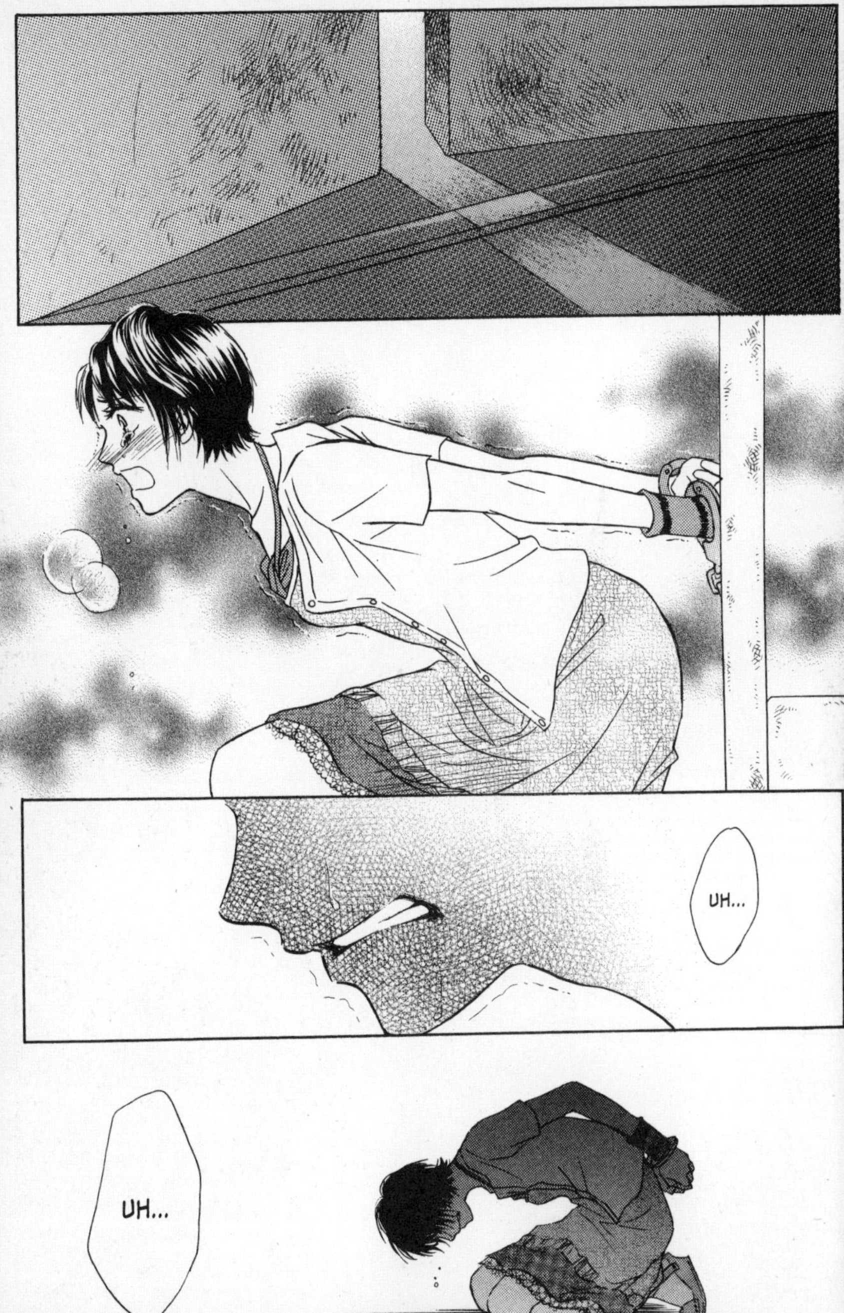
UH...
UH...

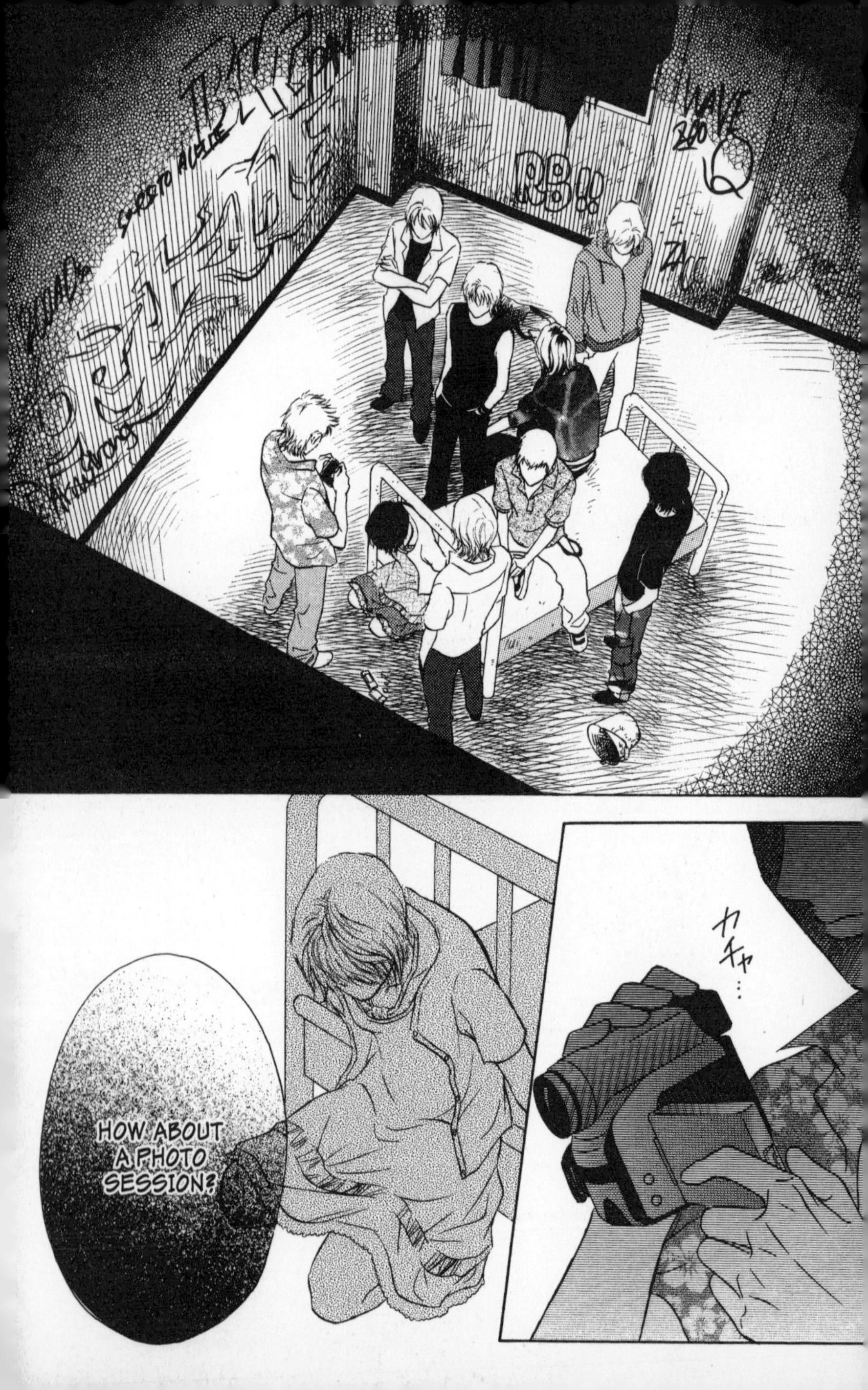

カチャ…
HOW ABOUT A PHOTO SESSION?

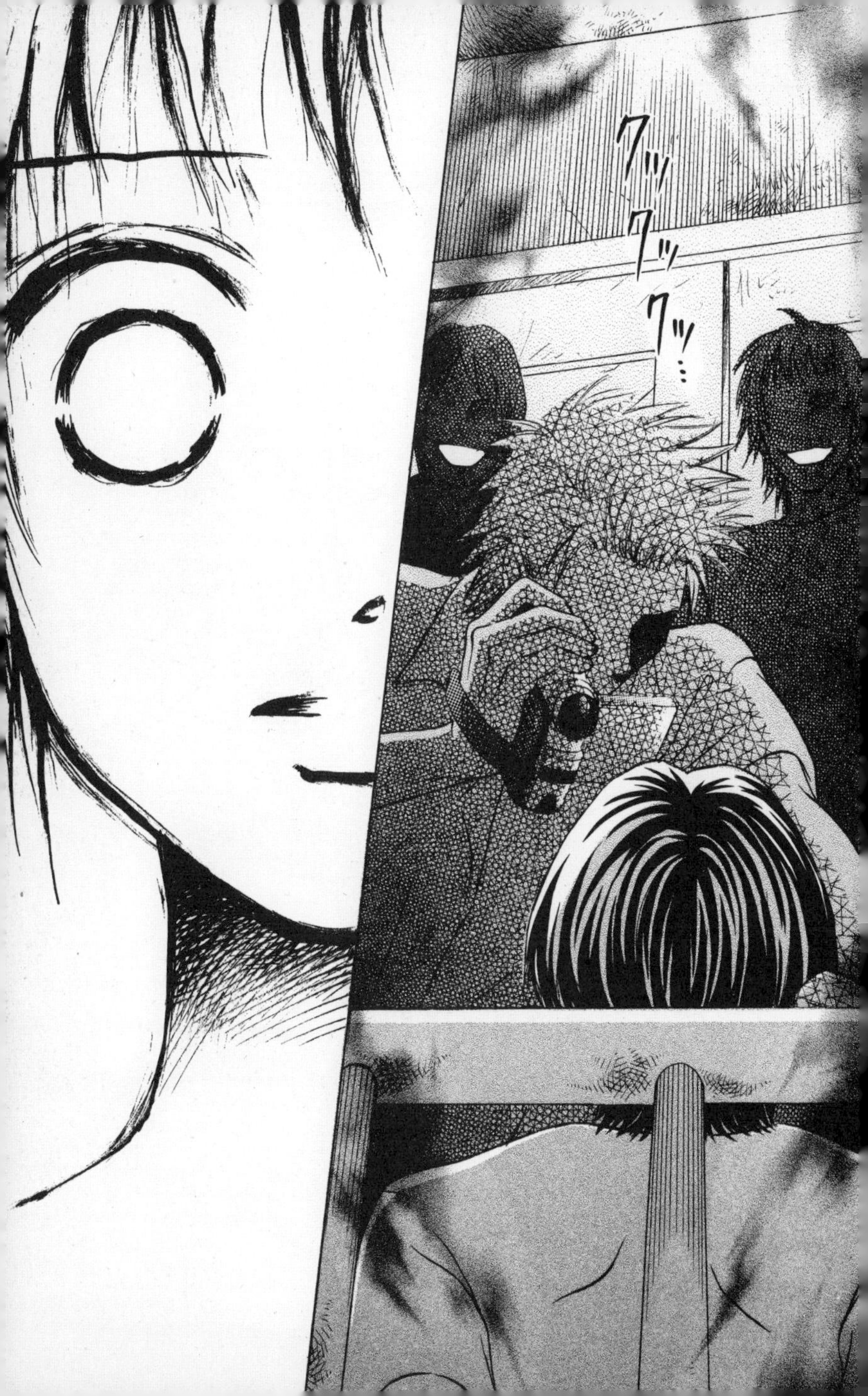
クッ
クッ
クッ…

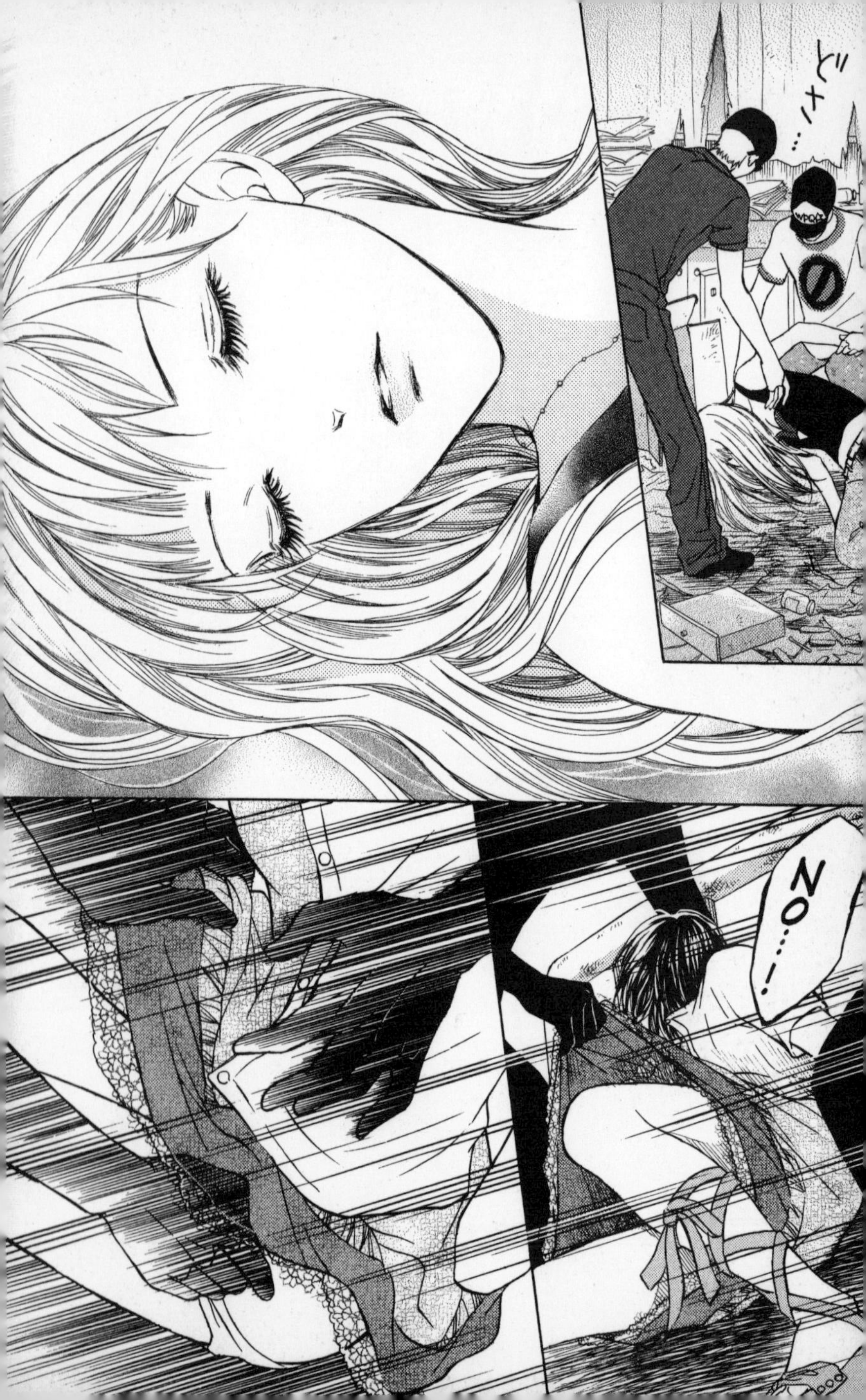

どメー…
NO…!

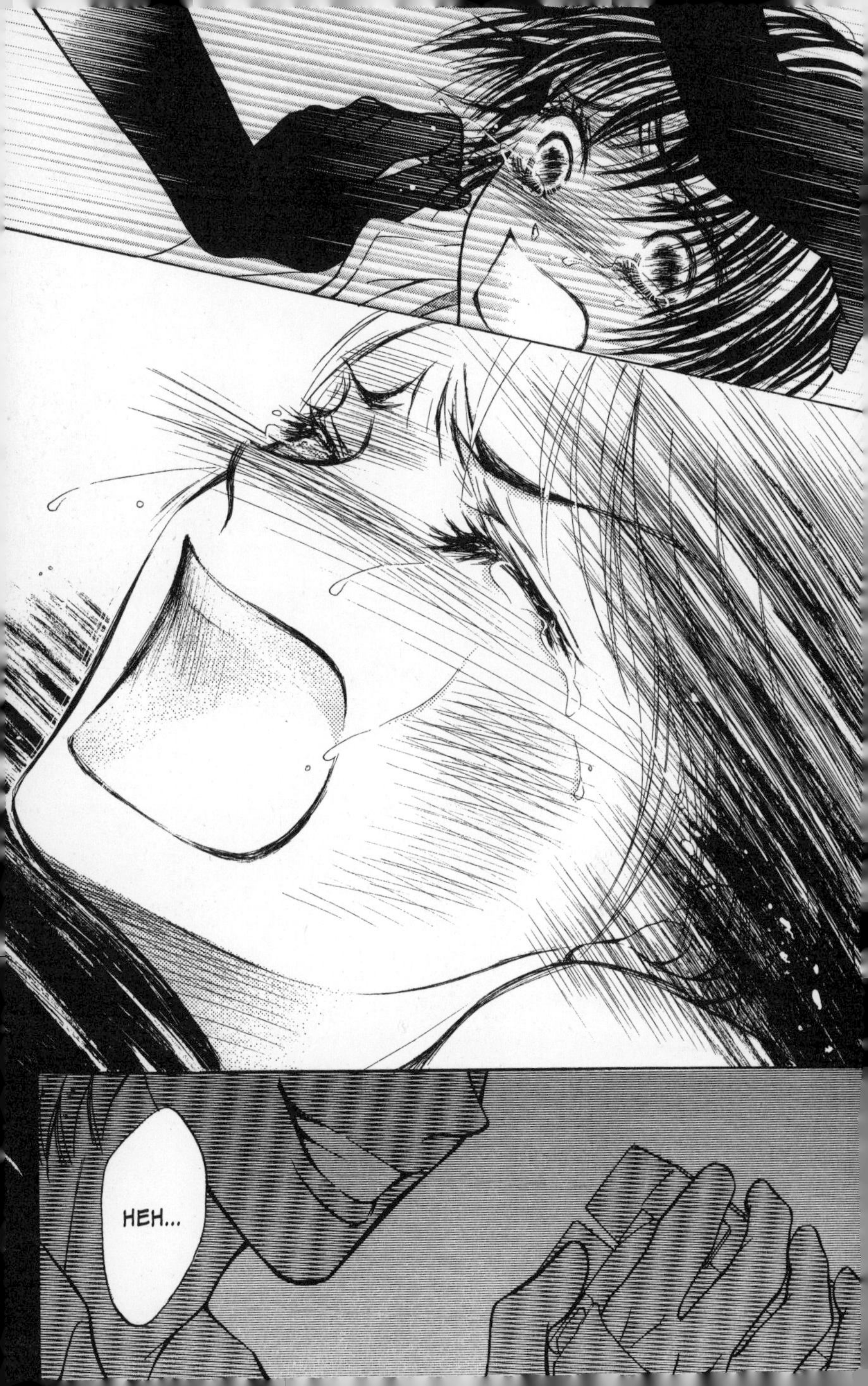
HEH...

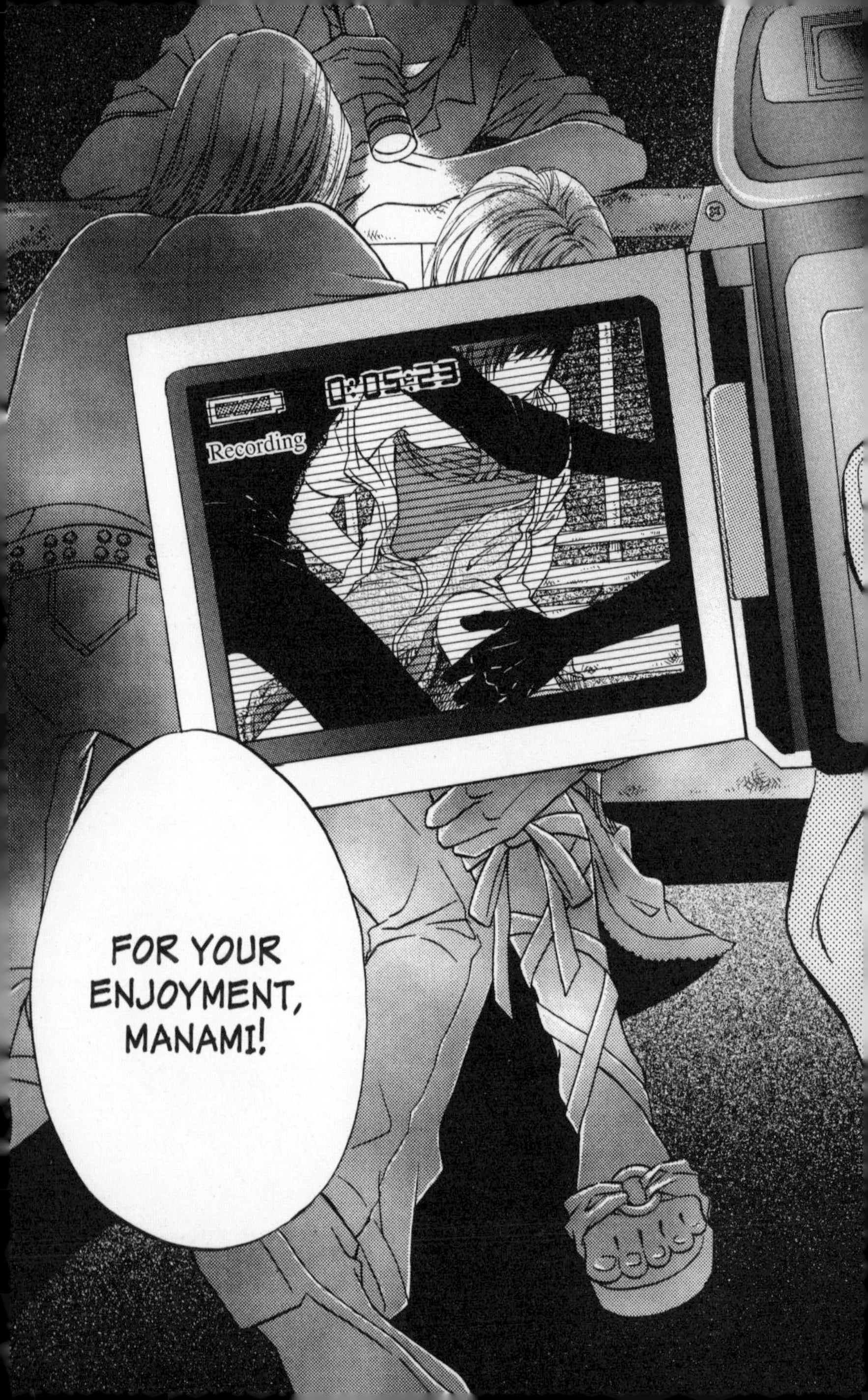
Recording
FOR YOUR ENJOYMENT, MANAMI!

Chapter 29: Heartless

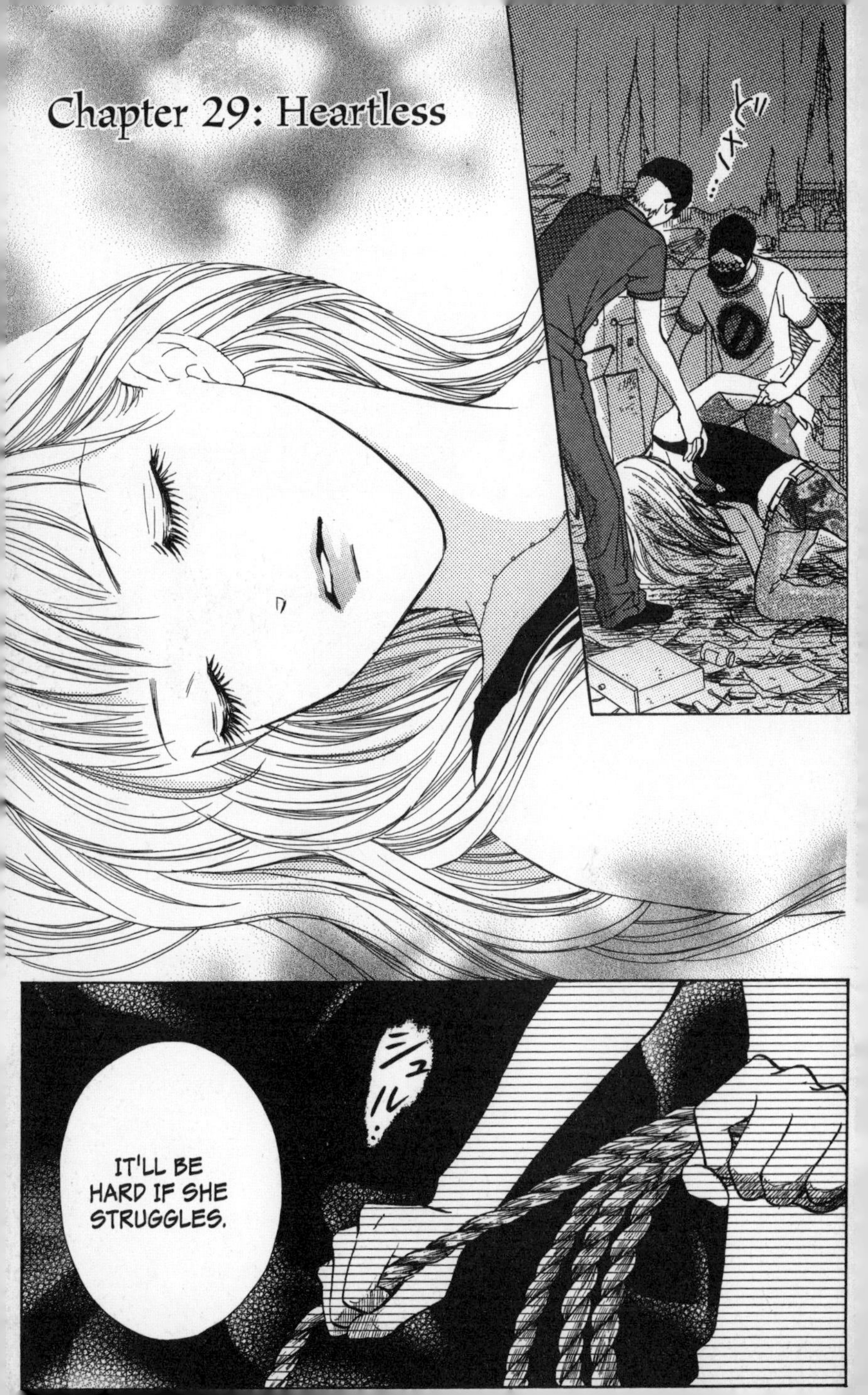
シュル…
IT'LL BE HARD IF SHE STRUGGLES.

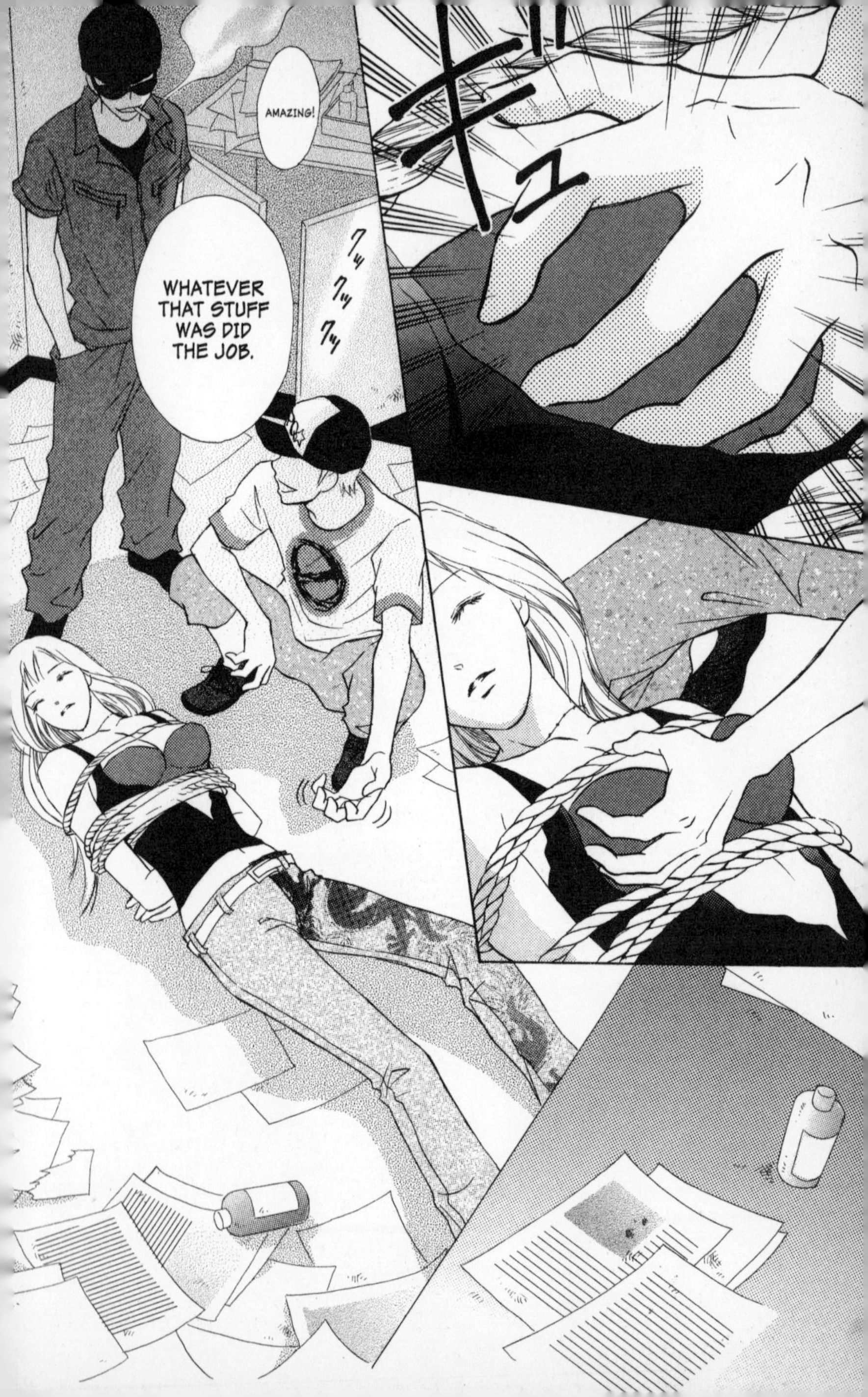
ギュ
AMAZING!
WHATEVER THAT STUFF WAS DID THE JOB.
クッ クッ クッ

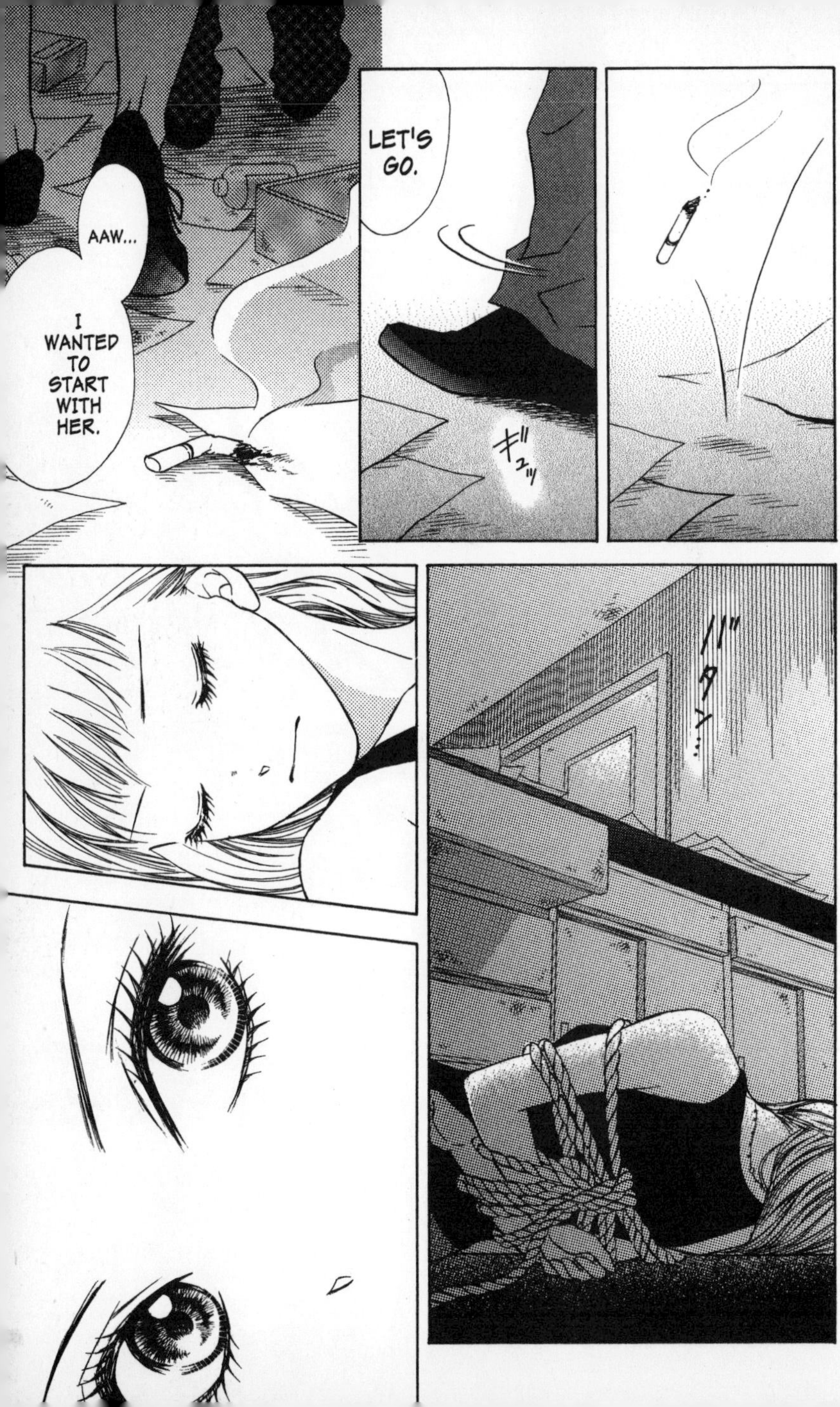
LET'S GO.
ギュッ
AAW...
I WANTED TO START WITH HER.
バタン…

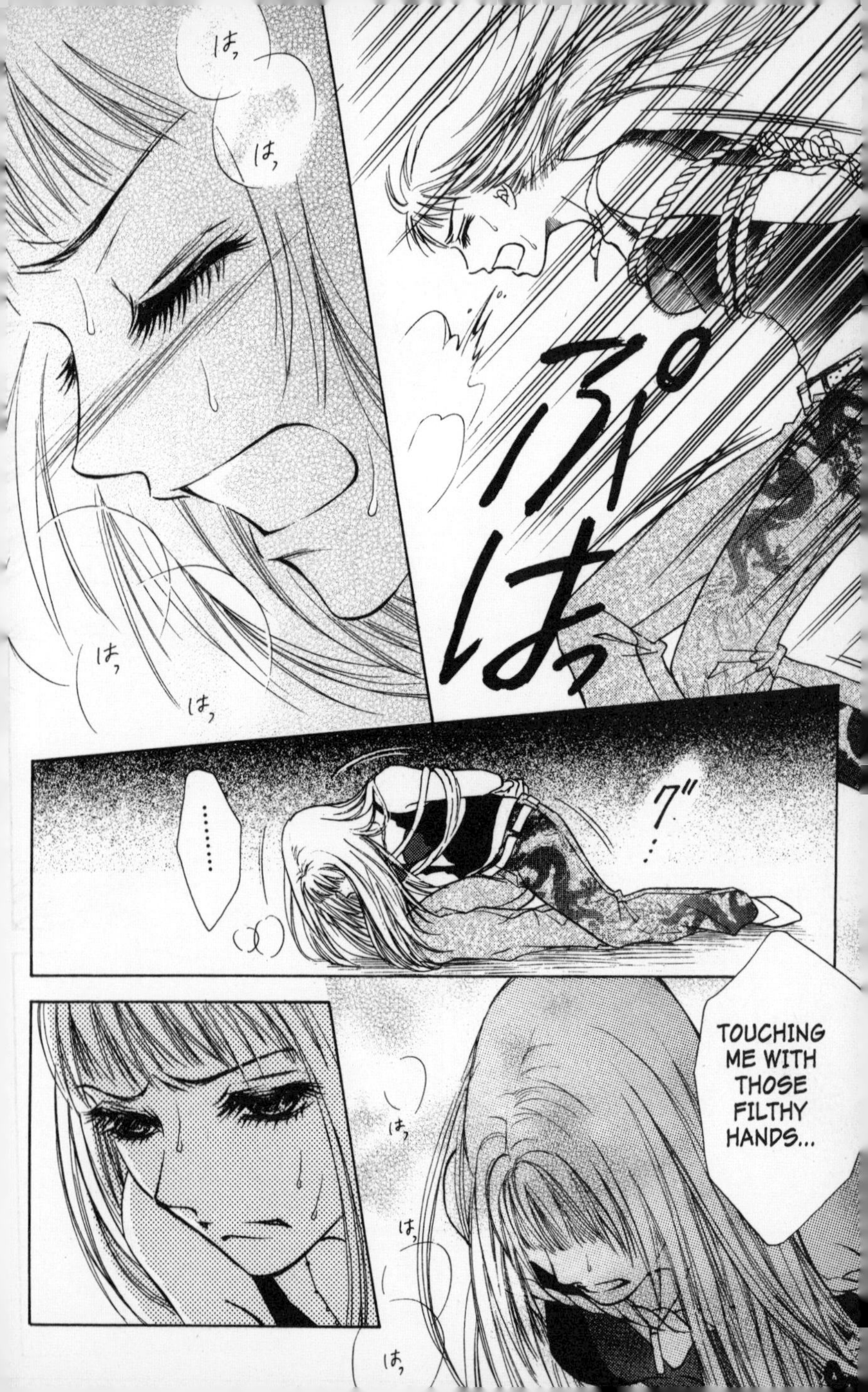
ぷはっ
はっ
はっ
はっ
はっ
グ…
……
TOUCHING ME WITH THOSE FILTHY HANDS...
はっ
はっ
はっ

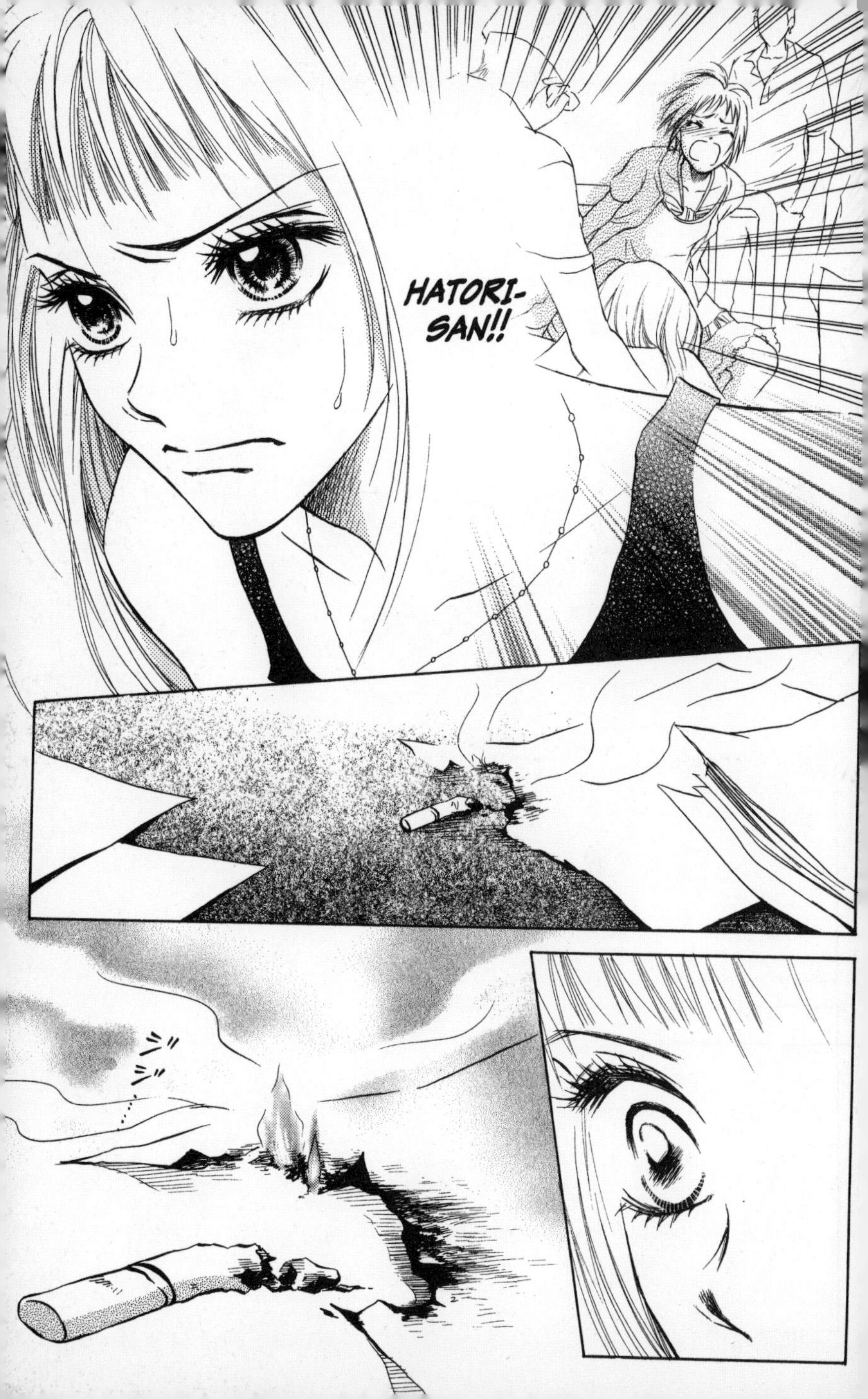
HATORI-SAN!!

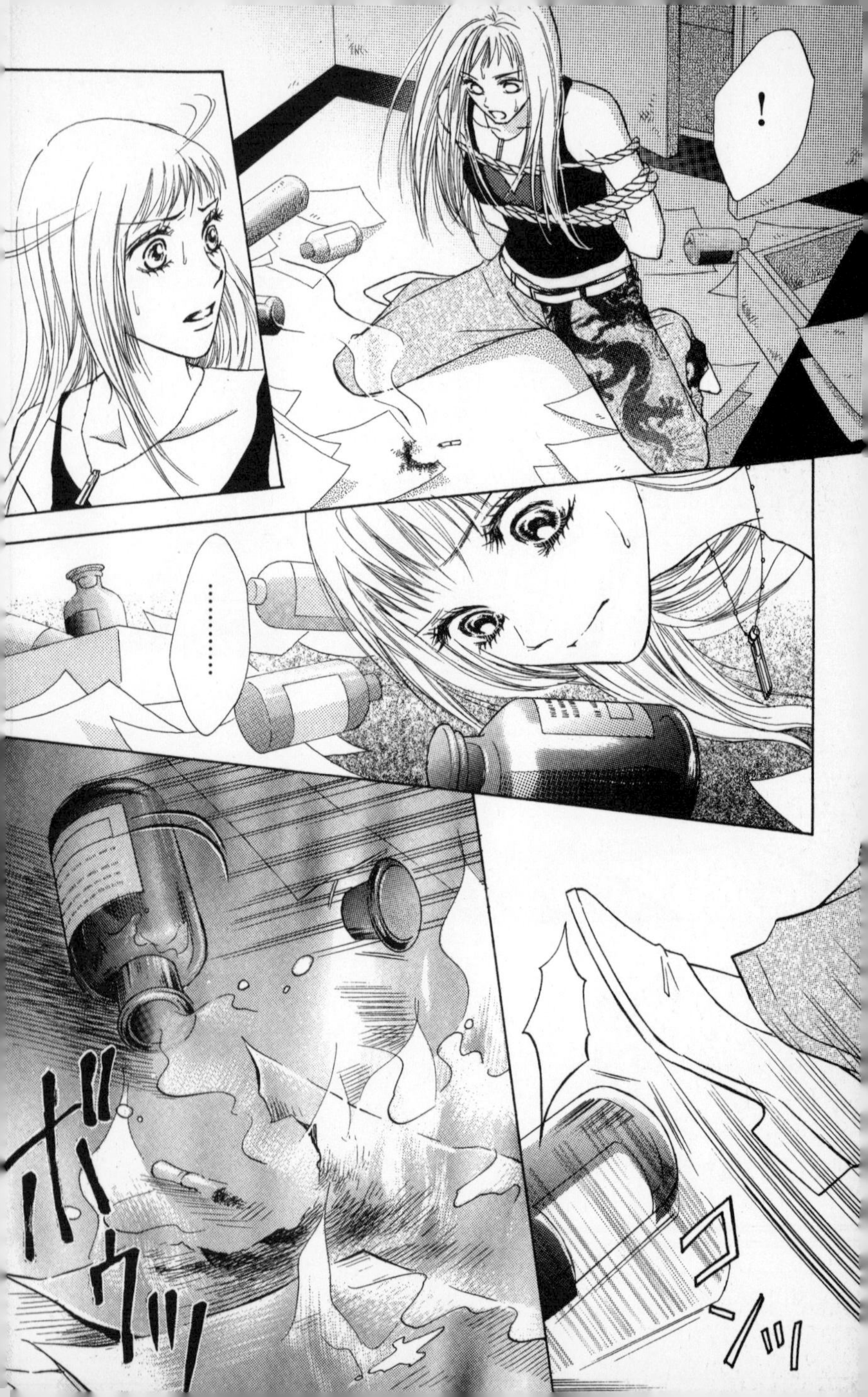
!
……
ボウッ

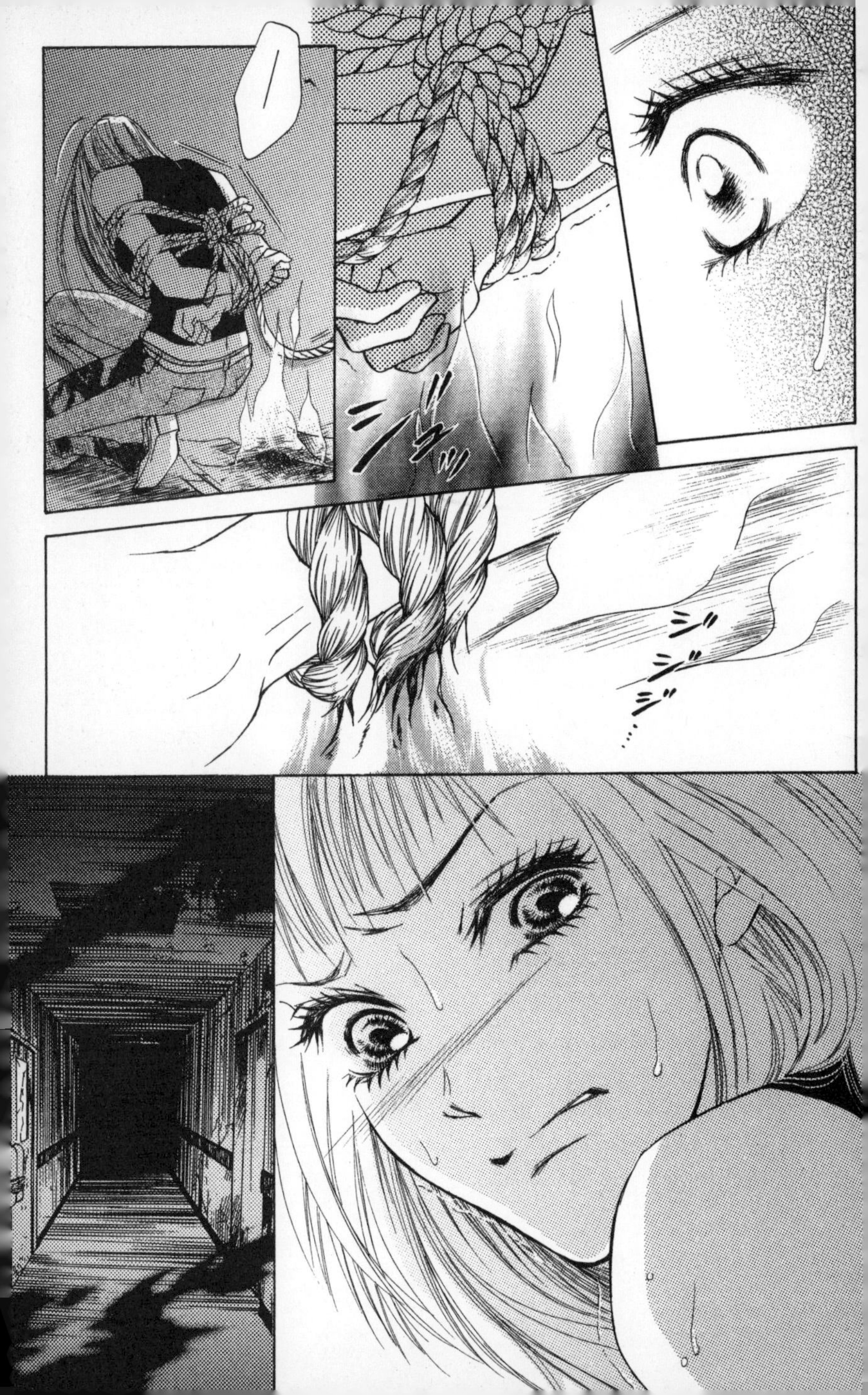
ジュッ
!
ジ
ジ
ジ
…

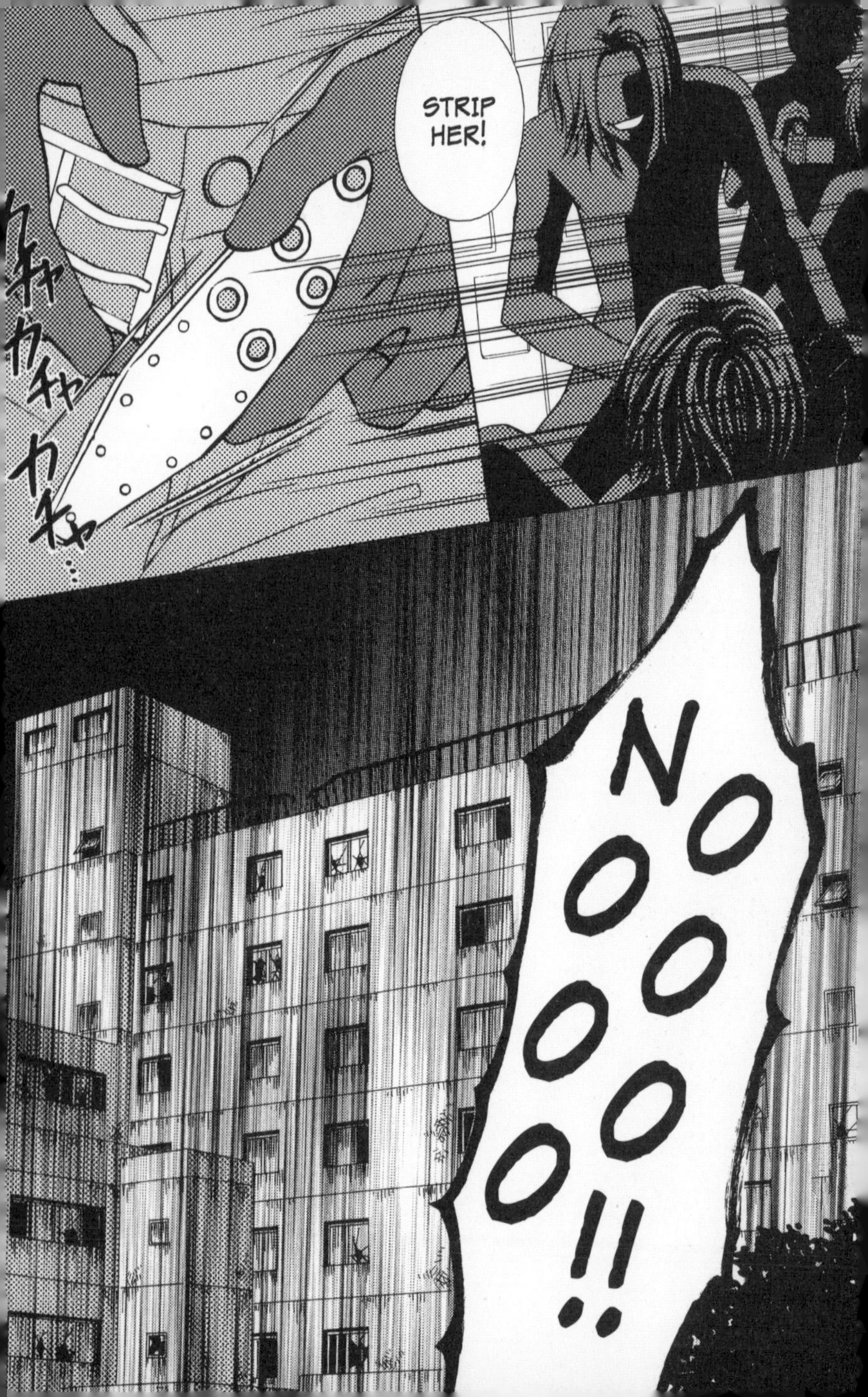
STRIP HER!
カチャカチャ
カチャ…
NOOOOOOO!!

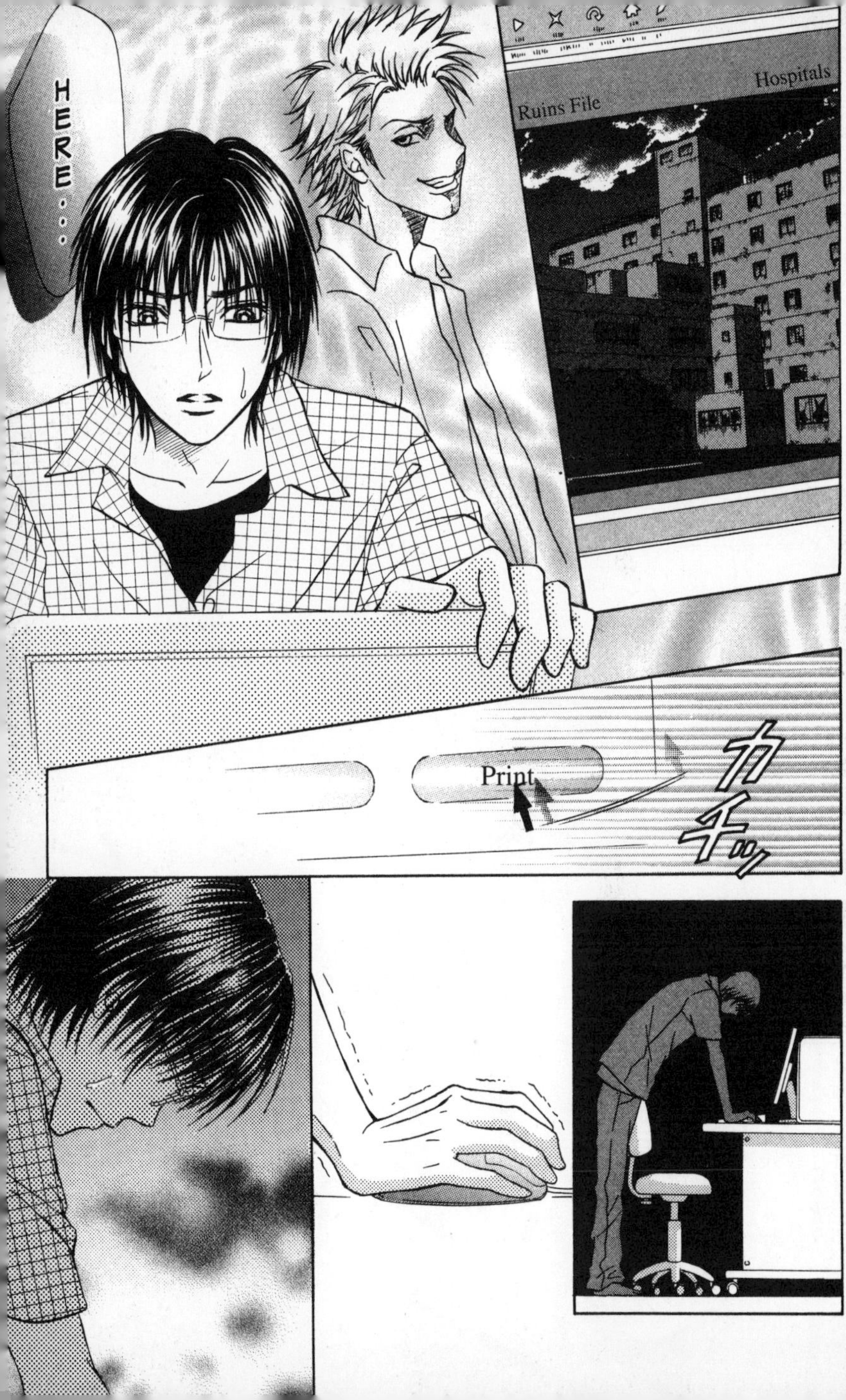
HERE...
Hospitals
Ruins File
Print
カチッ

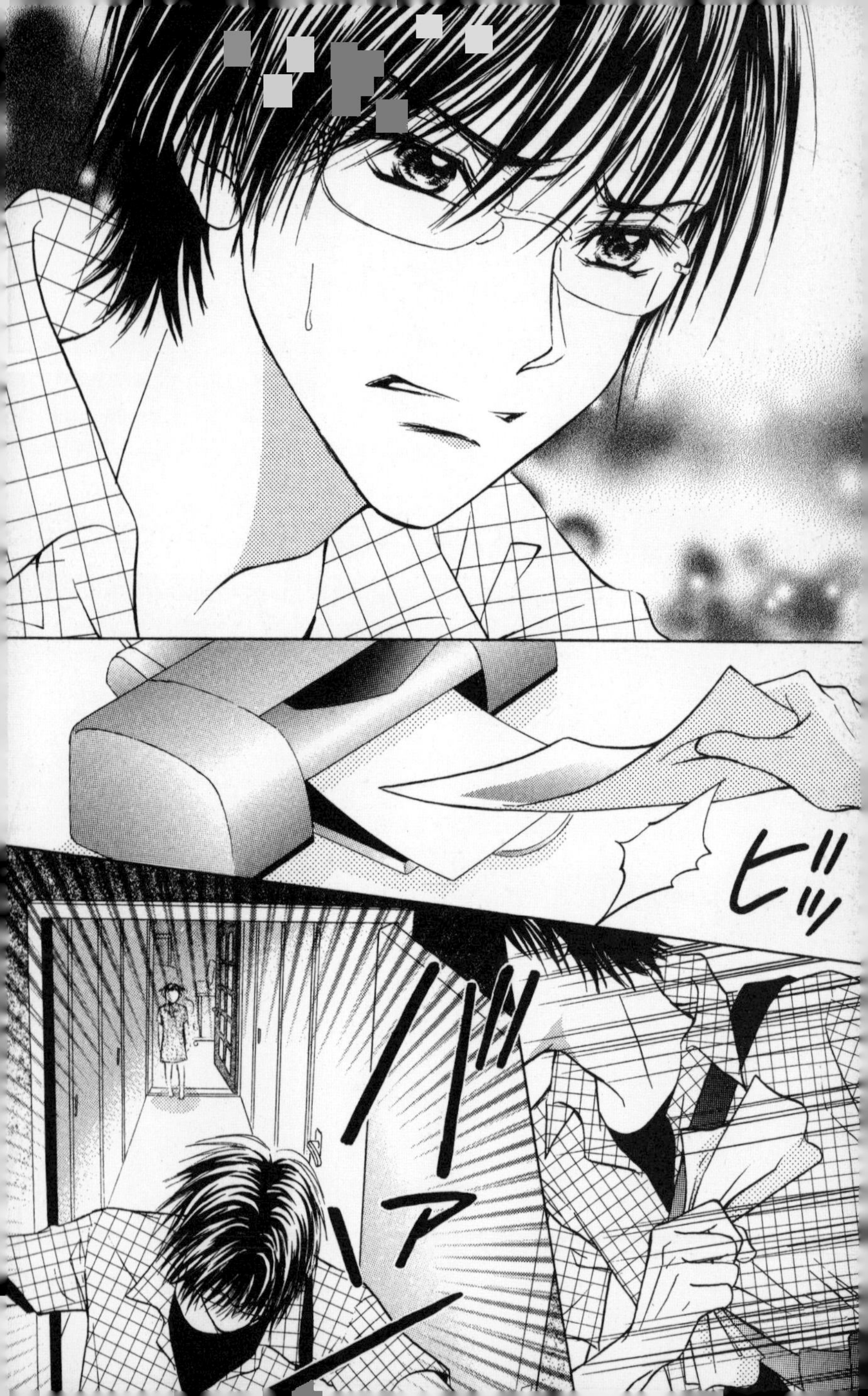
ビッ
バーア

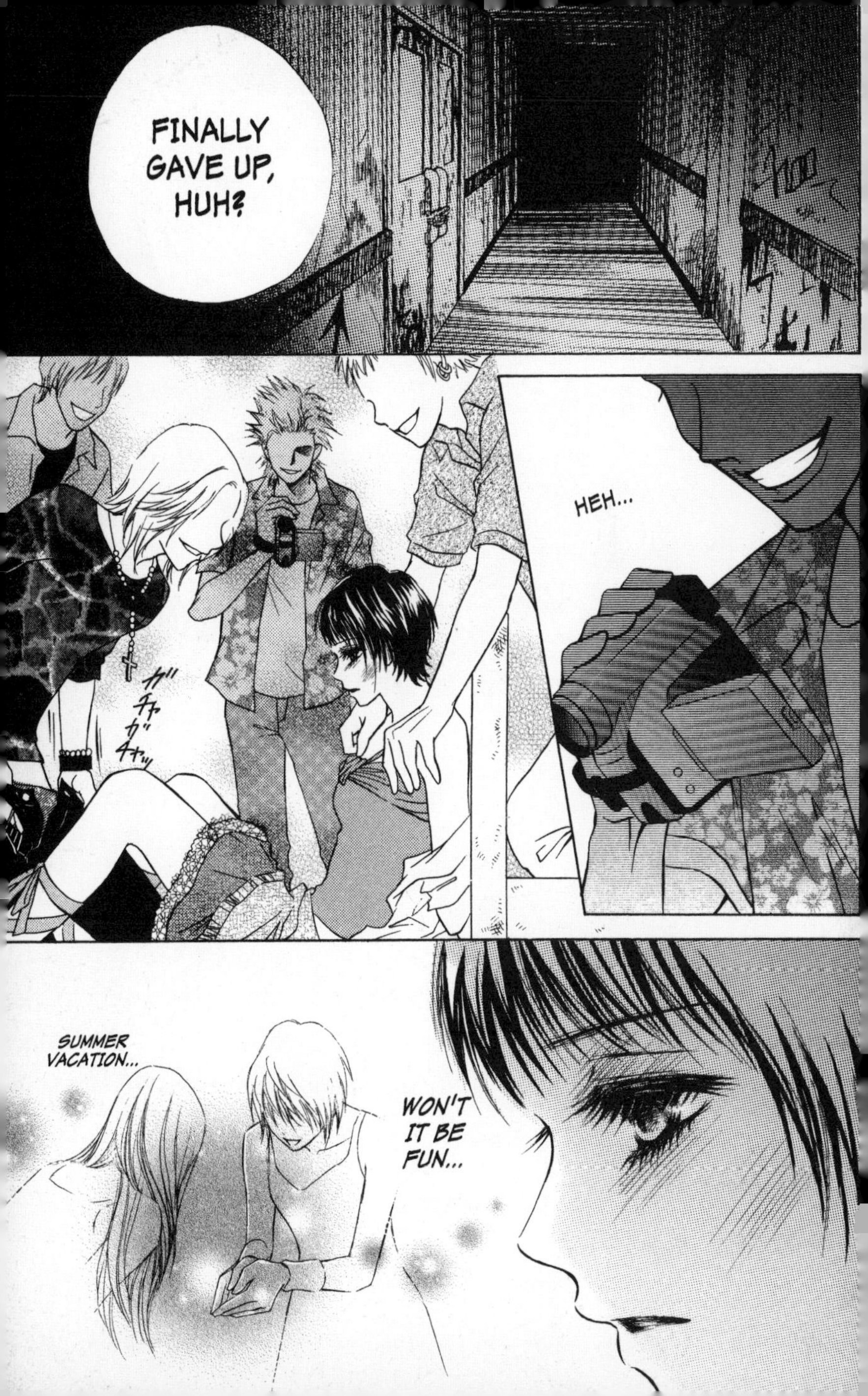
FINALLY GAVE UP, HUH?
HEH...
ガチャガチャッ
WON'T IT BE FUN...
SUMMER VACATION...

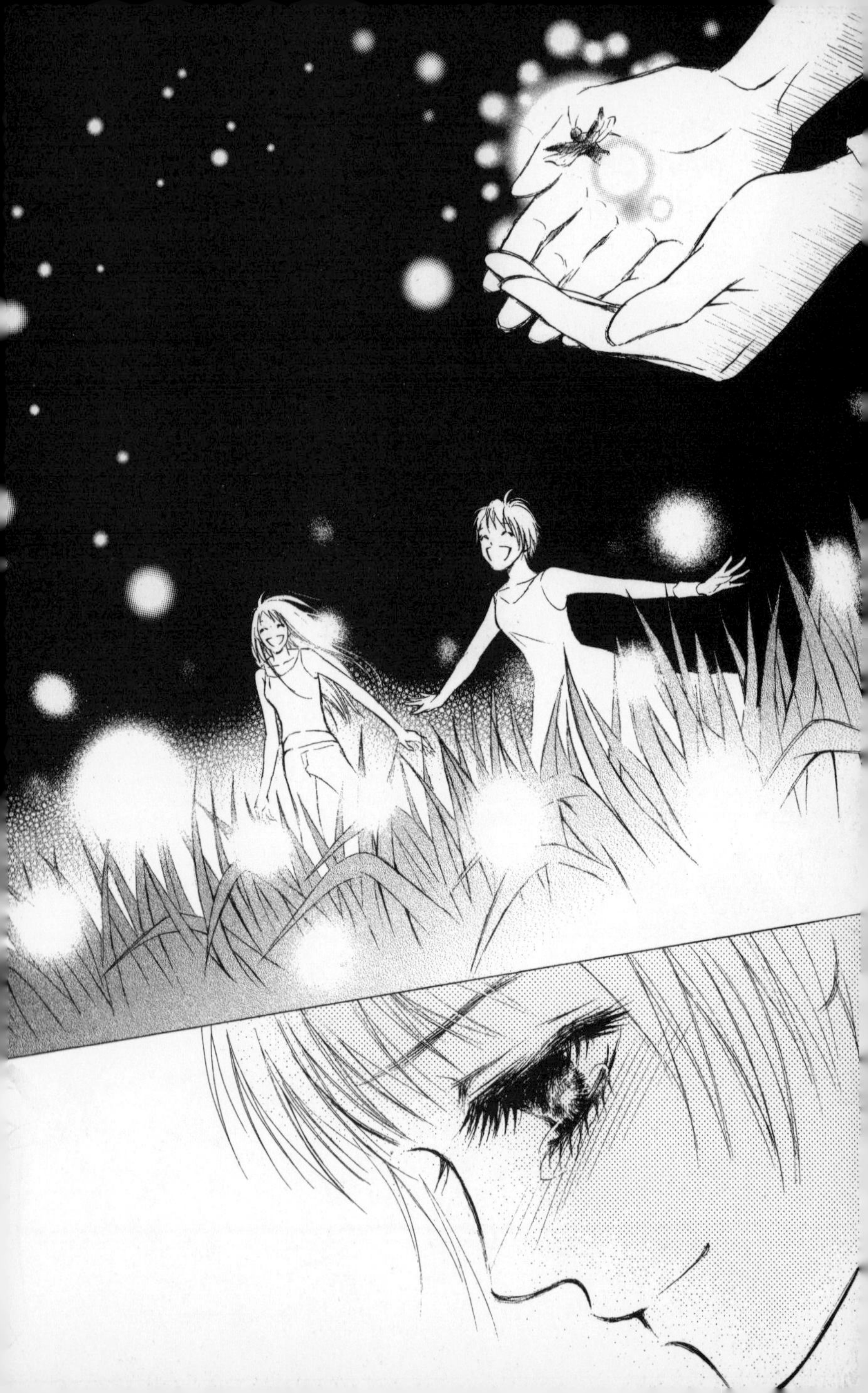

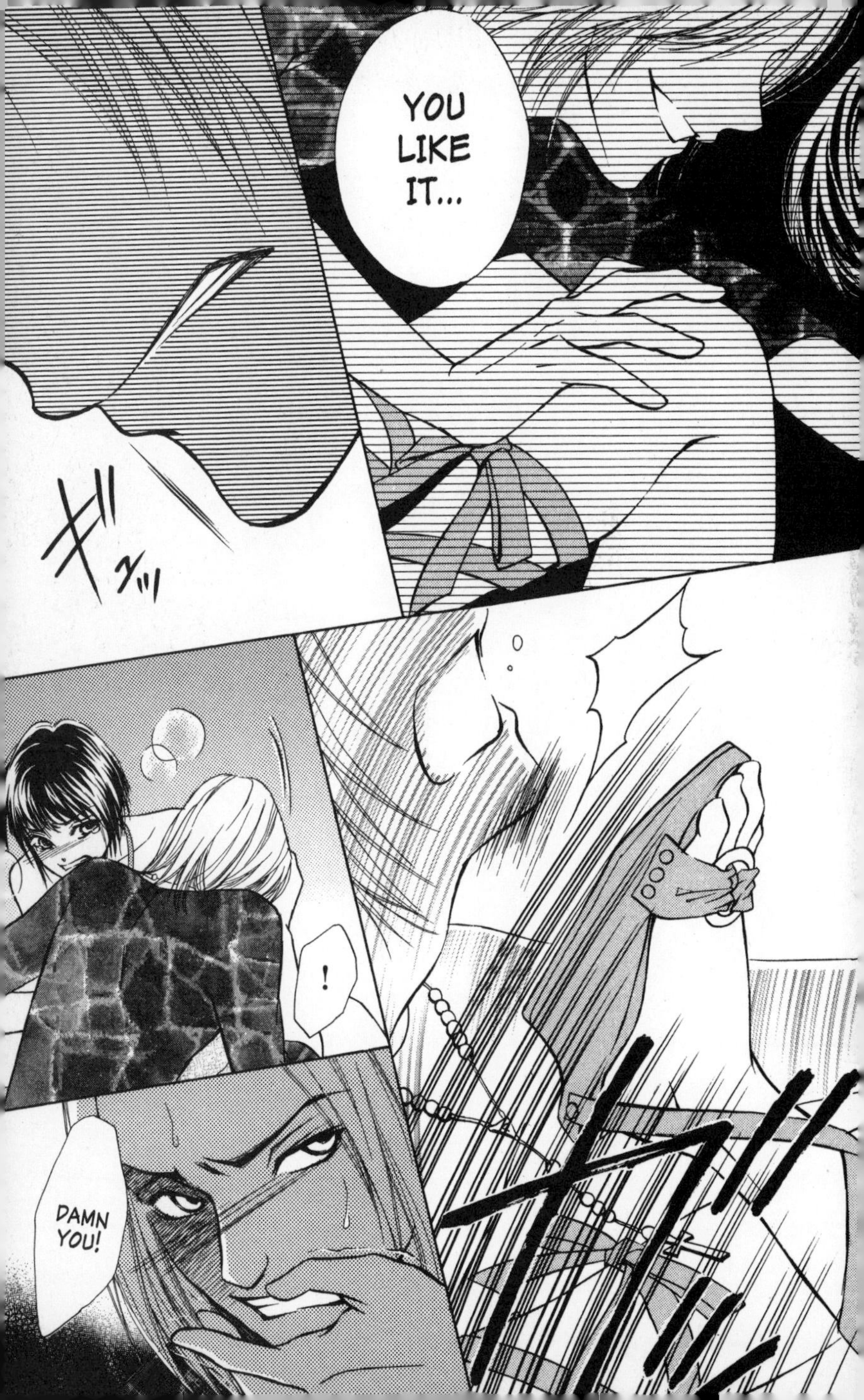
YOU LIKE IT...
!
DAMN YOU!

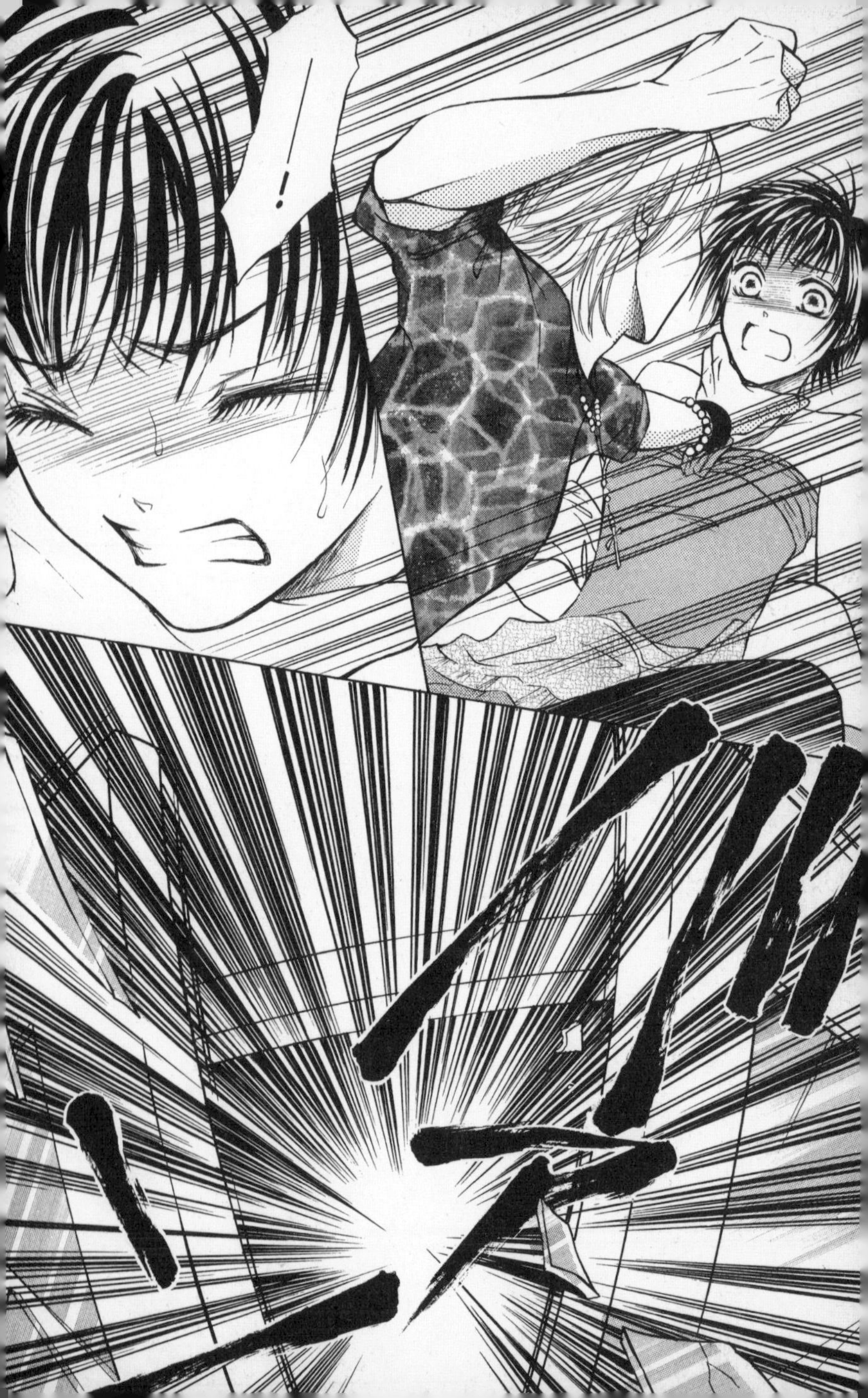
!

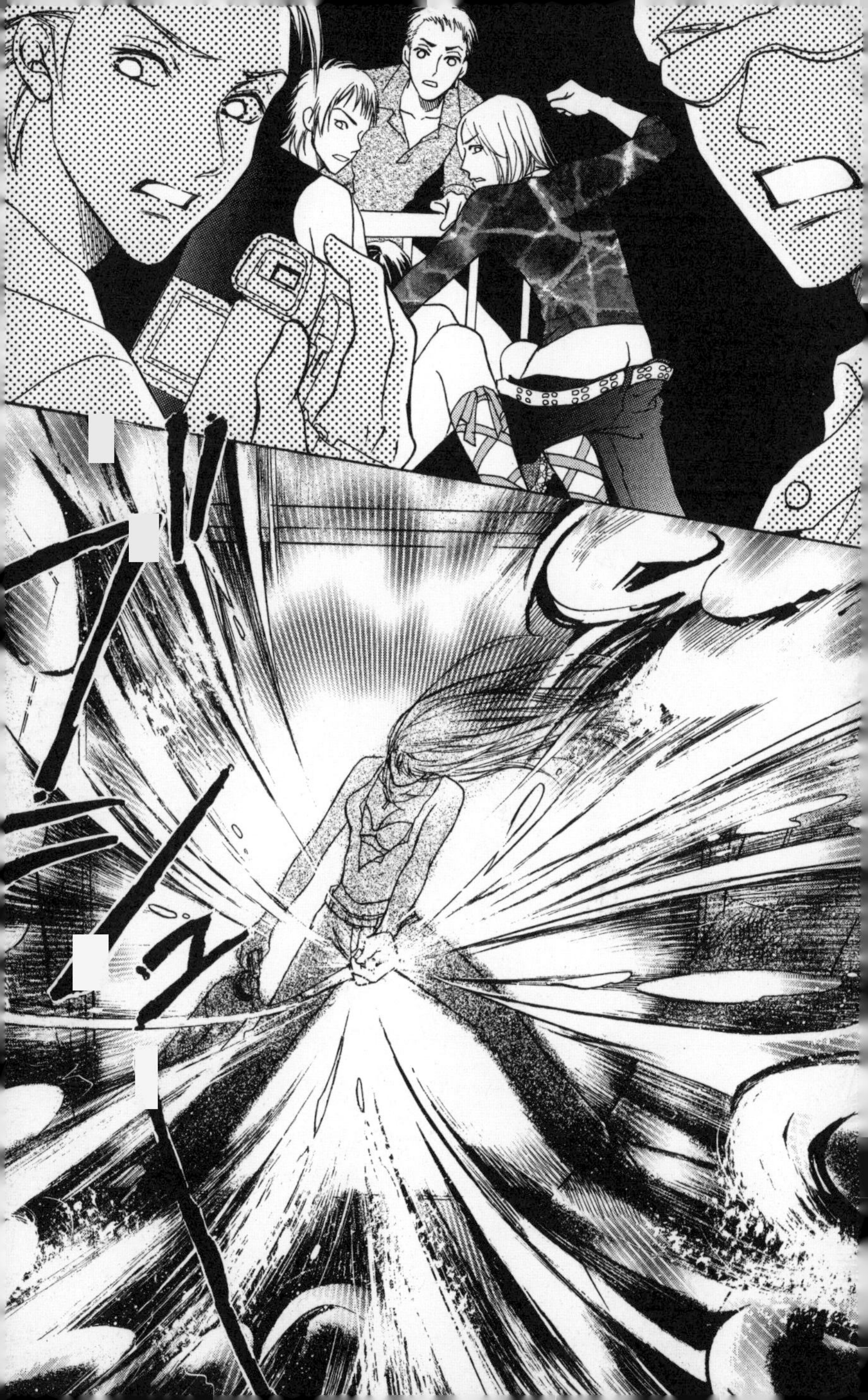

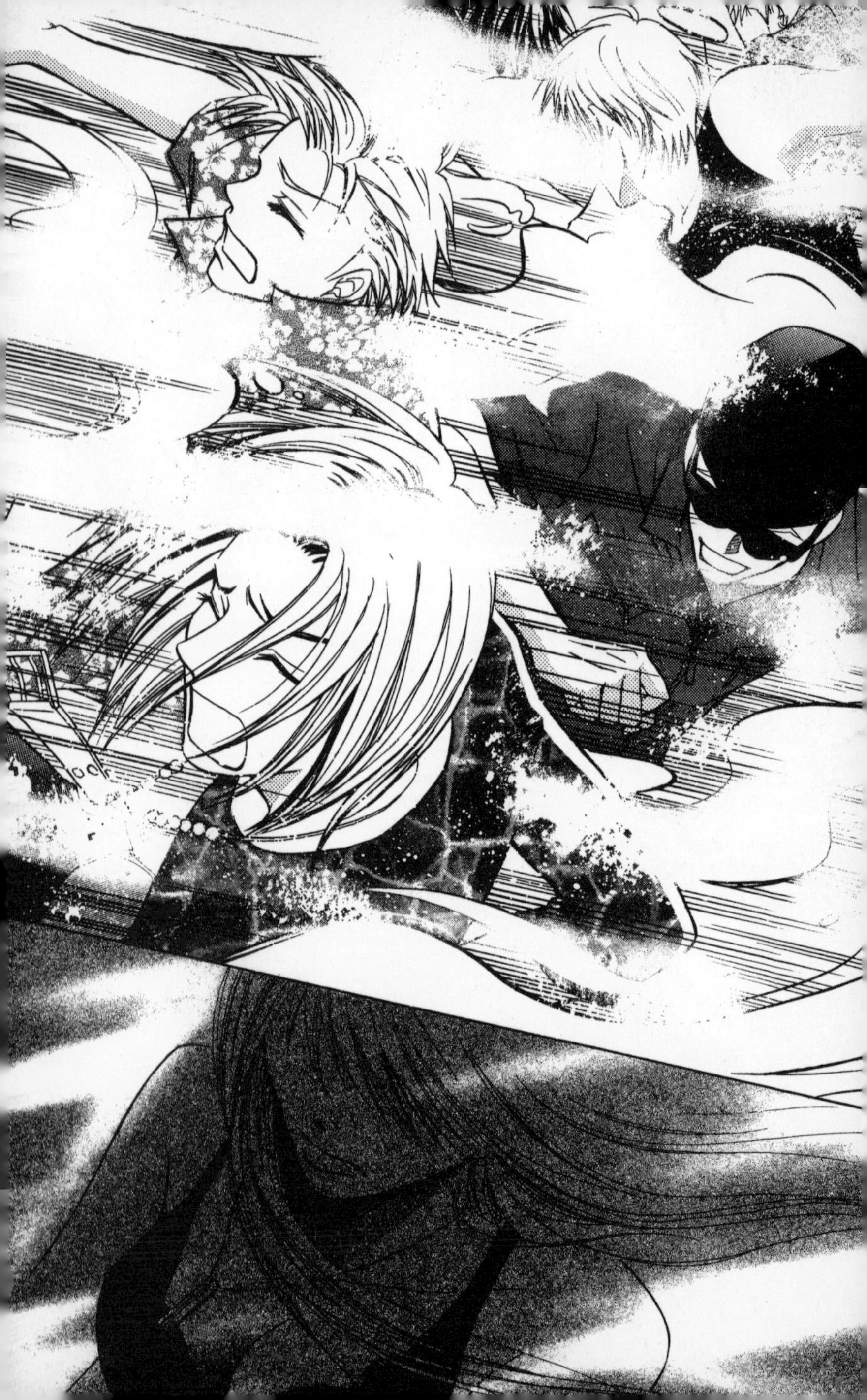

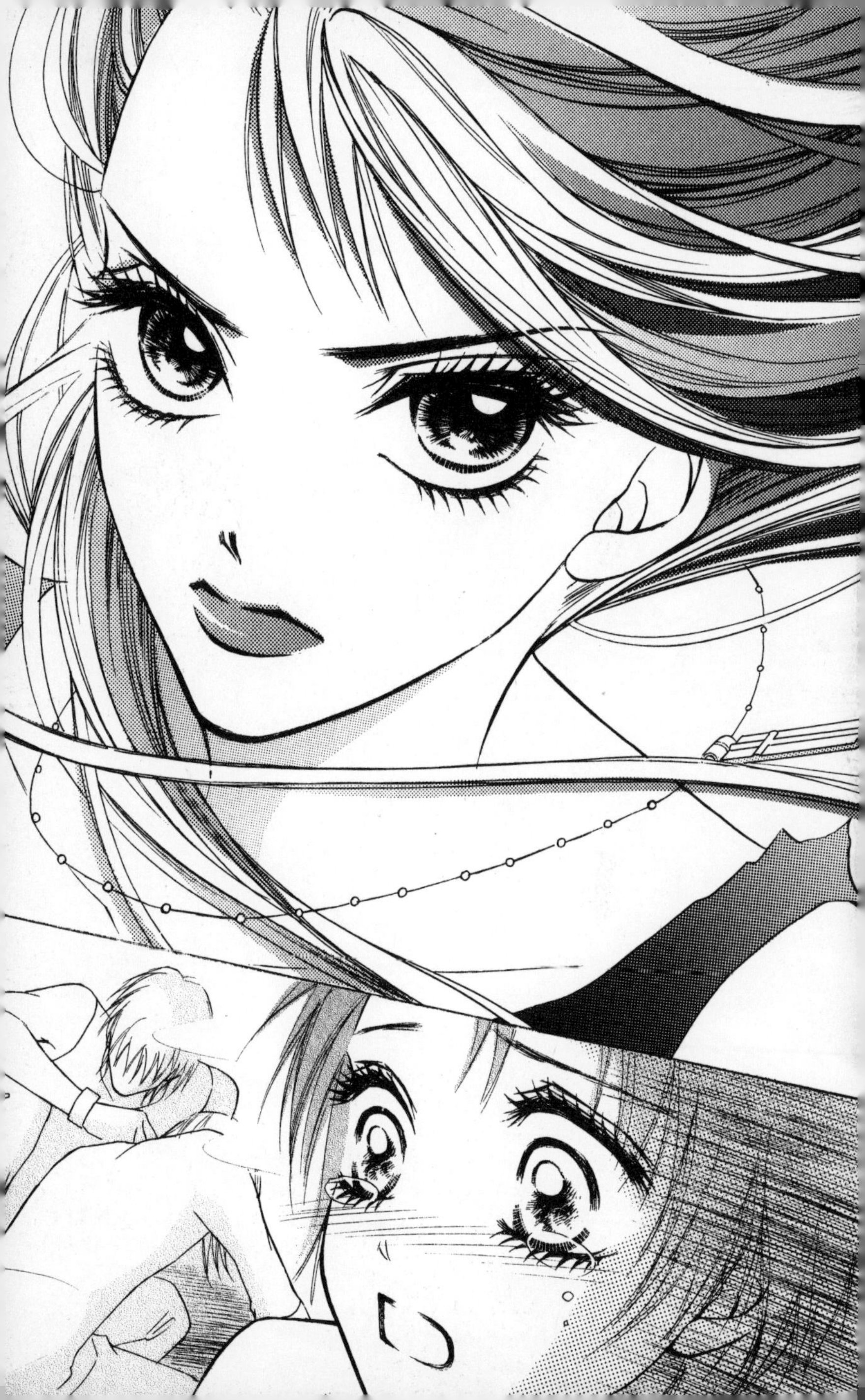

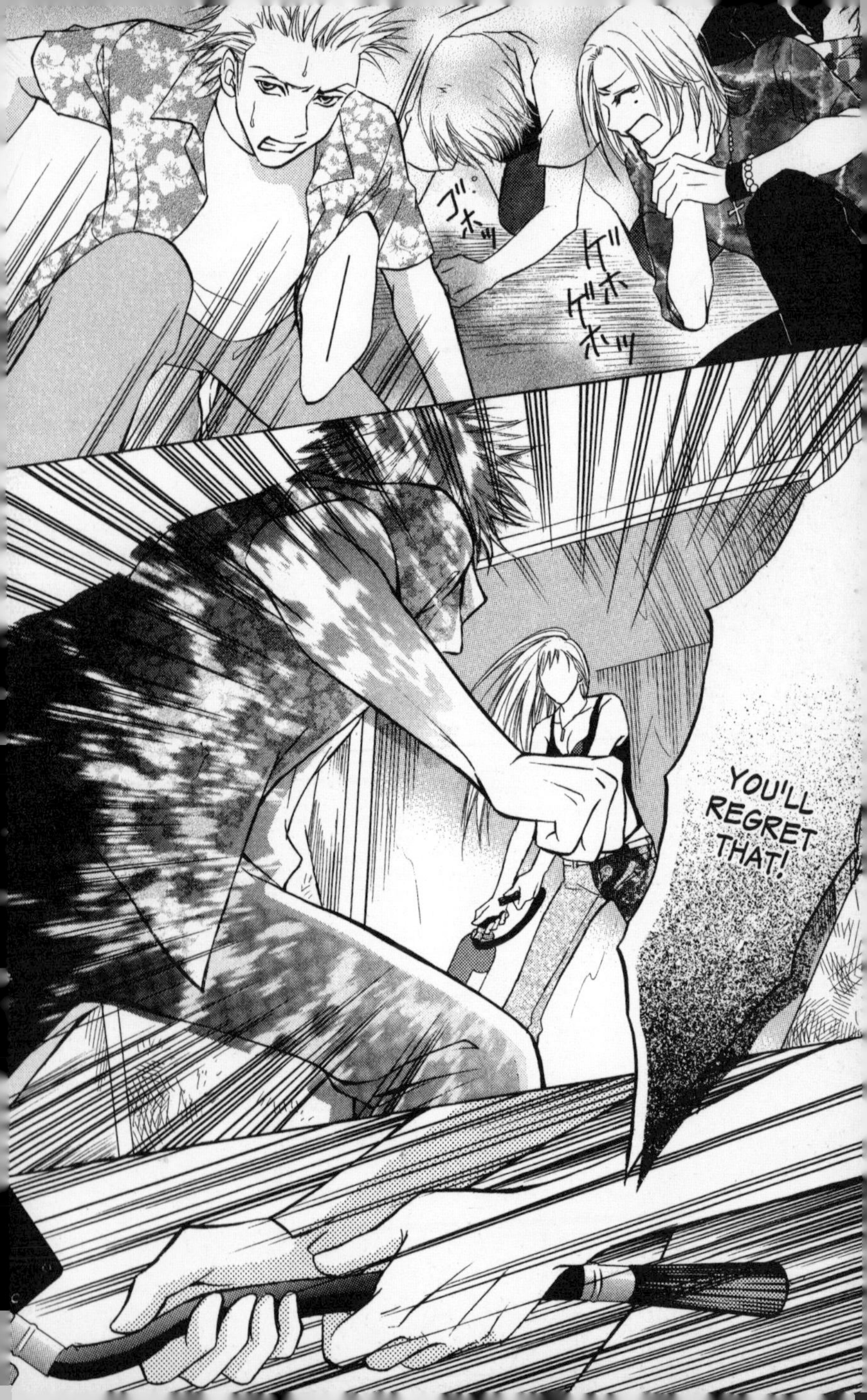
ゴホッ
ゲホゲホッ
YOU'LL REGRET THAT!

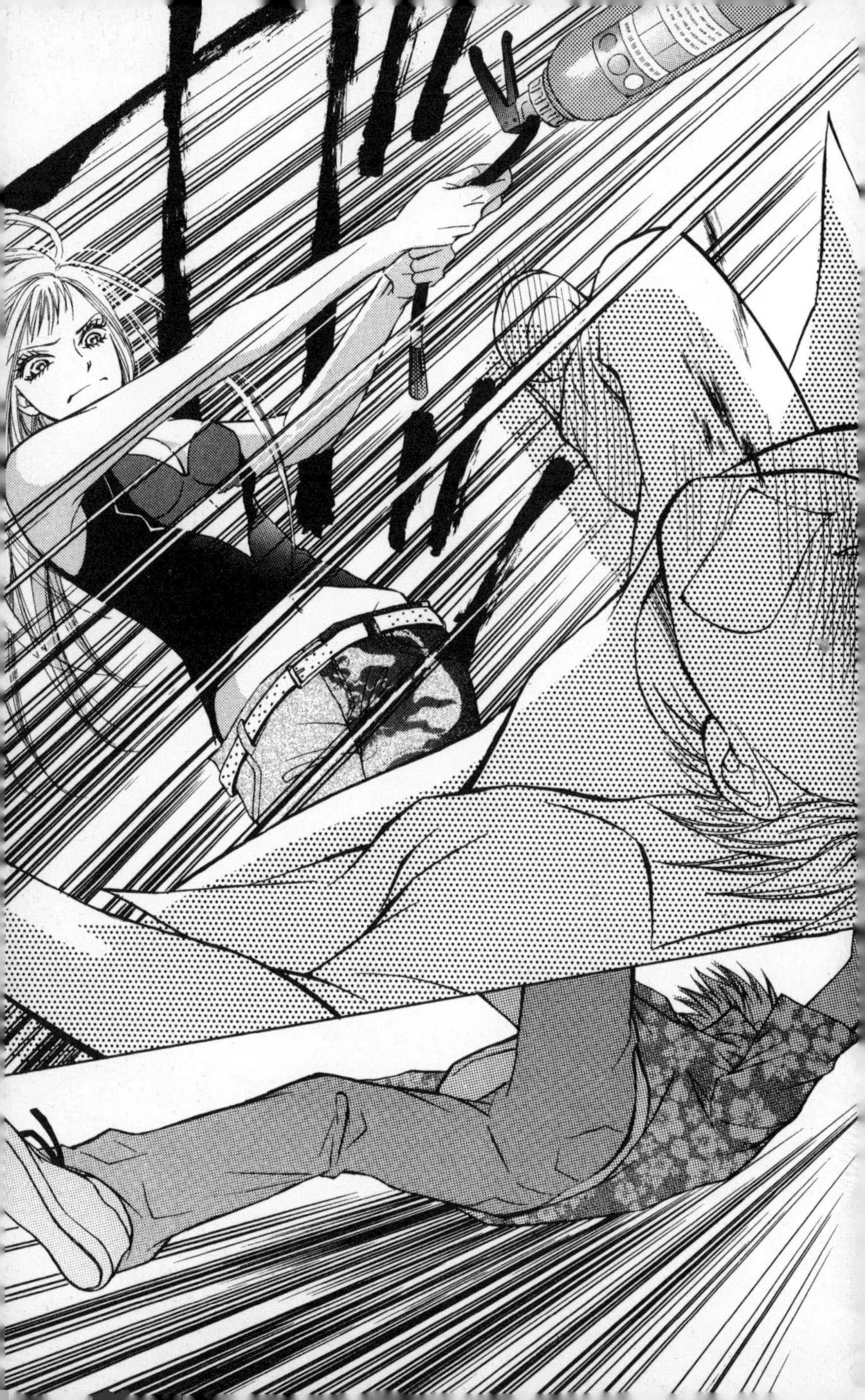

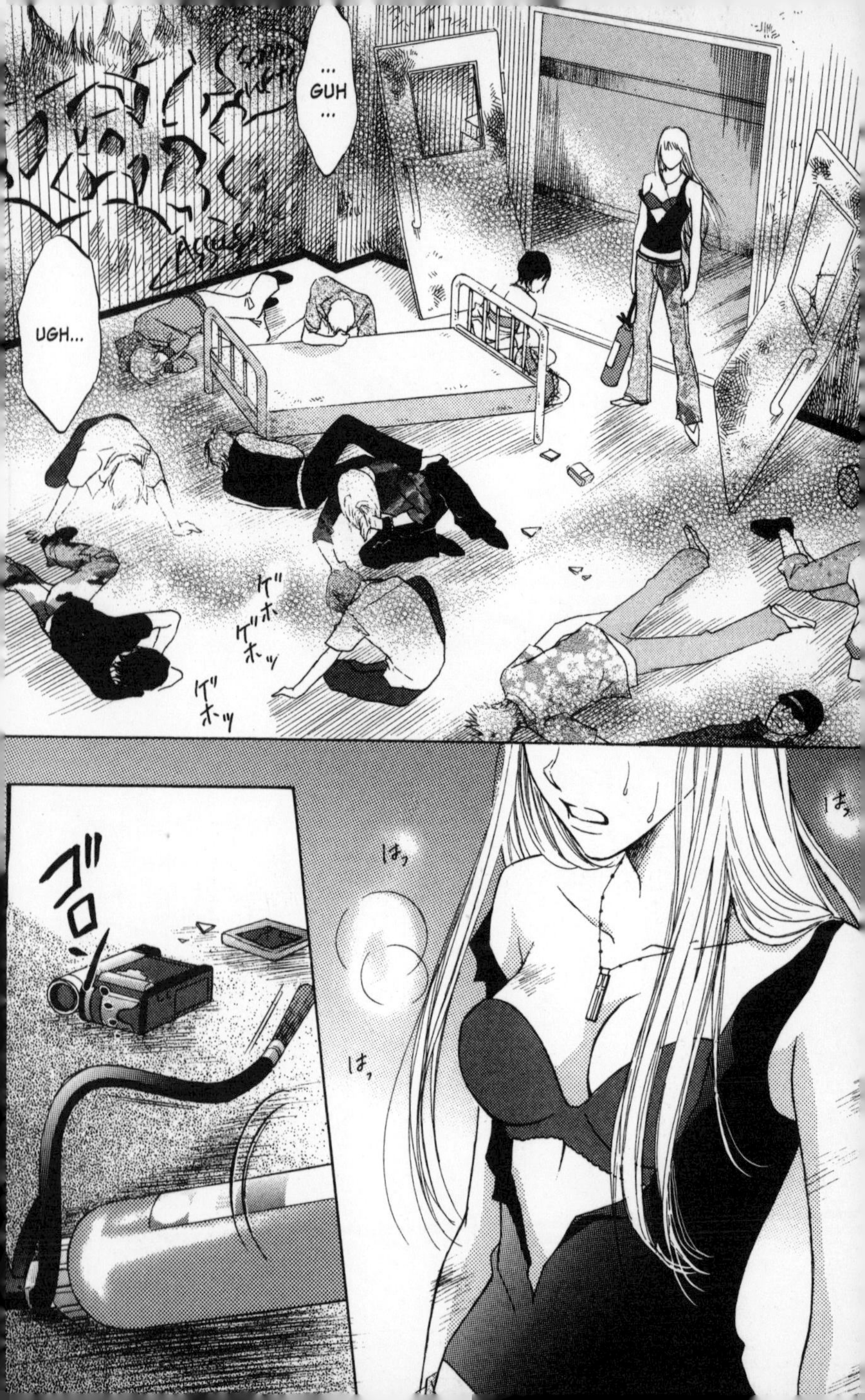

... GUH ...
UGH...
ゲホゲホッ
ゲホッ
はっ
はっ
はっ
ゴロ

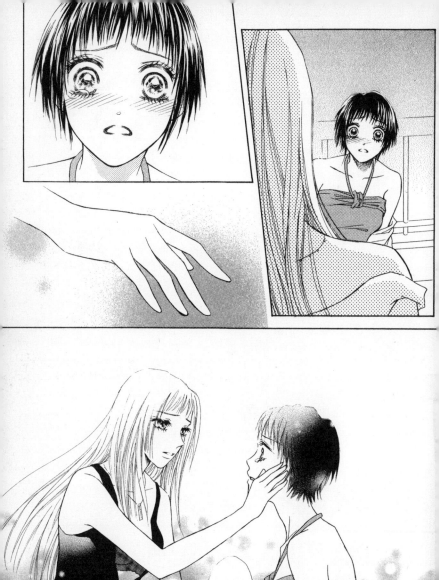

ARE
YOU
OKAY?

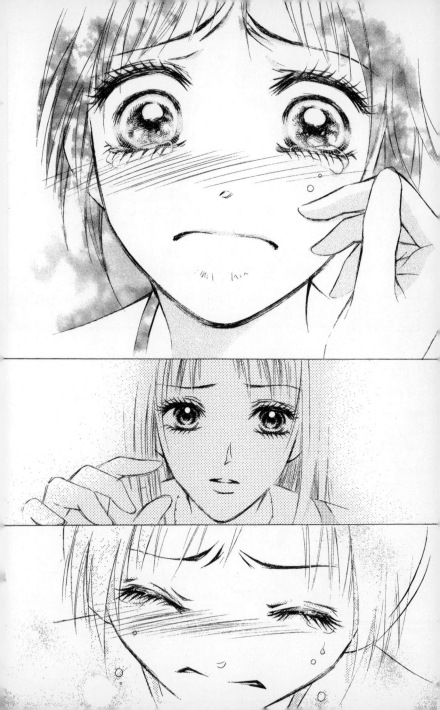

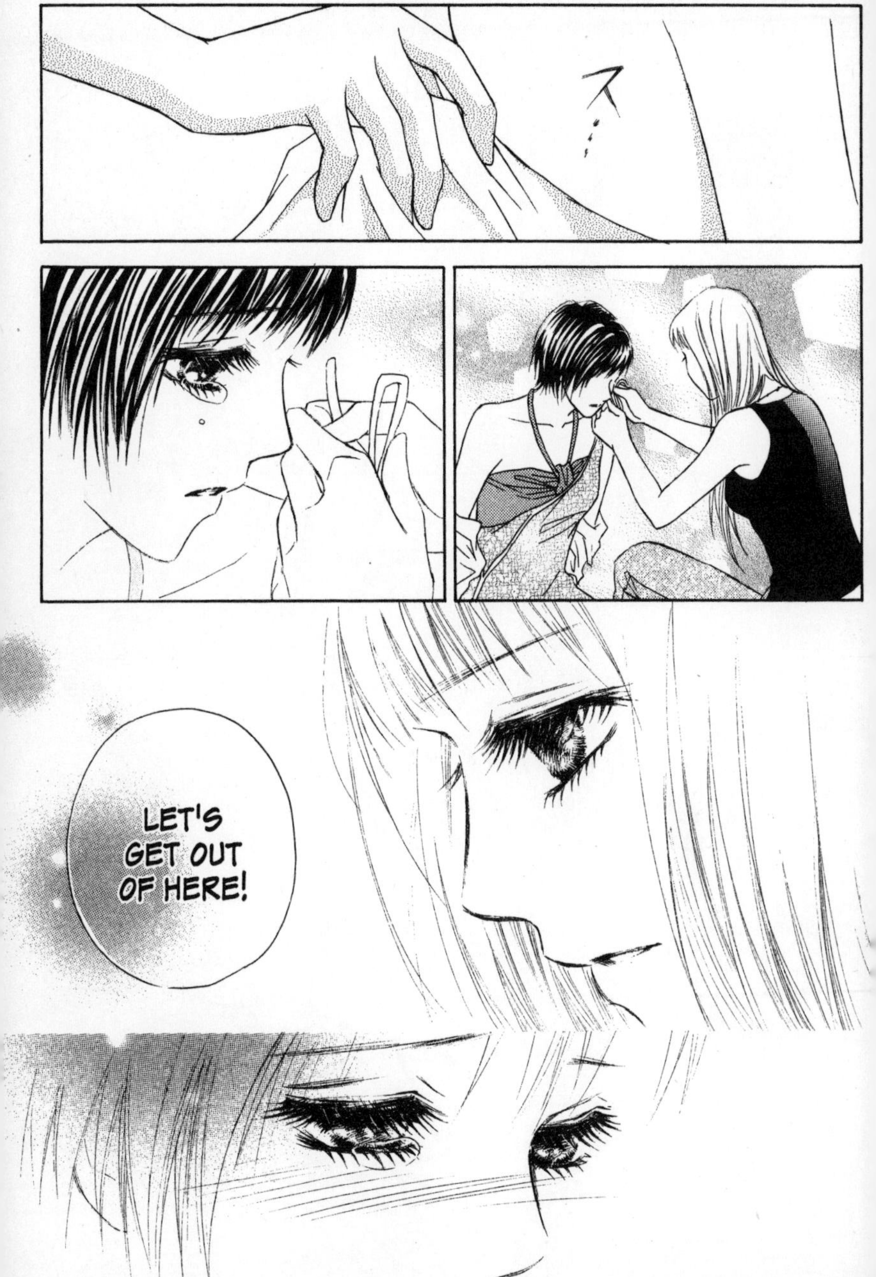
ス…
LET'S GET OUT OF HERE!

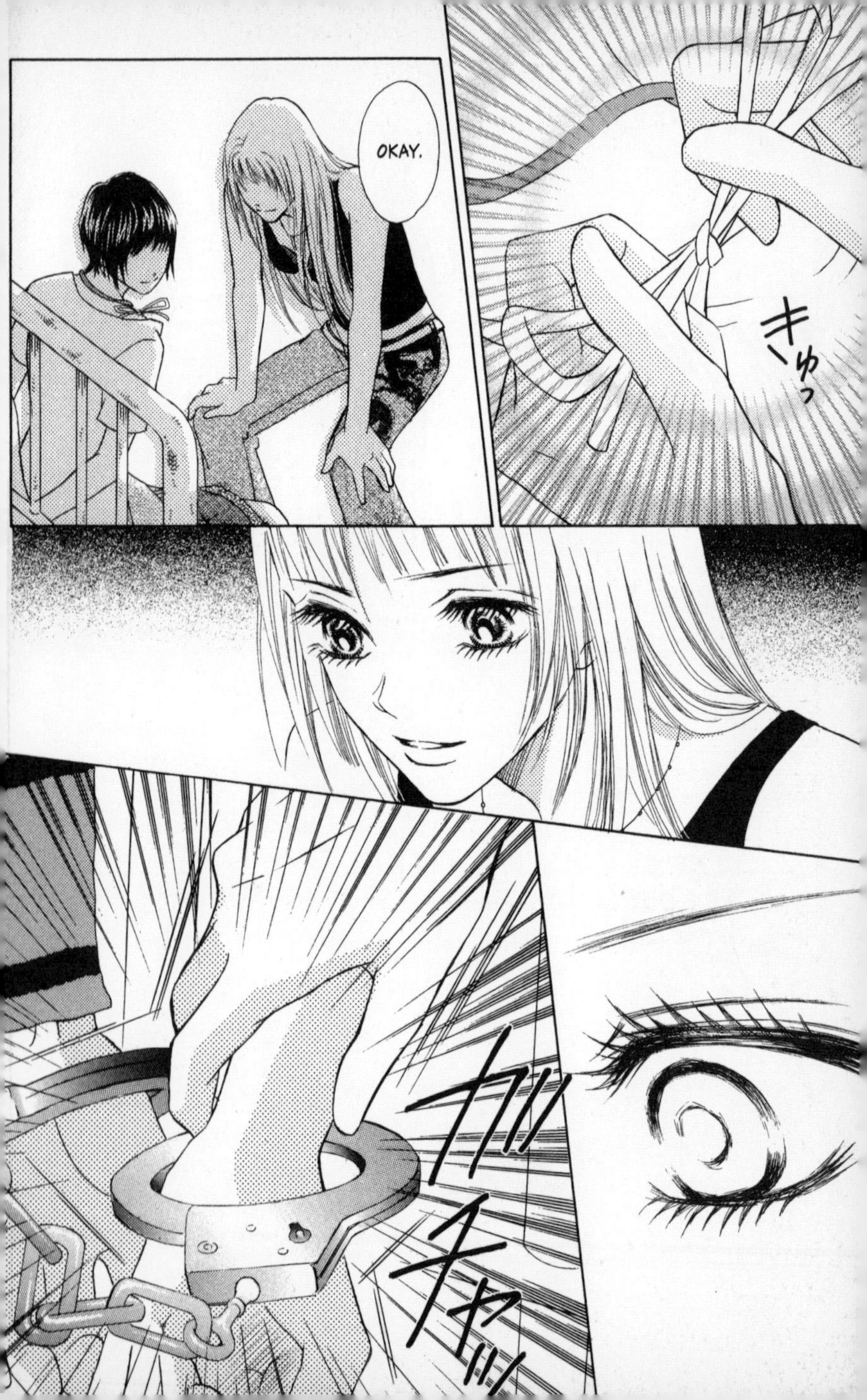
きゅっ
OKAY.
ガチャッ

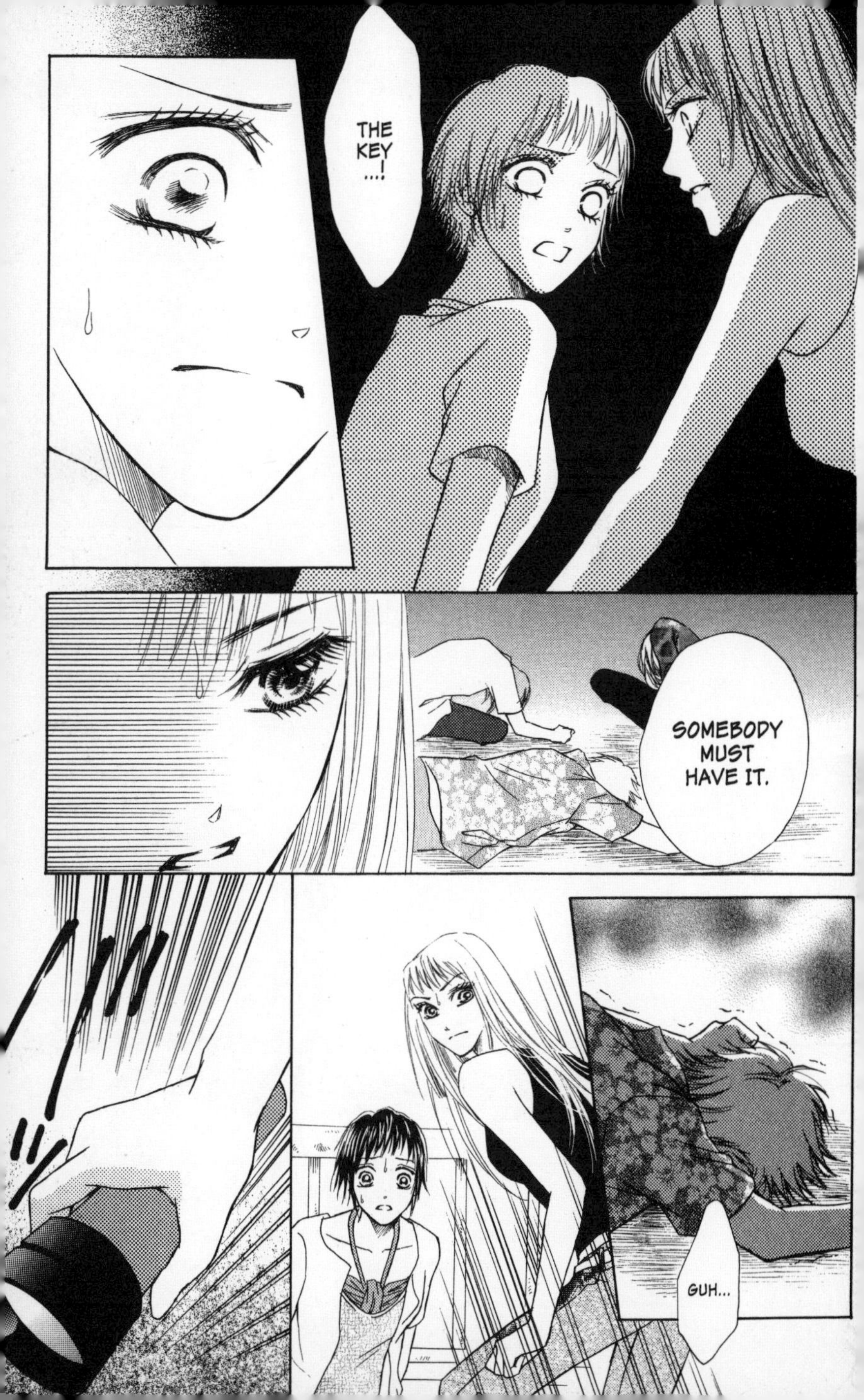
THE KEY ...!
SOMEBODY MUST HAVE IT.
GUH...

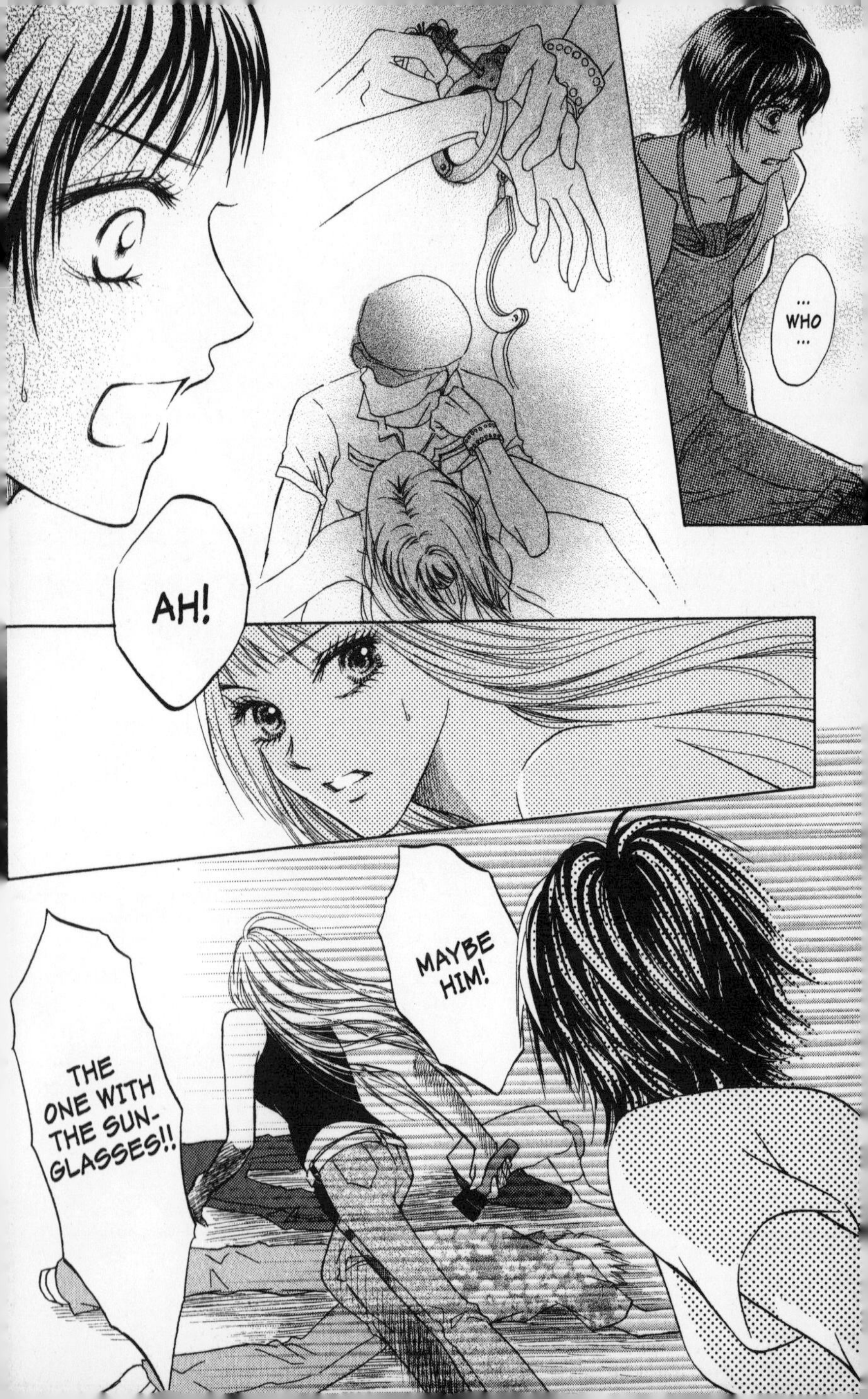
... WHO ...
AH!
MAYBE HIM!
THE ONE WITH THE SUN-GLASSES!!

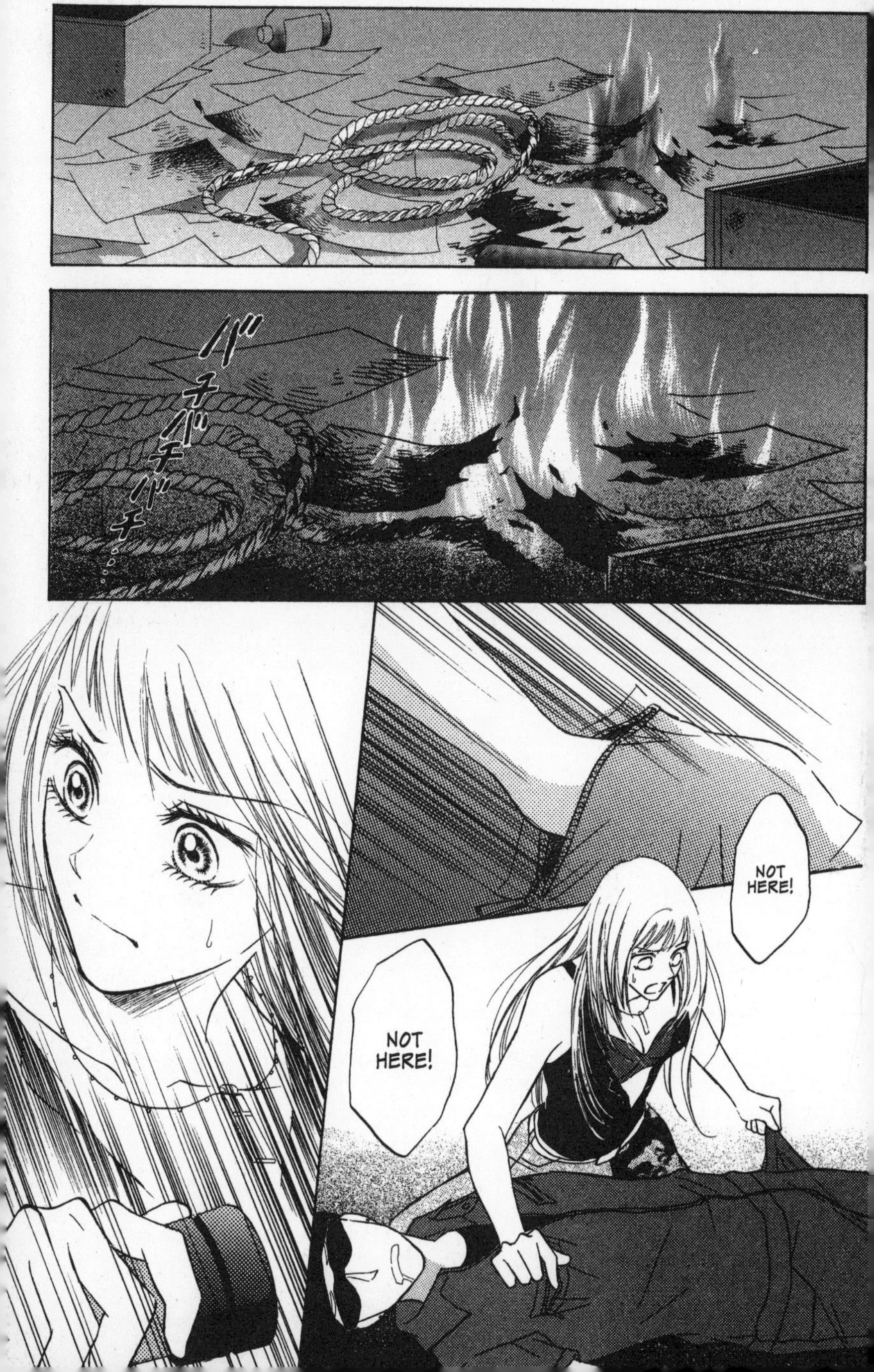
バチバチバチ
NOT HERE!
NOT HERE!

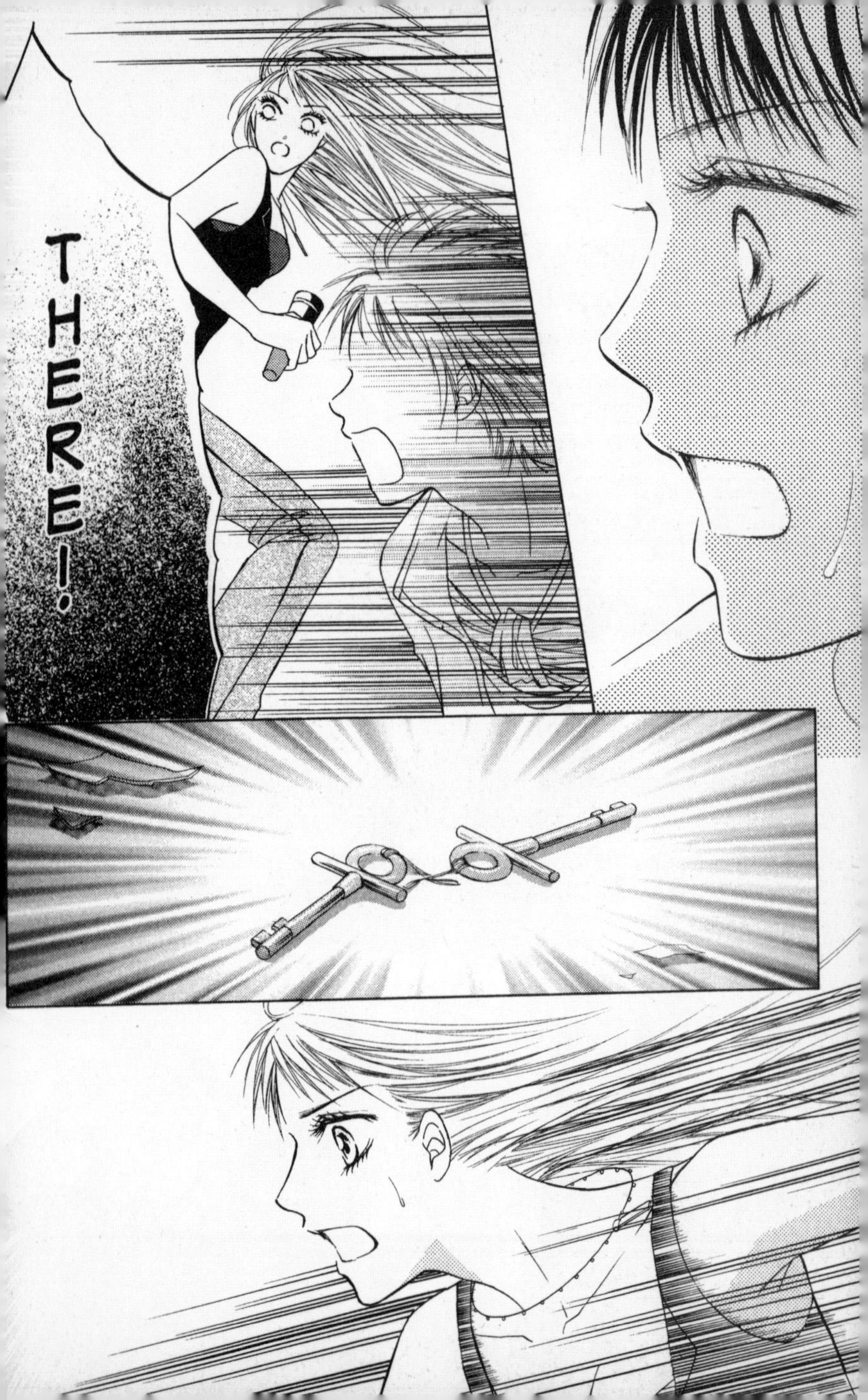
THERE!

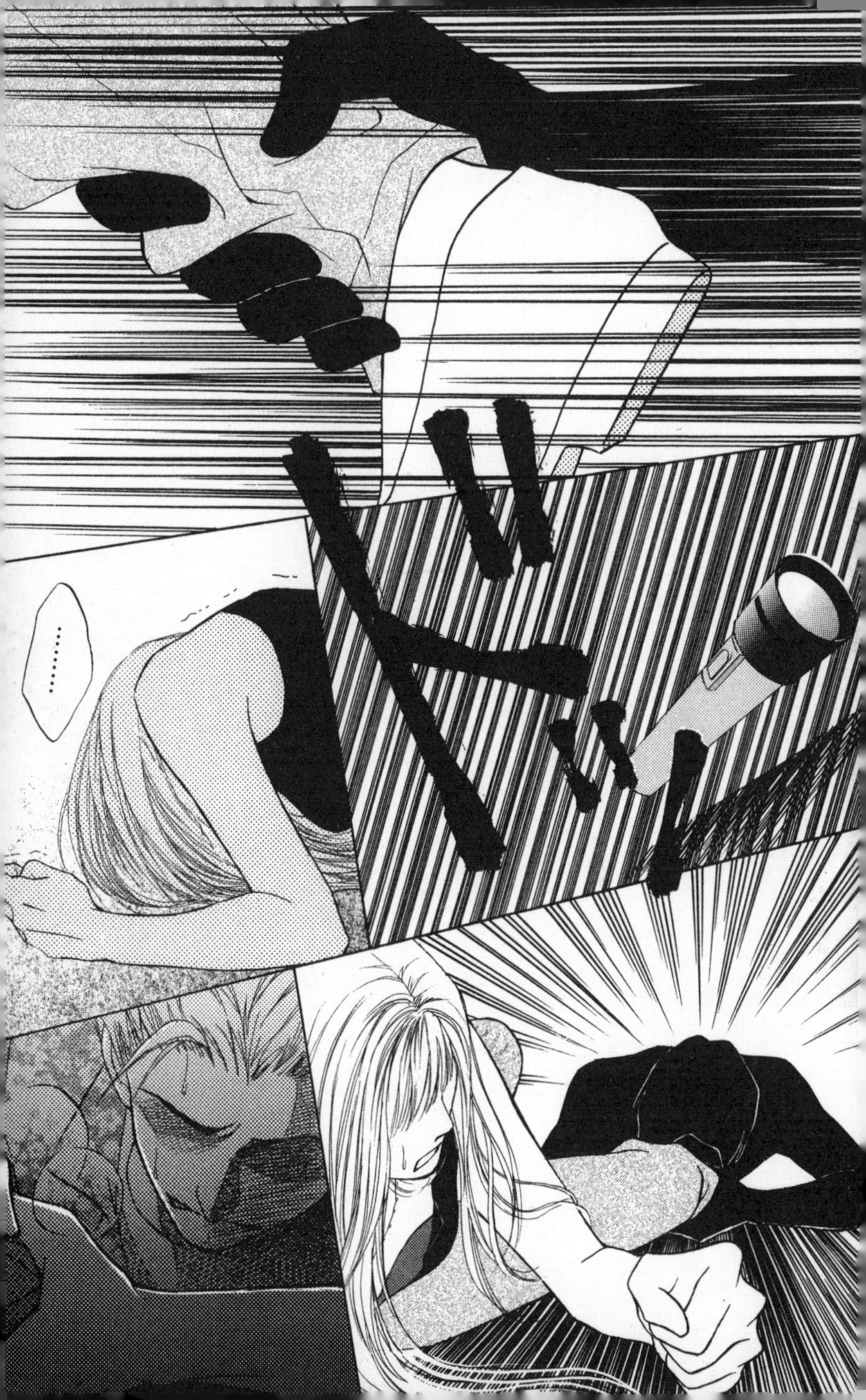
......

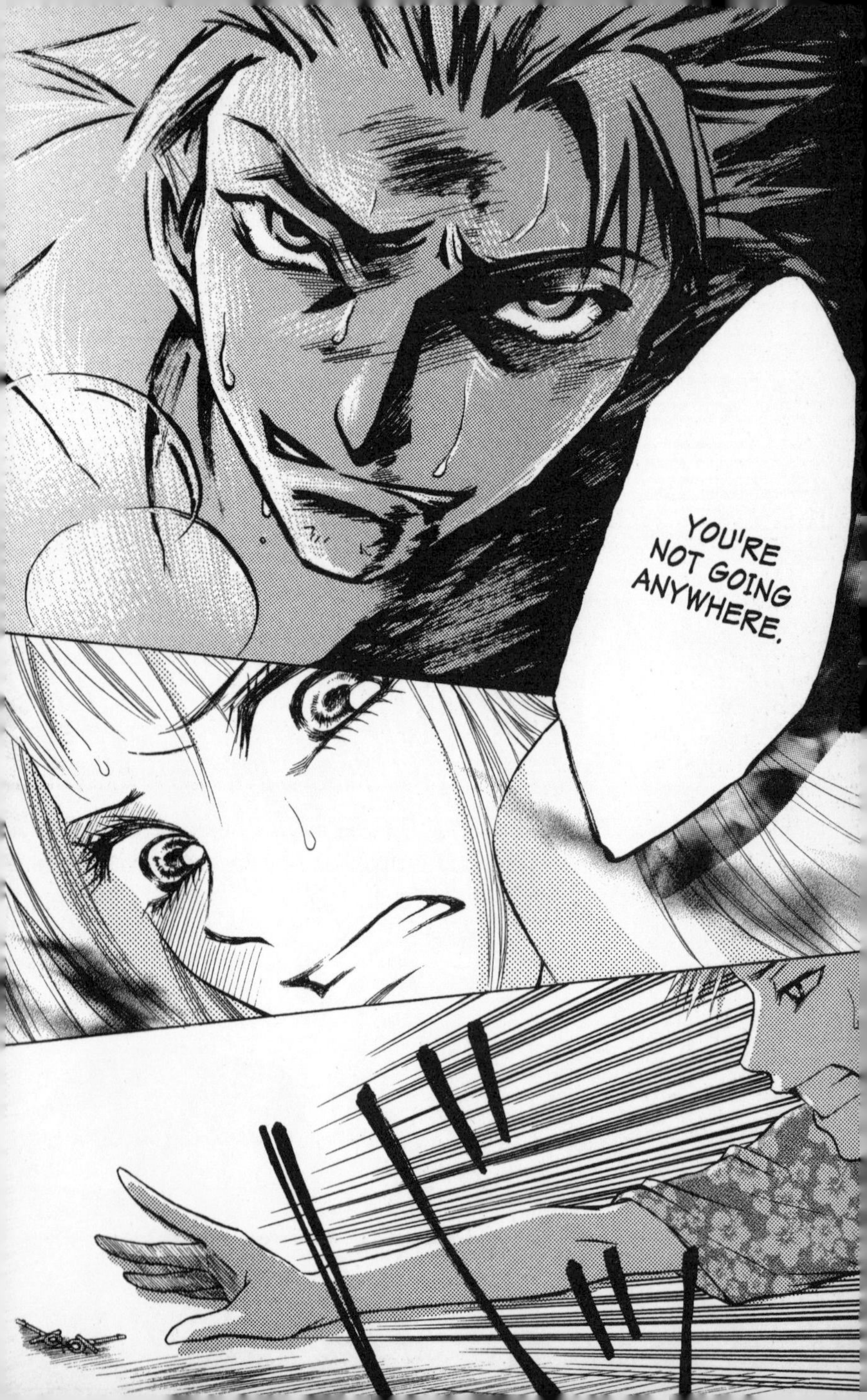
YOU'RE NOT GOING ANYWHERE.

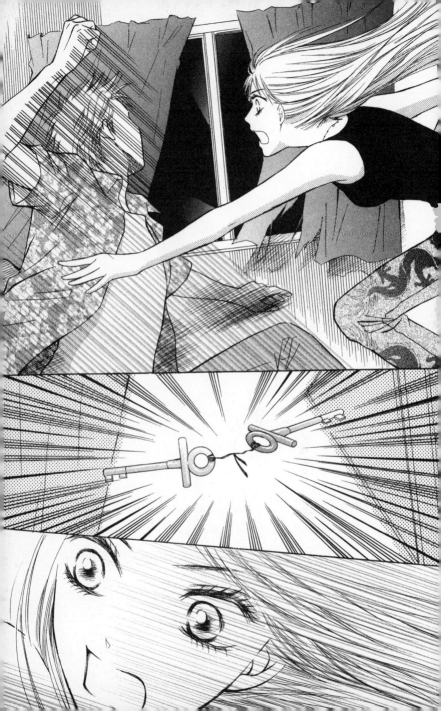

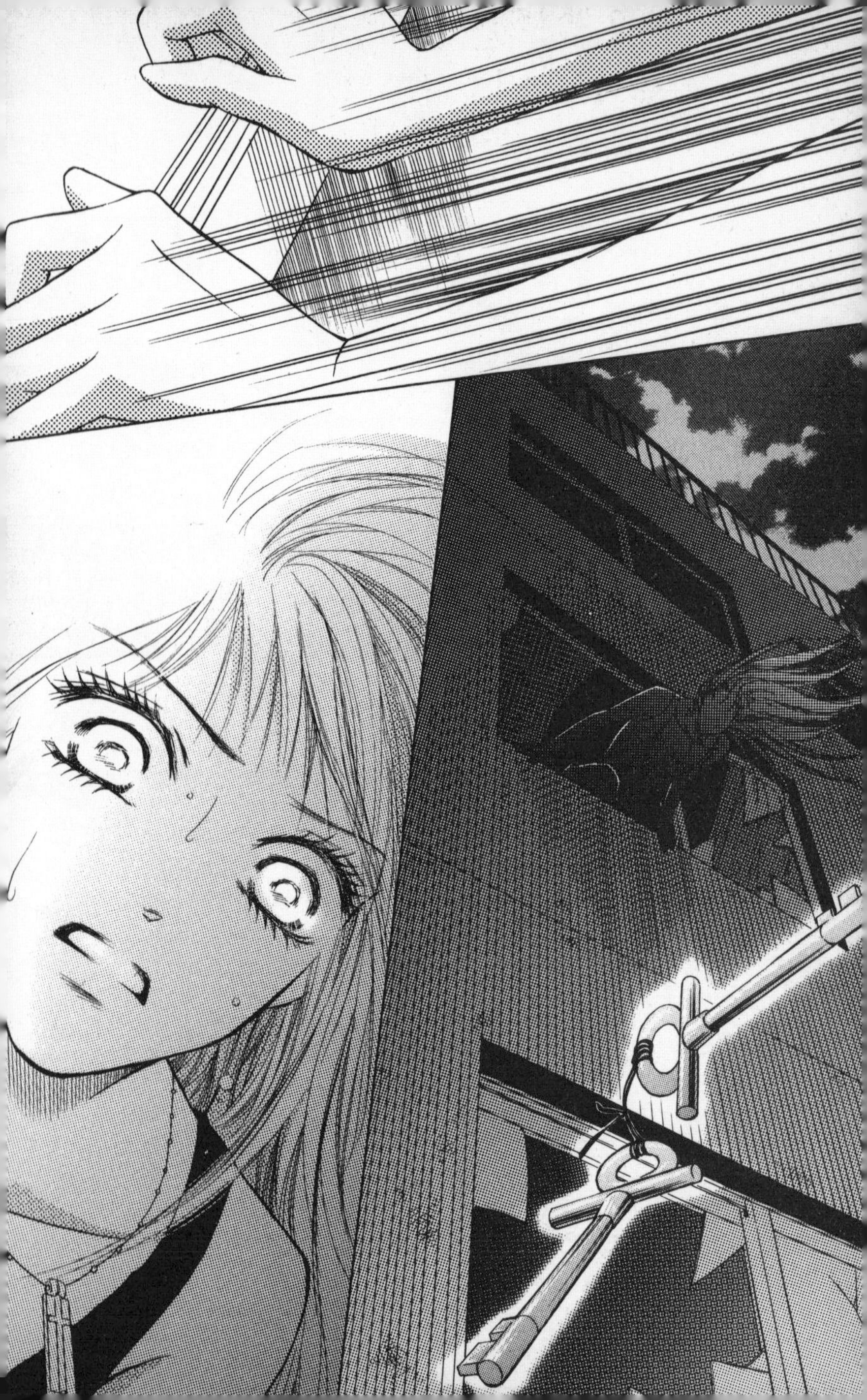

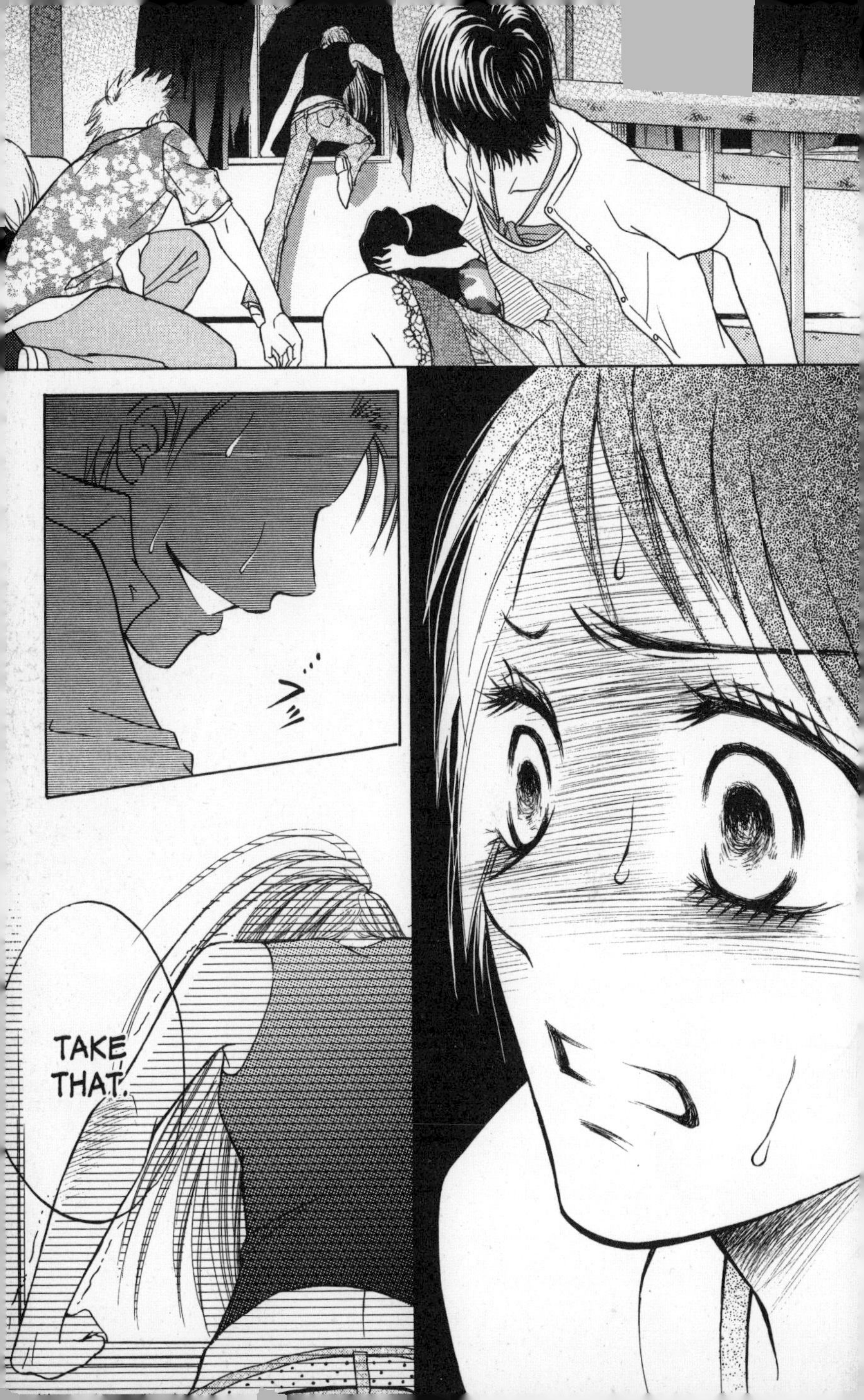
TAKE THAT.

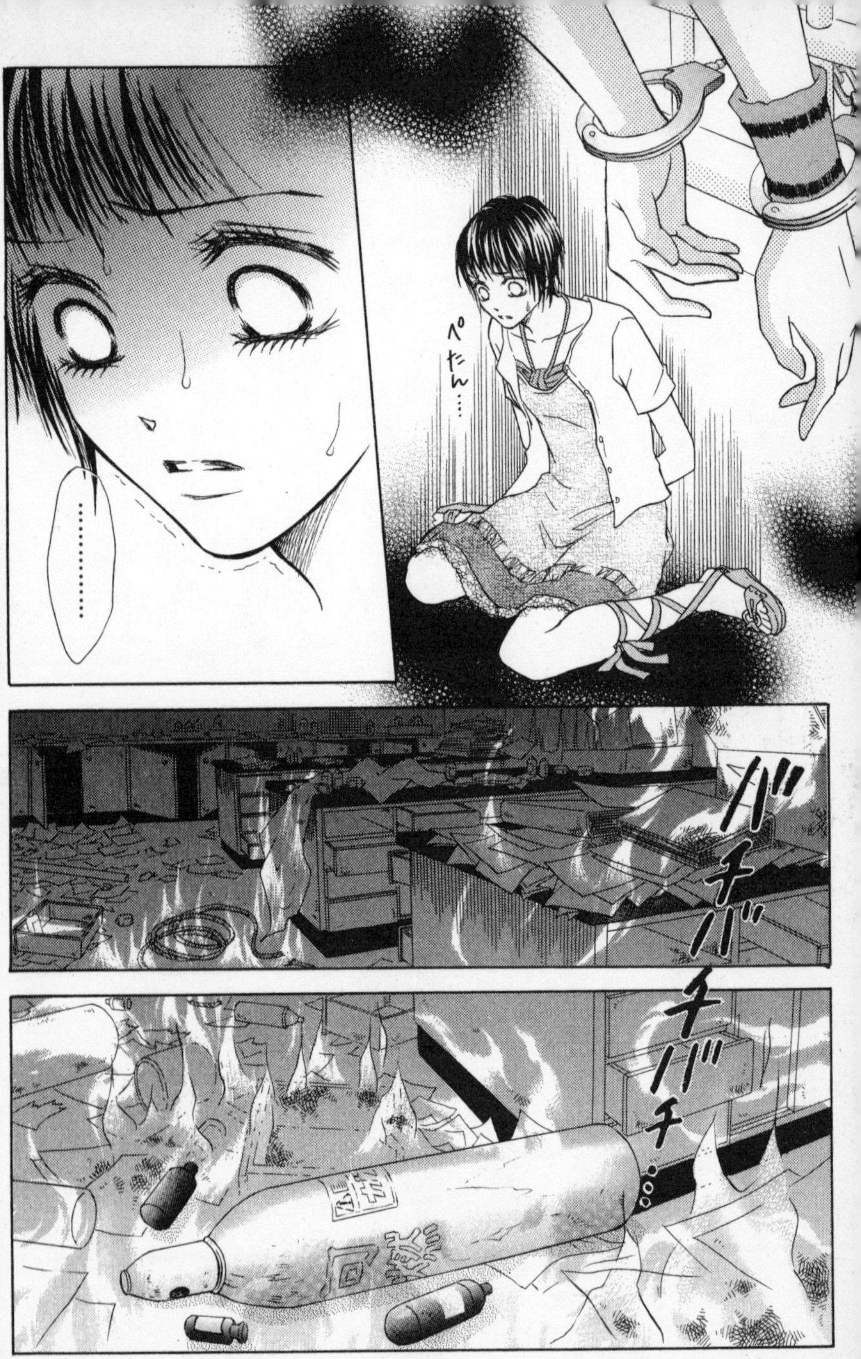
ぺたん…
…………
バチバチバチ…

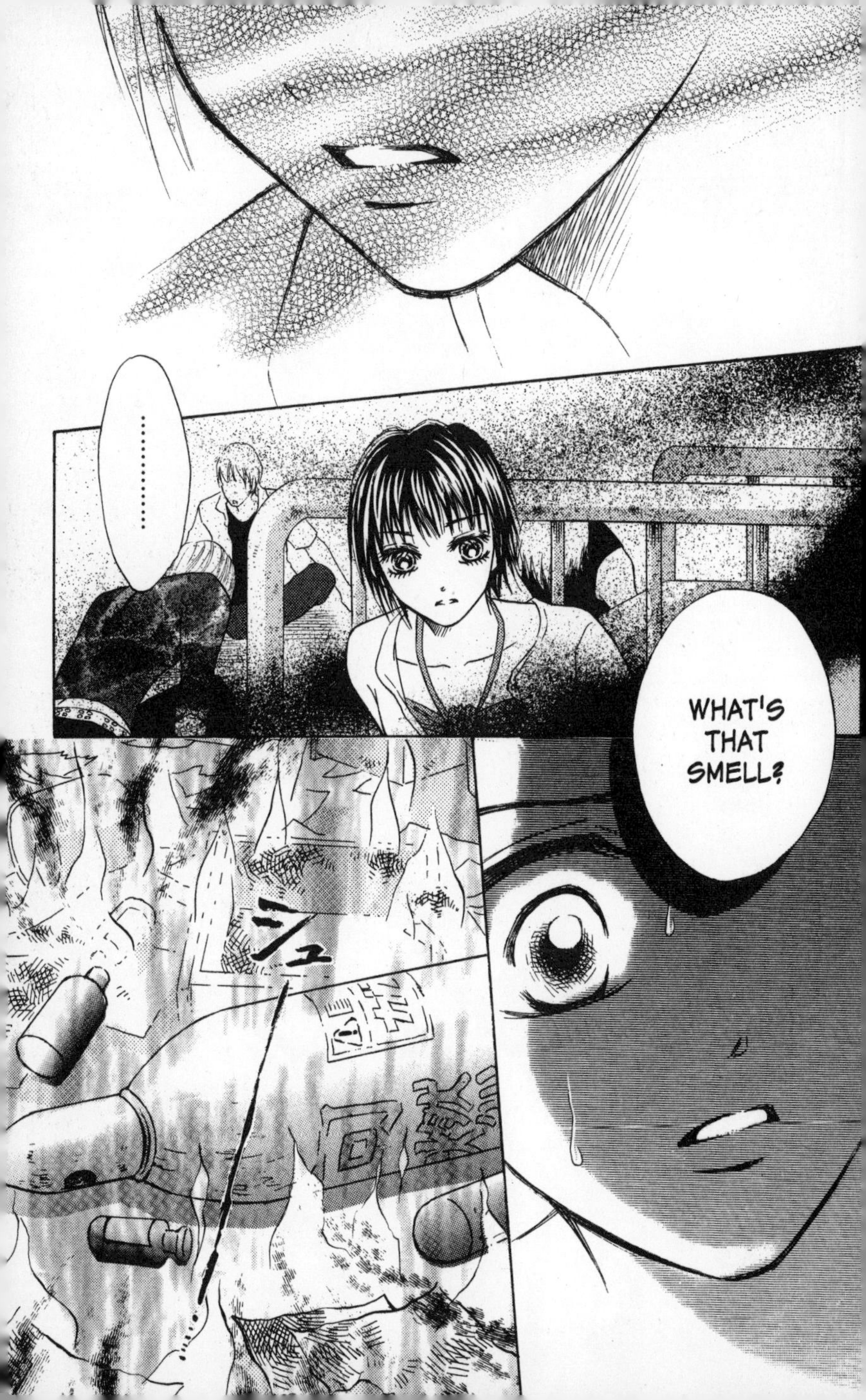
......
WHAT'S THAT SMELL?
シュ
......

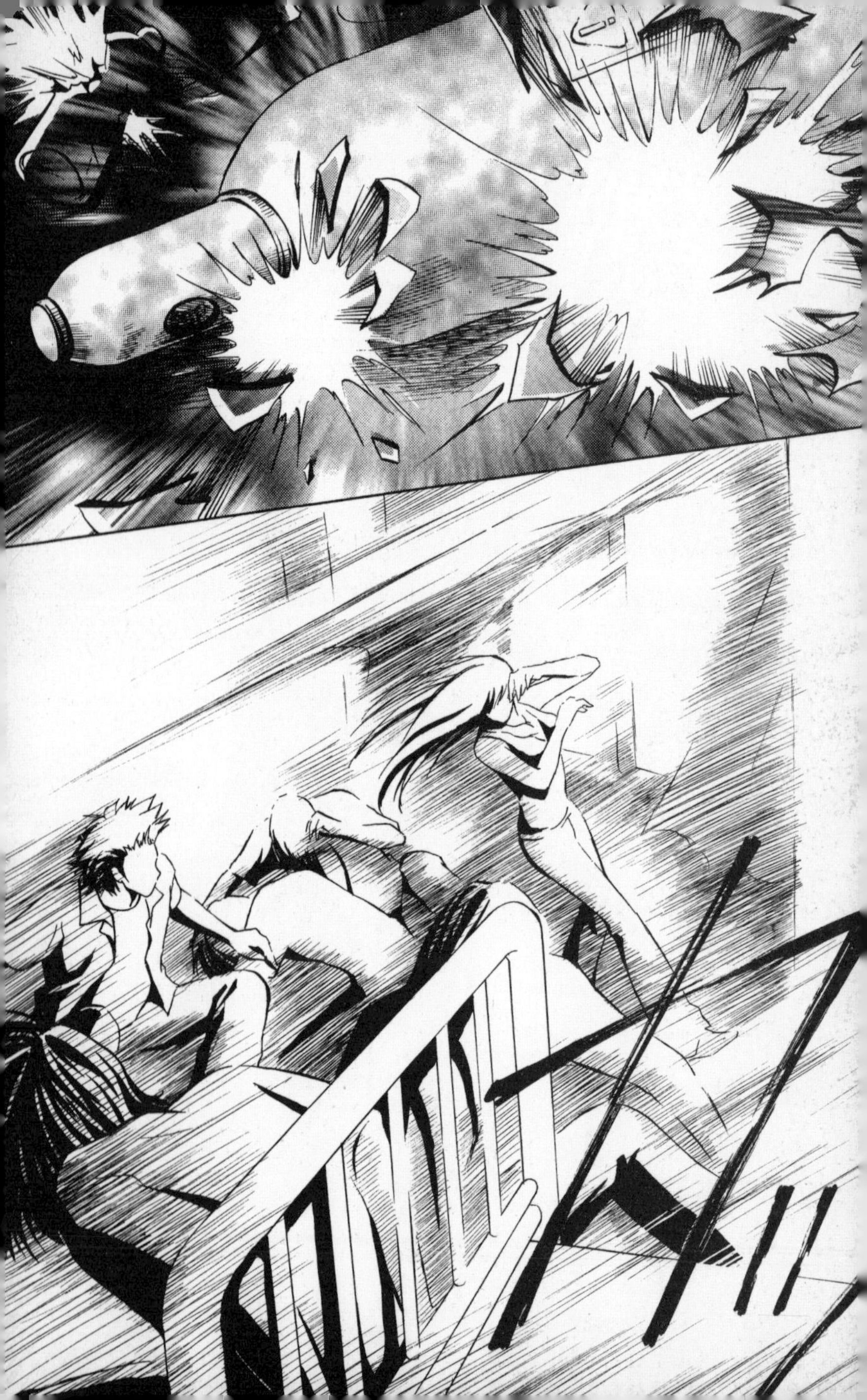

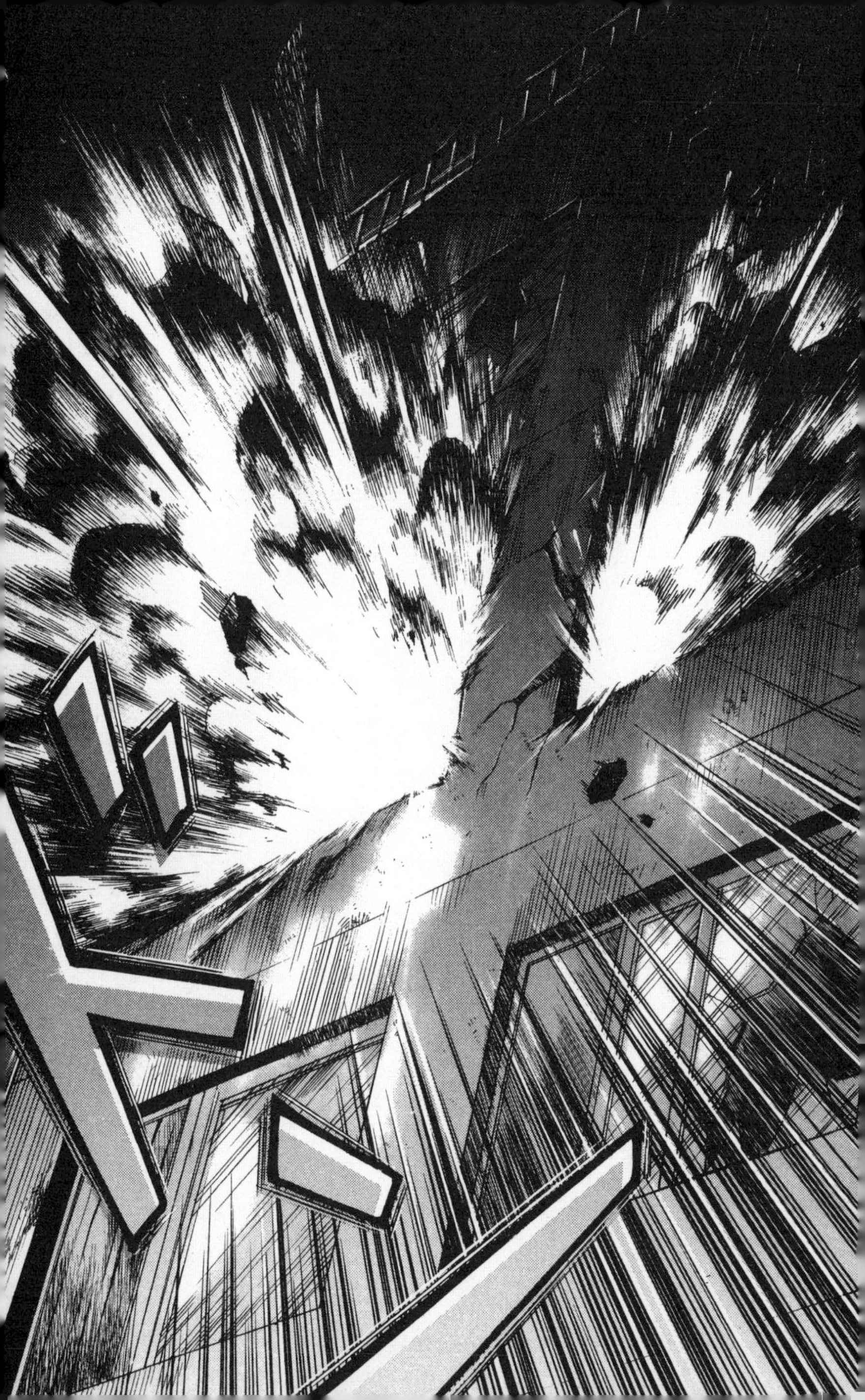

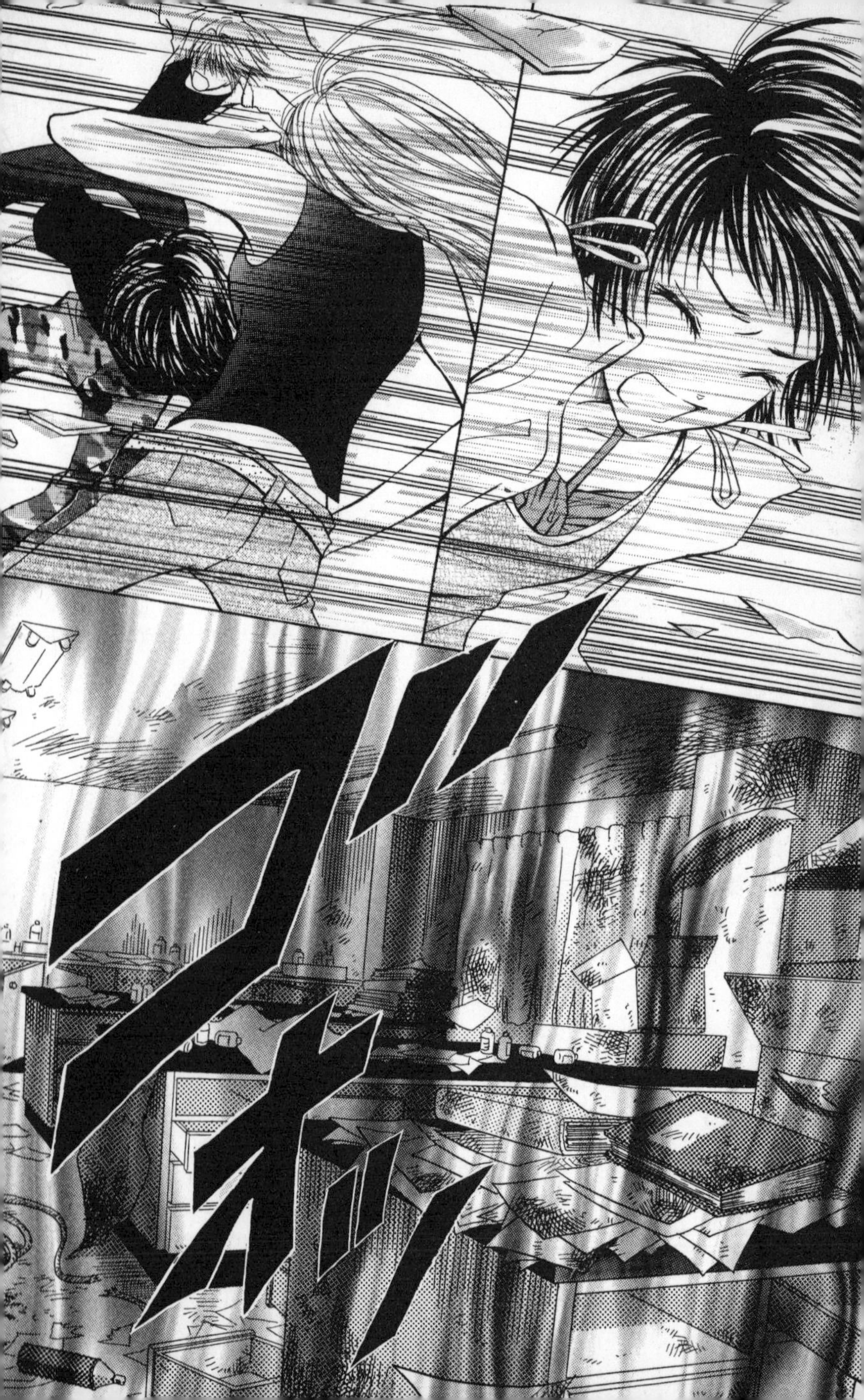

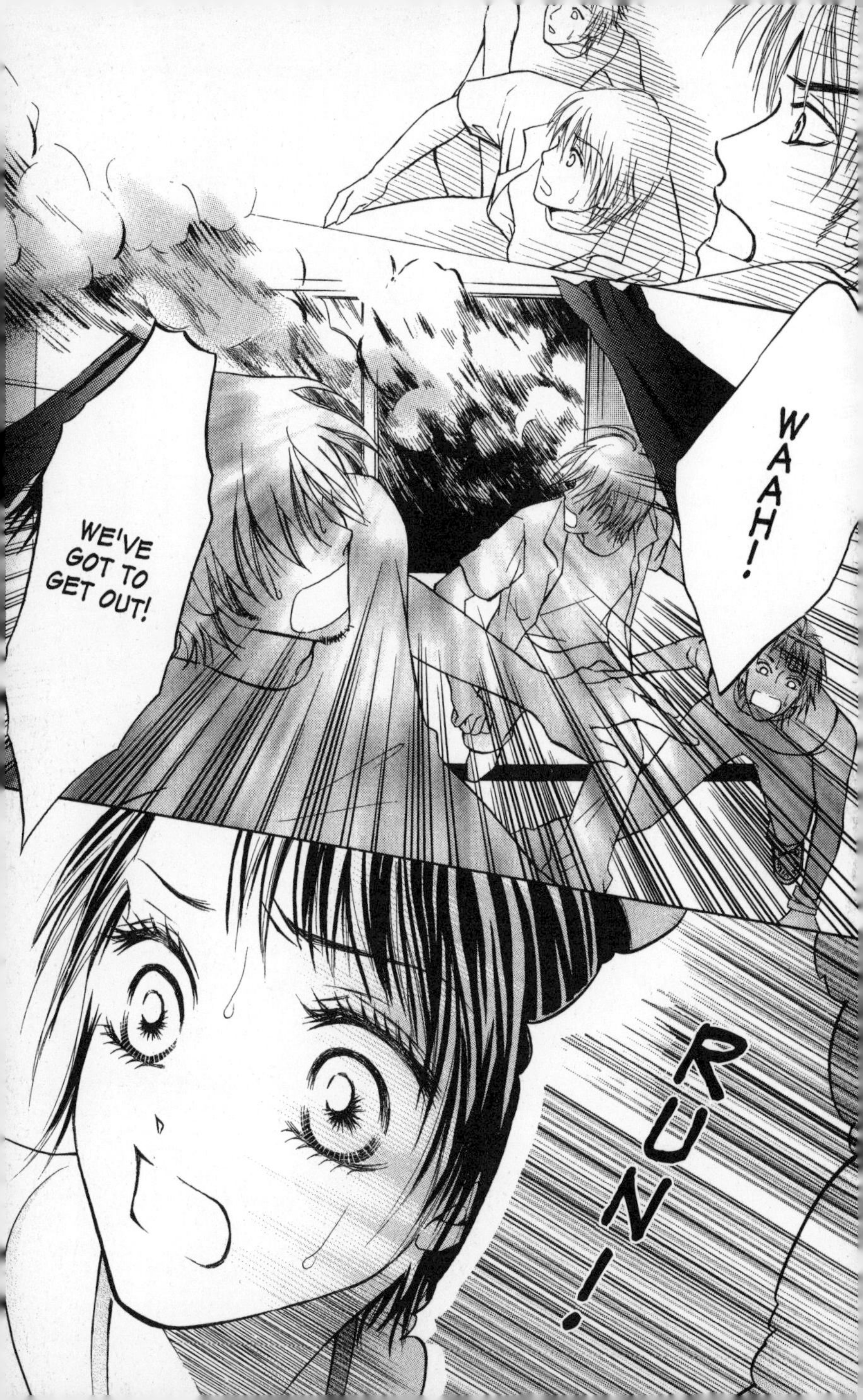
WAAH!
WE'VE GOT TO GET OUT!
RUN!

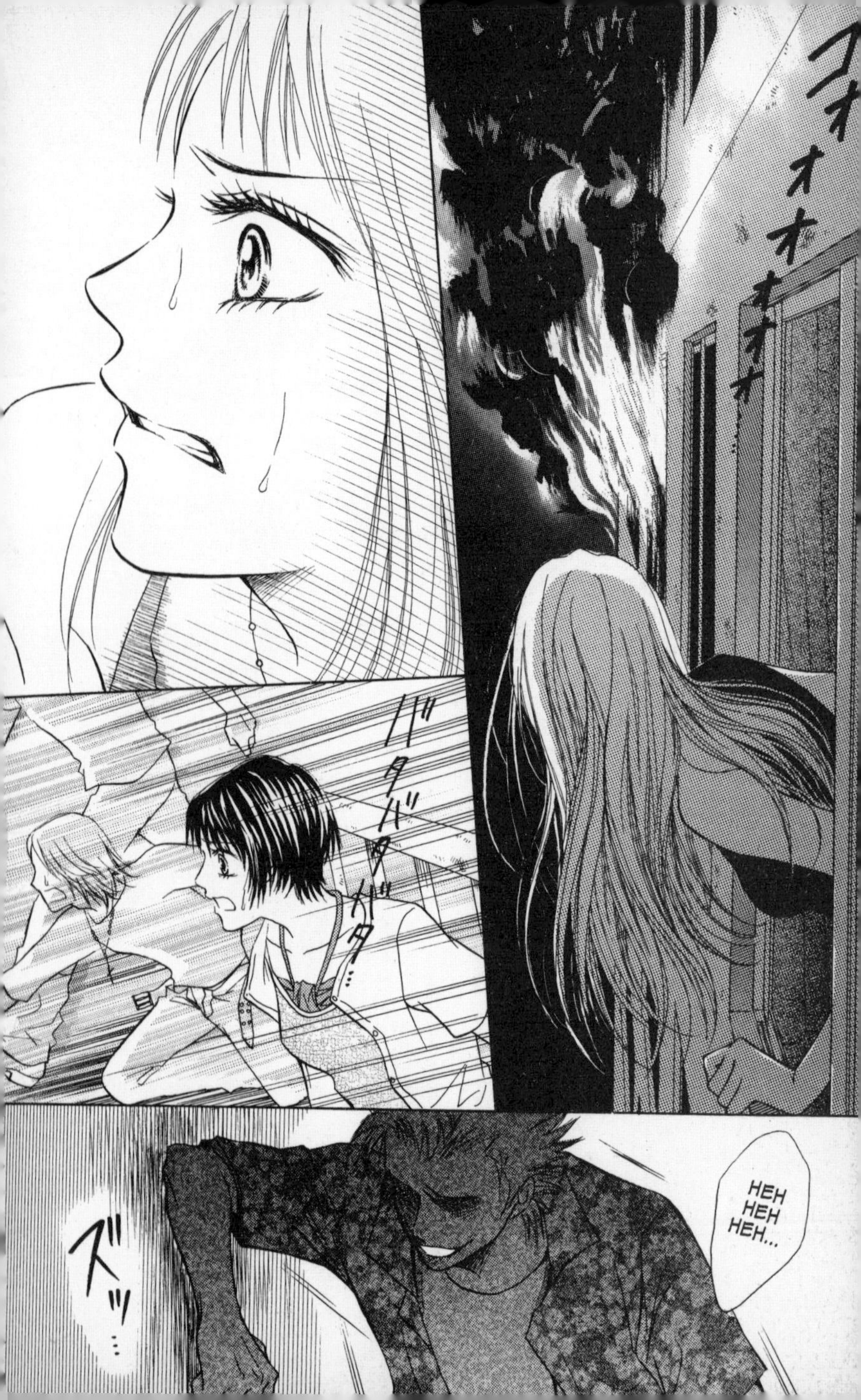
ゴオオオオオオ
バタバタバタ…
HEH HEH HEH...
ズッ…

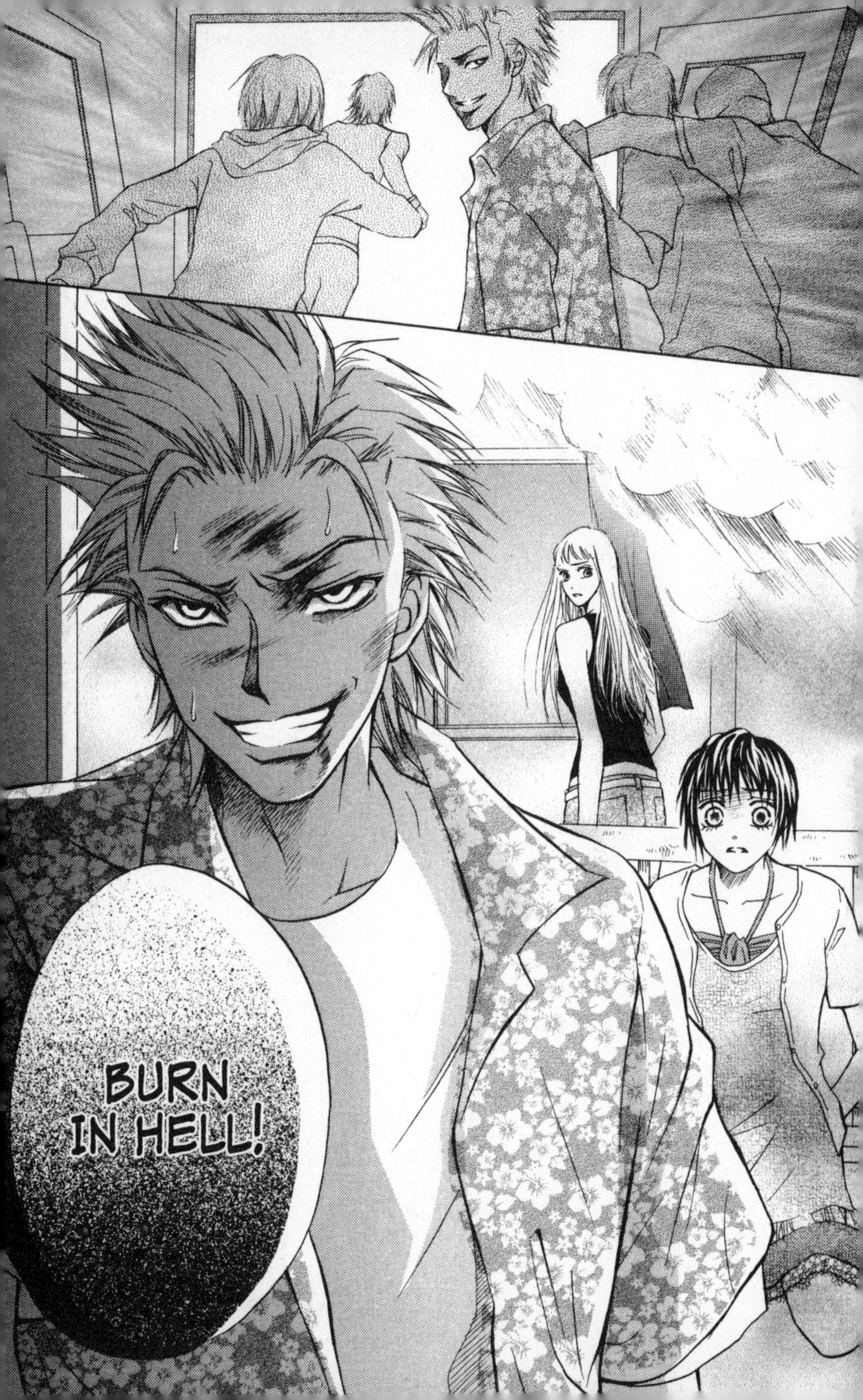
BURN IN HELL!

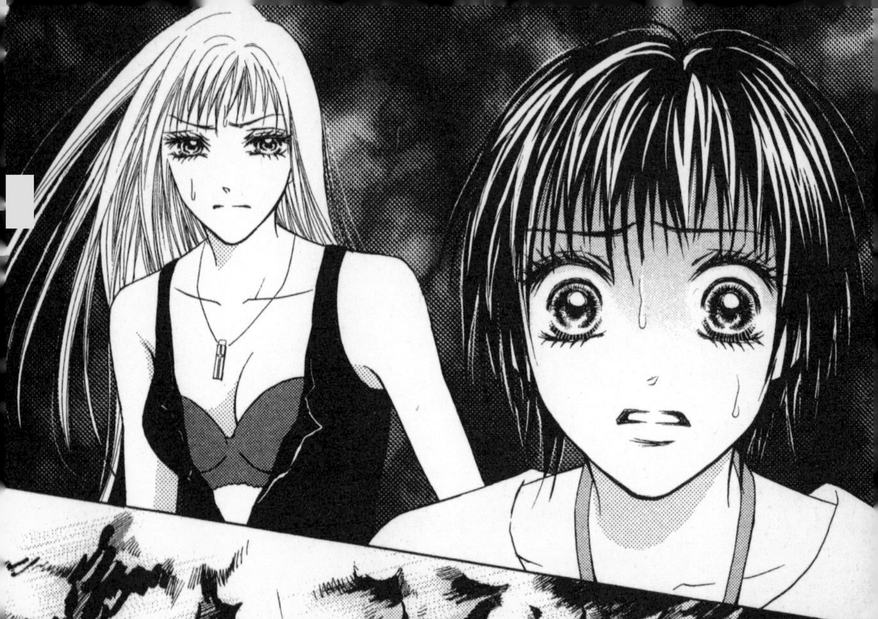

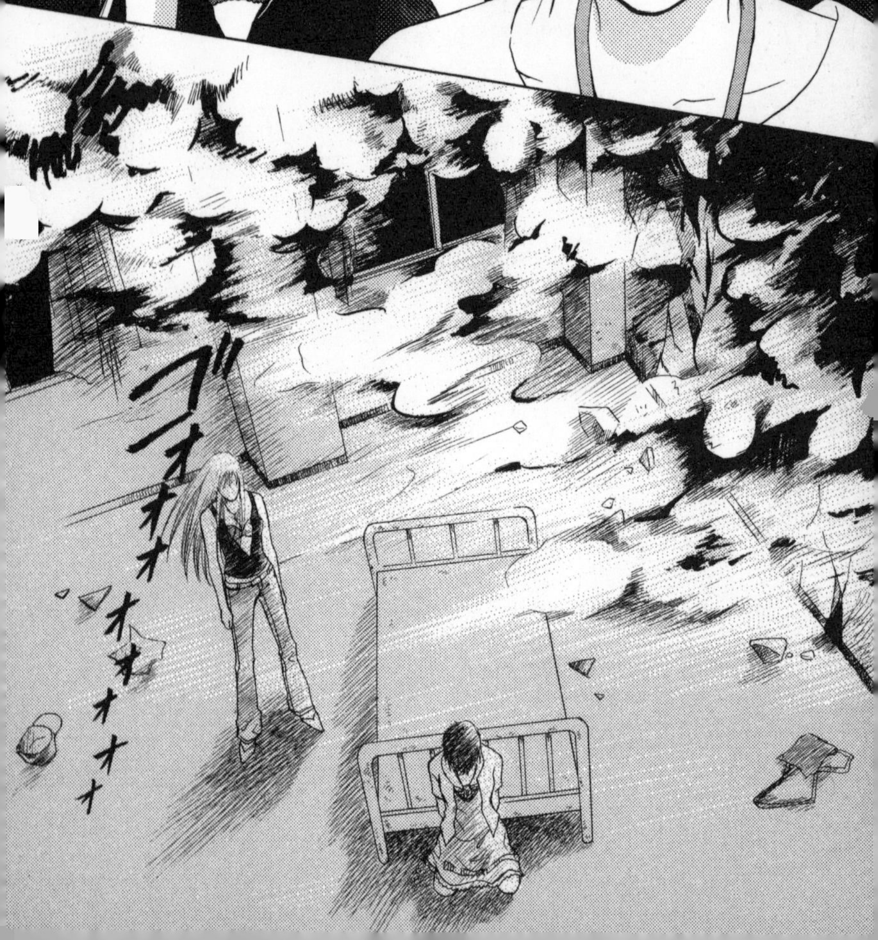
ゴオオオオオオオオ

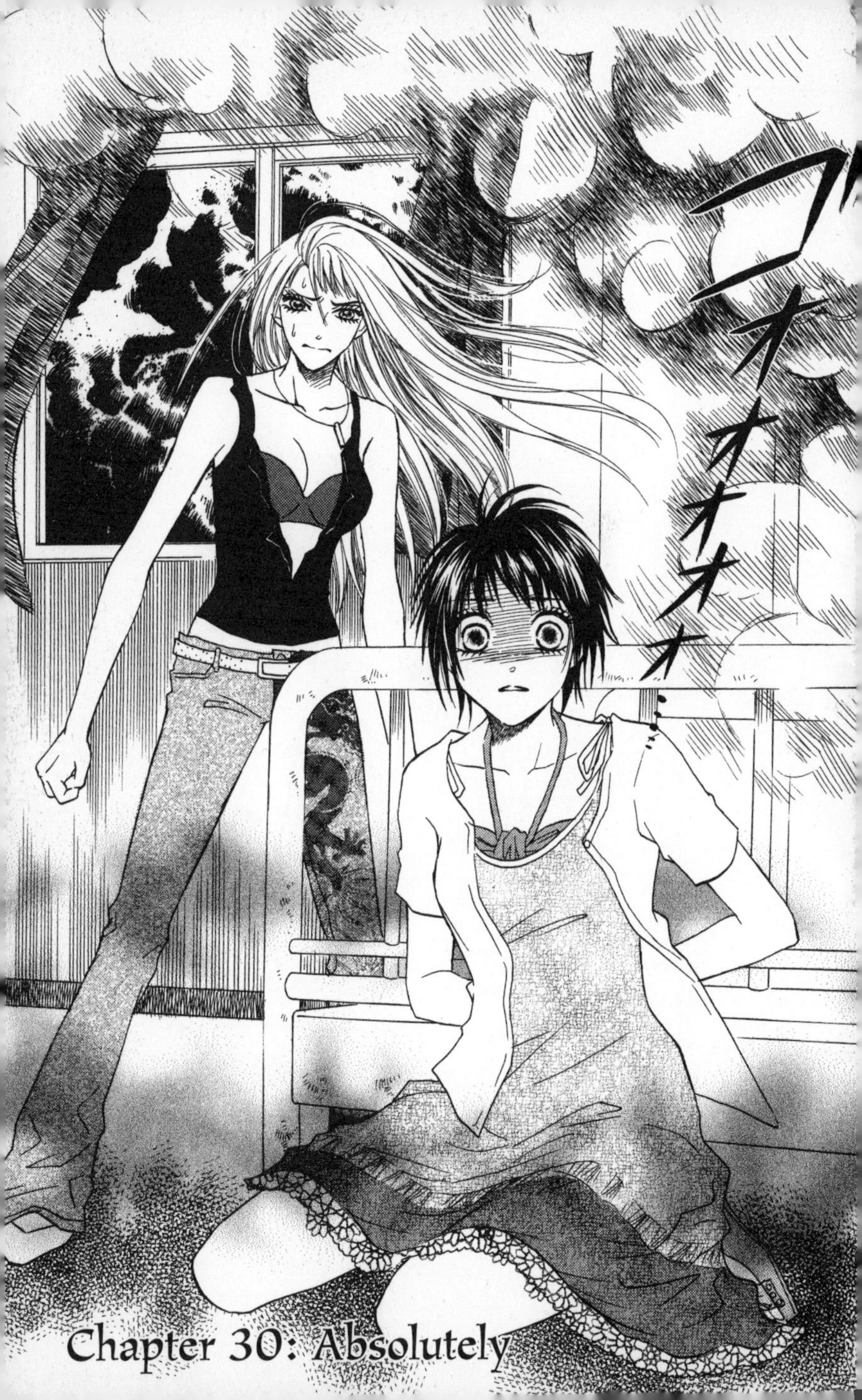

Chapter 30: Absolutely

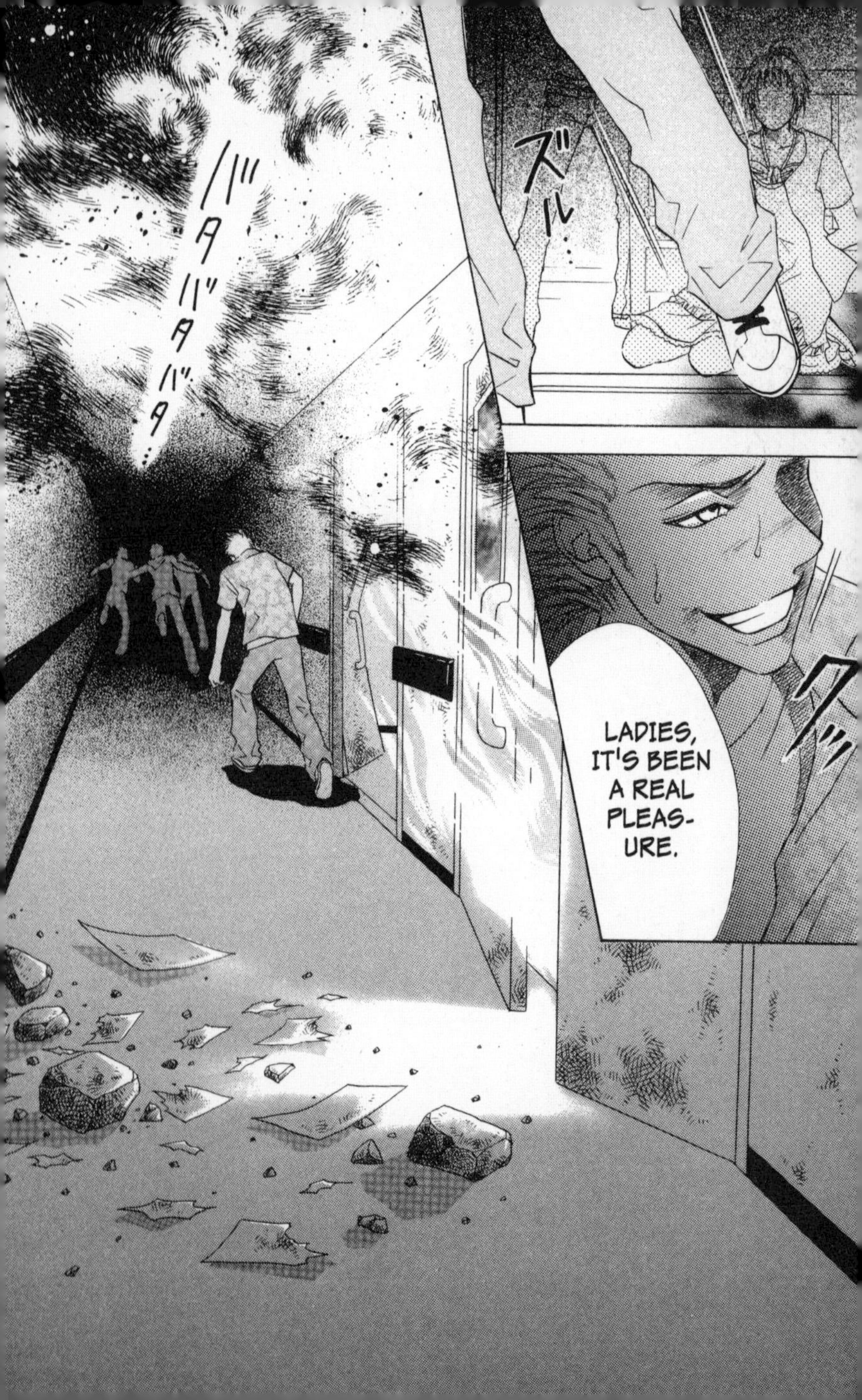
ズル
LADIES, IT'S BEEN A REAL PLEAS-URE.
クッ
バタバタバタ

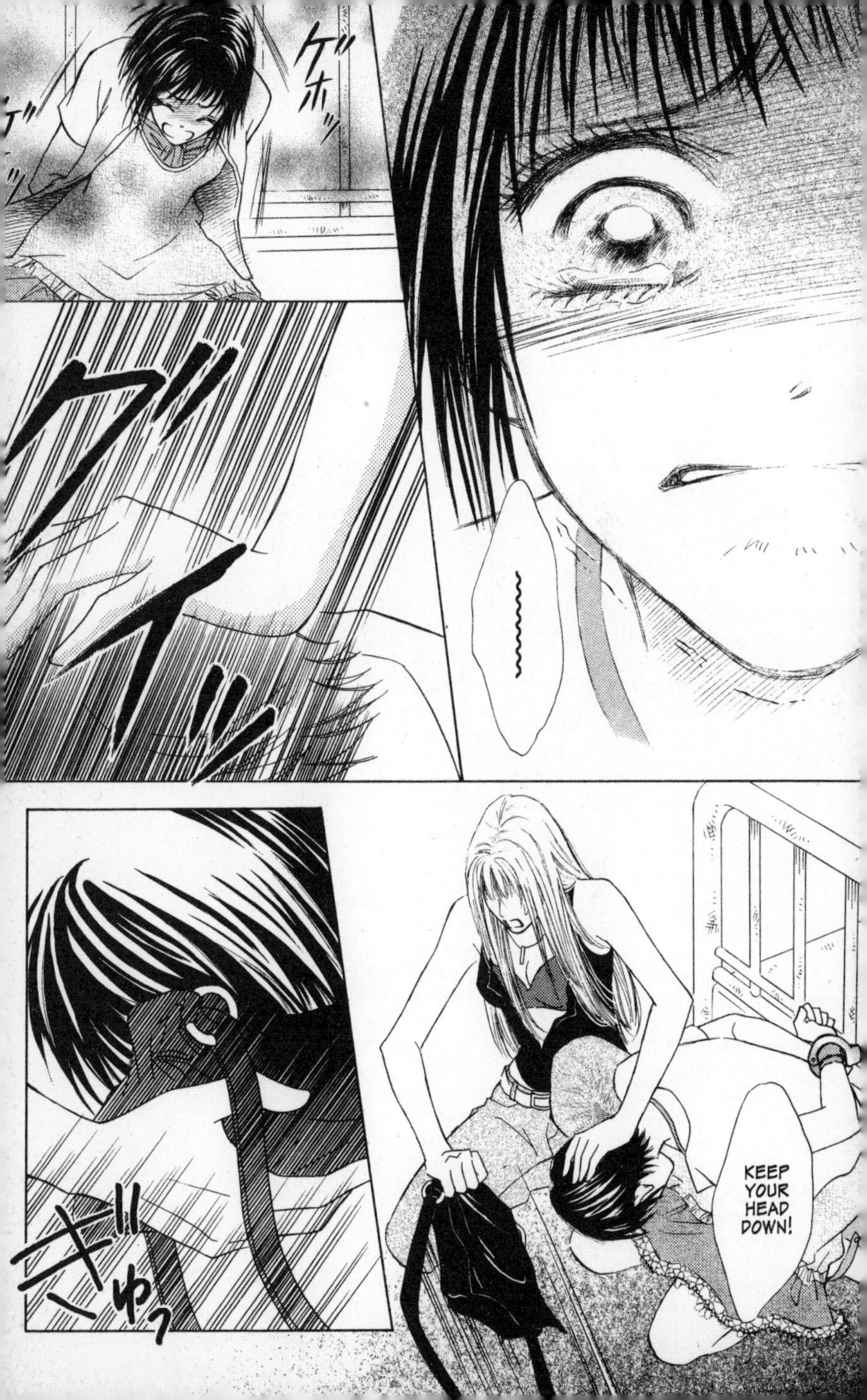
ゲボッ
グイッ
KEEP YOUR HEAD DOWN!
ギゅっ

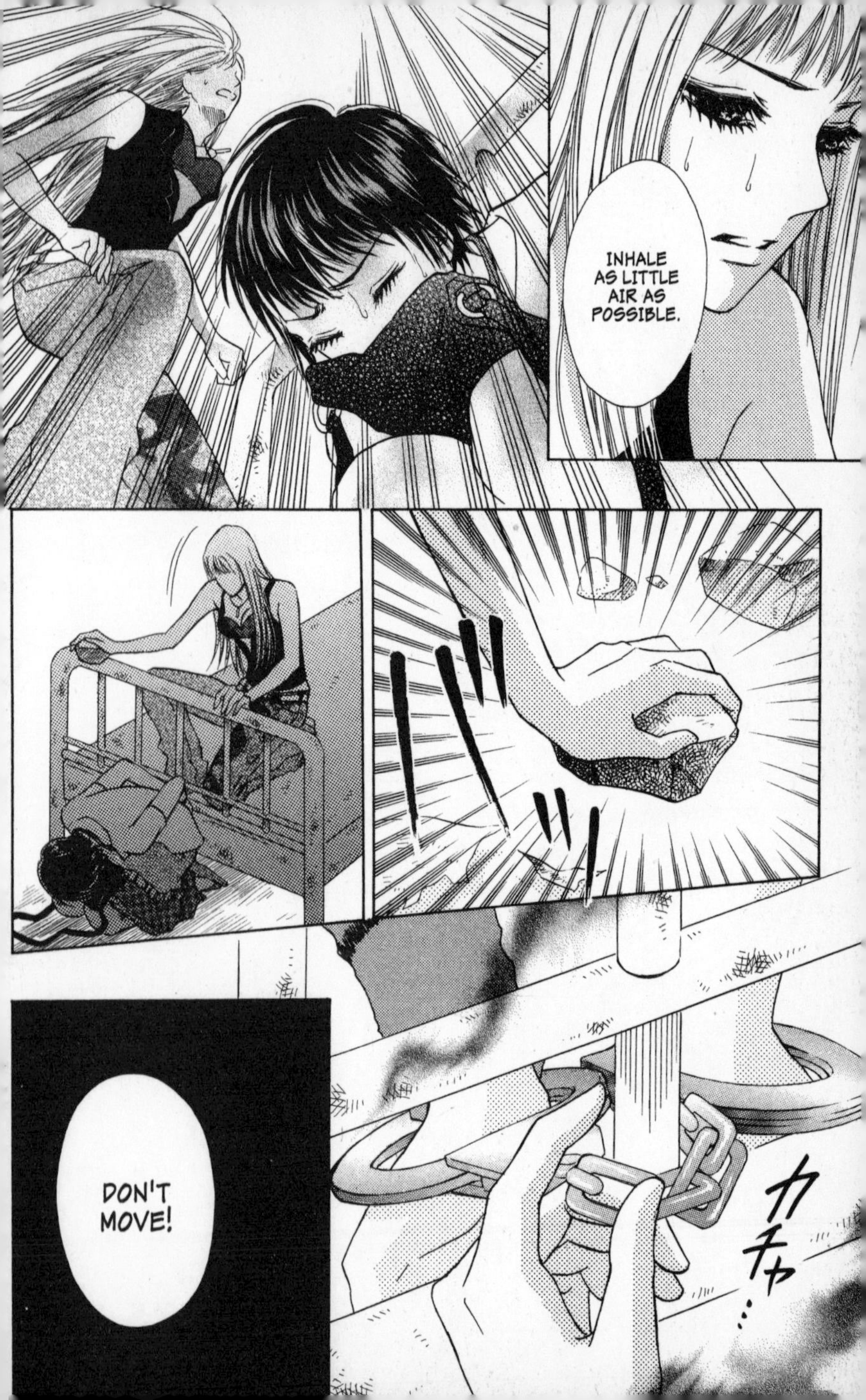
INHALE AS LITTLE AIR AS POSSIBLE.
DON'T MOVE!
カチャ…

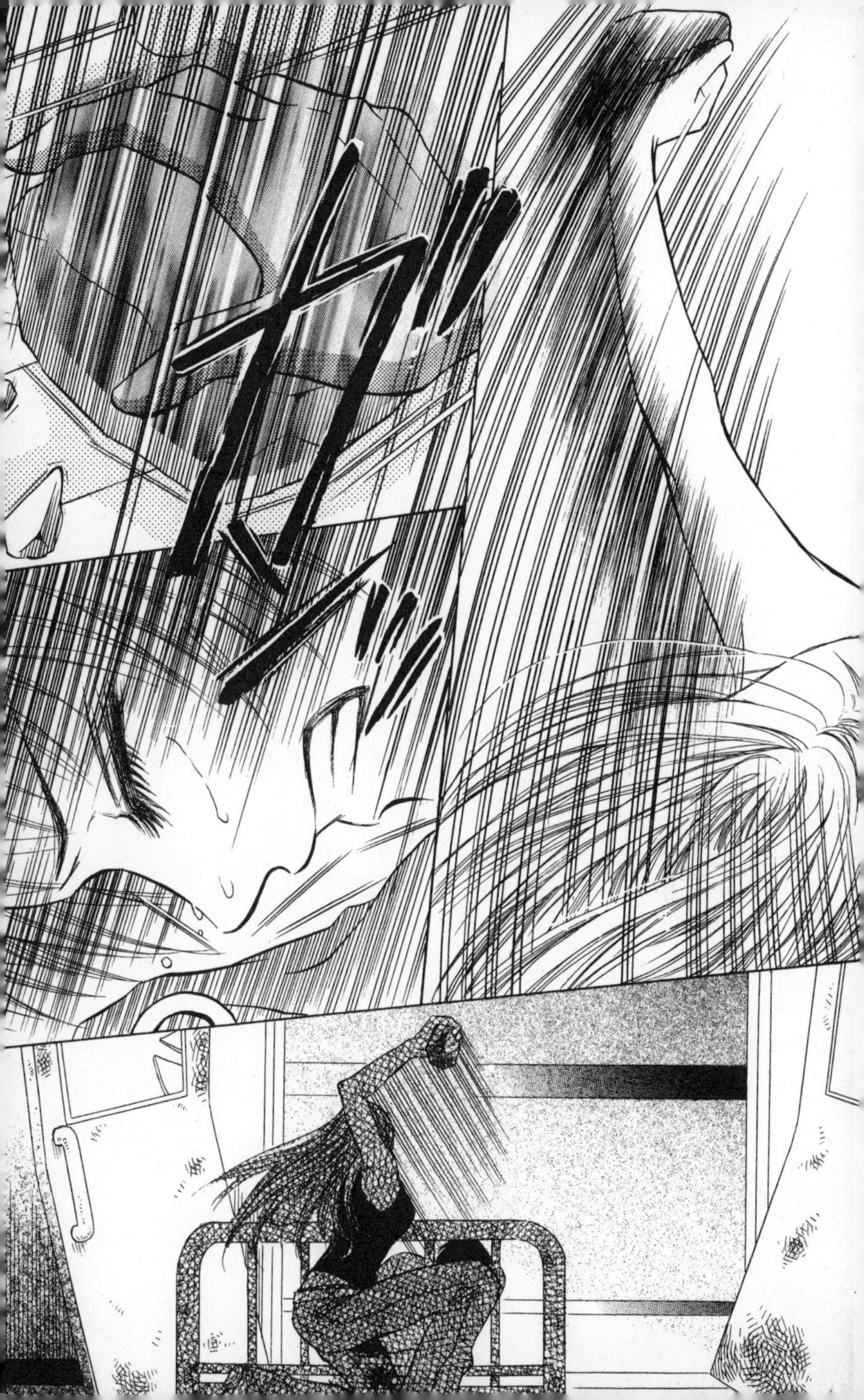

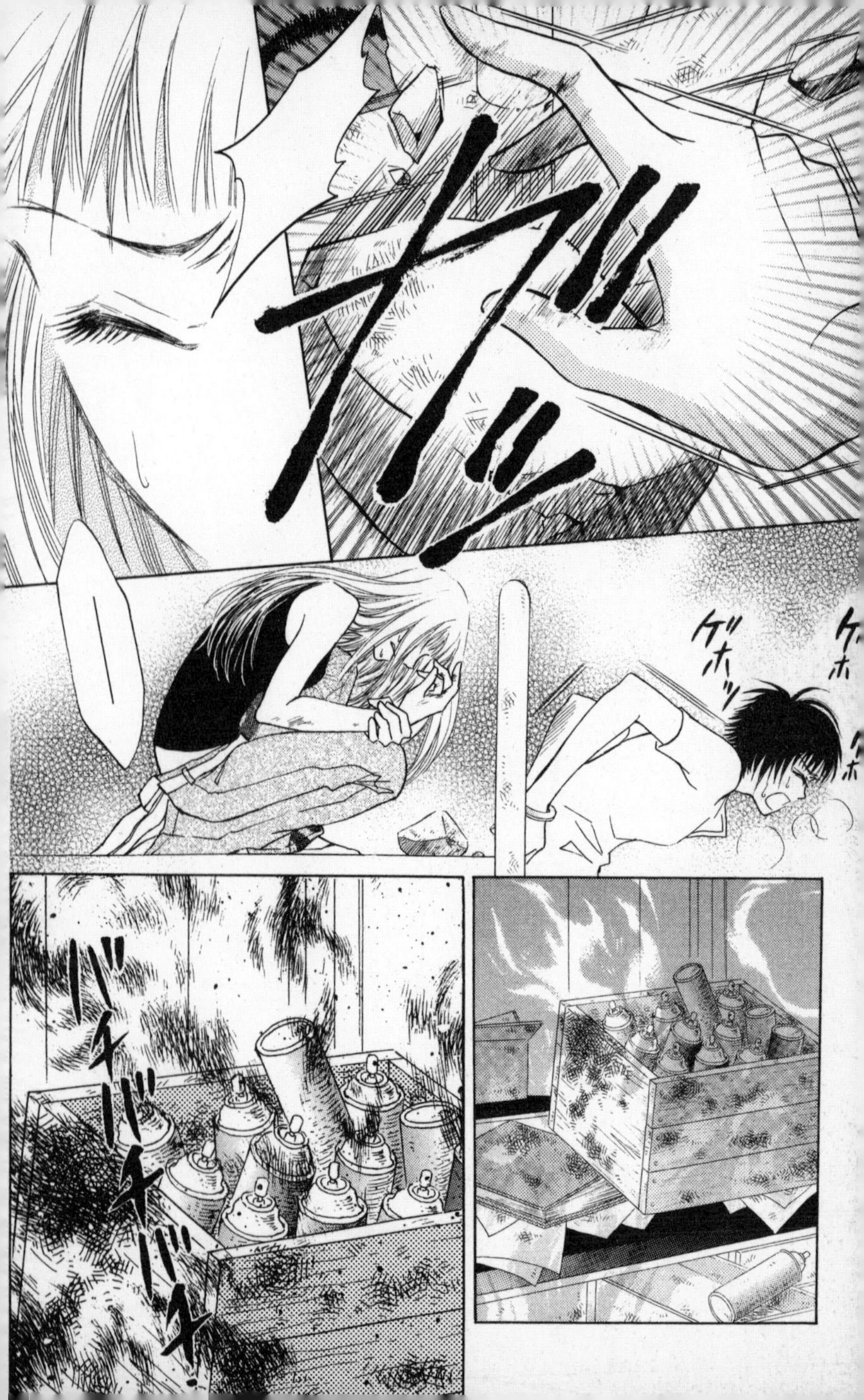
ガッ
ケホ
ケホ
ゲホッ
ー
バチバチバチ!

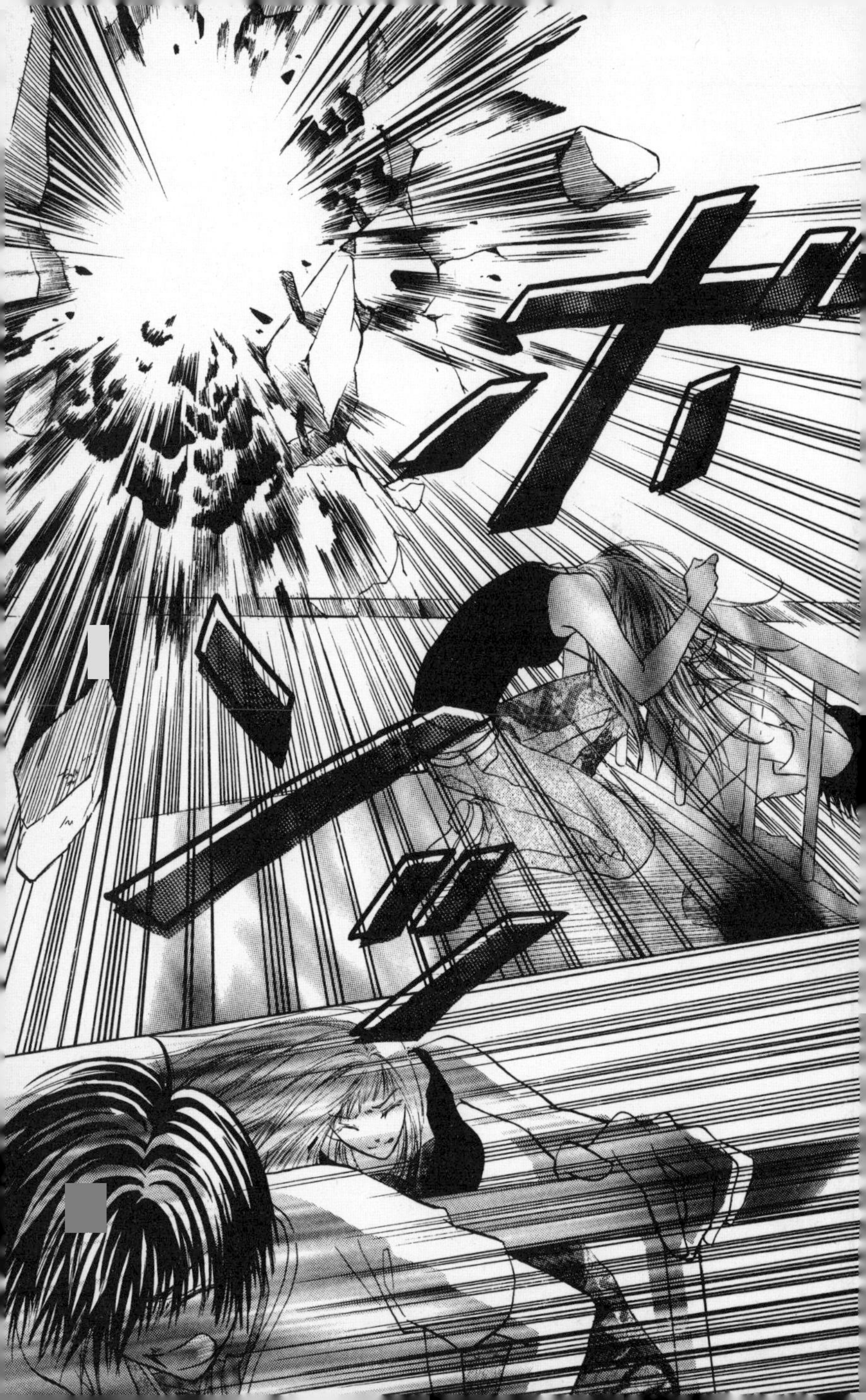

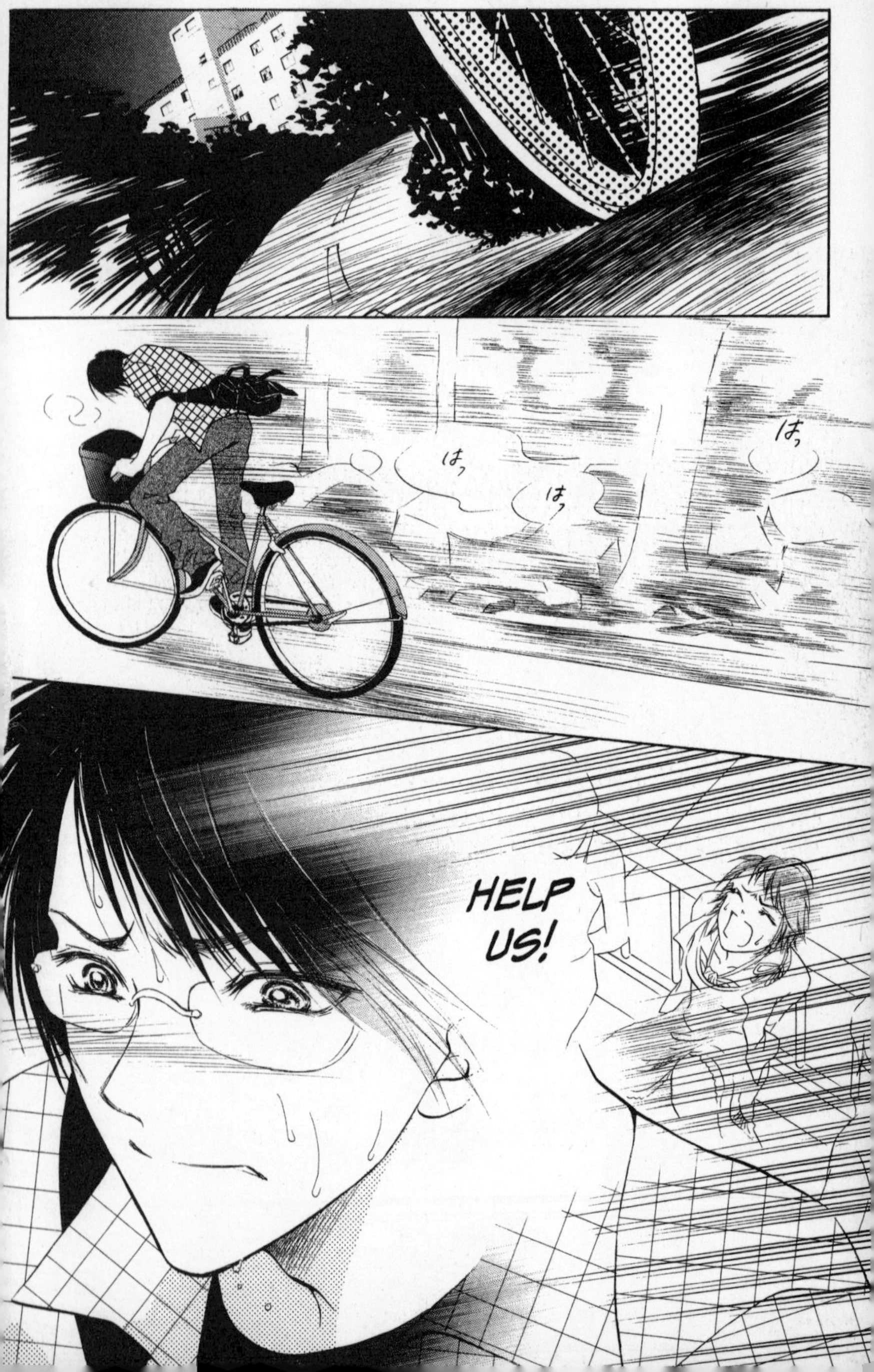
はっ
はっ
はっ
HELP US!

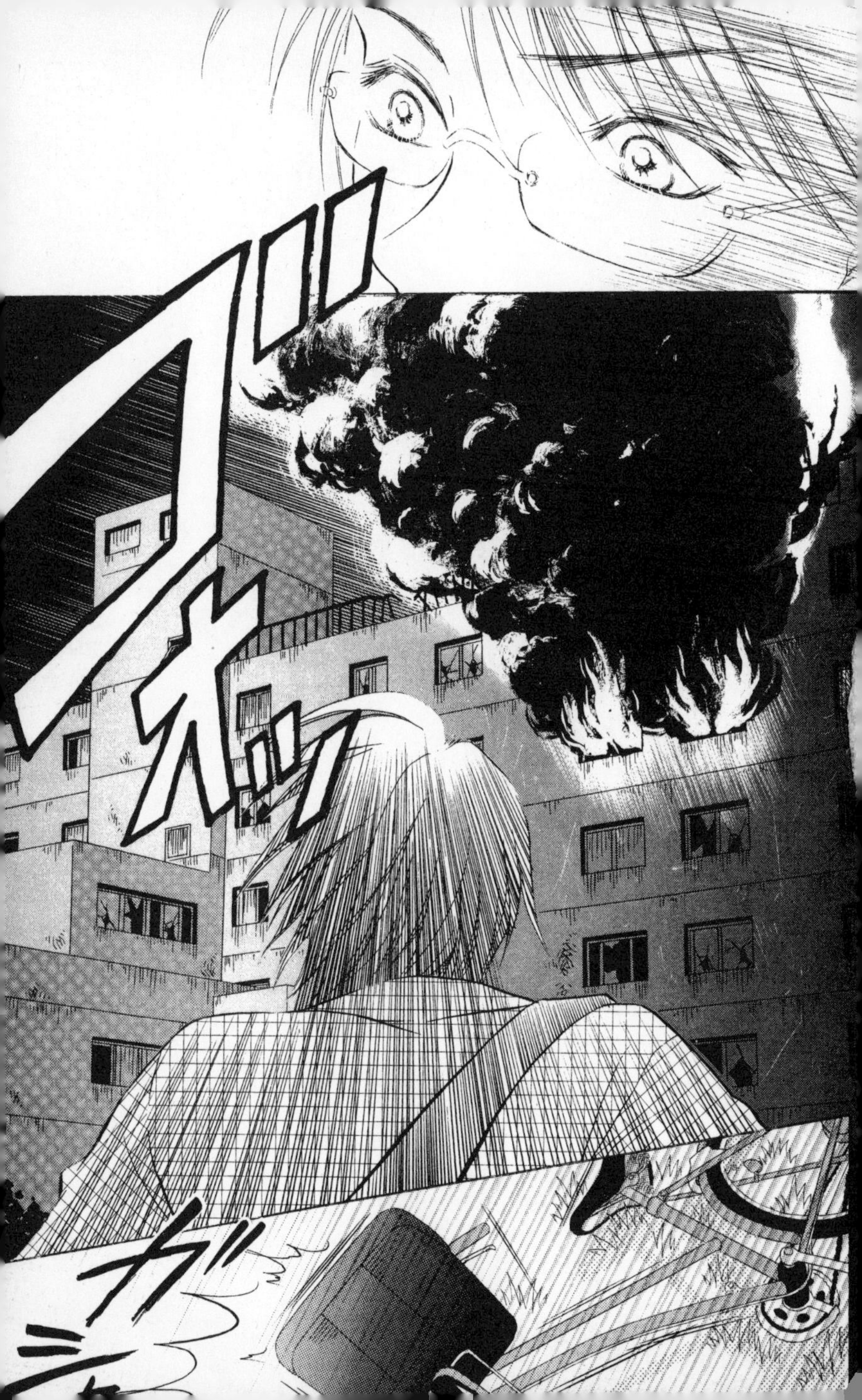
ブオ…
ガ

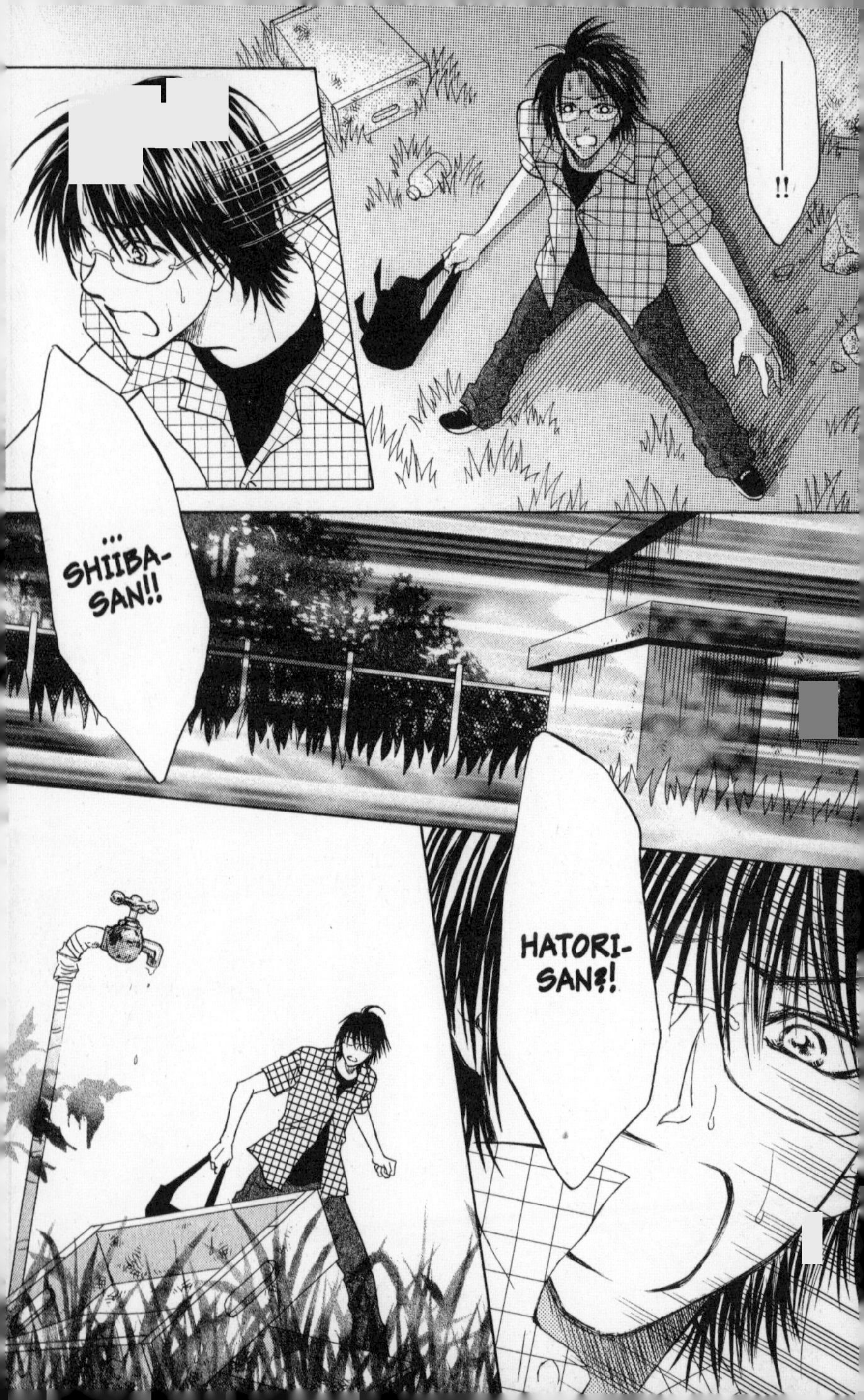
—!!
...SHIIBA-SAN!!
HATORI-SAN?!

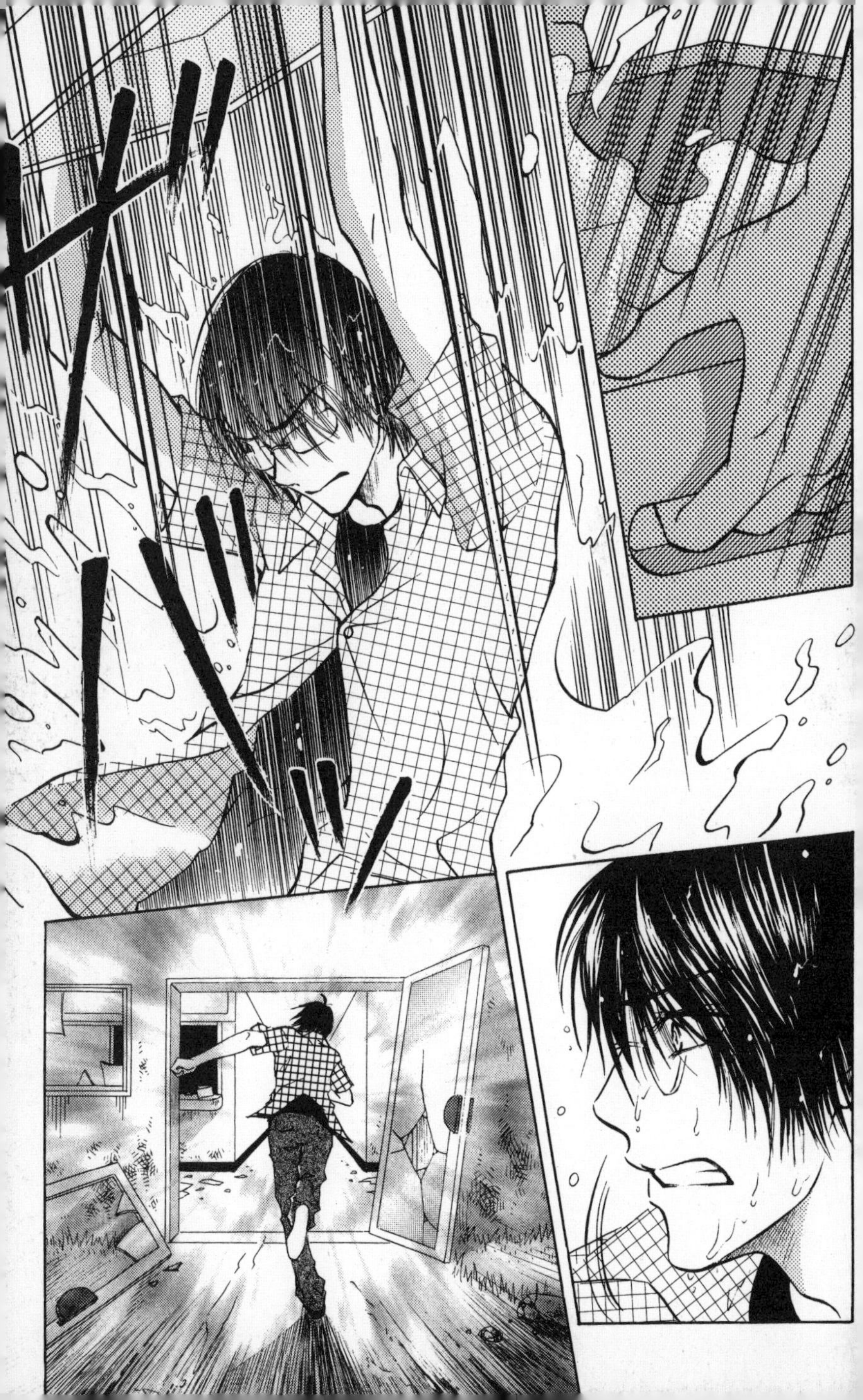

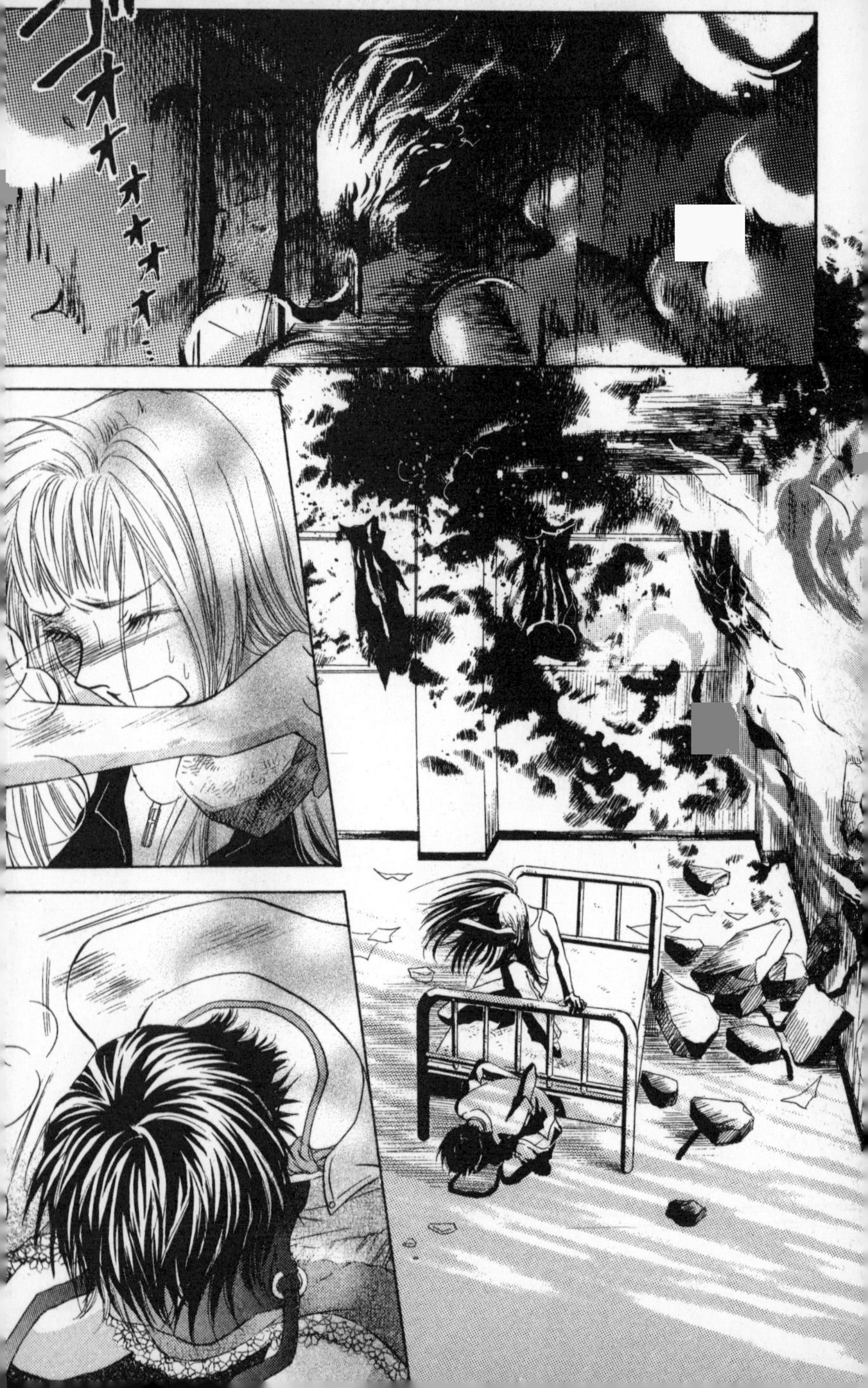
ゴオオオオオオオ…

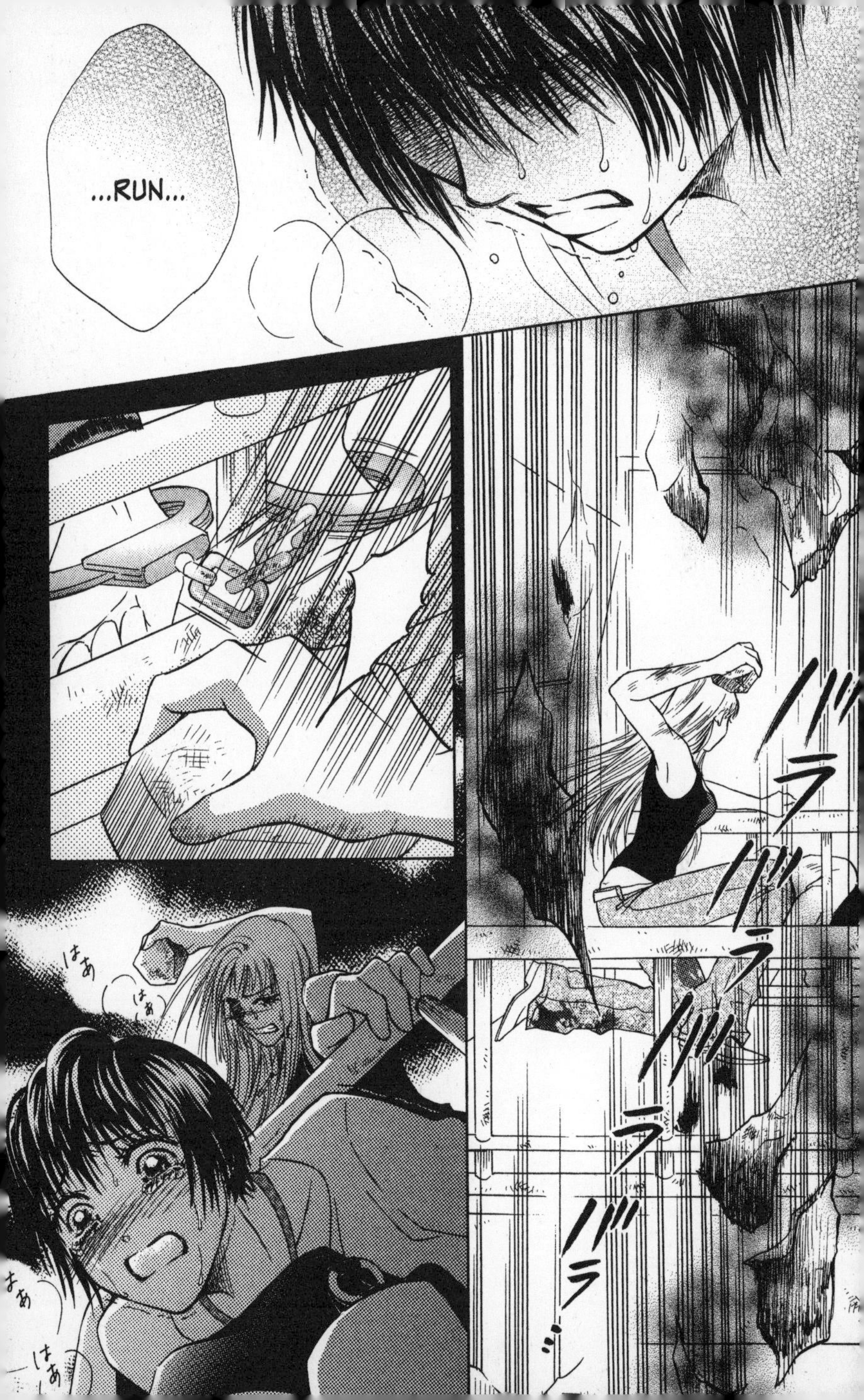
...RUN...
はあ はあ
はあ

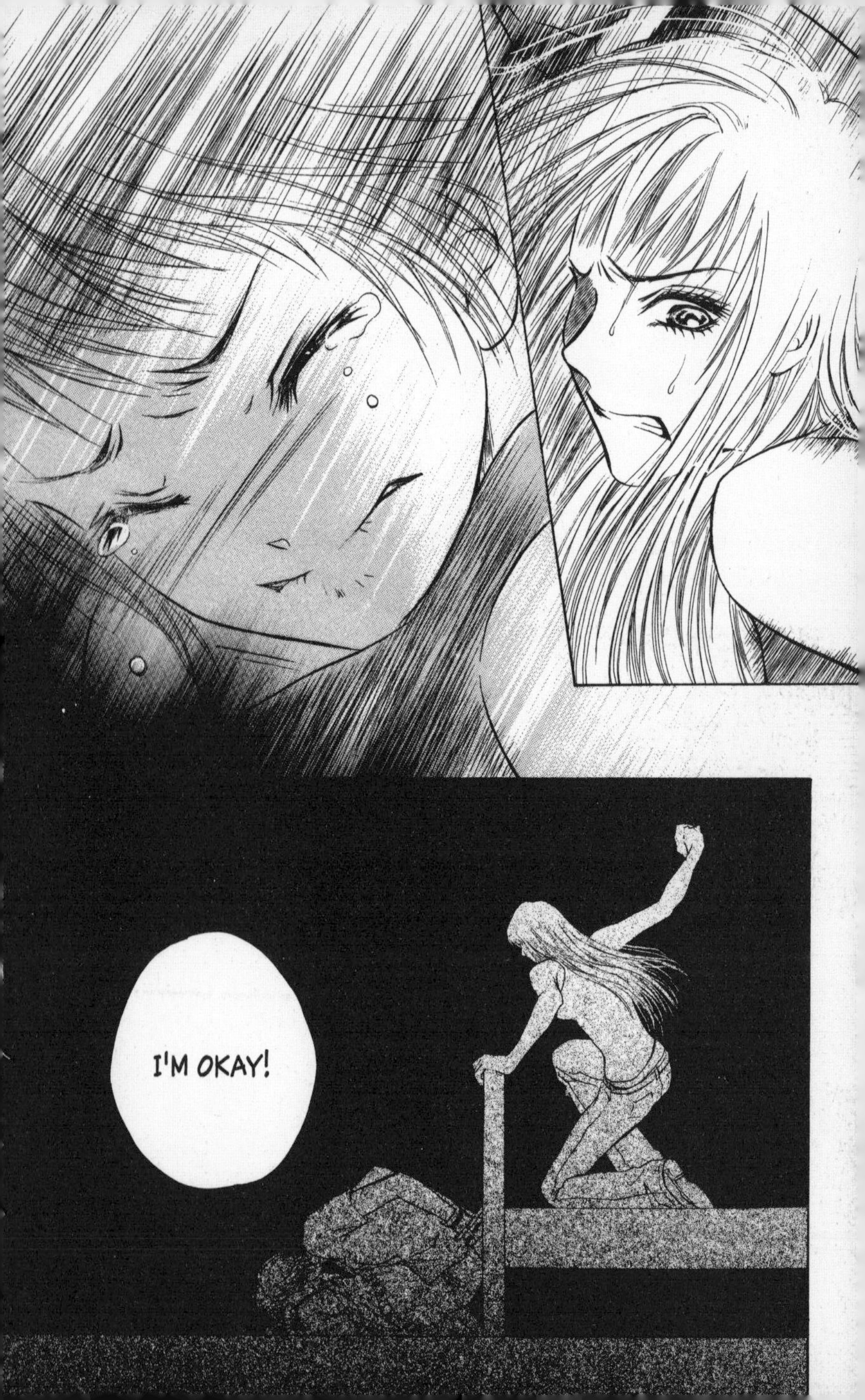
I'M OKAY!

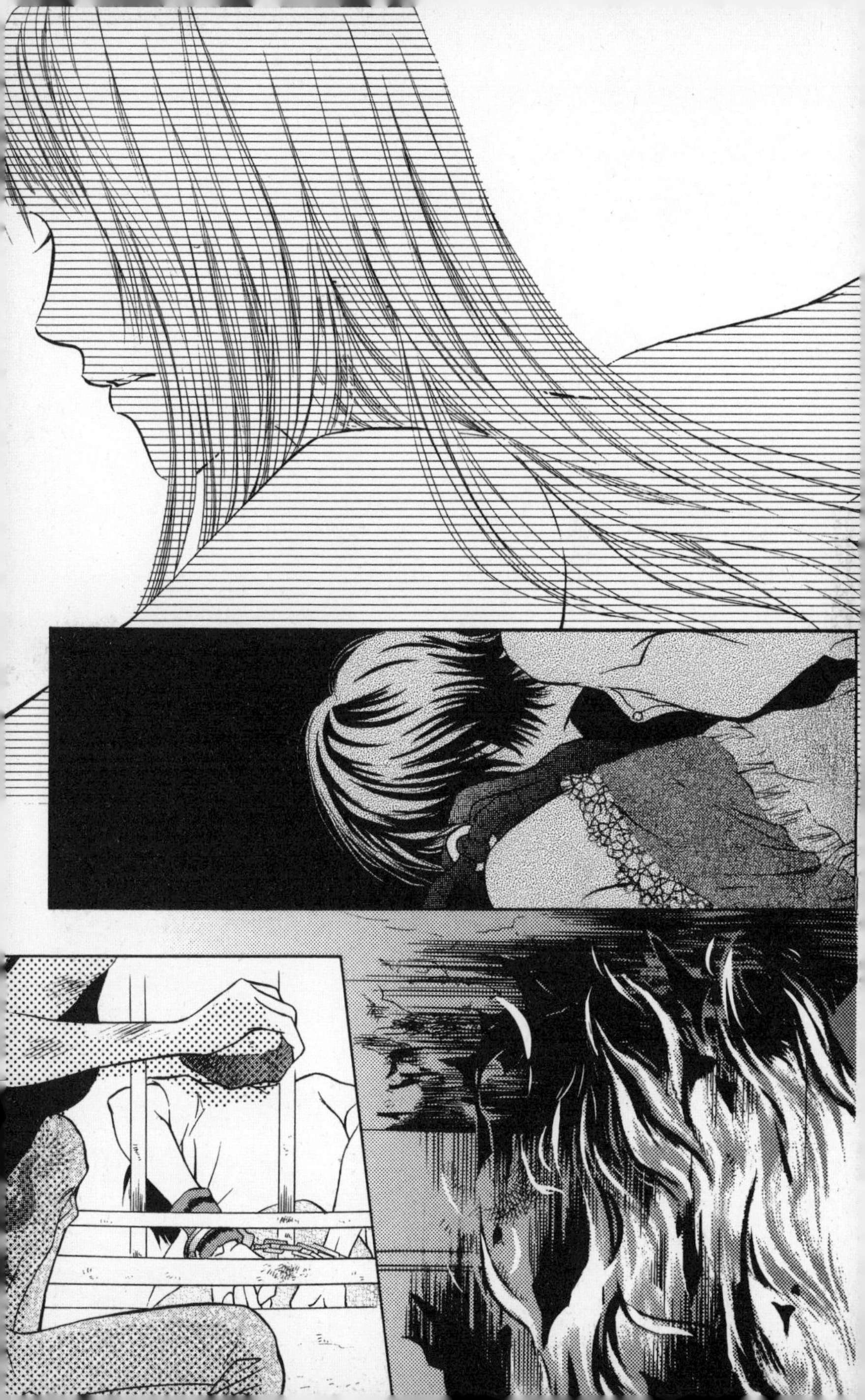

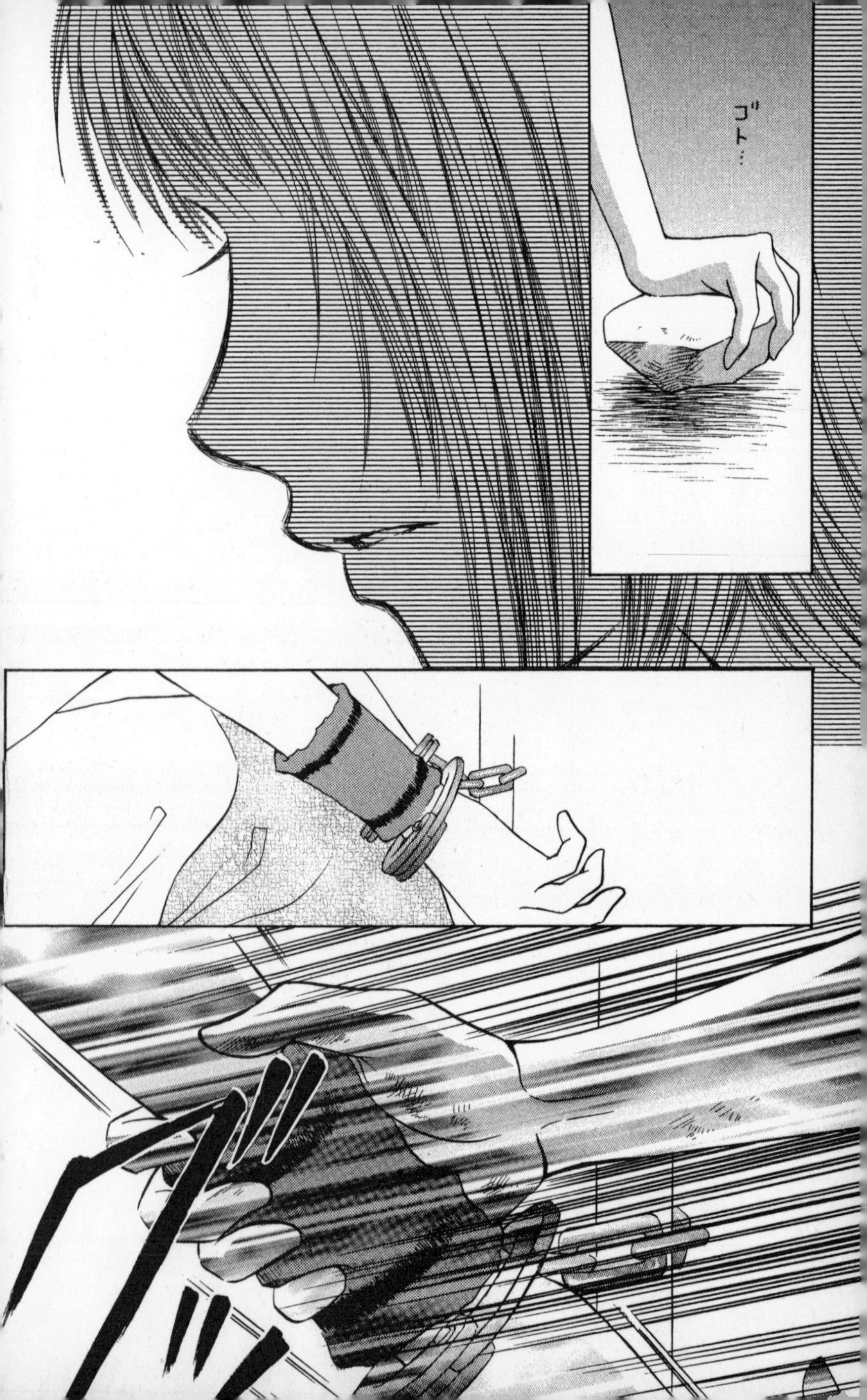
ゴト…

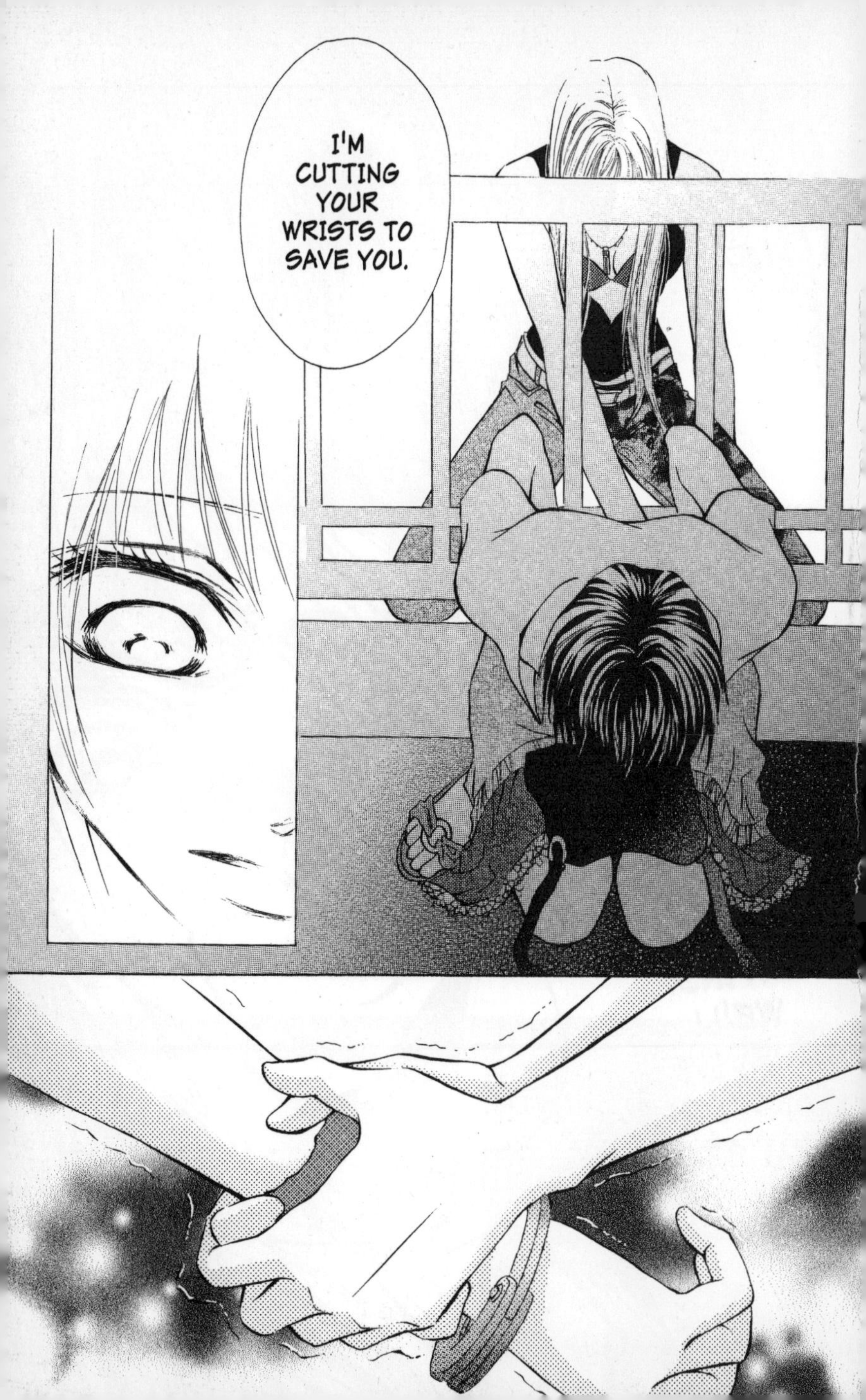
I'M CUTTING YOUR WRISTS TO SAVE YOU.

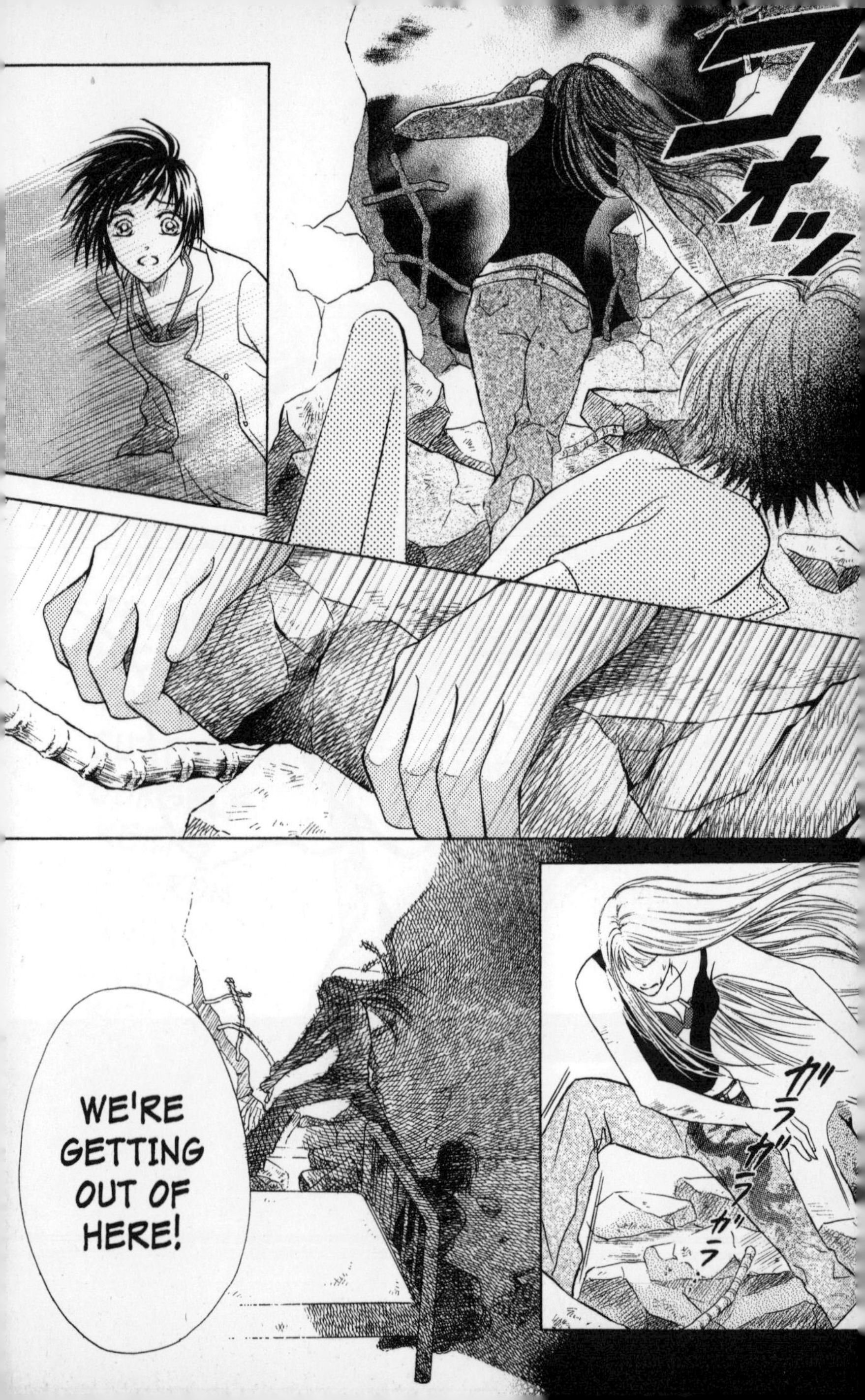
ガラガラガラ
WE'RE GETTING OUT OF HERE!

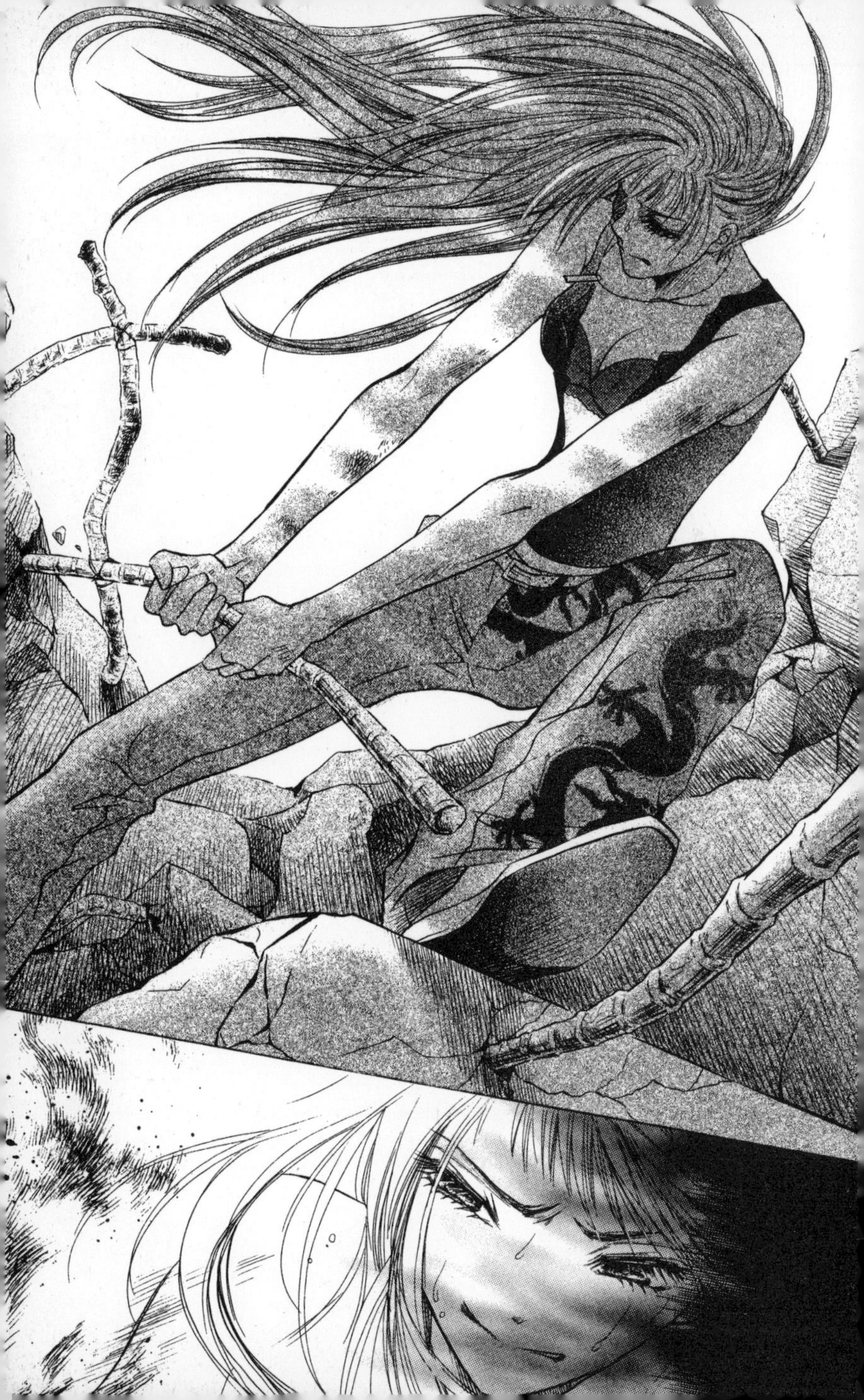

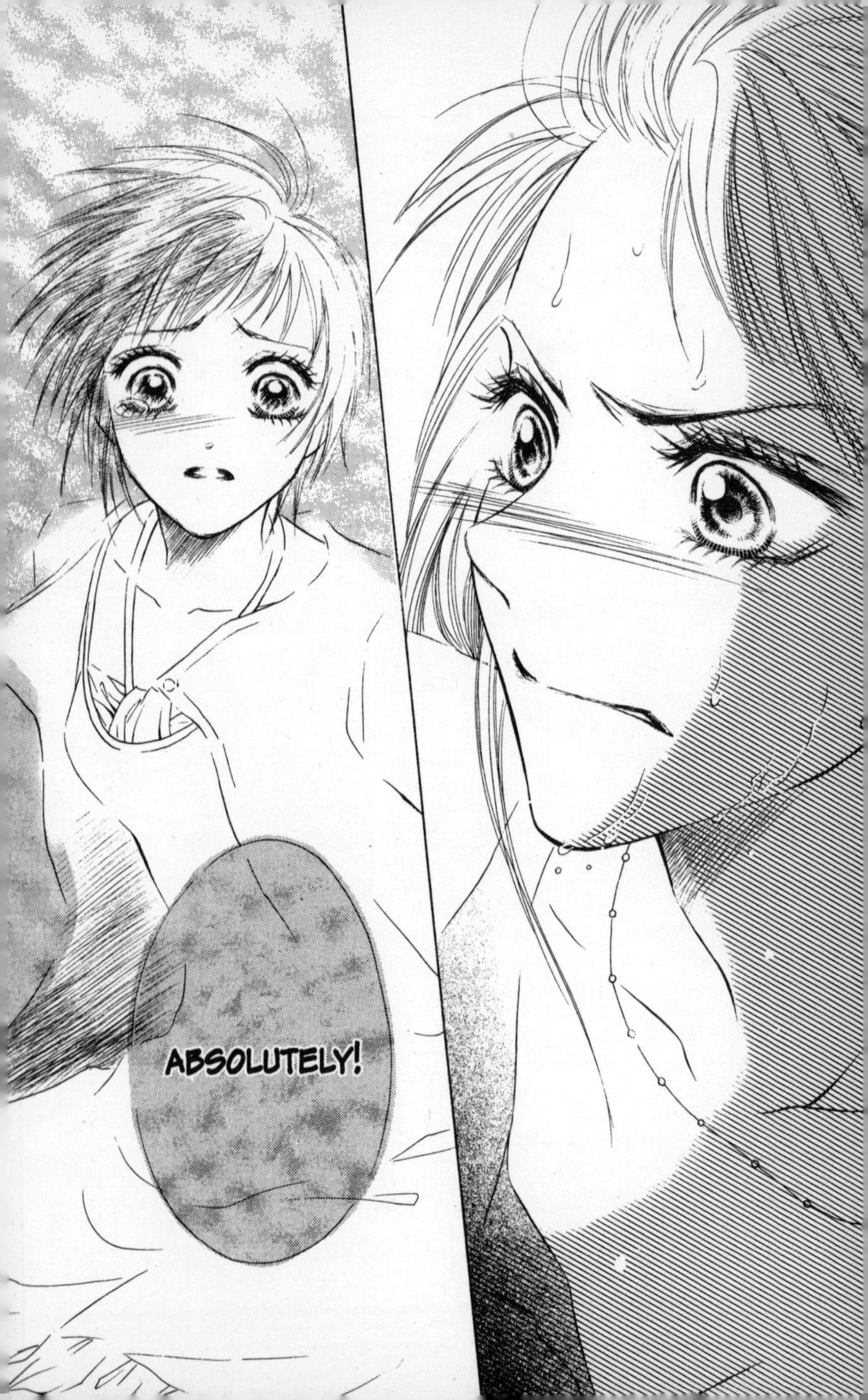
ABSOLUTELY!

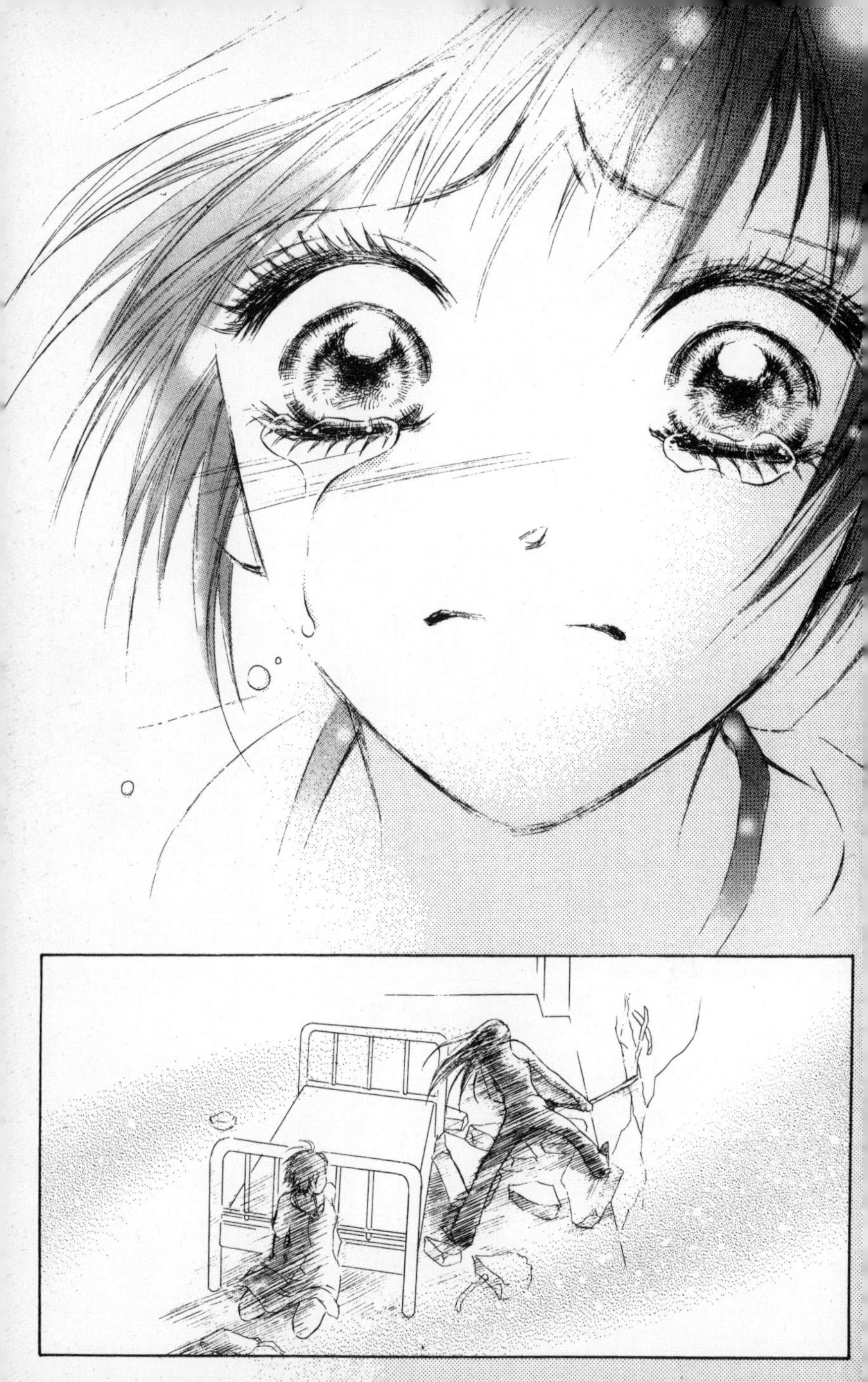

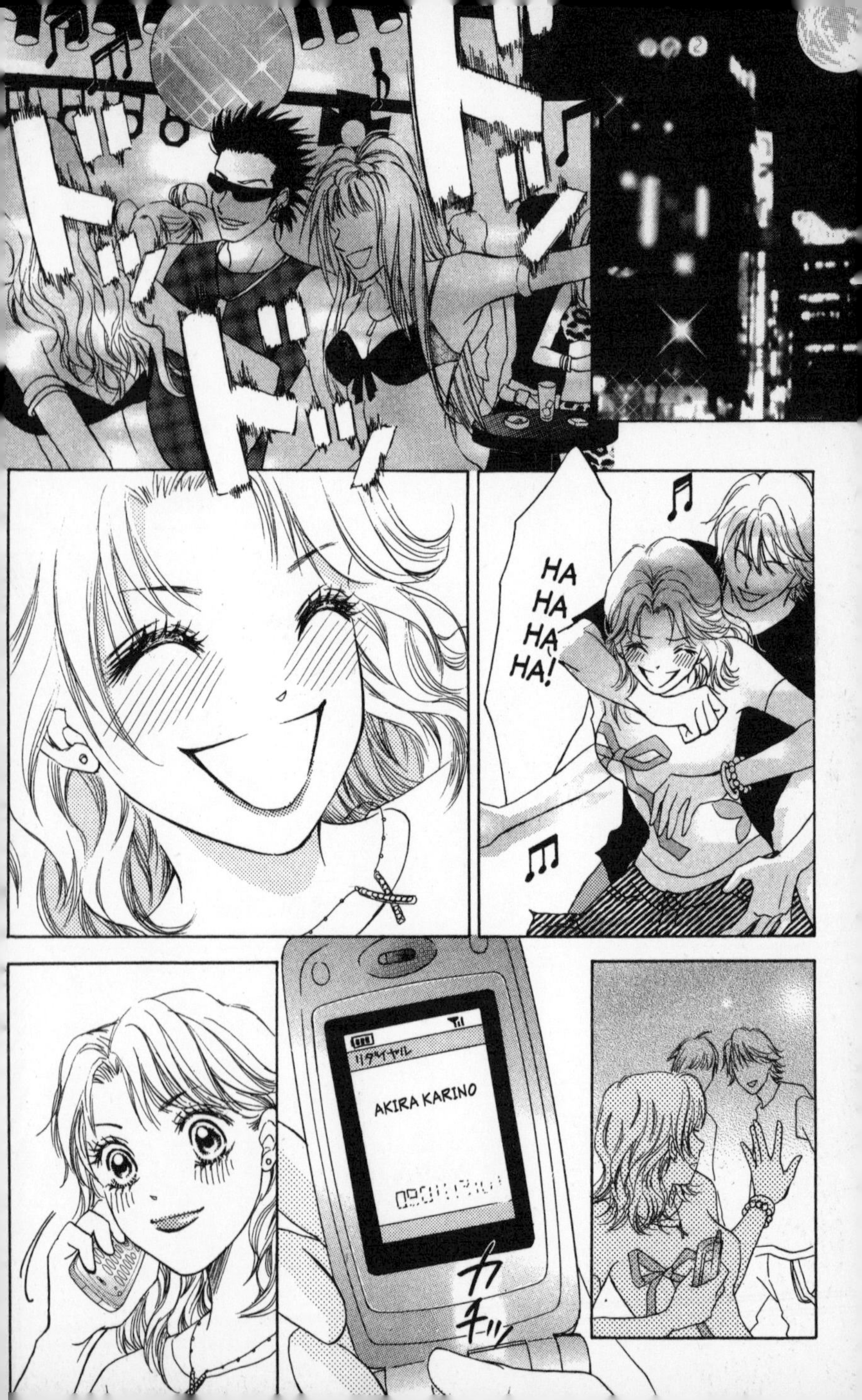
HA
HA
HA
HA!
AKIRA KARINO

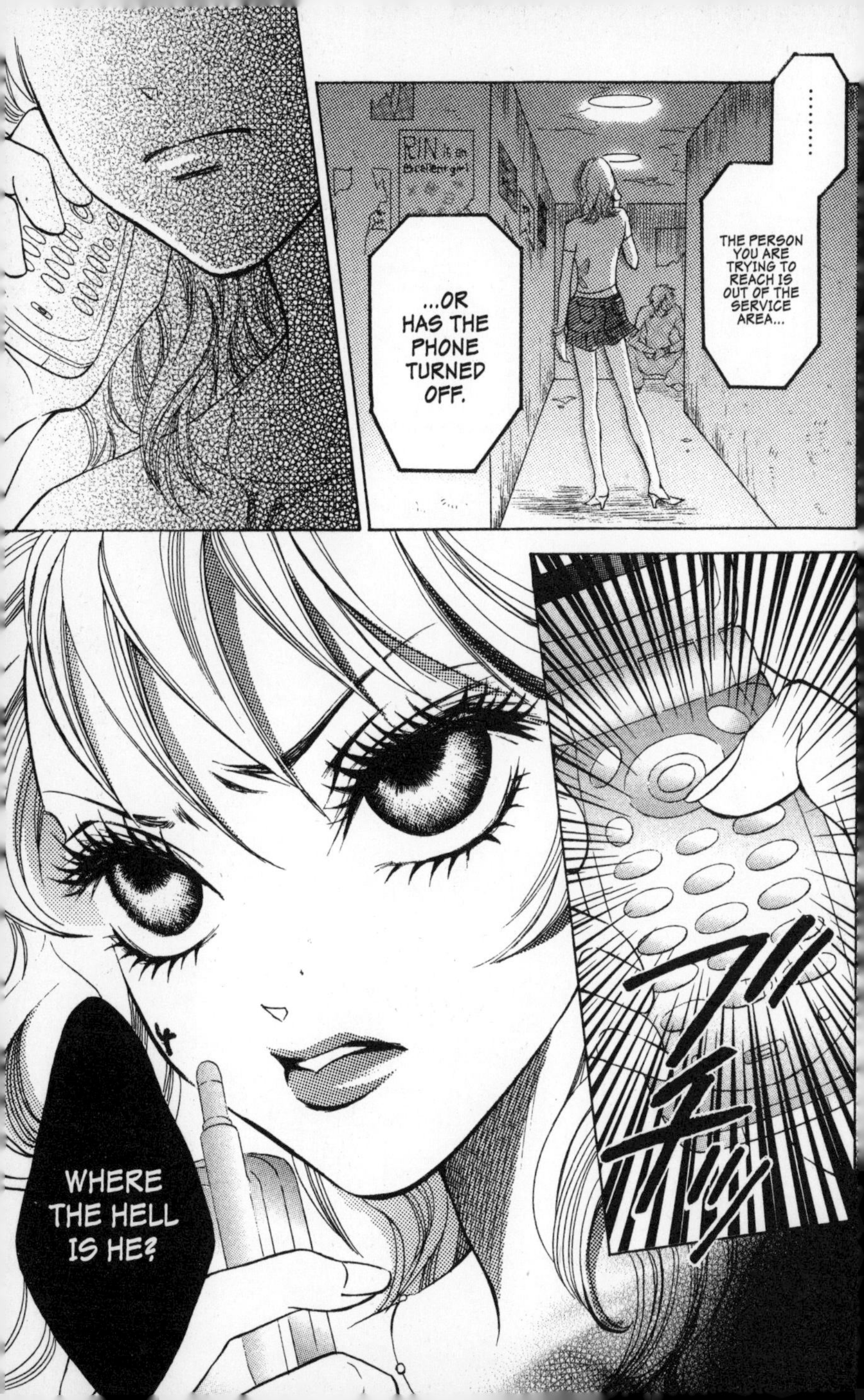
......
THE PERSON YOU ARE TRYING TO REACH IS OUT OF THE SERVICE AREA...
...OR HAS THE PHONE TURNED OFF.
WHERE THE HELL IS HE?

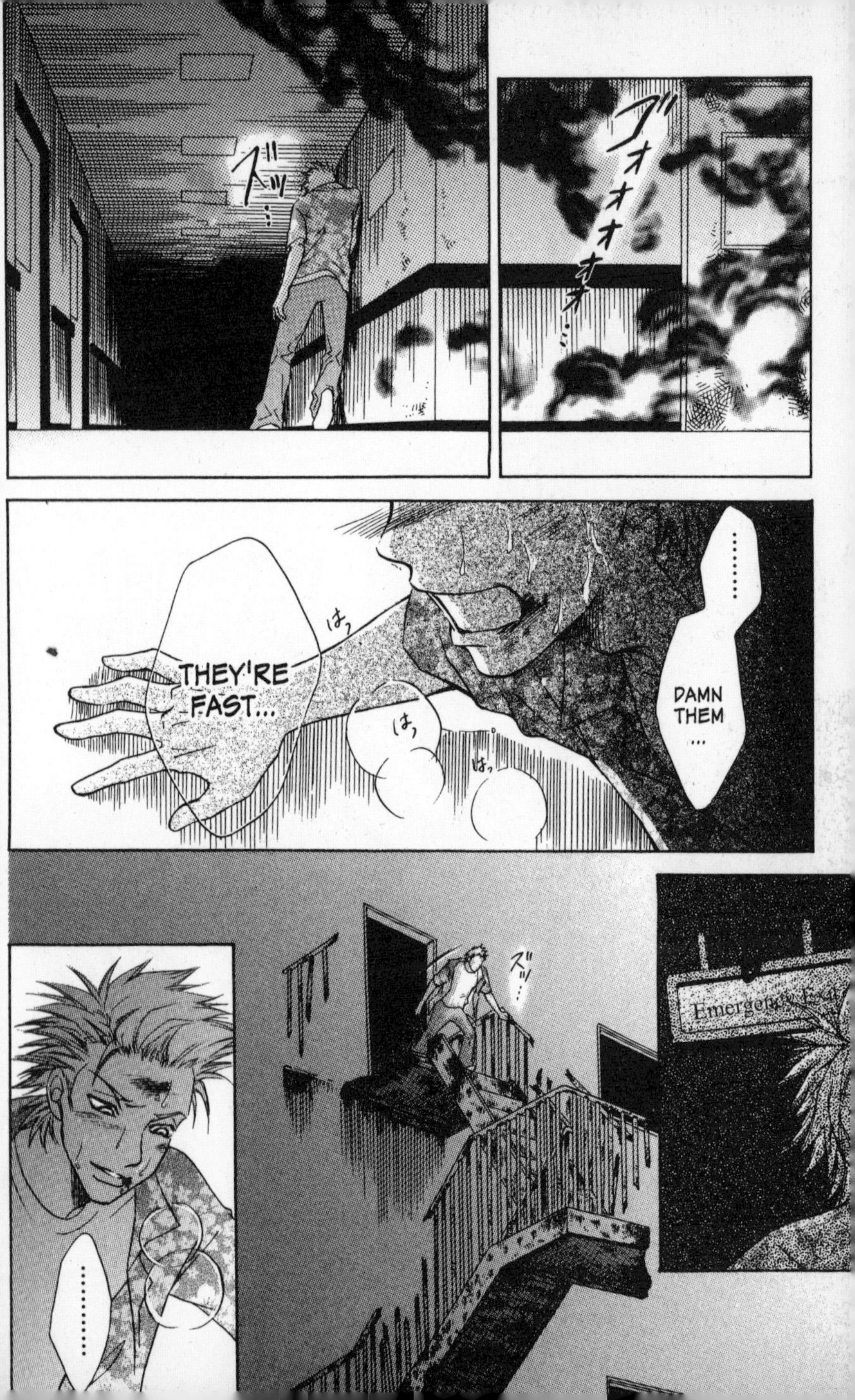
ズッ…
……
DAMN THEM …
はっ
THEY'RE FAST…
はっ
はっ
Emergen
ズッ…
……

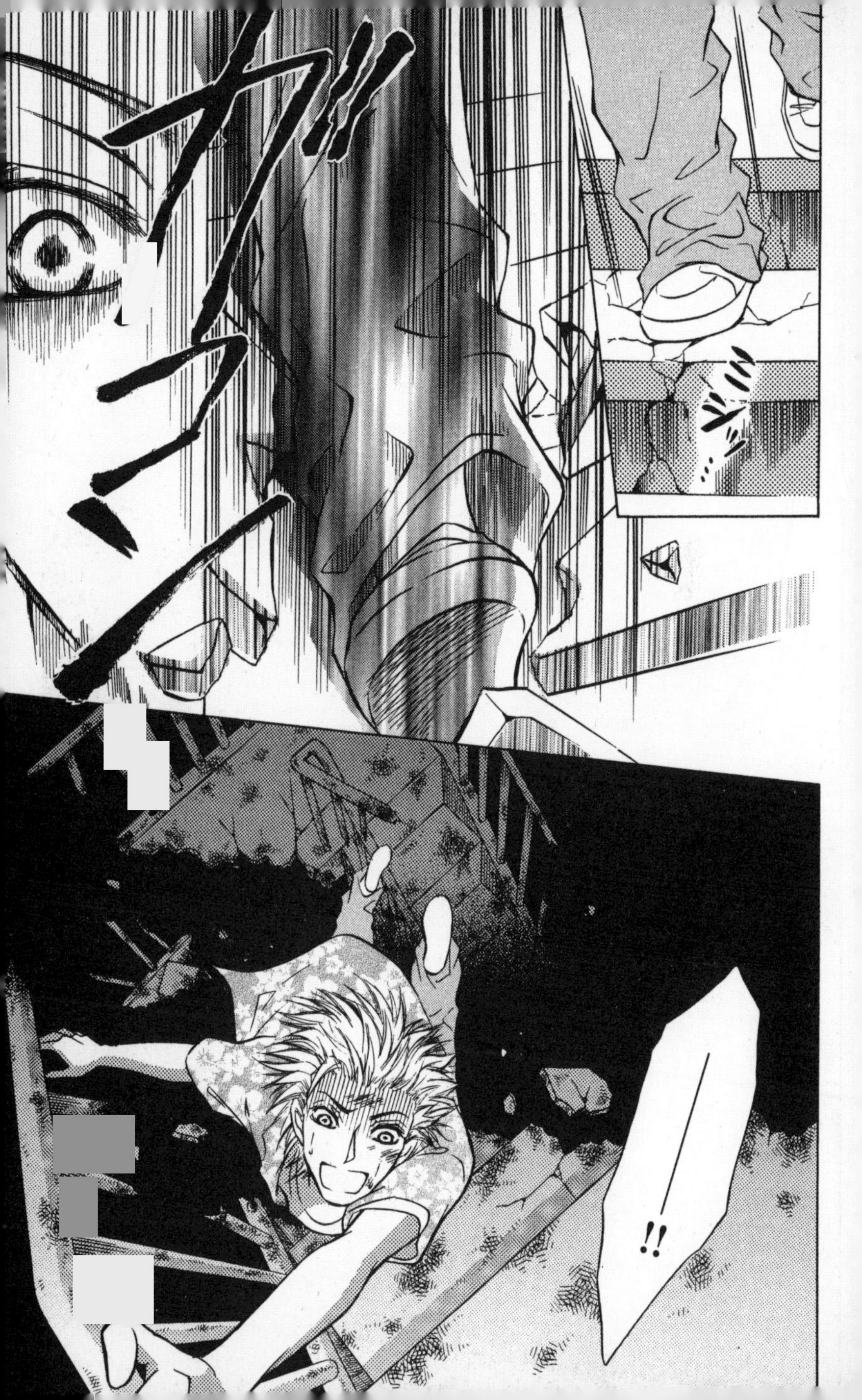
!!

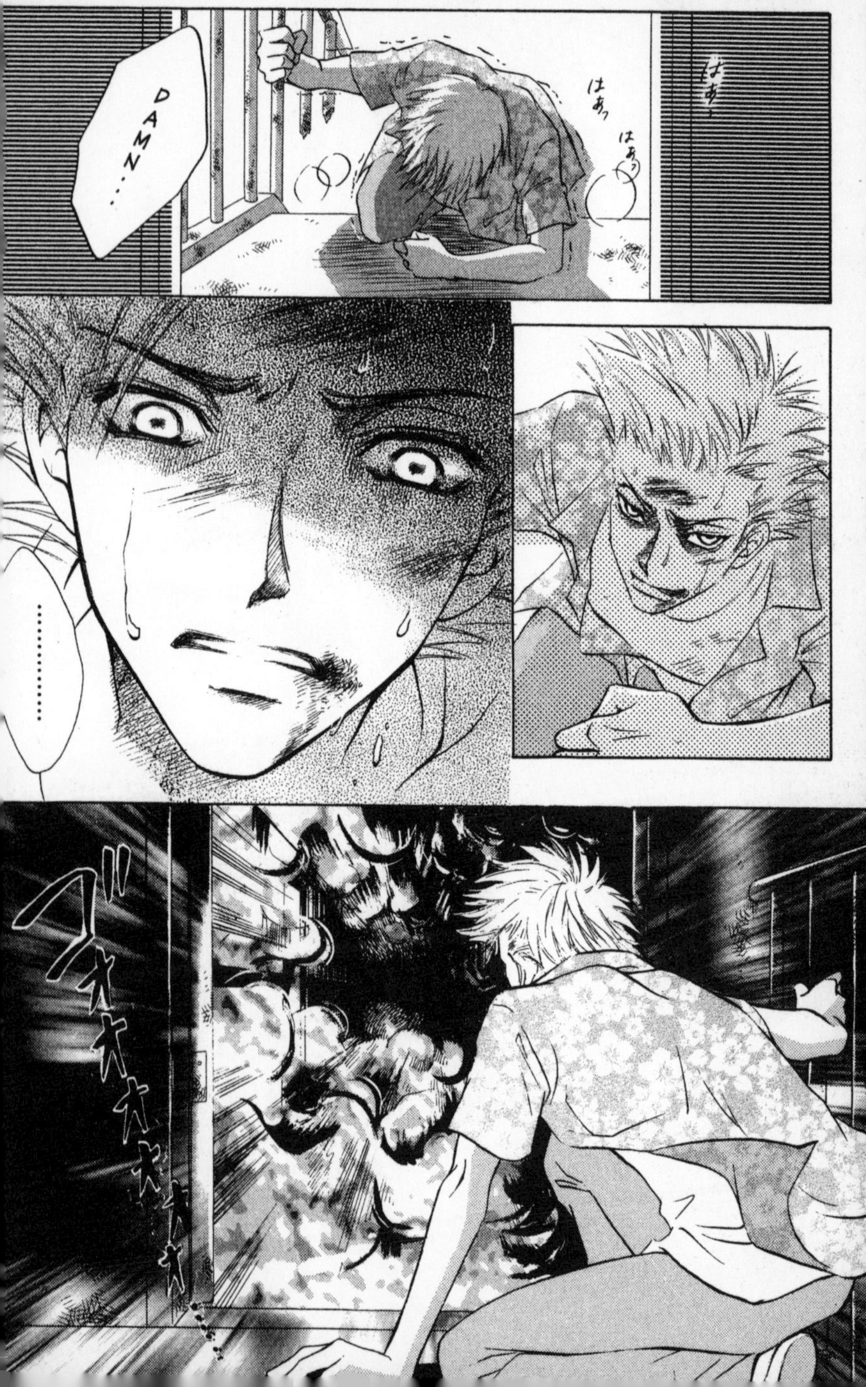
はあっ
はあっ
はあっ
DAMN...
......

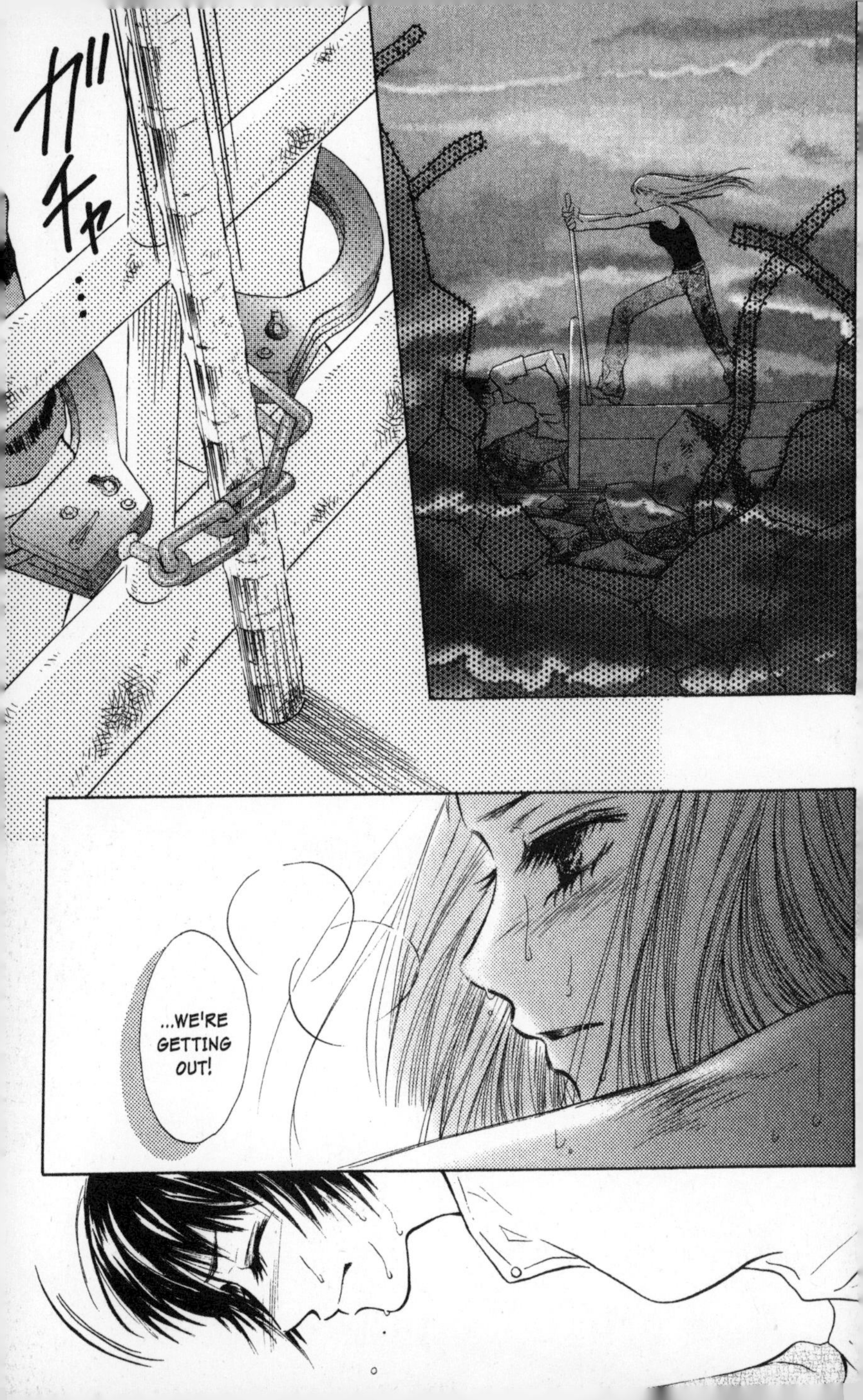
ガチャ…
...WE'RE GETTING OUT!

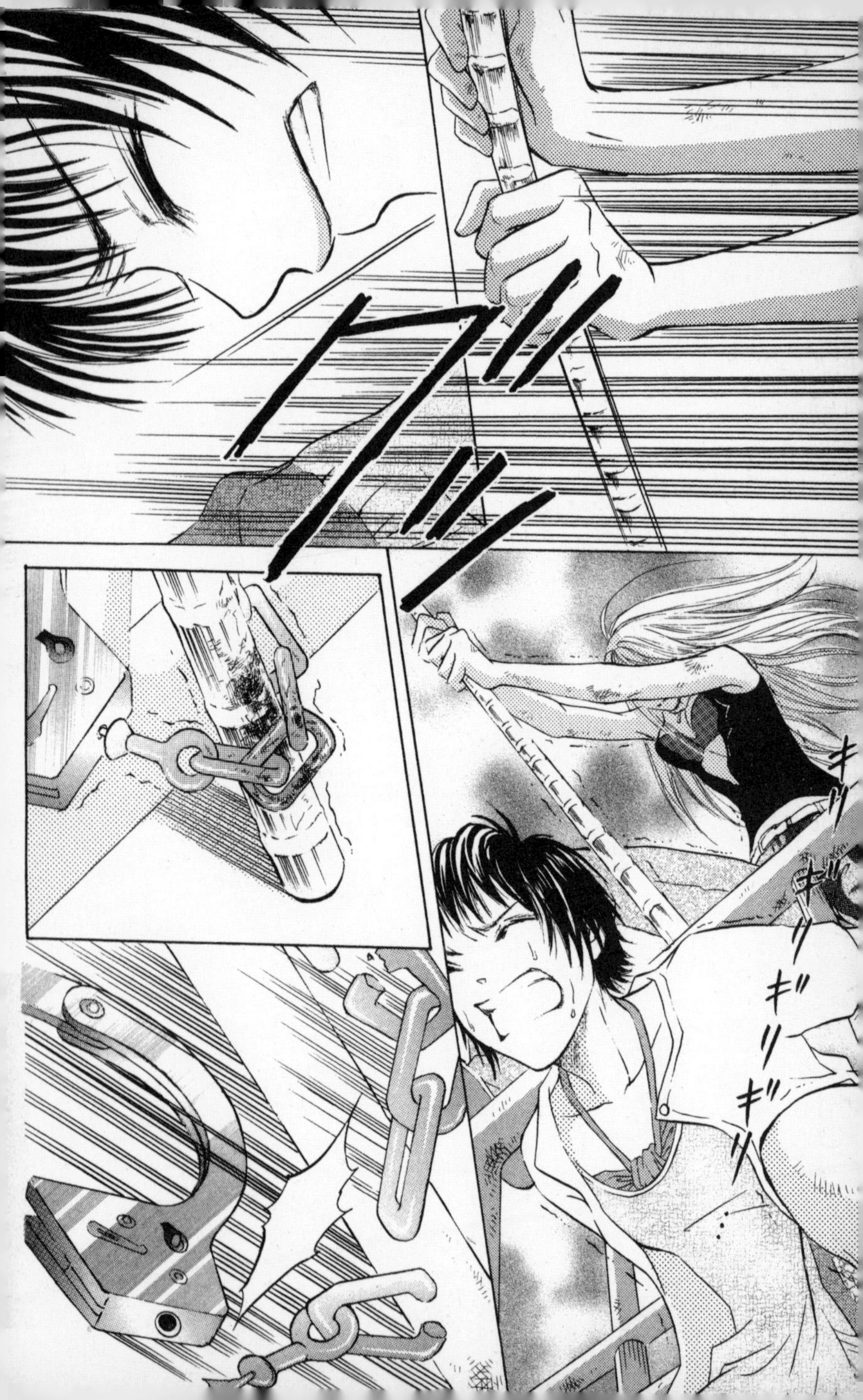
ガッ
ギリギリギリギリ

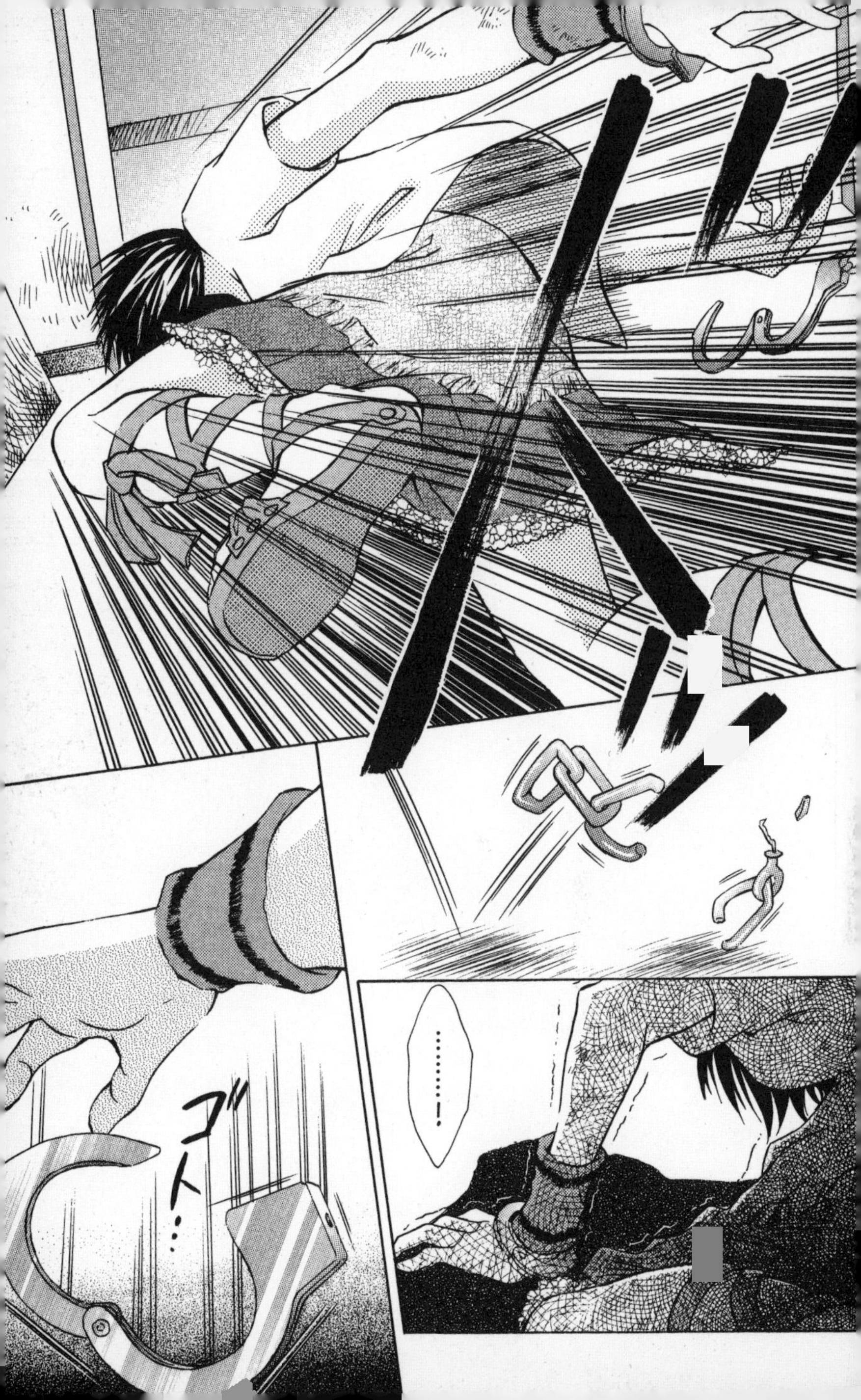
……!
ゴト…

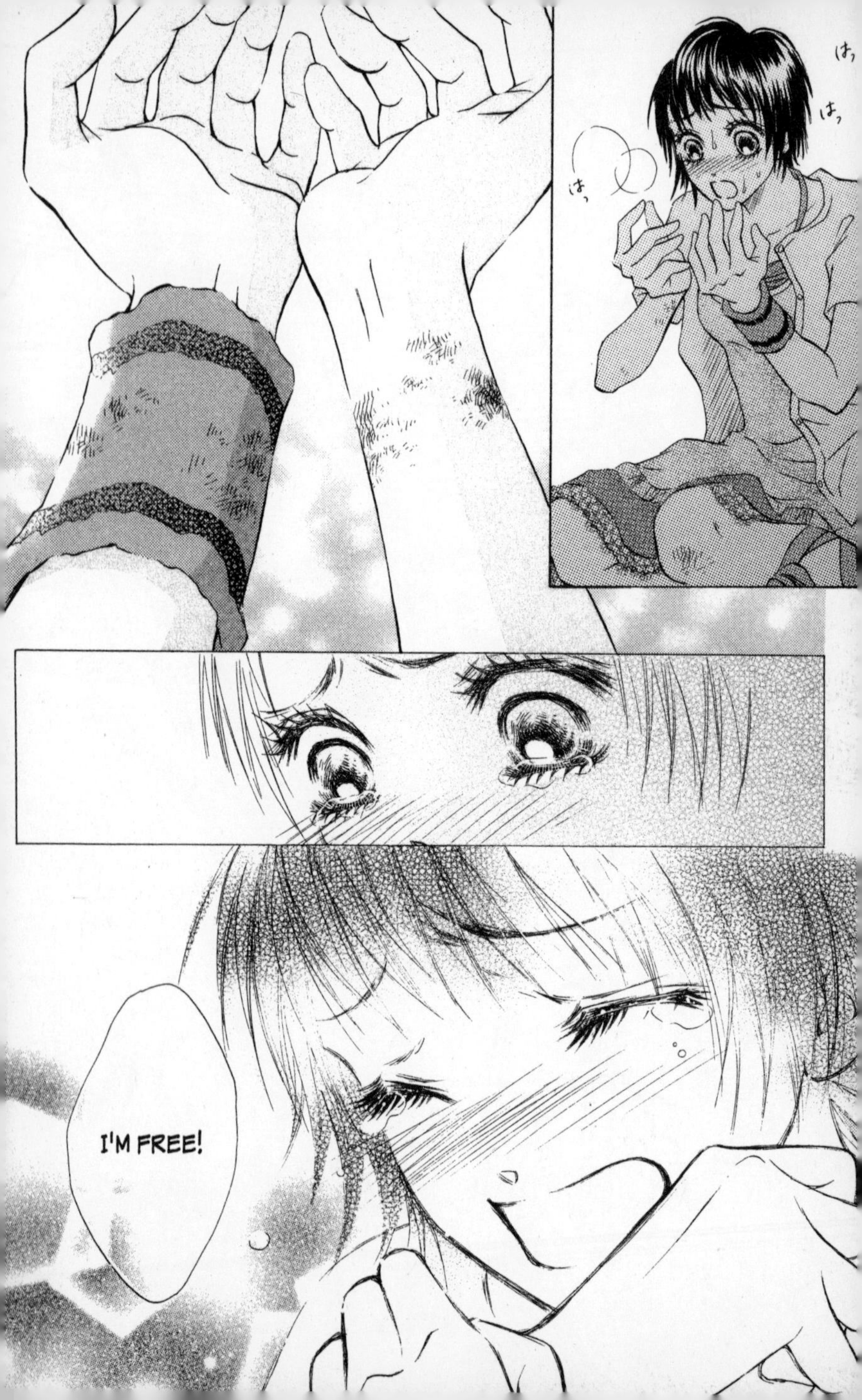
はっ
はっ
はっ
I'M FREE!

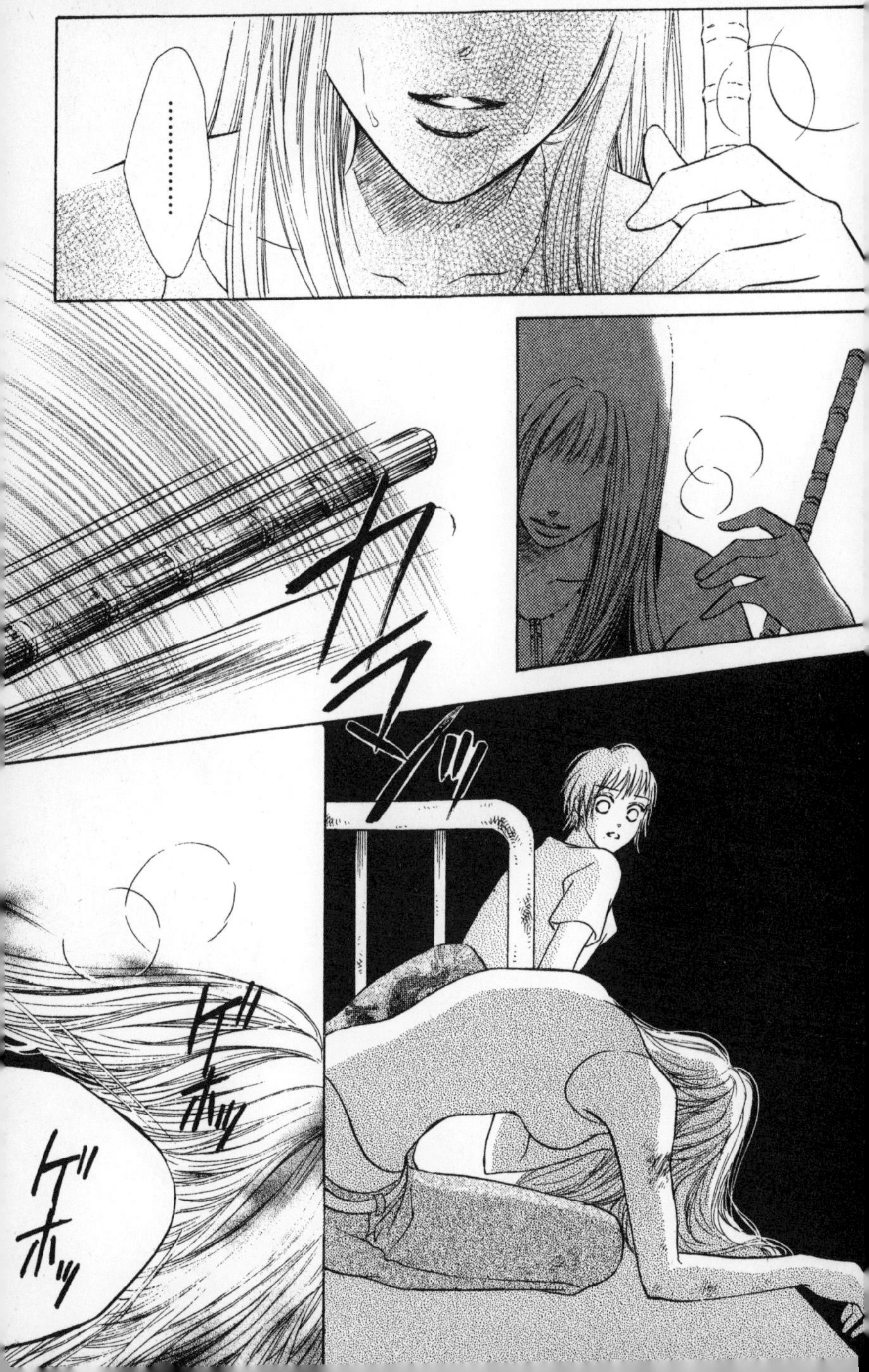
……
ゲホッ
ゲホッ

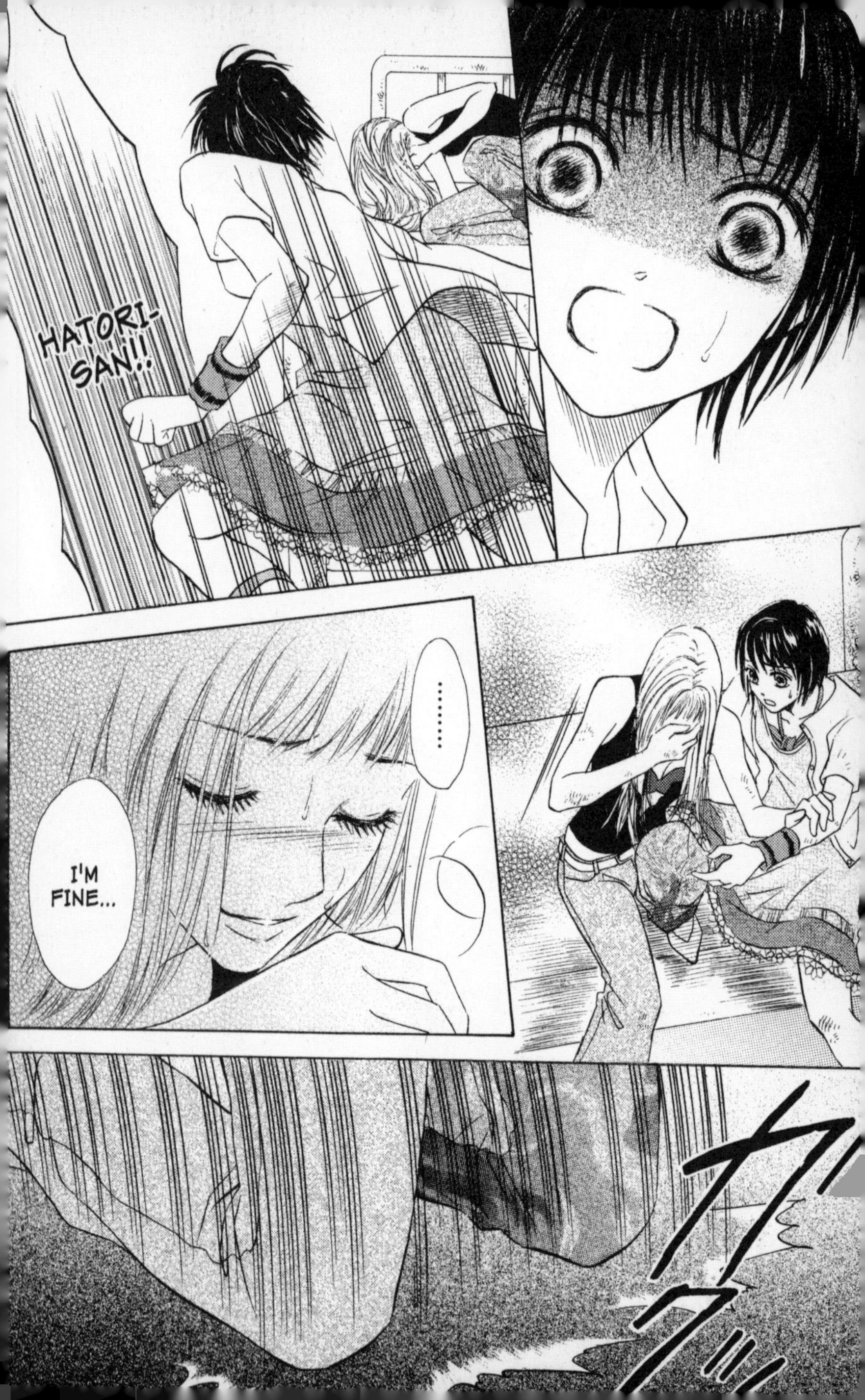
HATORI-SAN!!
......
I'M FINE...

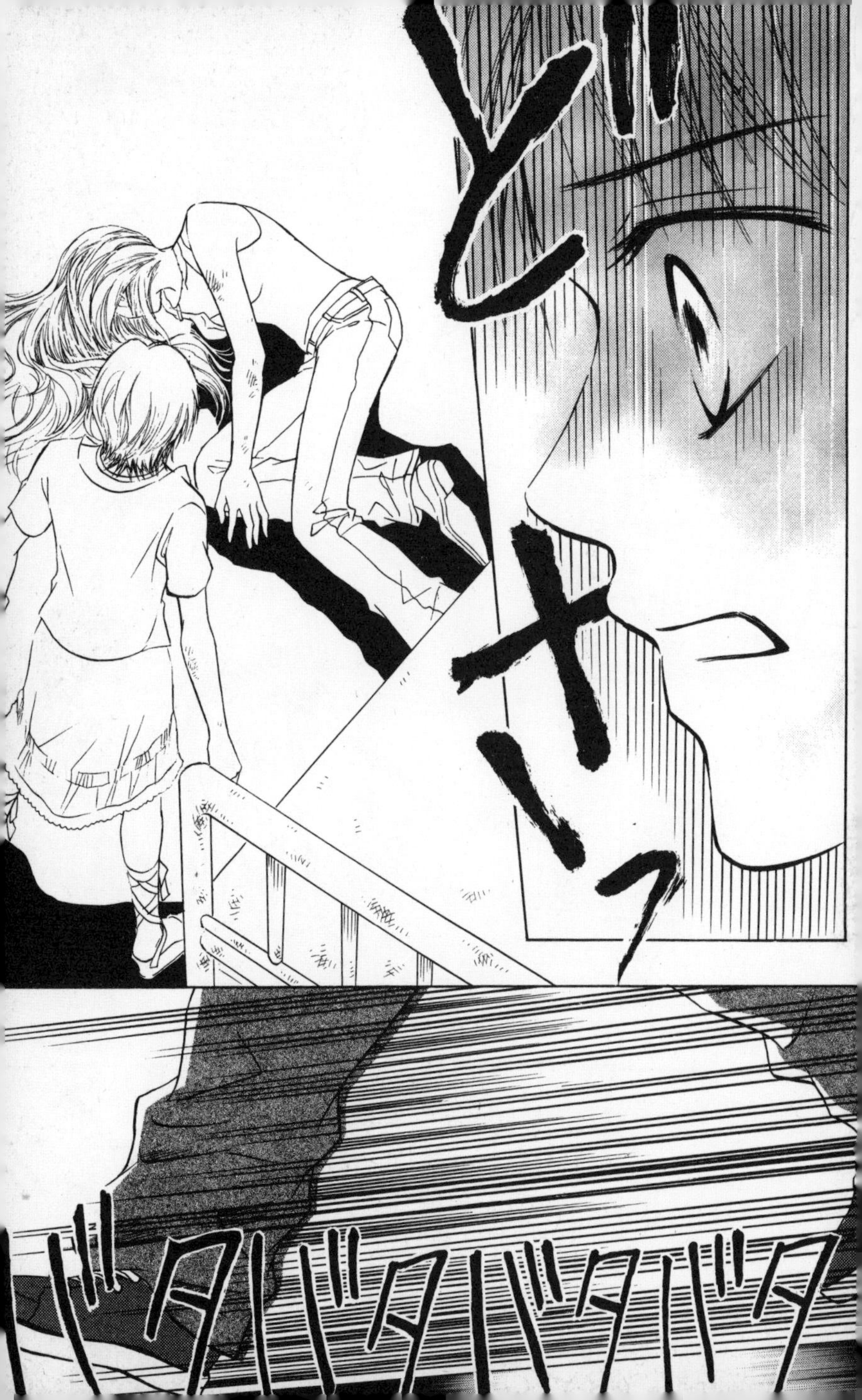
ヒ!!
サーッ
ドタバタバタバタ

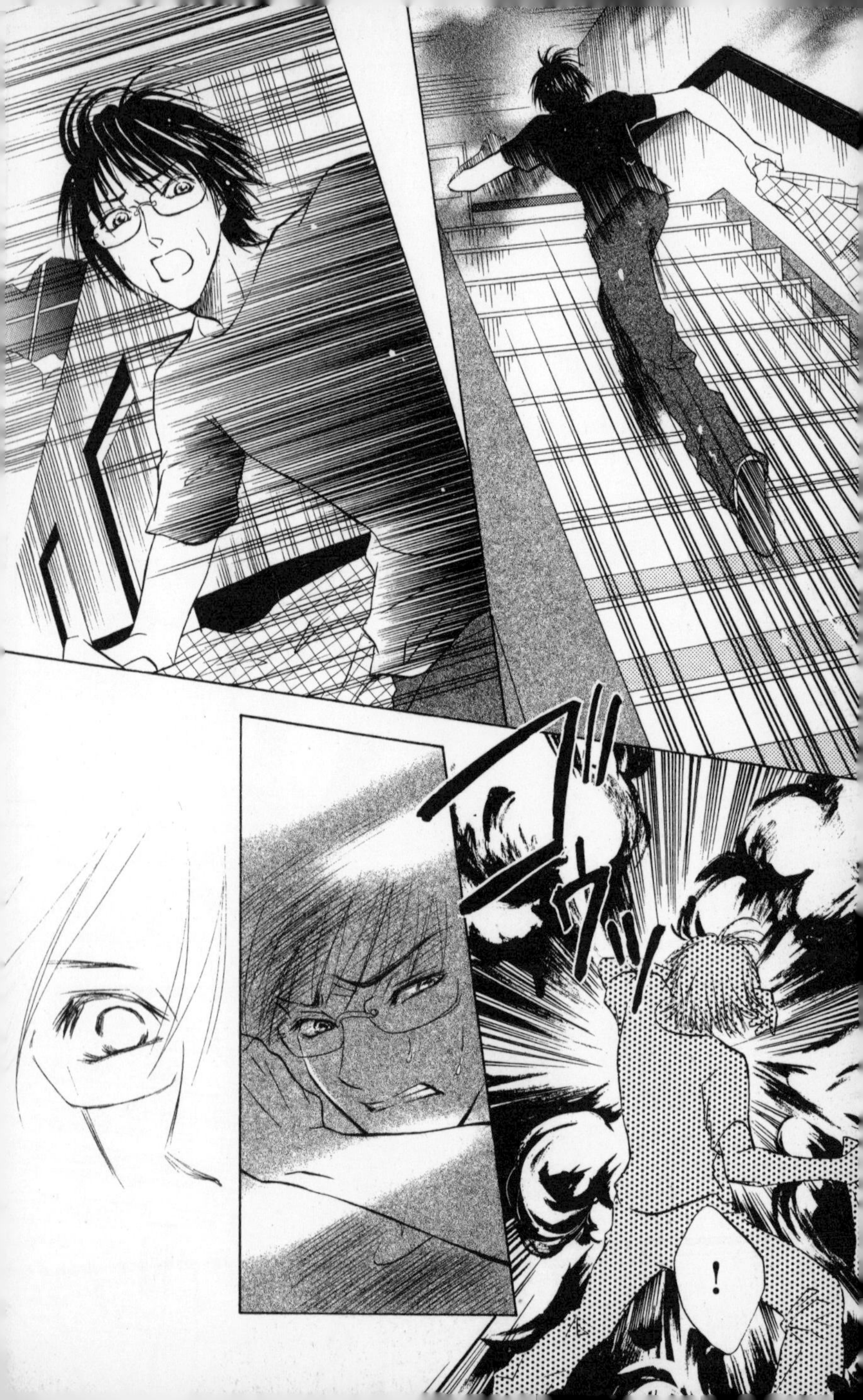
!

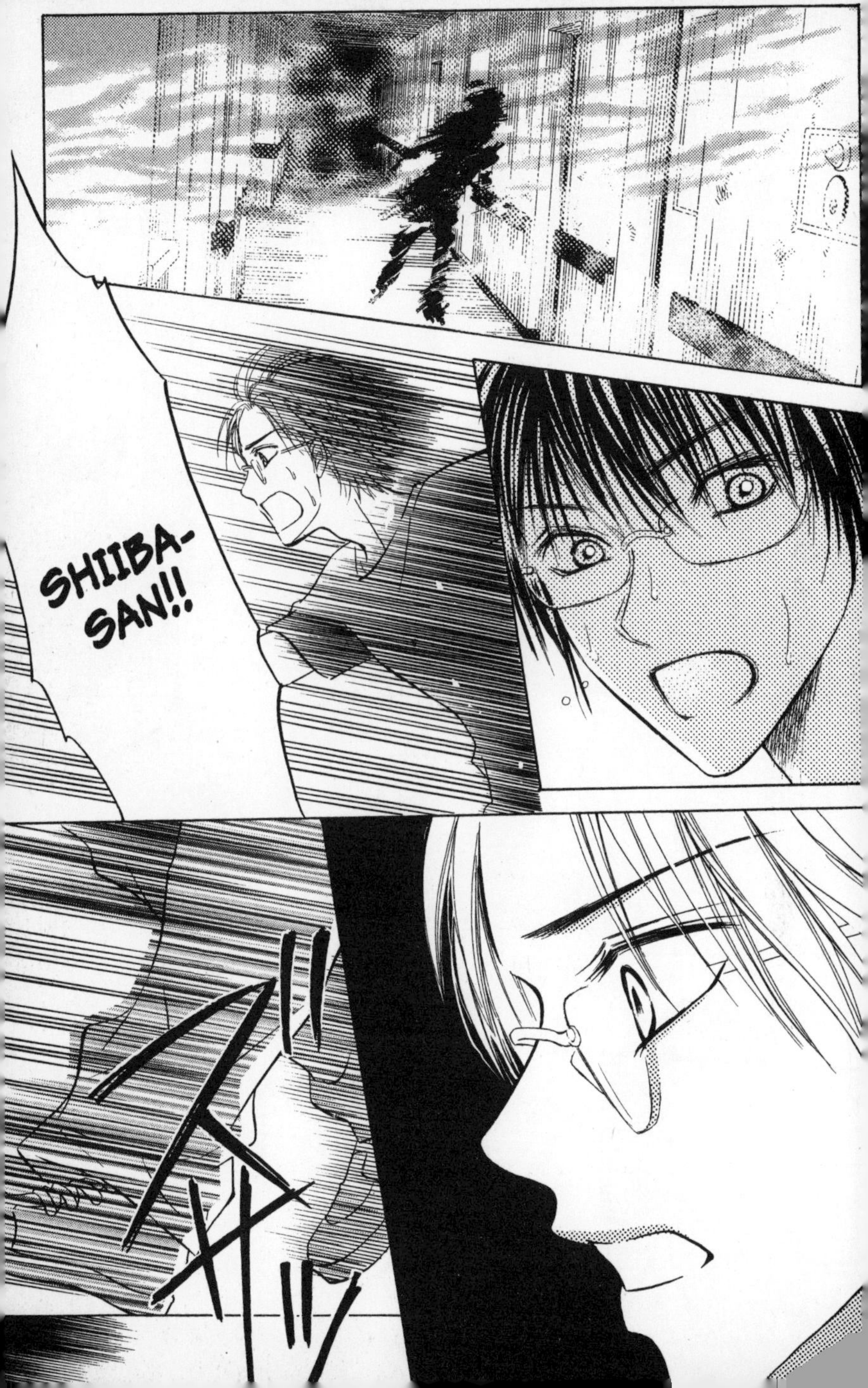
SHIIBA-SAN!!

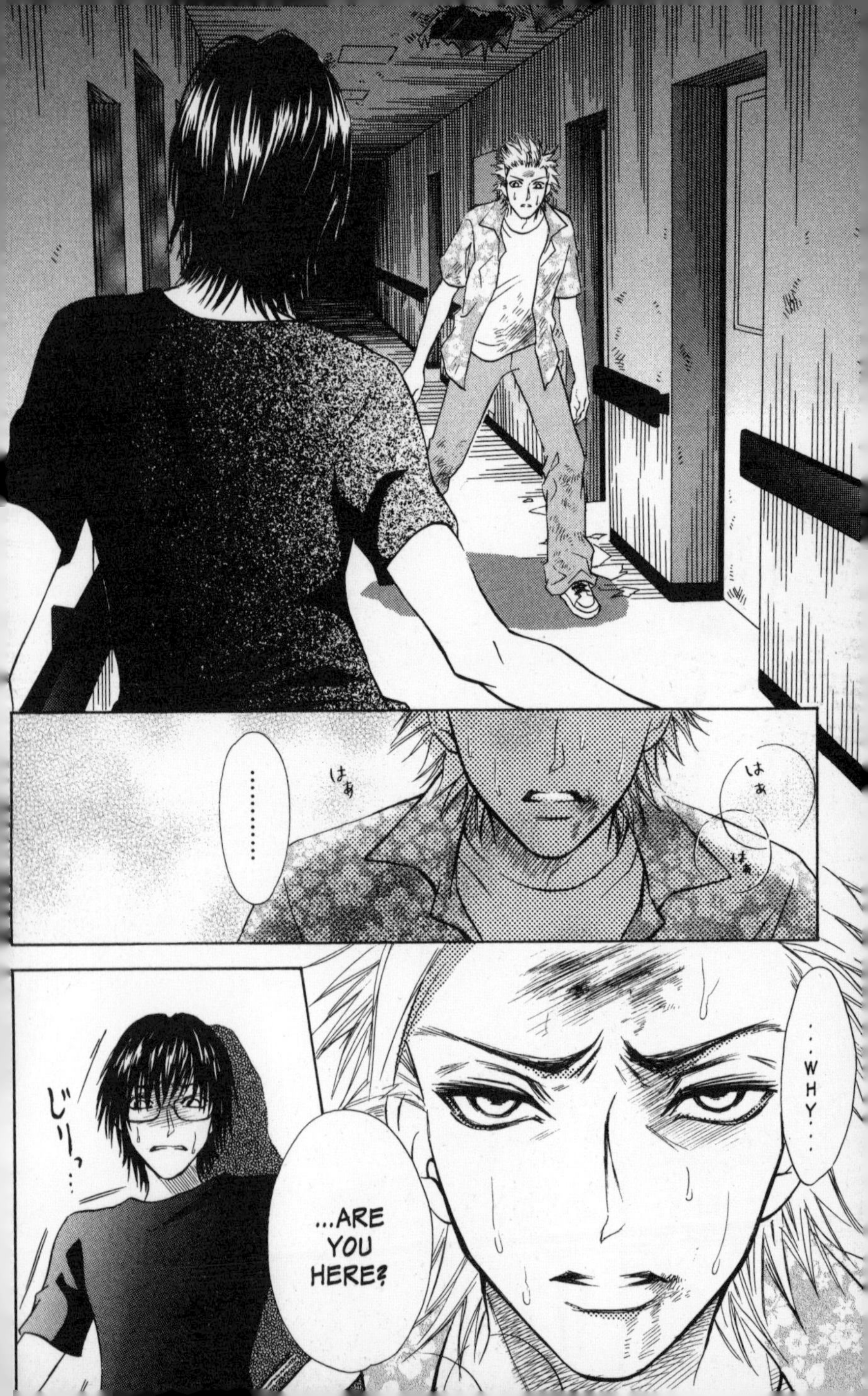

はぁ
はぁ
......
はぁ
...WHY...
...ARE YOU HERE?
じりっ...

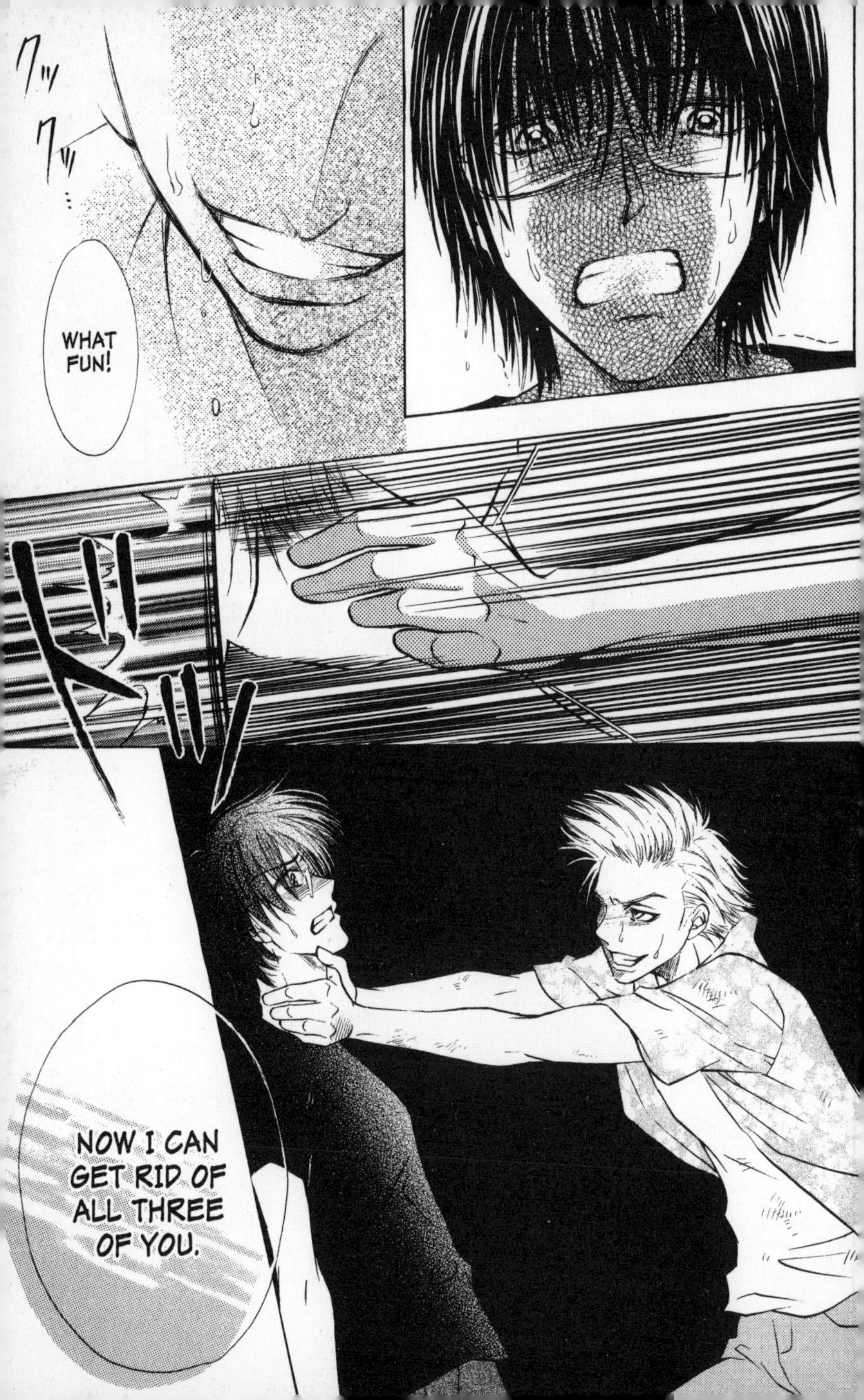
WHAT FUN!
NOW I CAN GET RID OF ALL THREE OF YOU.

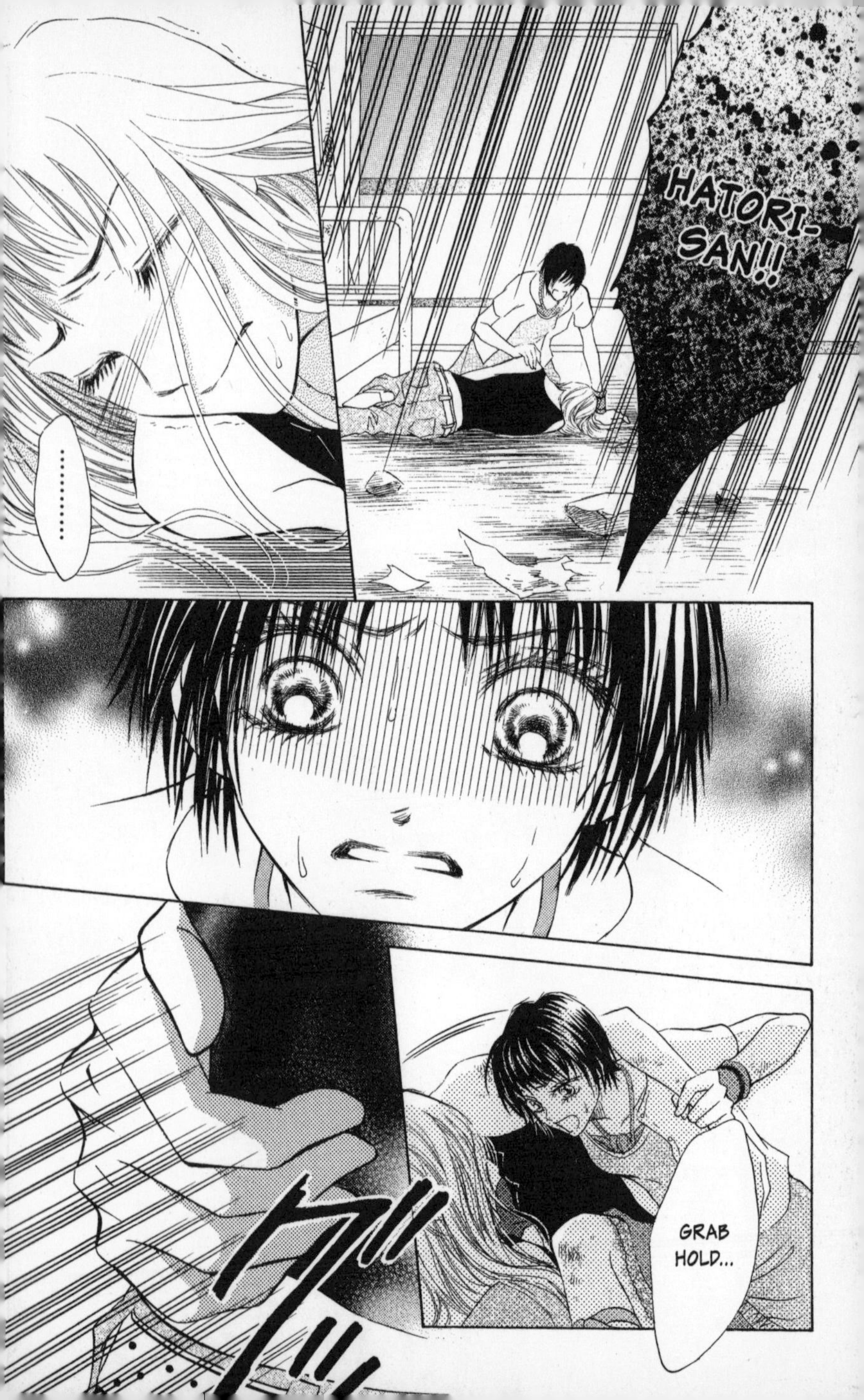
HATORI-SAN!!
……
GRAB HOLD...

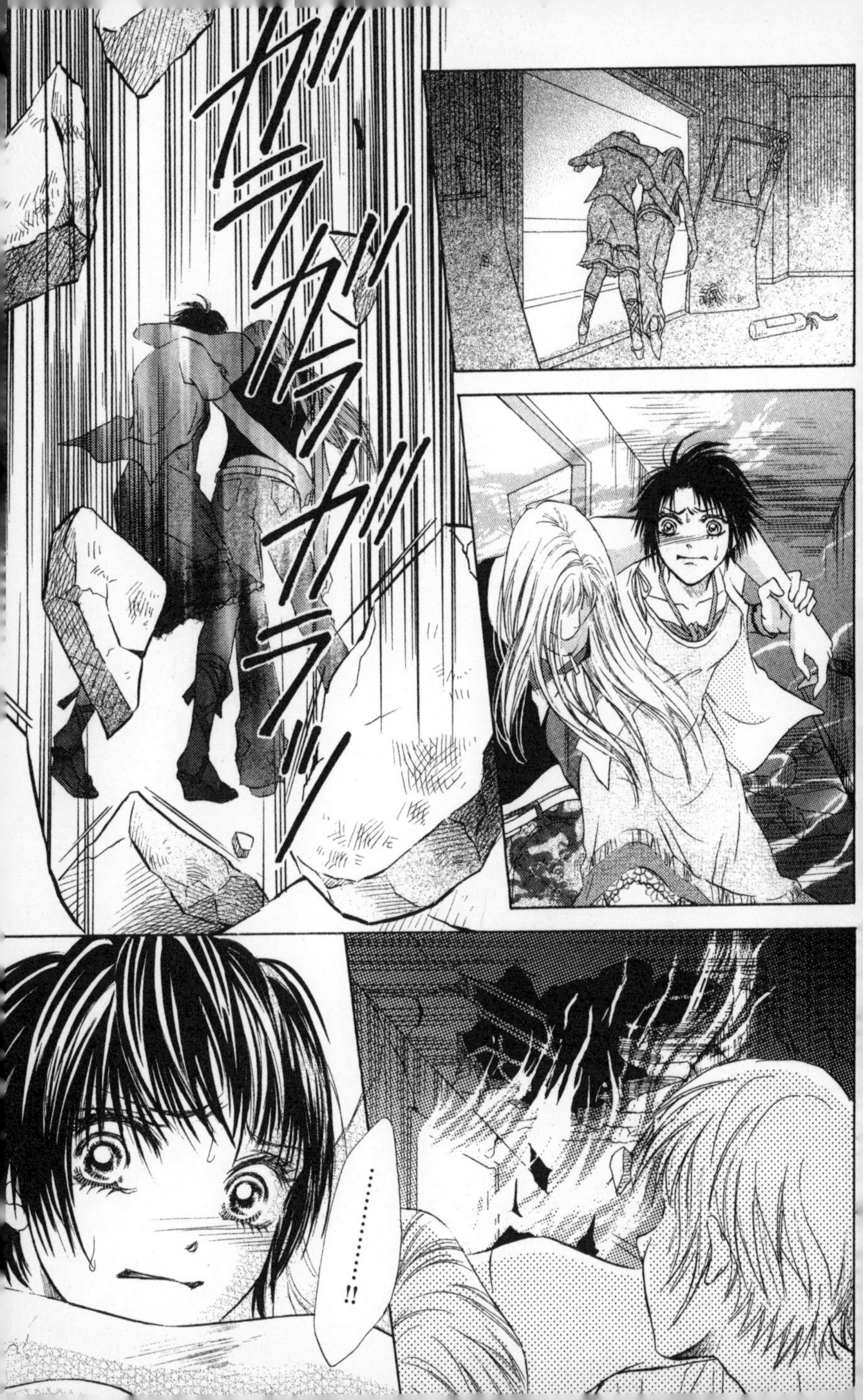
ガラガラガラッ
……!!

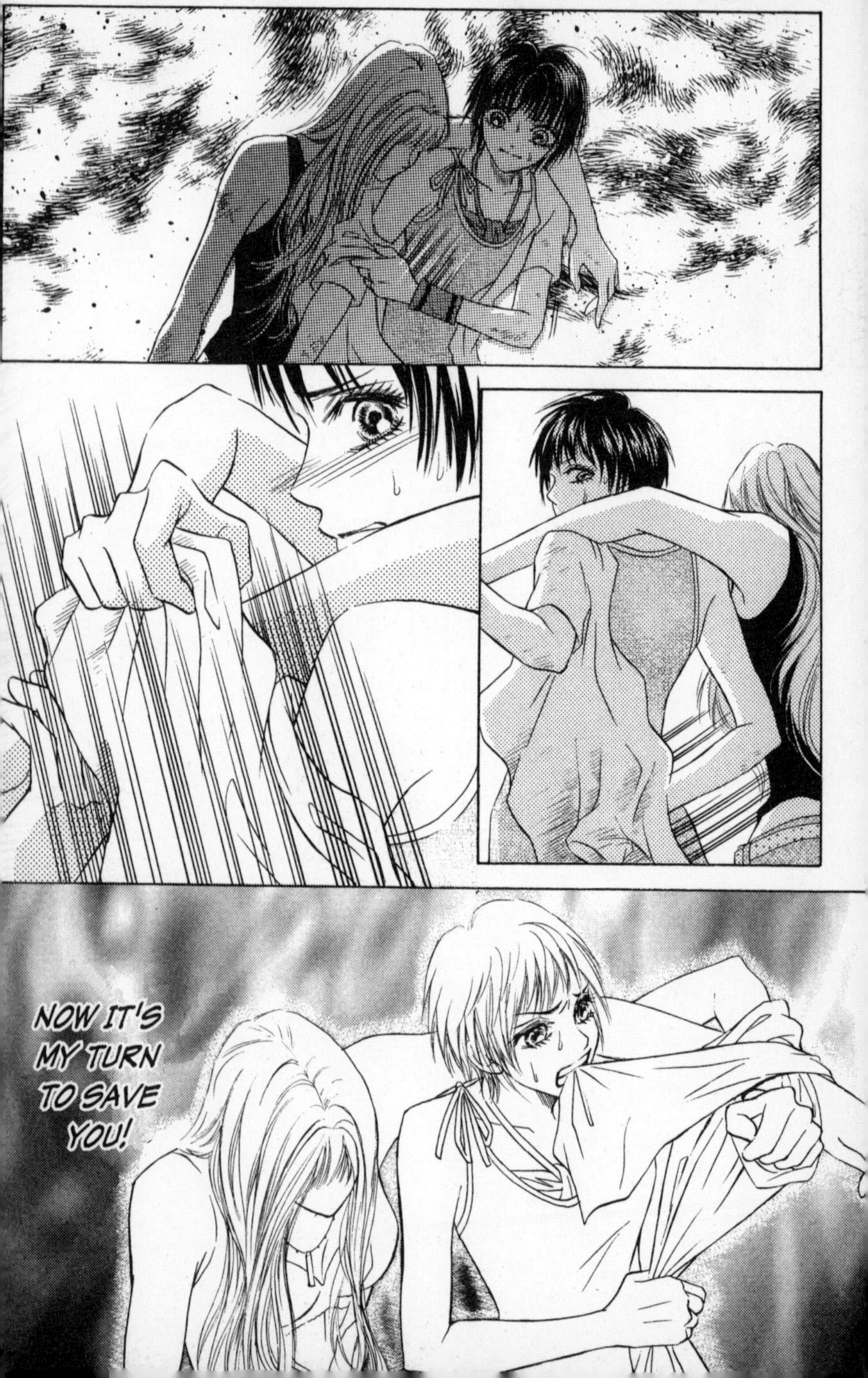
NOW IT'S MY TURN TO SAVE YOU!

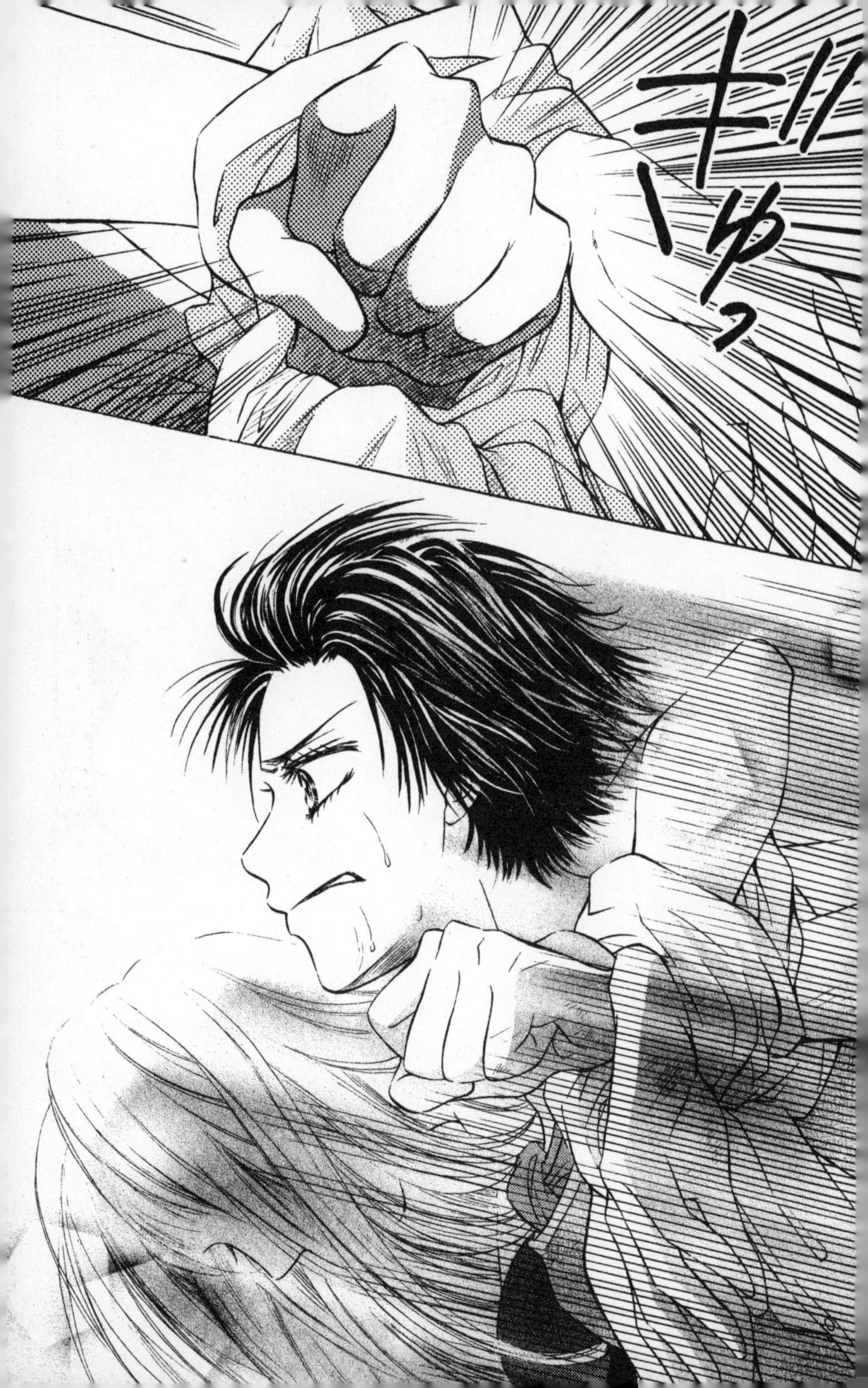
ギリーゅっ

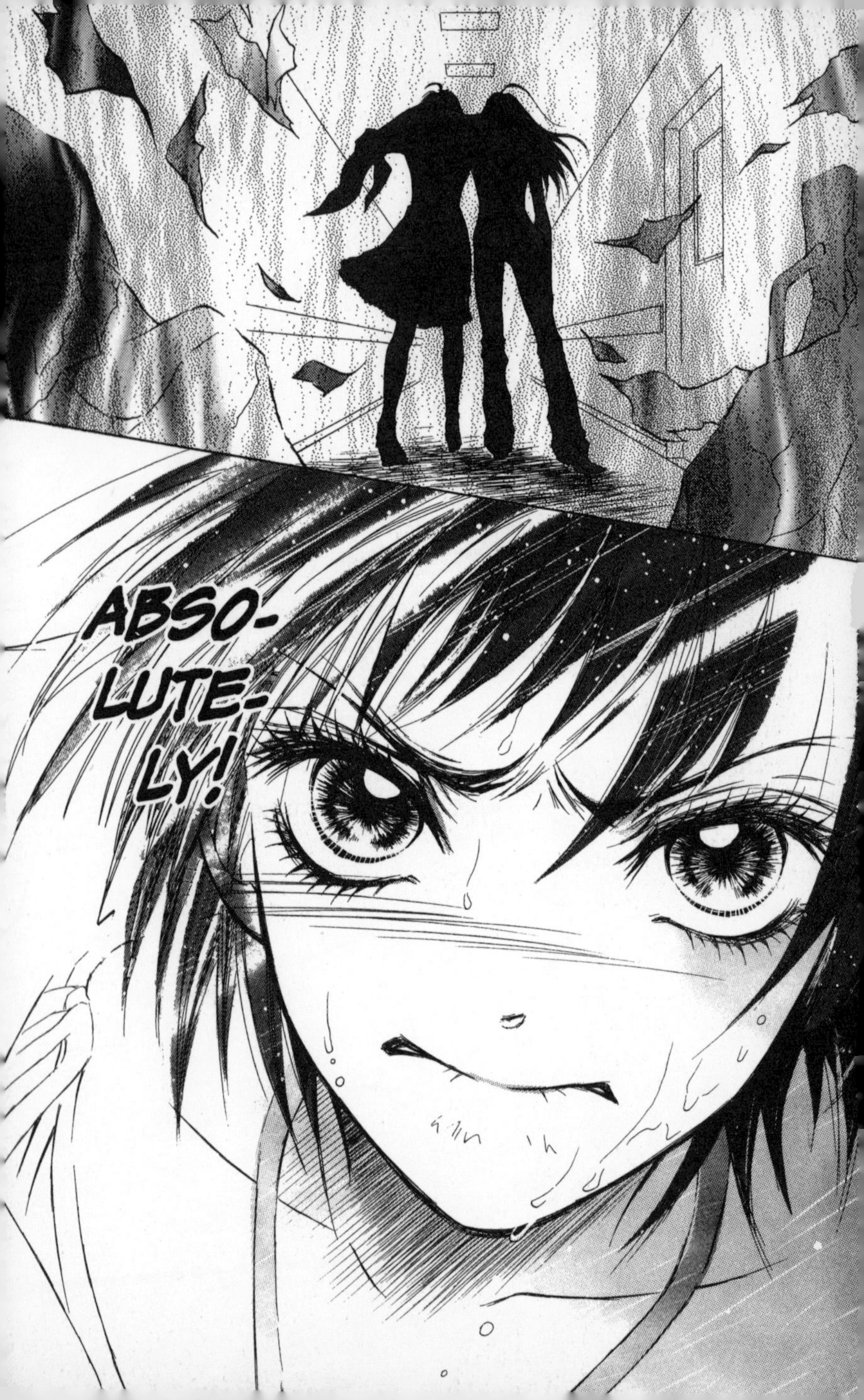
ABSO-
LUTE-
LY!

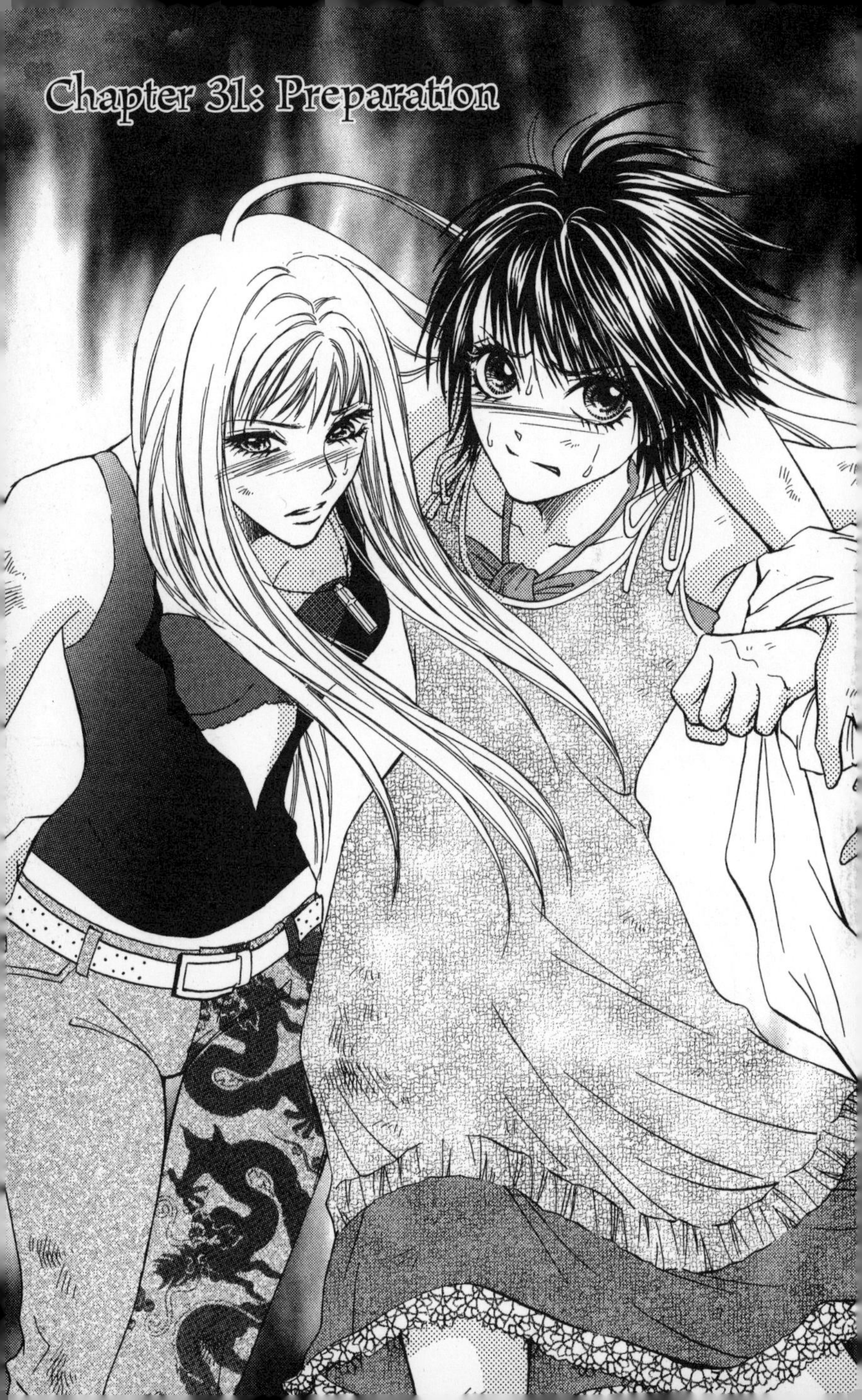
Chapter 31: Preparation

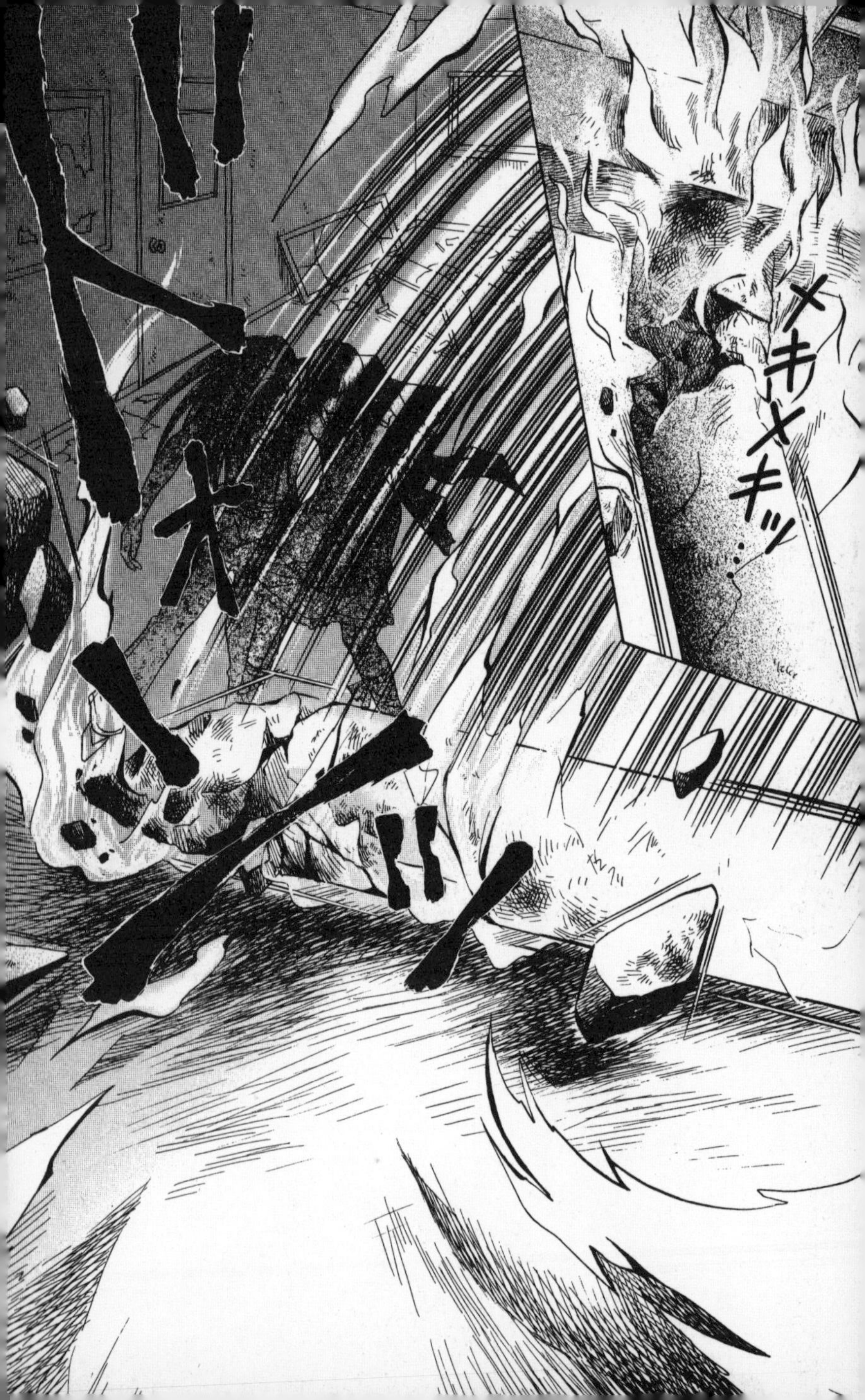
メキメキッ…

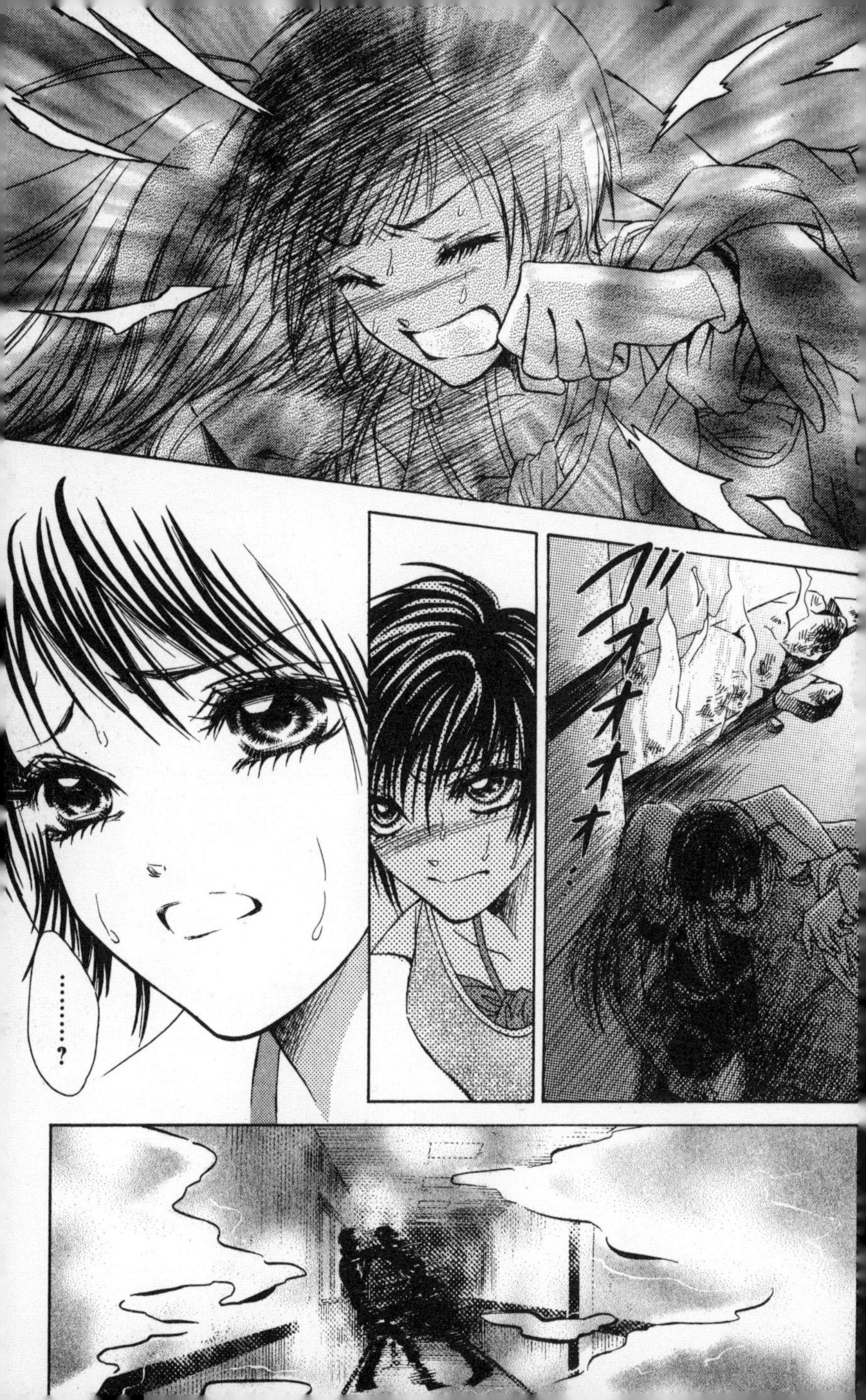
ゴオオオオ…
……？

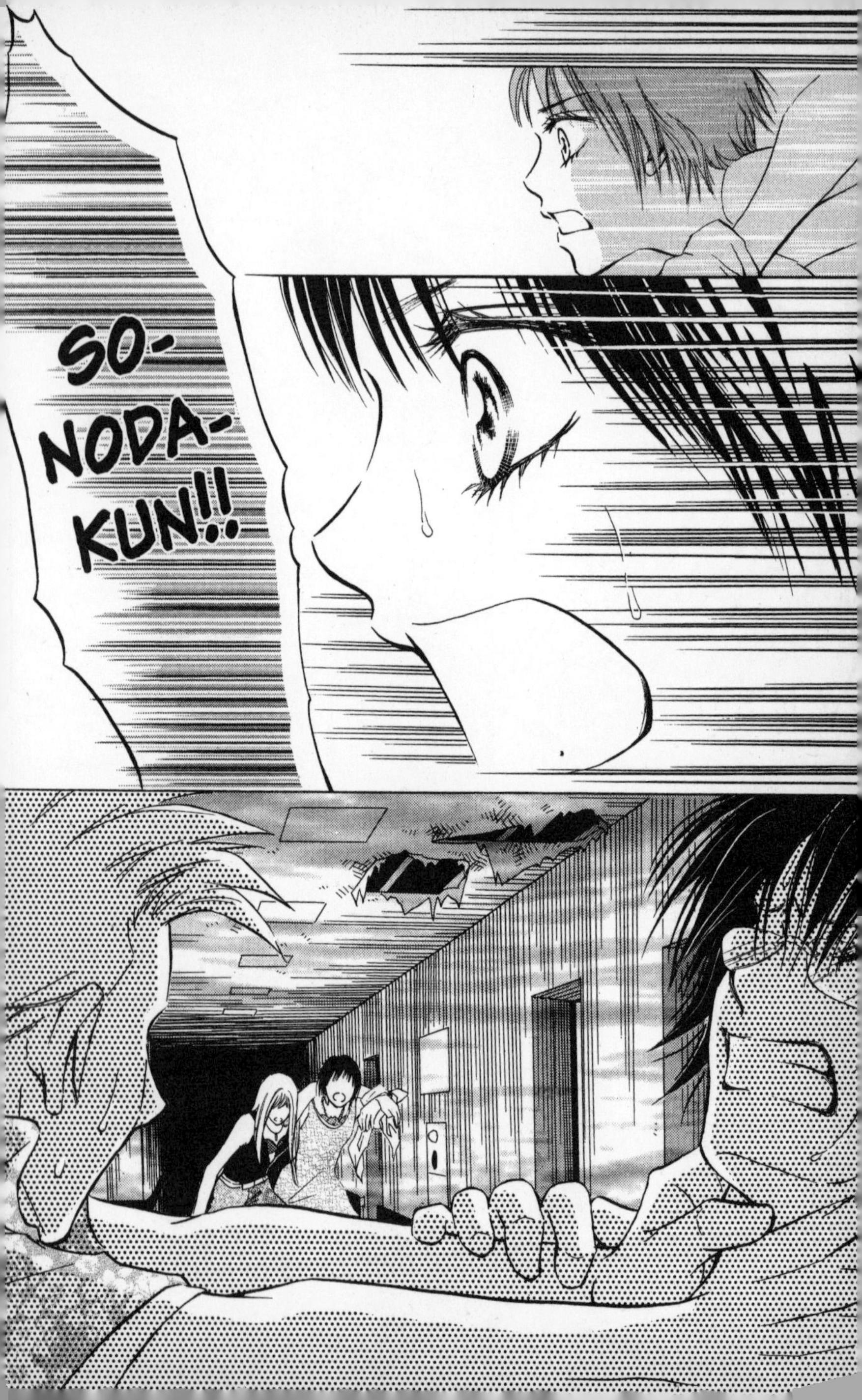
SO-NODA-KUN!!

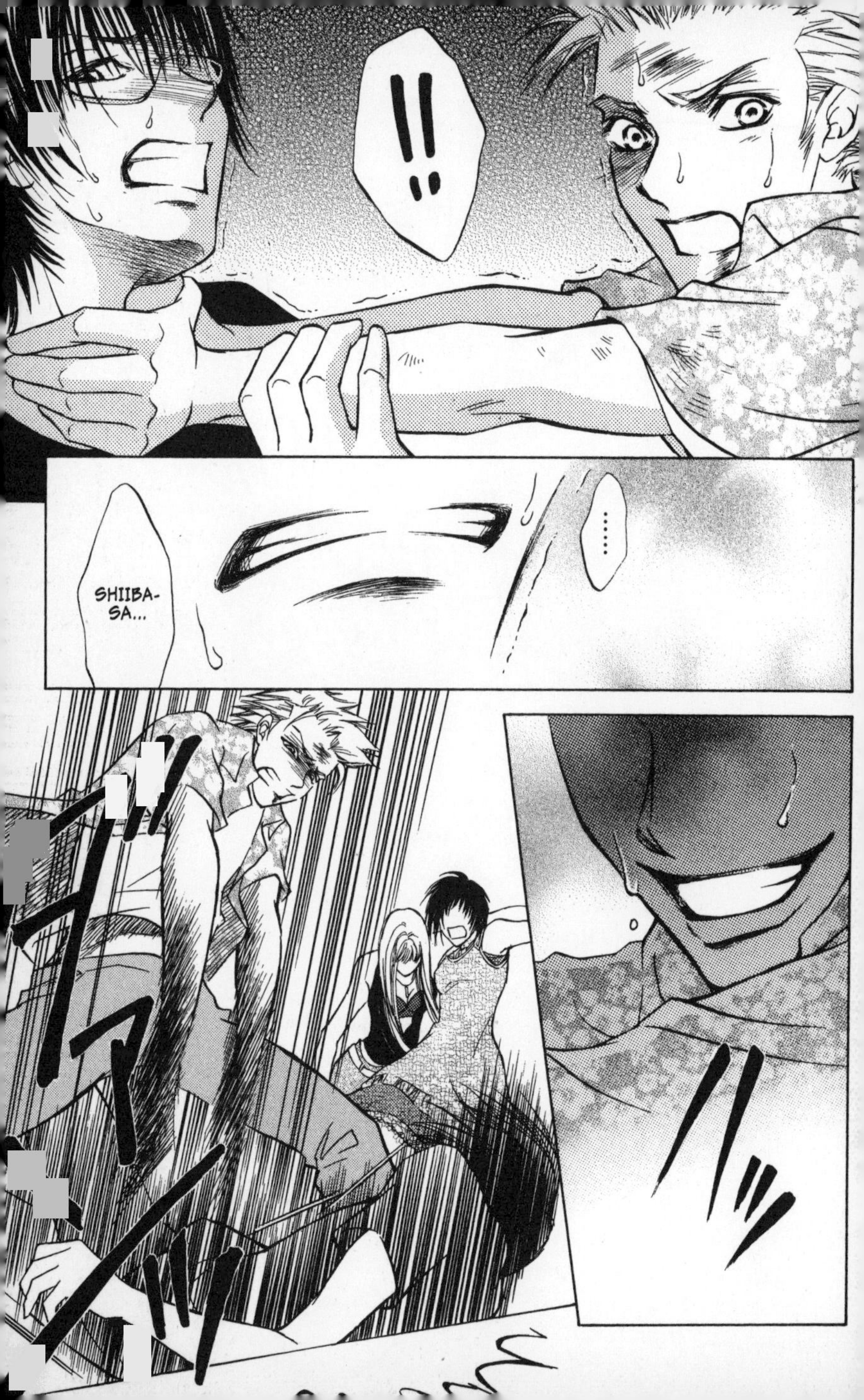
!!
......
SHIIBA-SA...

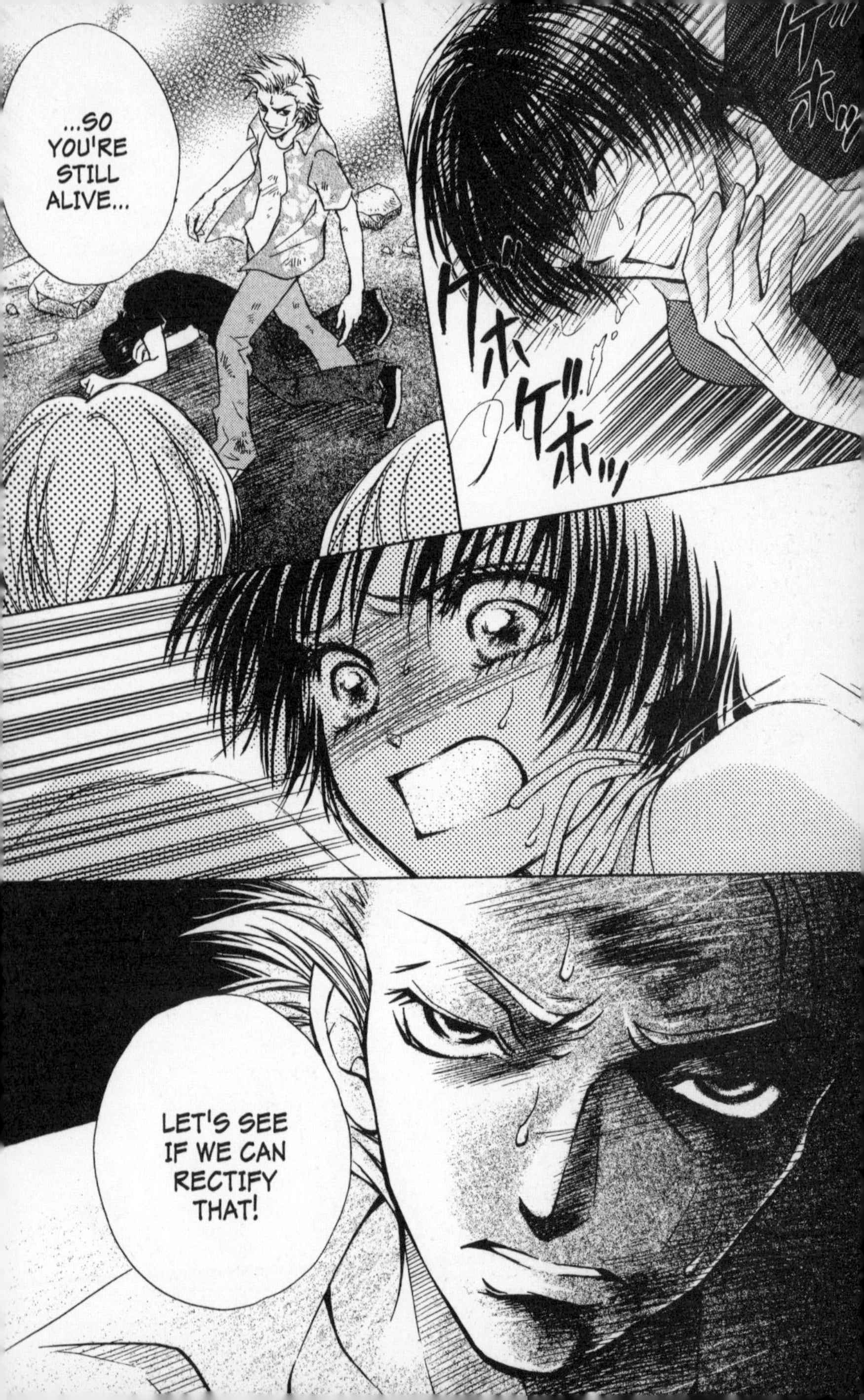
...SO YOU'RE STILL ALIVE...
LET'S SEE IF WE CAN RECTIFY THAT!

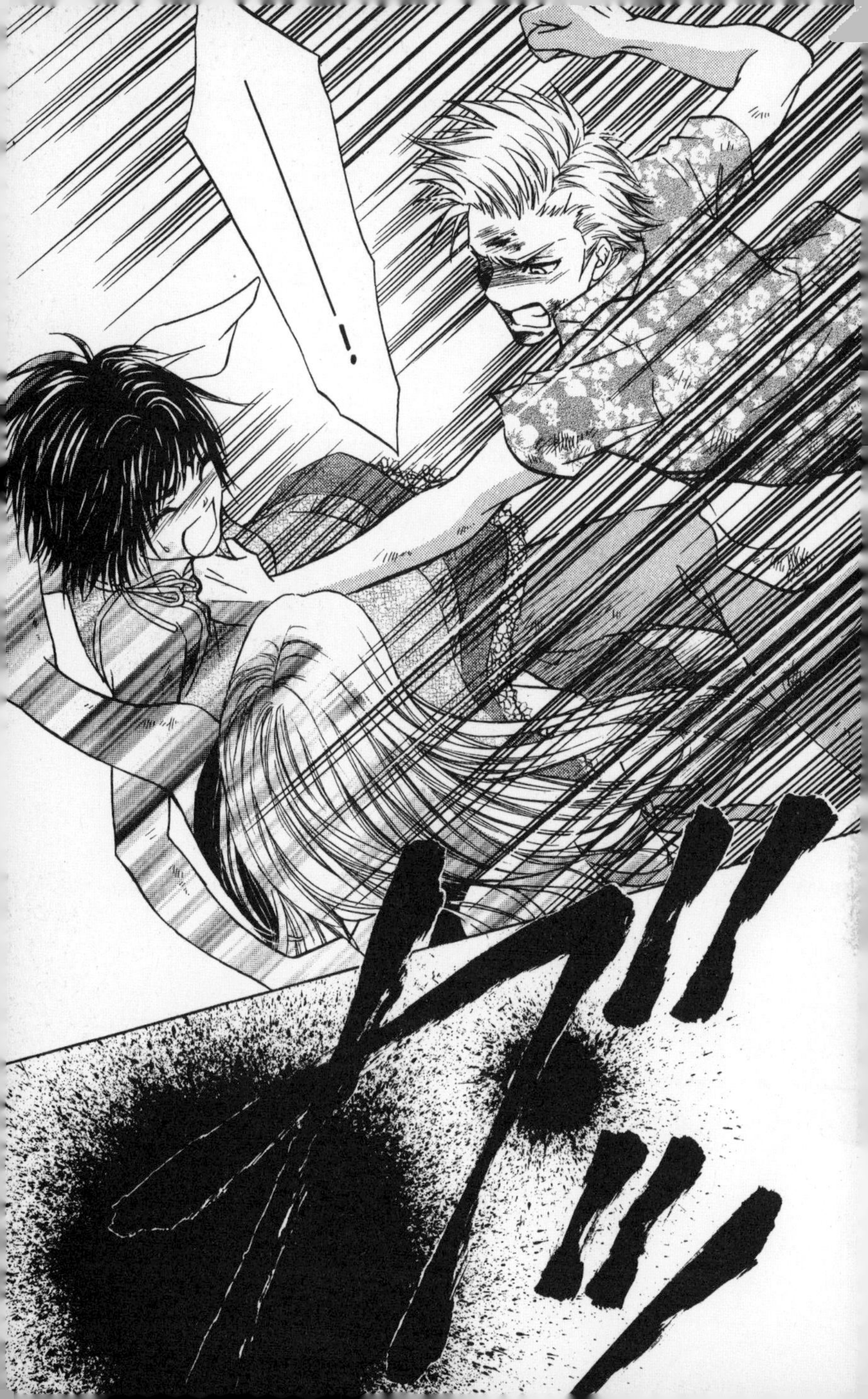
!

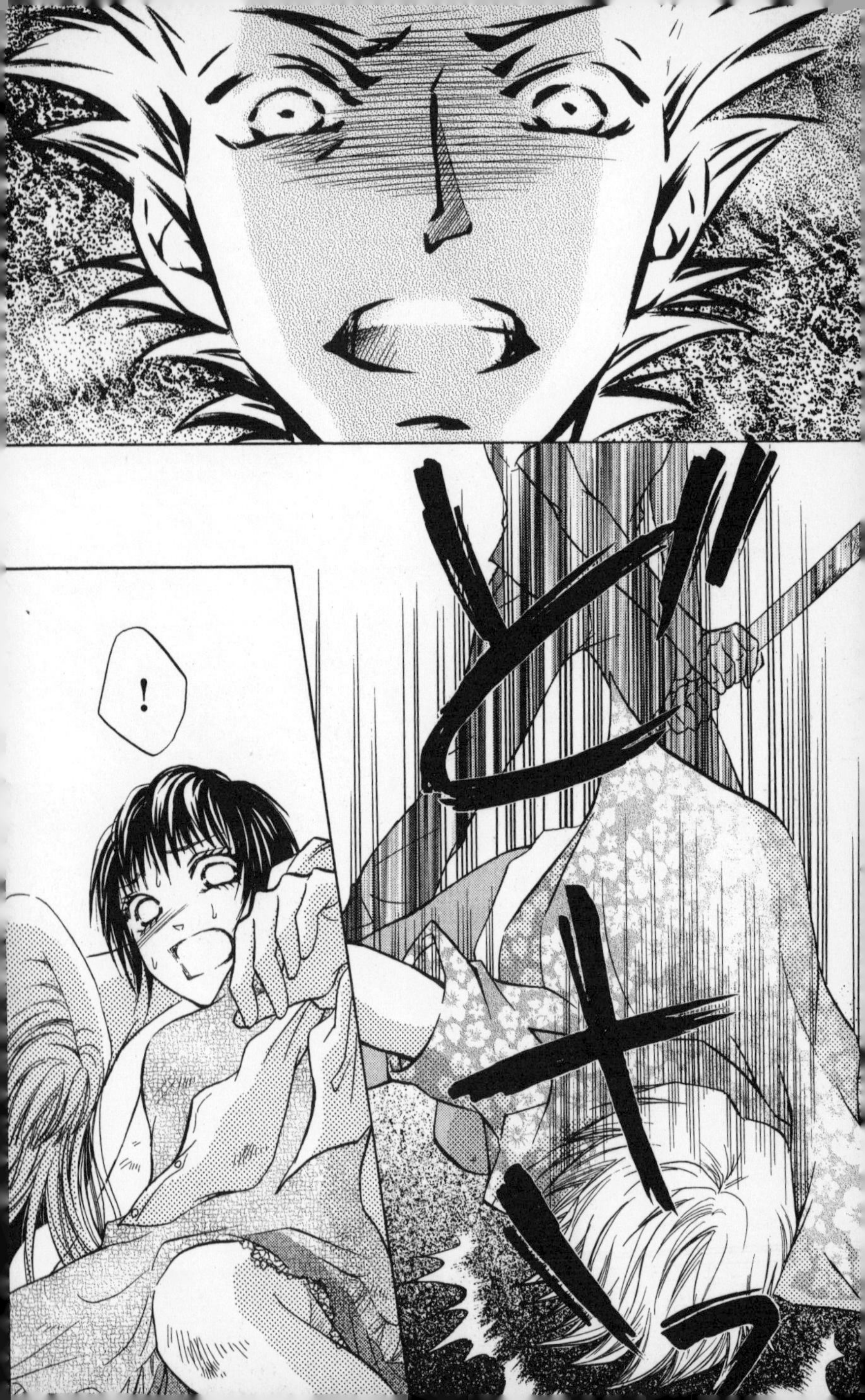
!

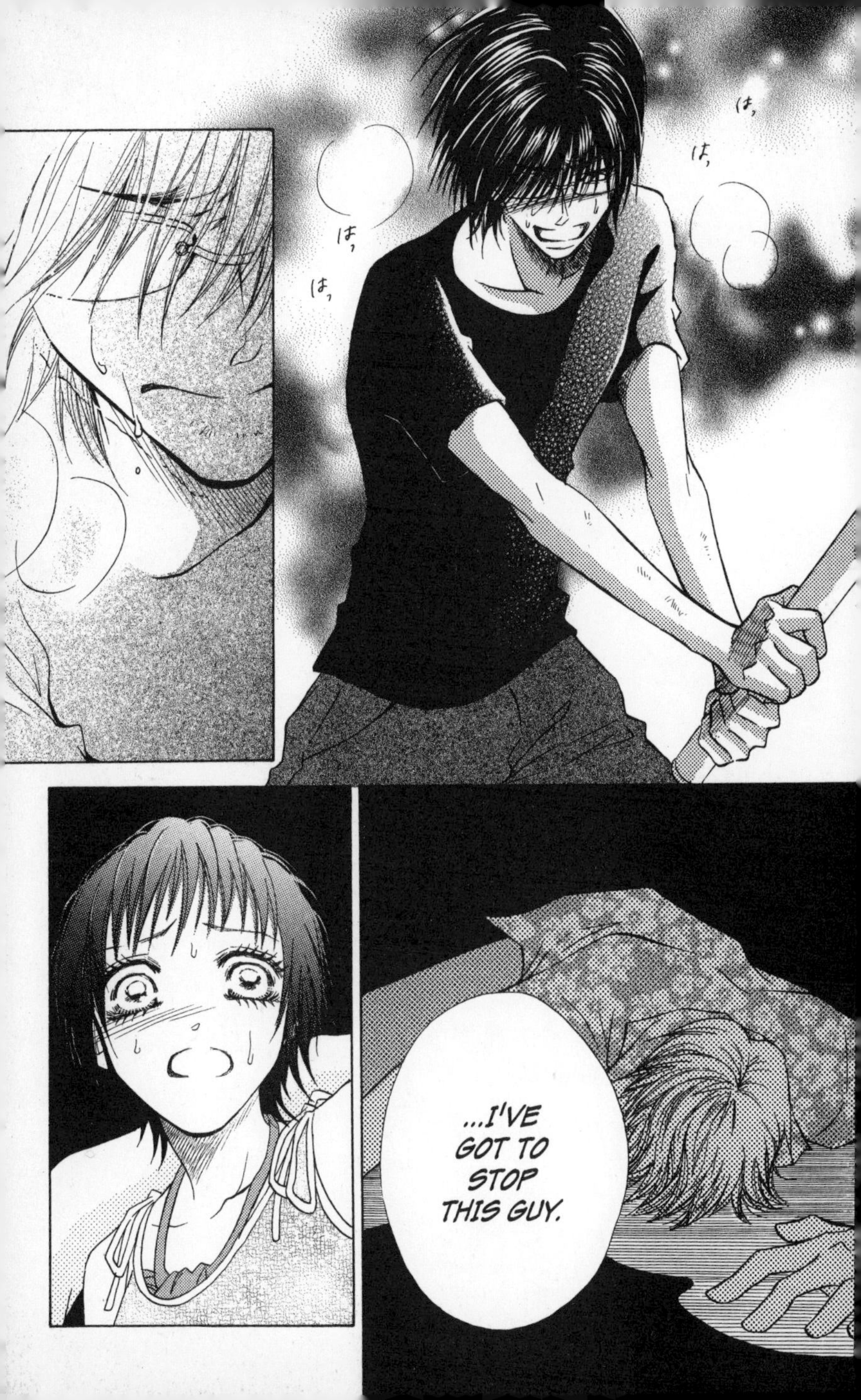
はっ
はっ
はっ
はっ
...I'VE GOT TO STOP THIS GUY.

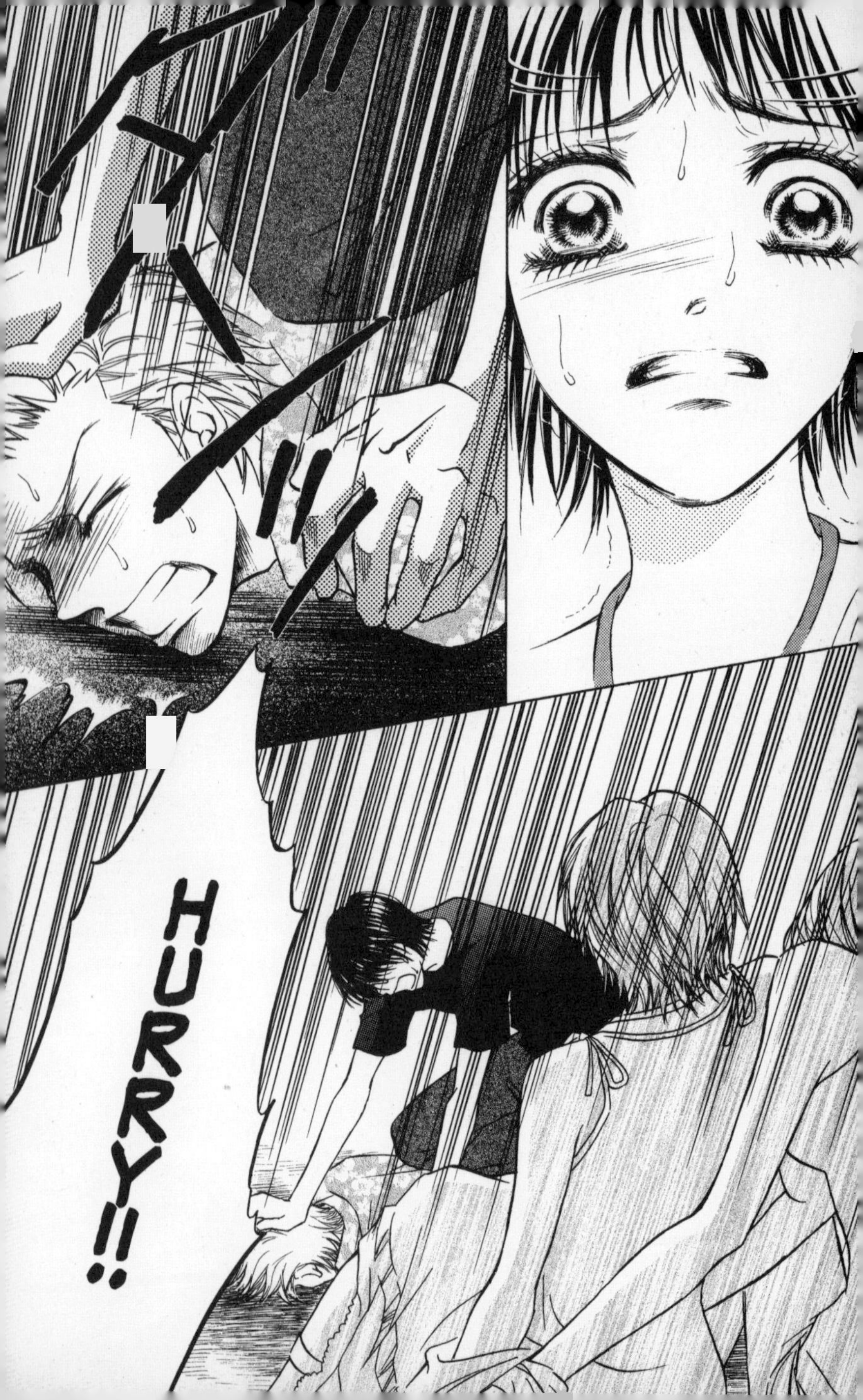
HURRY!!

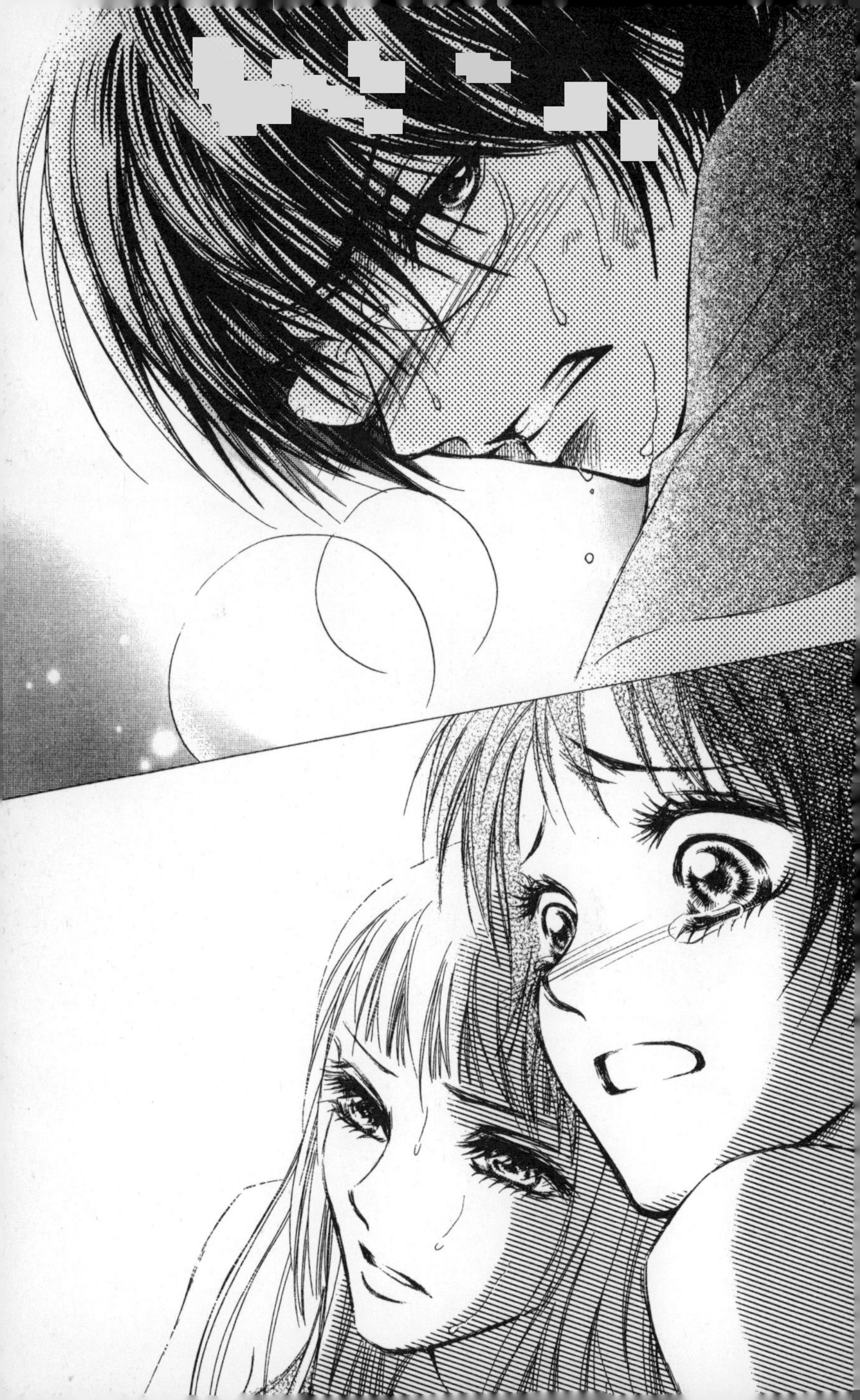

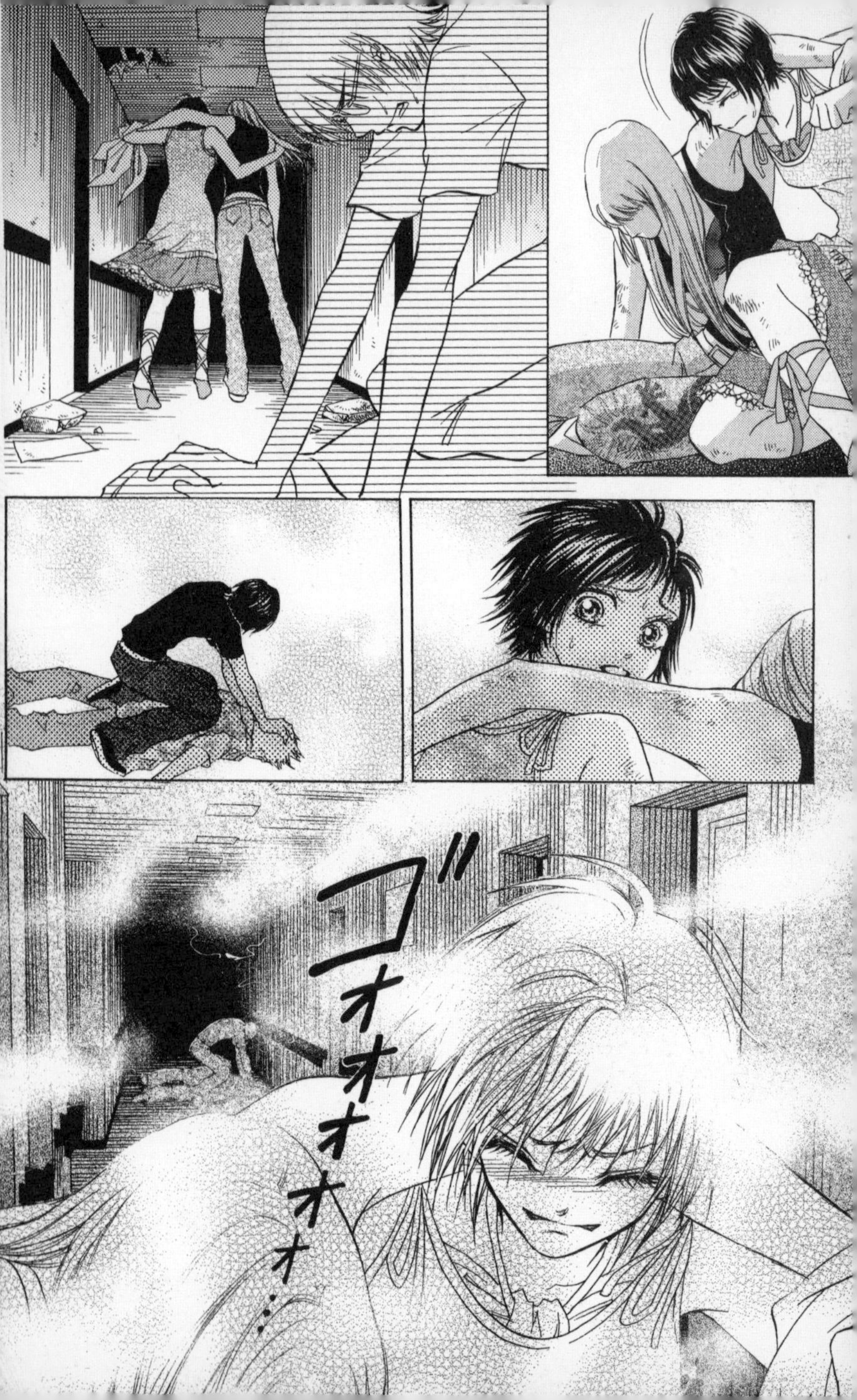
ゴオオオオ…

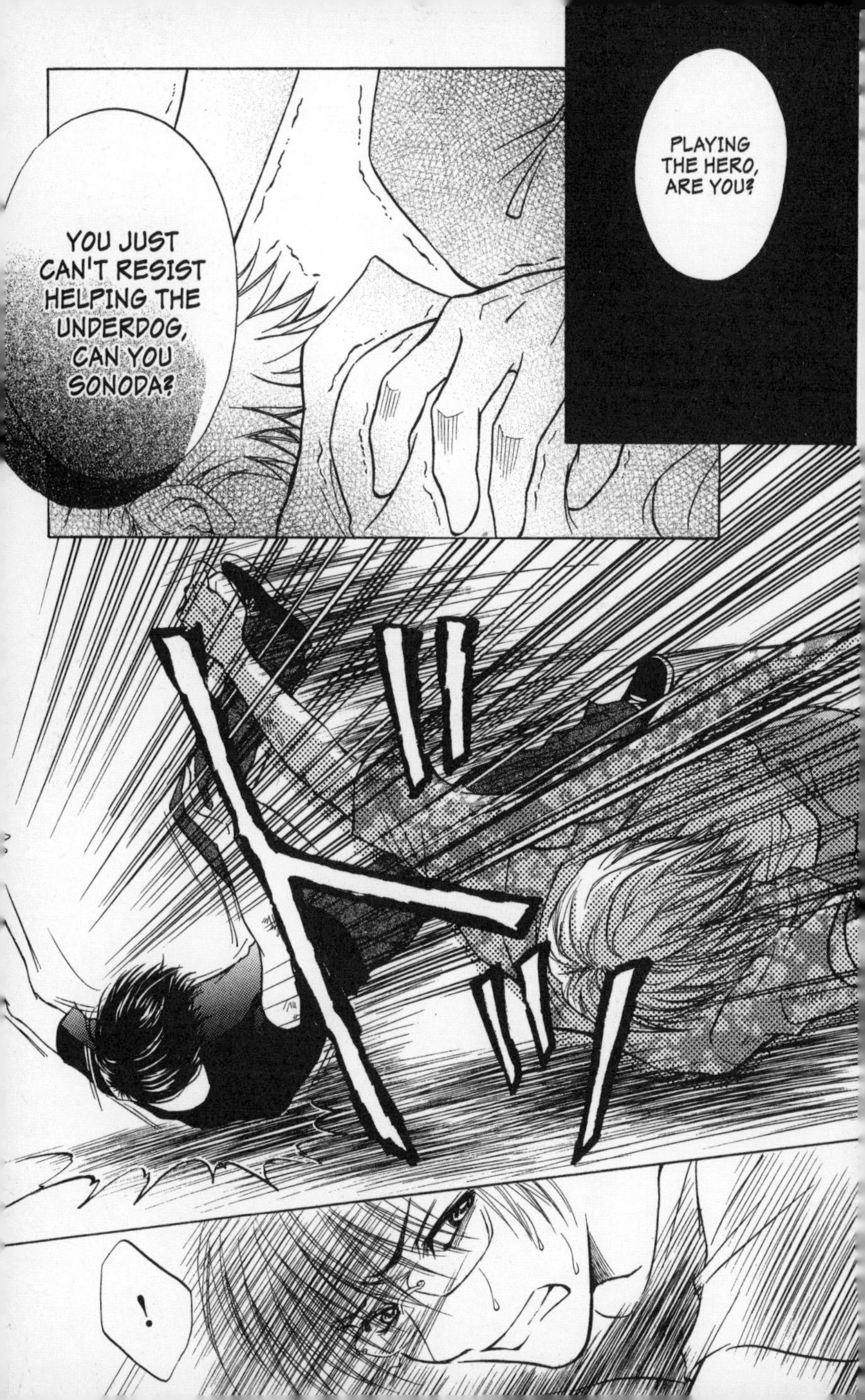
PLAYING THE HERO, ARE YOU?
YOU JUST CAN'T RESIST HELPING THE UNDERDOG, CAN YOU SONODA?
!

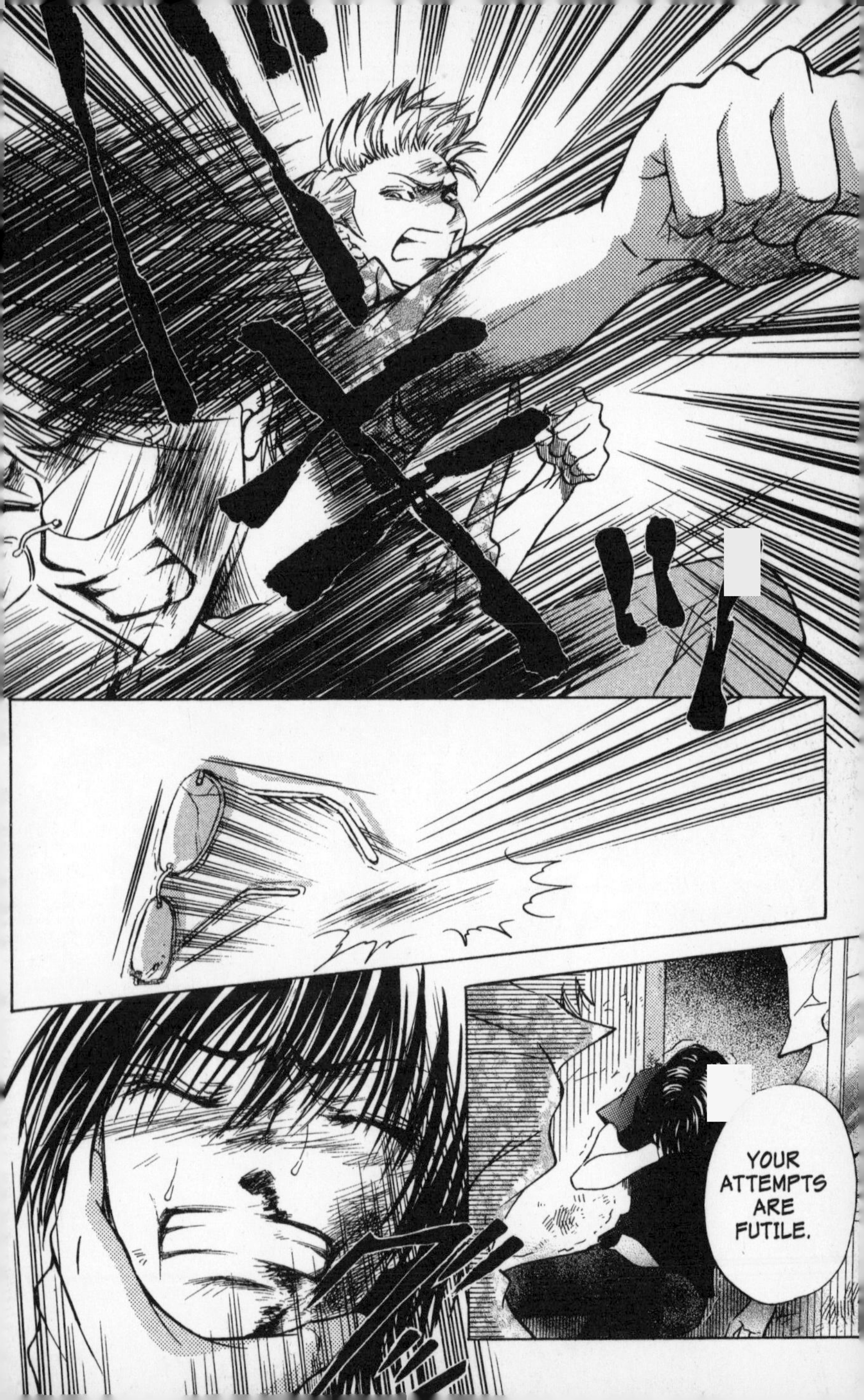
YOUR ATTEMPTS ARE FUTILE.

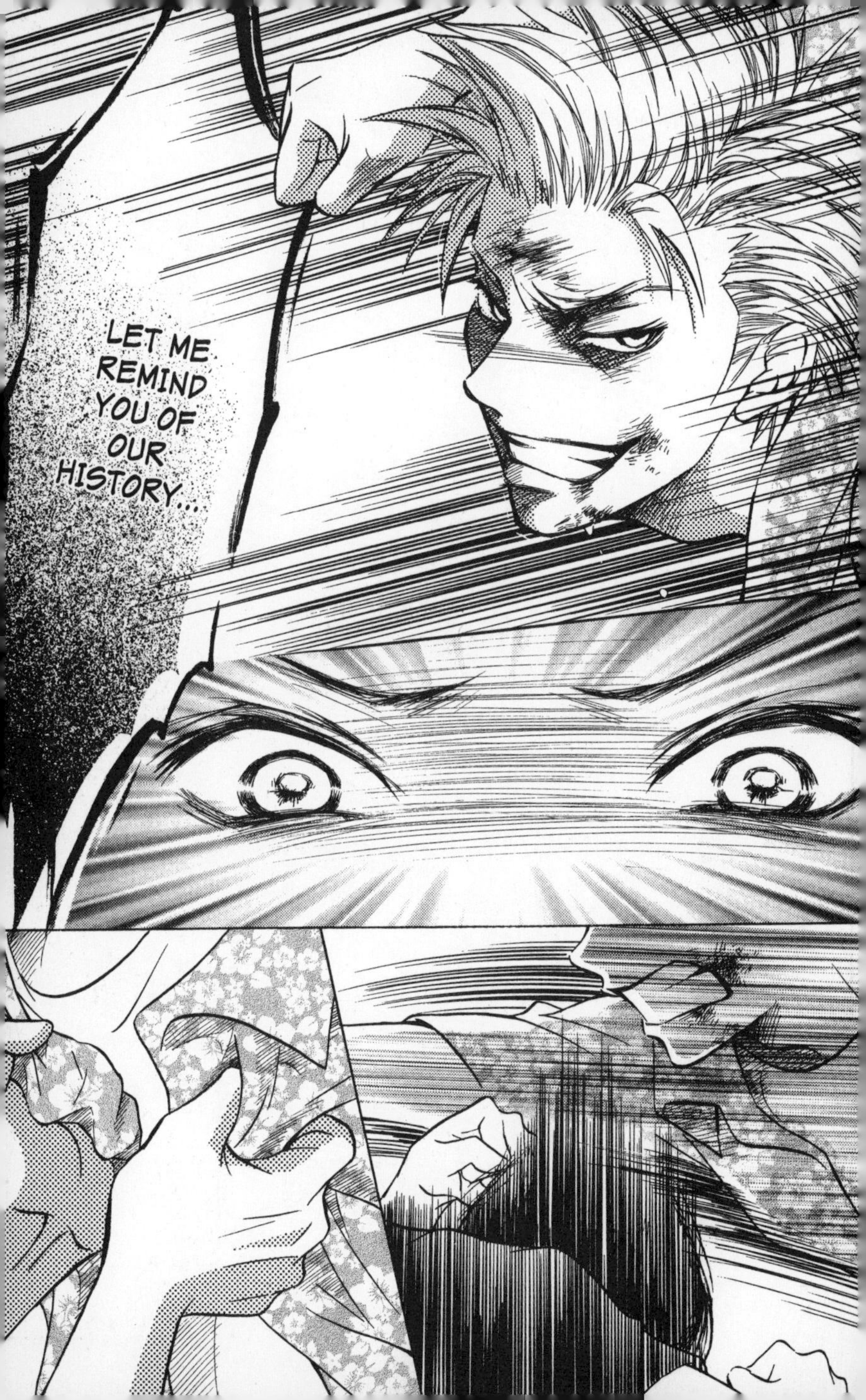
LET ME REMIND YOU OF OUR HISTORY...

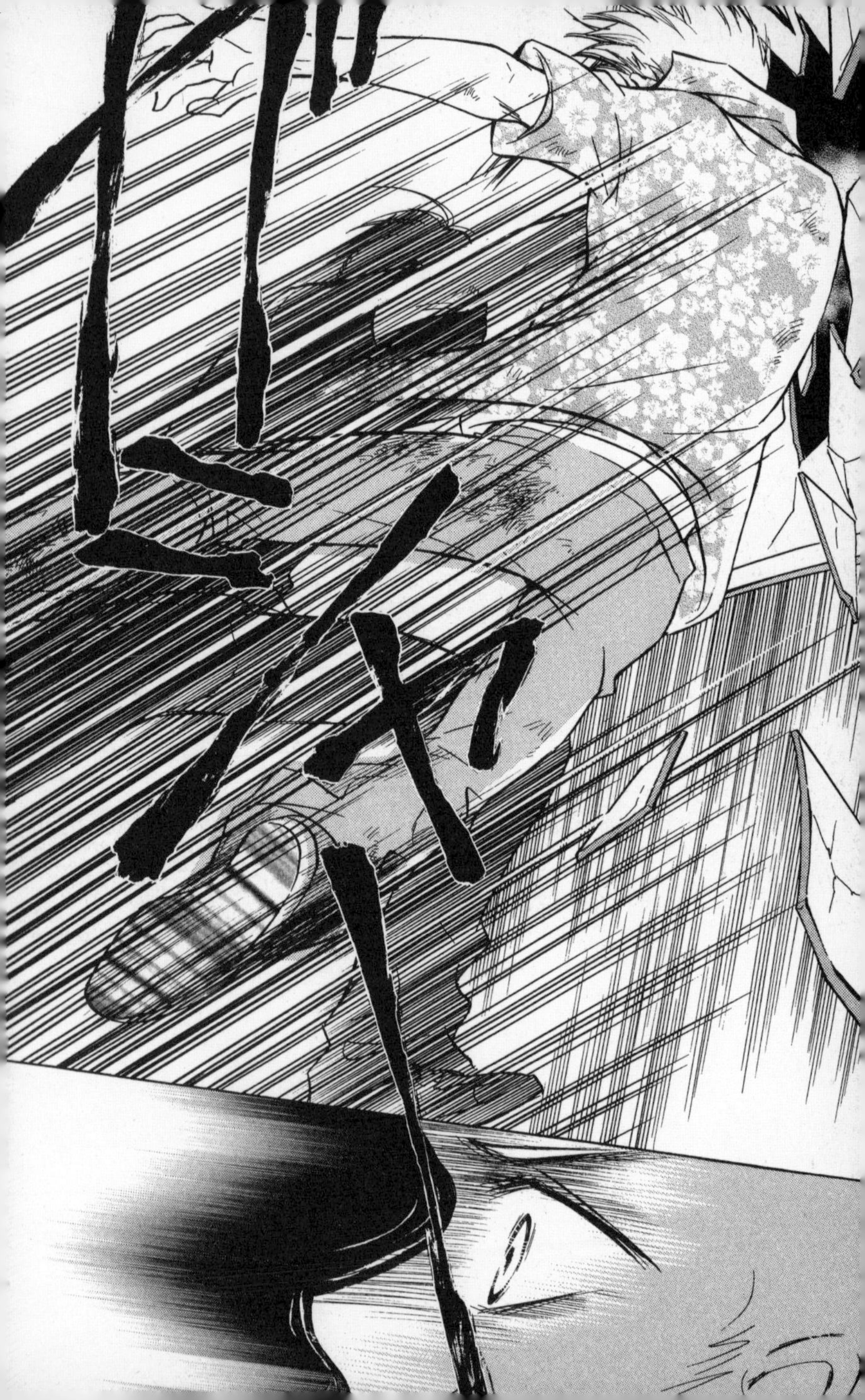

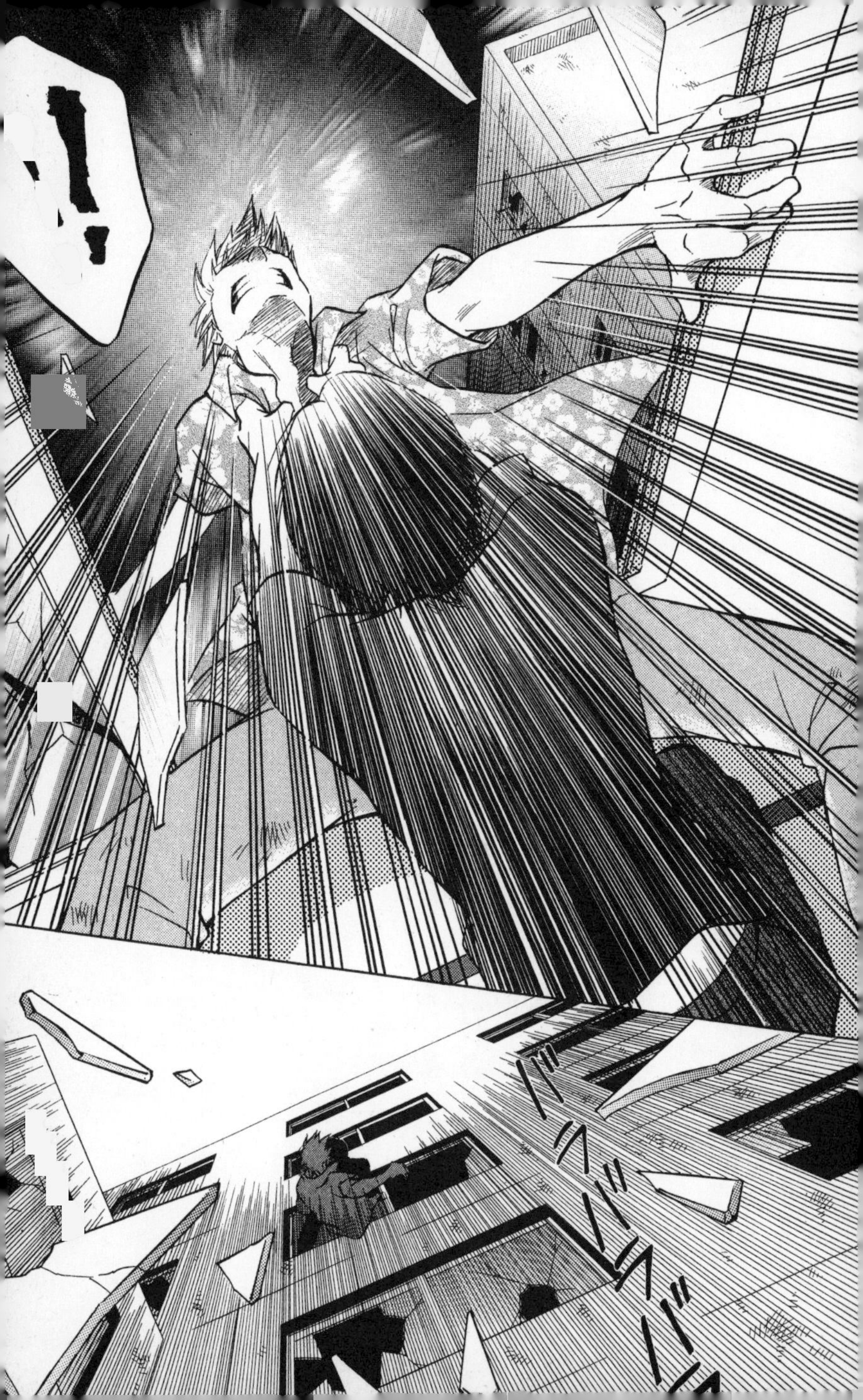
!

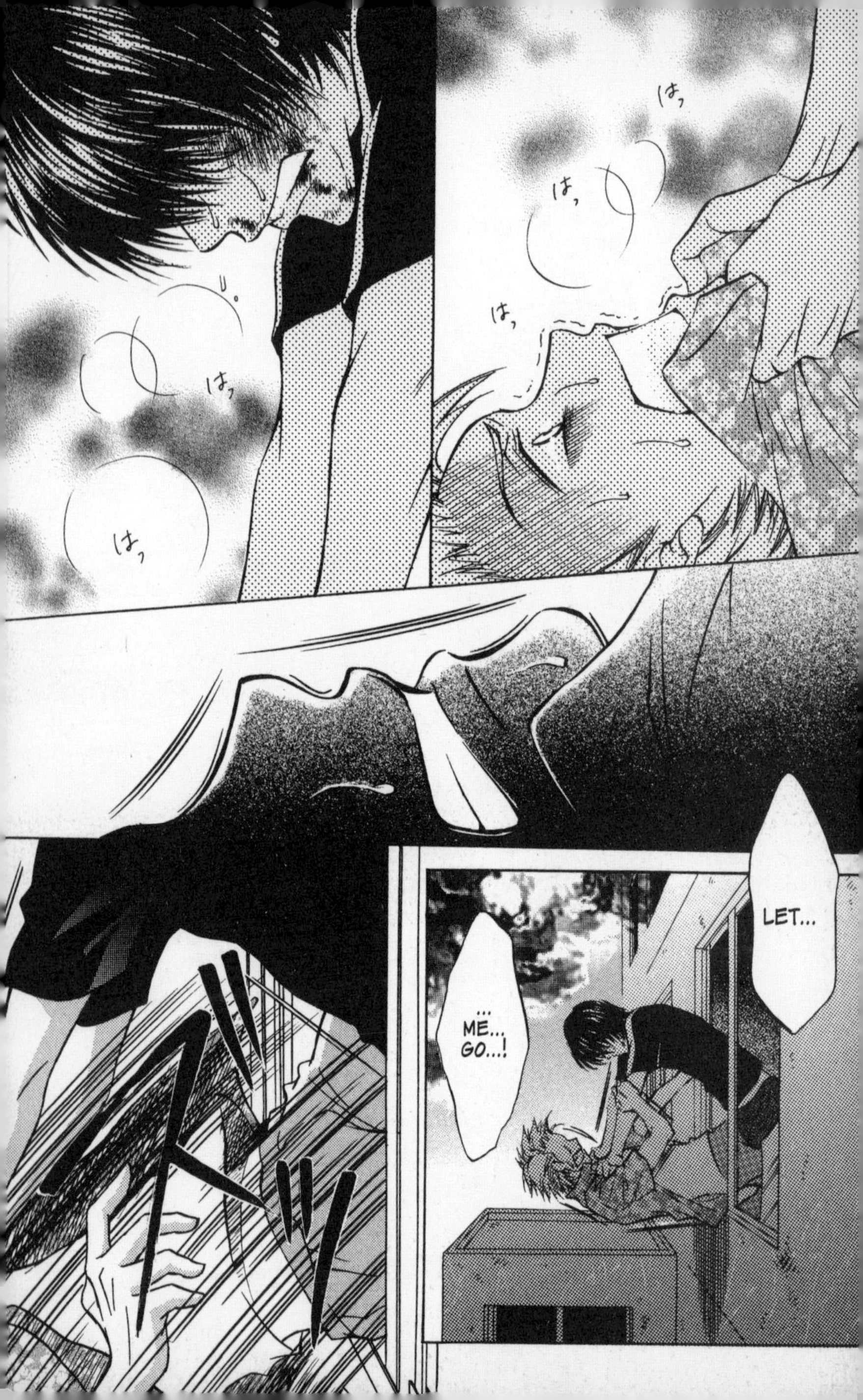
はっ
はっ
はっ
はっ
はっ
LET...
... ME... GO...!

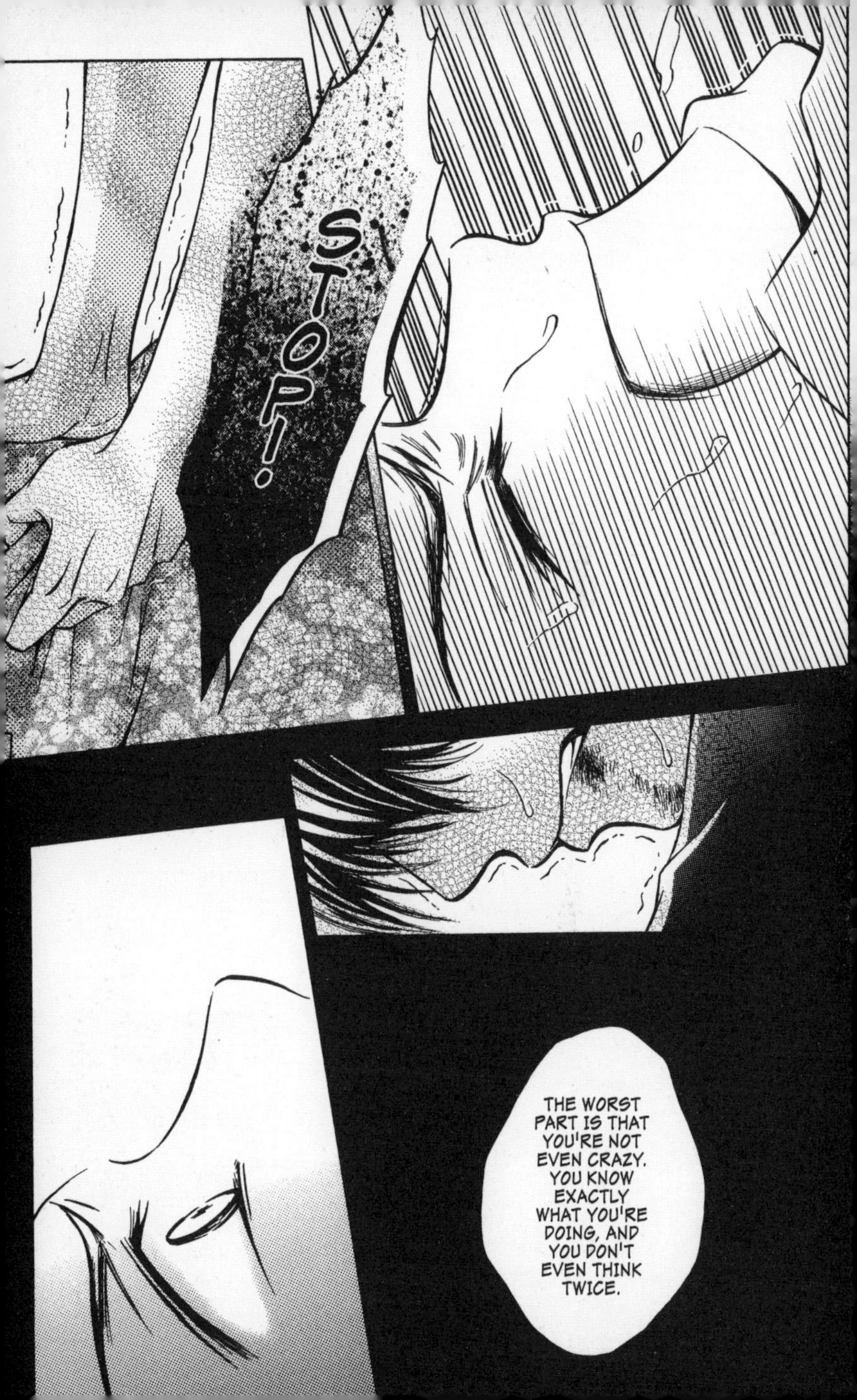
STOP!
THE WORST PART IS THAT YOU'RE NOT EVEN CRAZY. YOU KNOW EXACTLY WHAT YOU'RE DOING, AND YOU DON'T EVEN THINK TWICE.

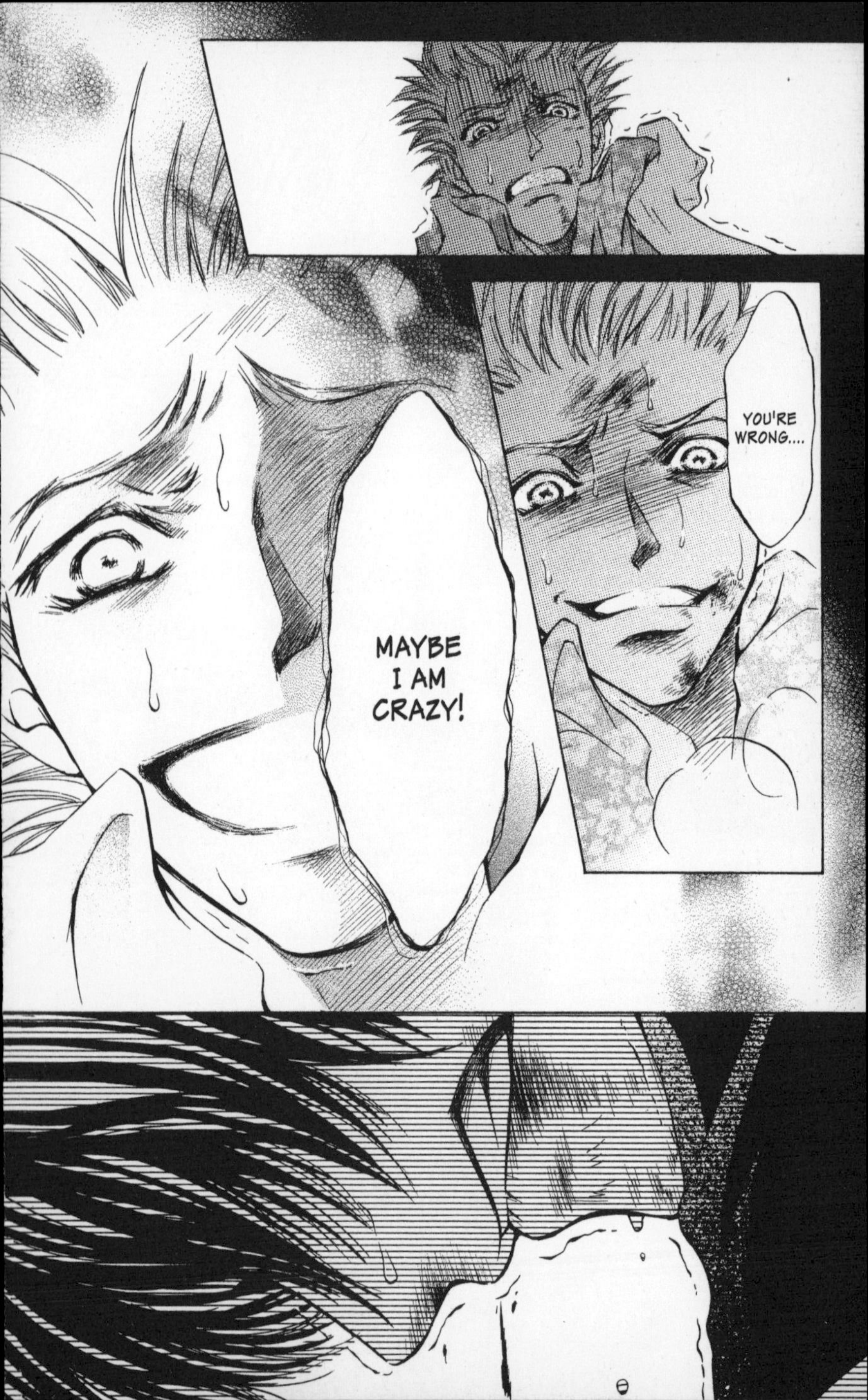
YOU'RE WRONG....
MAYBE I AM CRAZY!

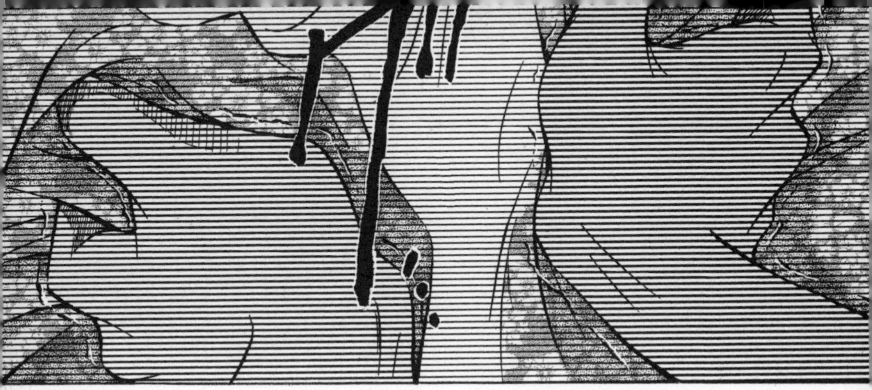
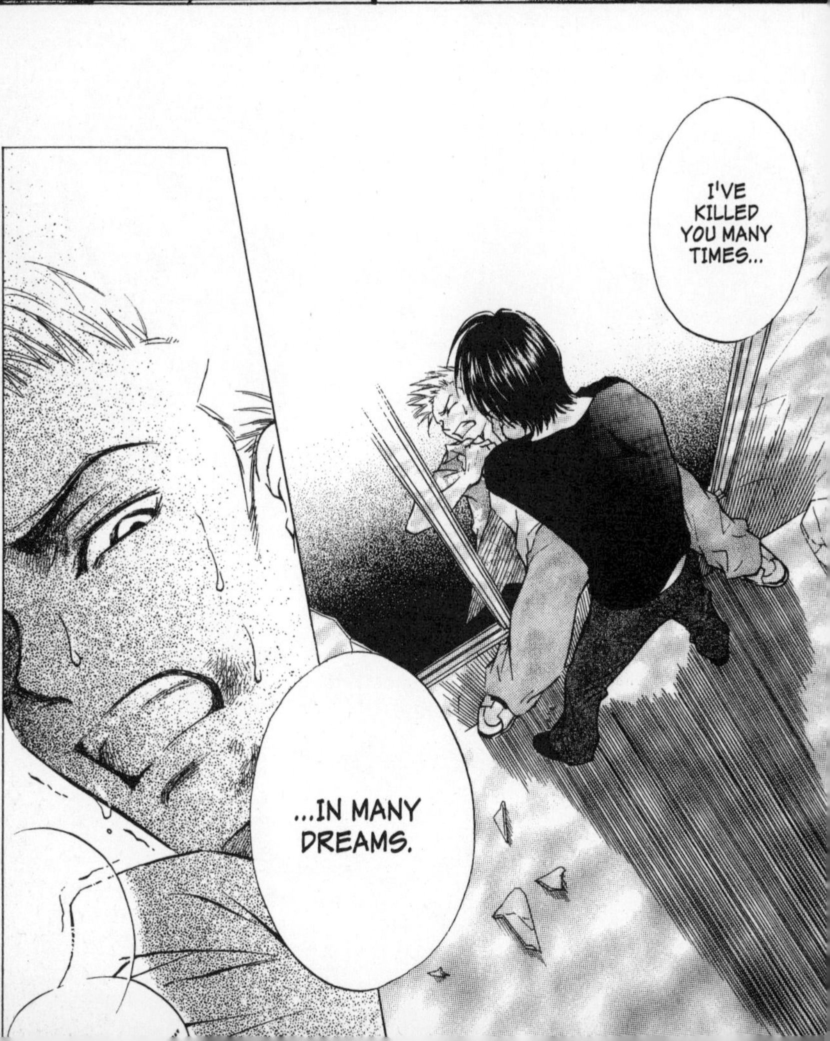
I'VE KILLED YOU MANY TIMES...
...IN MANY DREAMS.

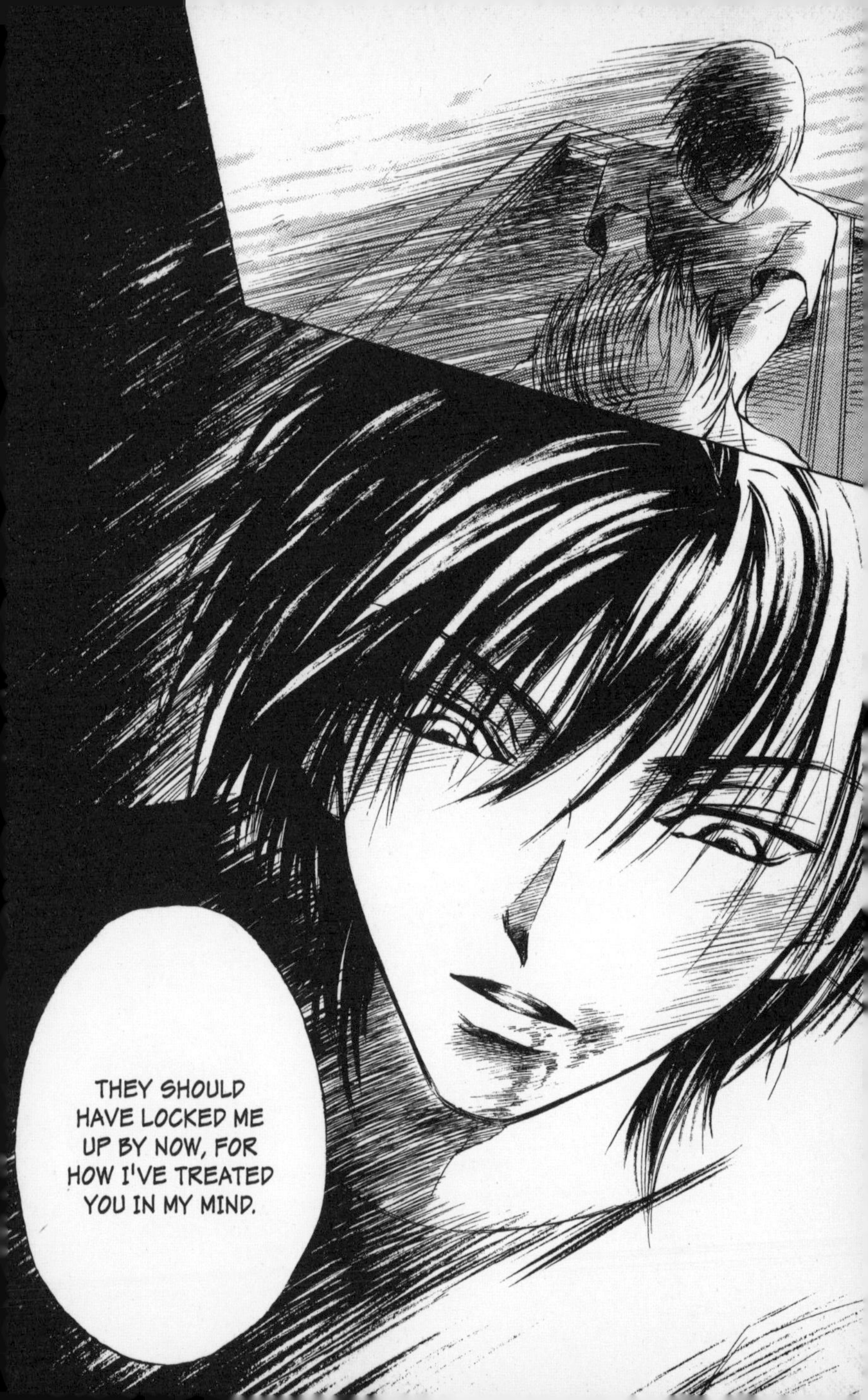
THEY SHOULD HAVE LOCKED ME UP BY NOW, FOR HOW I'VE TREATED YOU IN MY MIND.

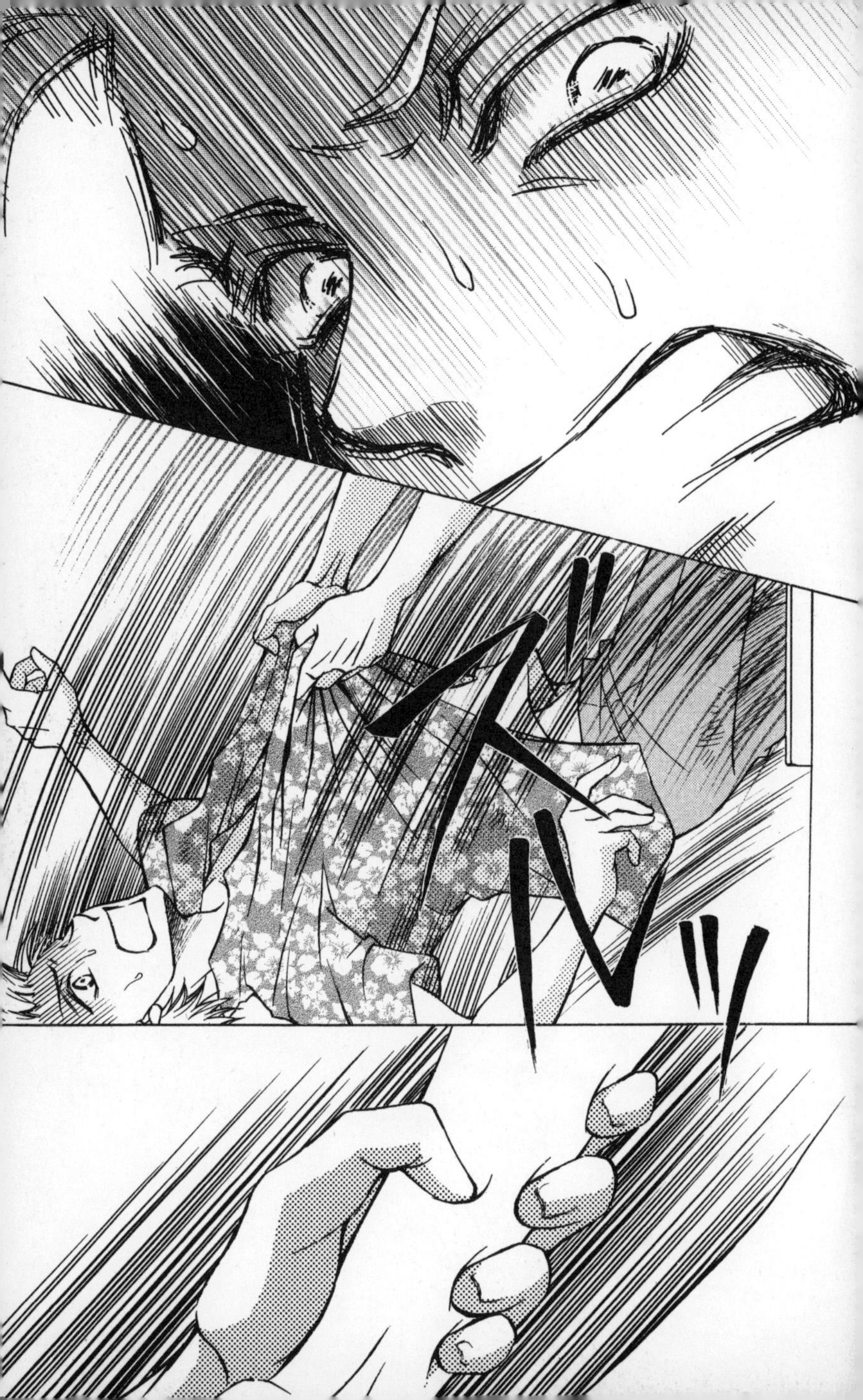
ズバッ

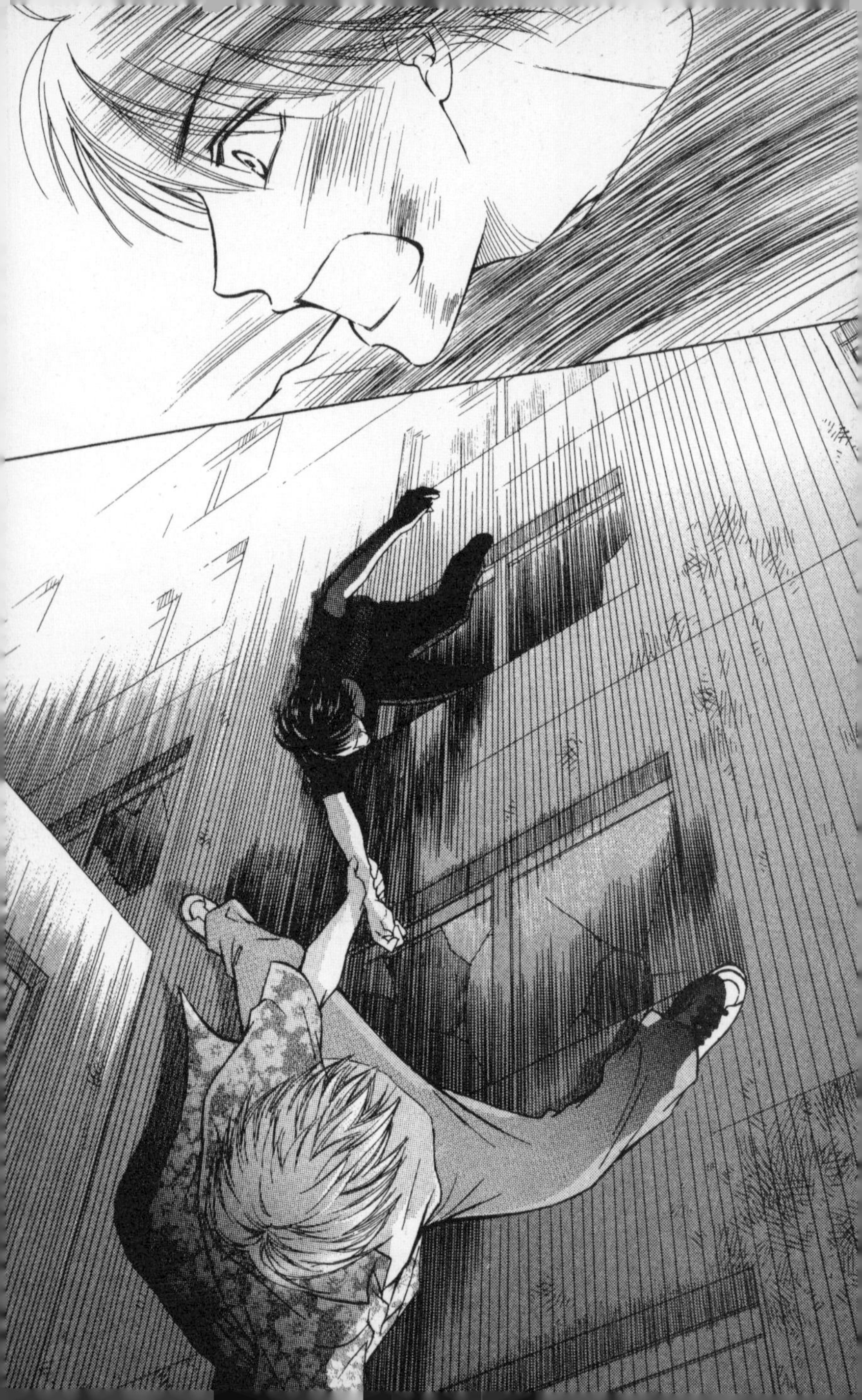

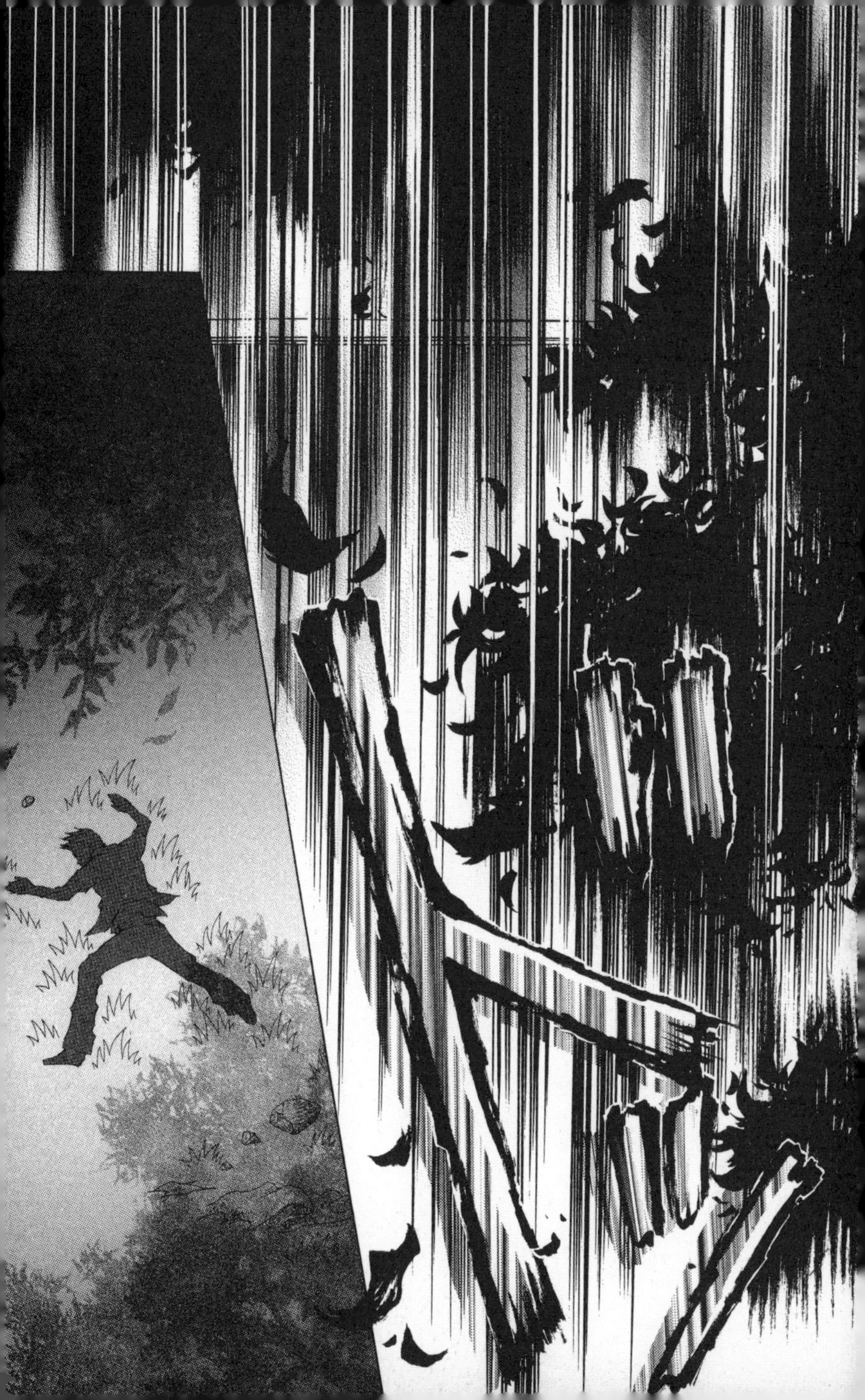

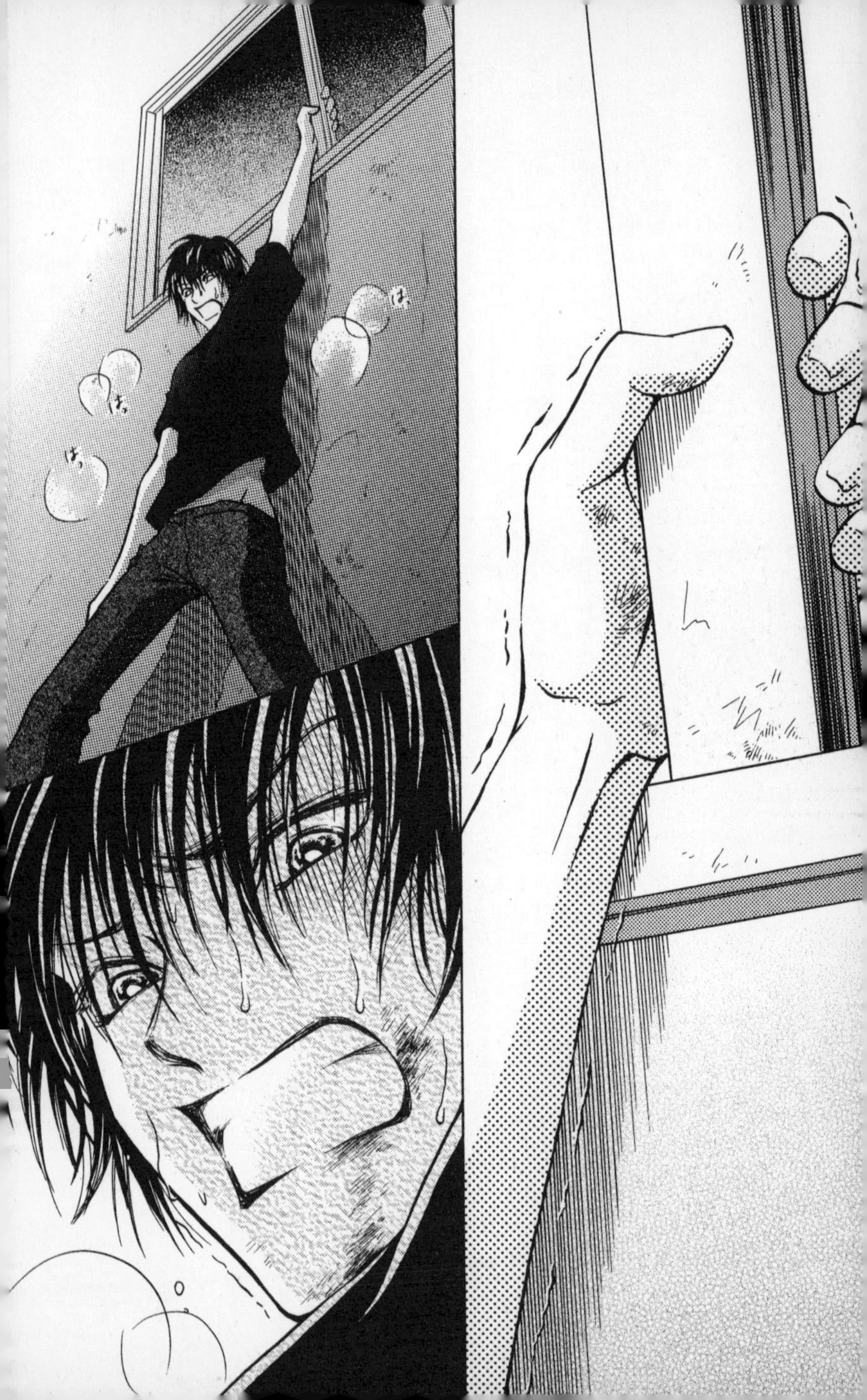
は
は
は

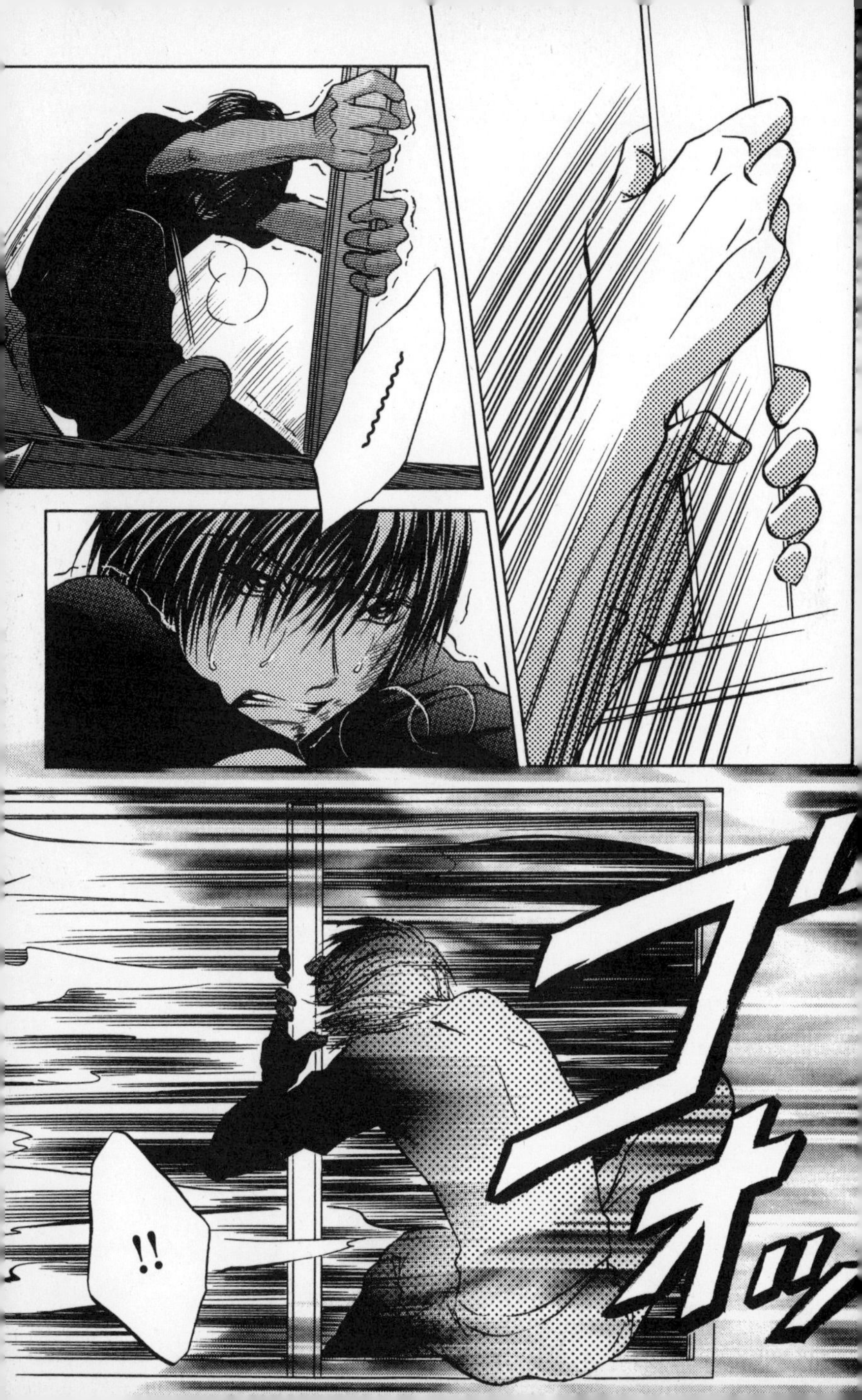
ブオッ
!!

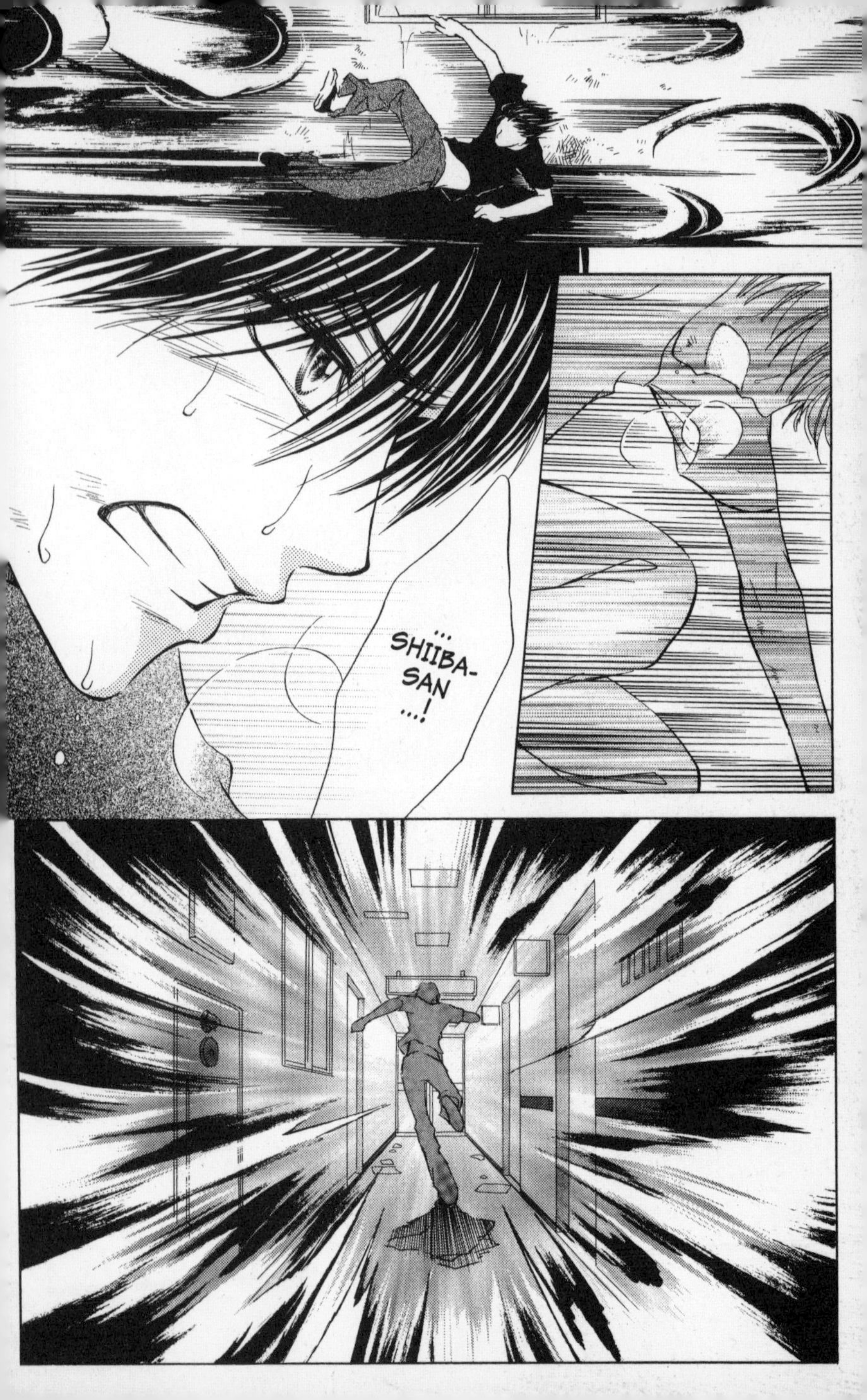
...SHIIBA-SAN ...!

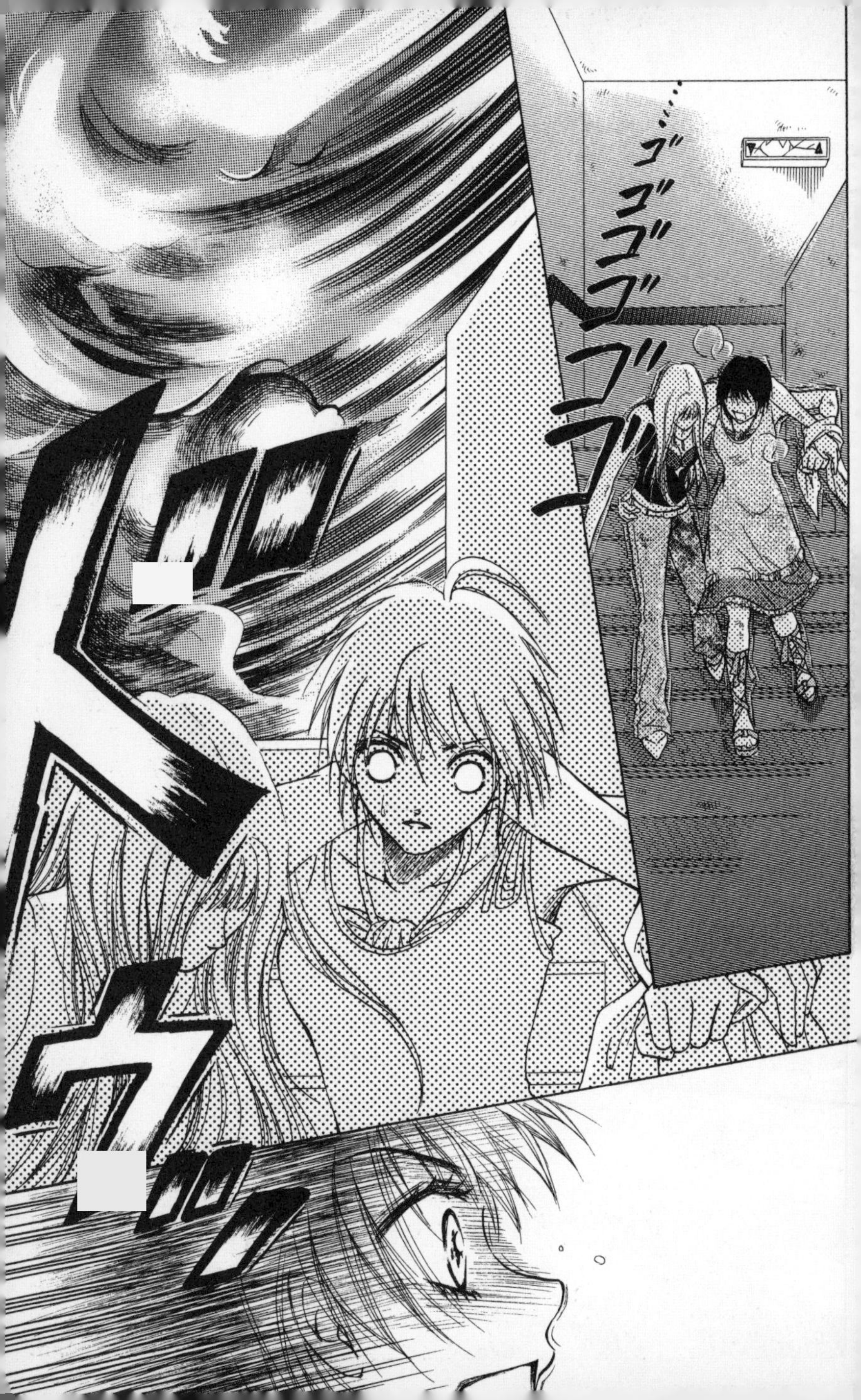
…ゴゴゴゴゴゴ

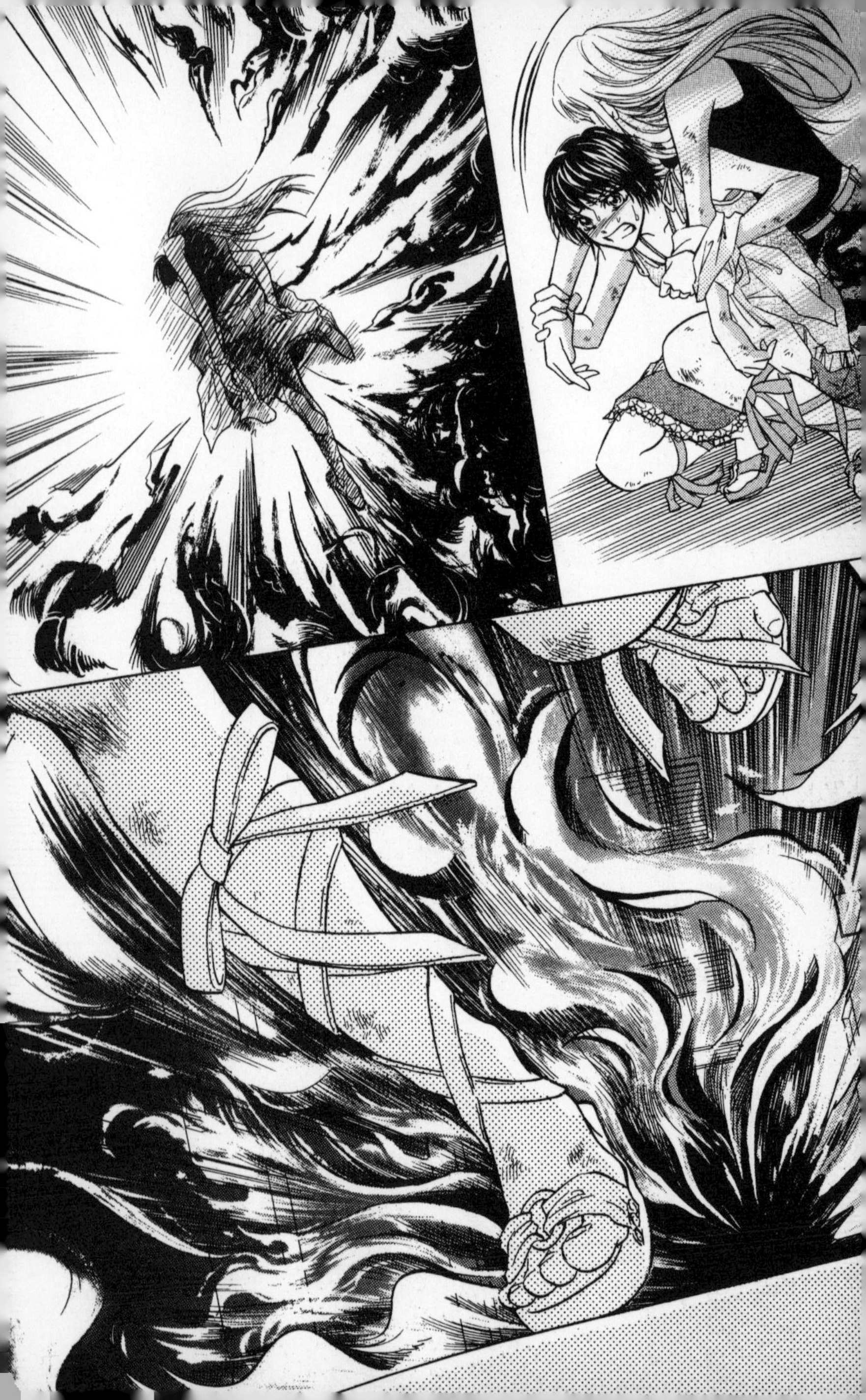

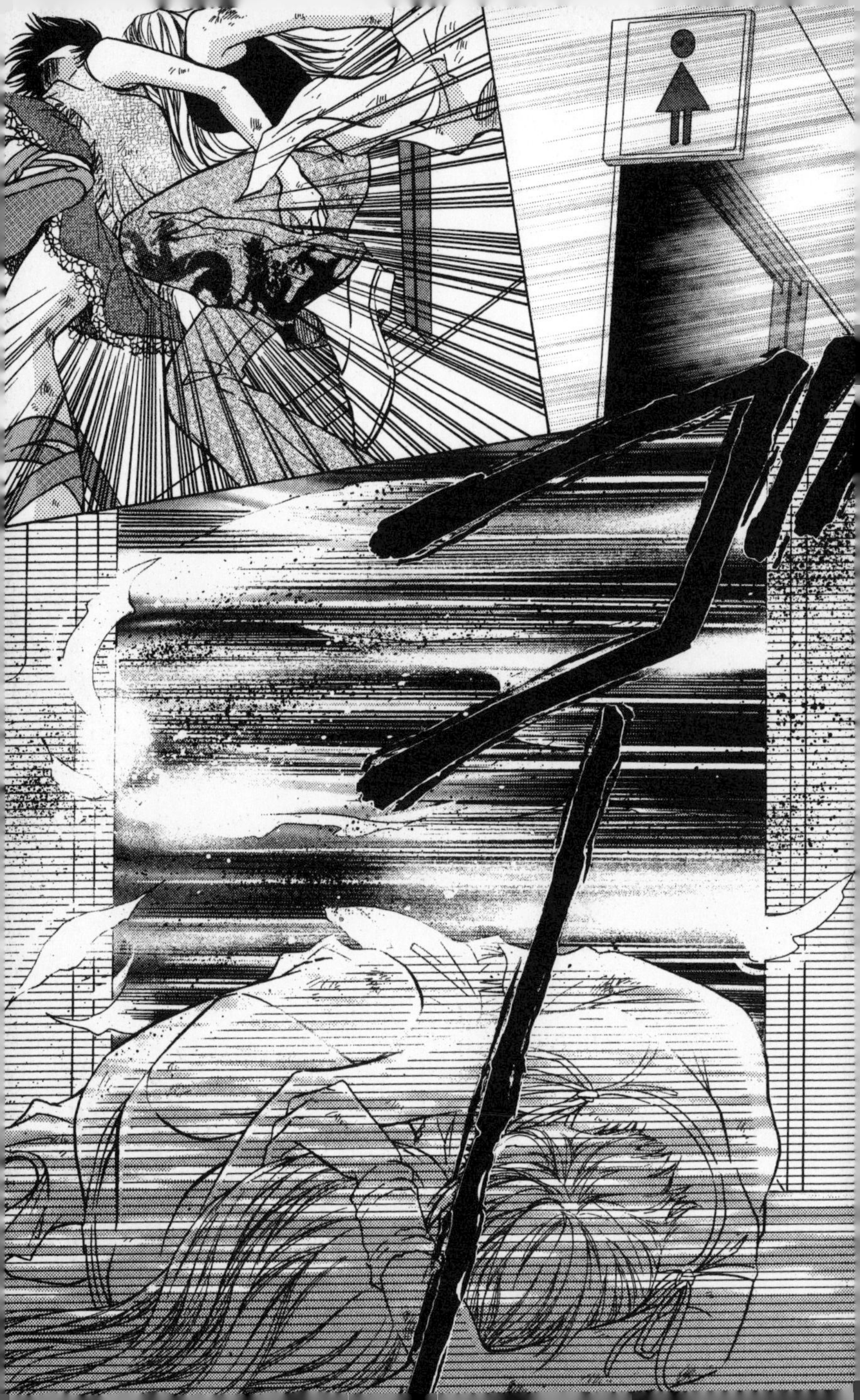

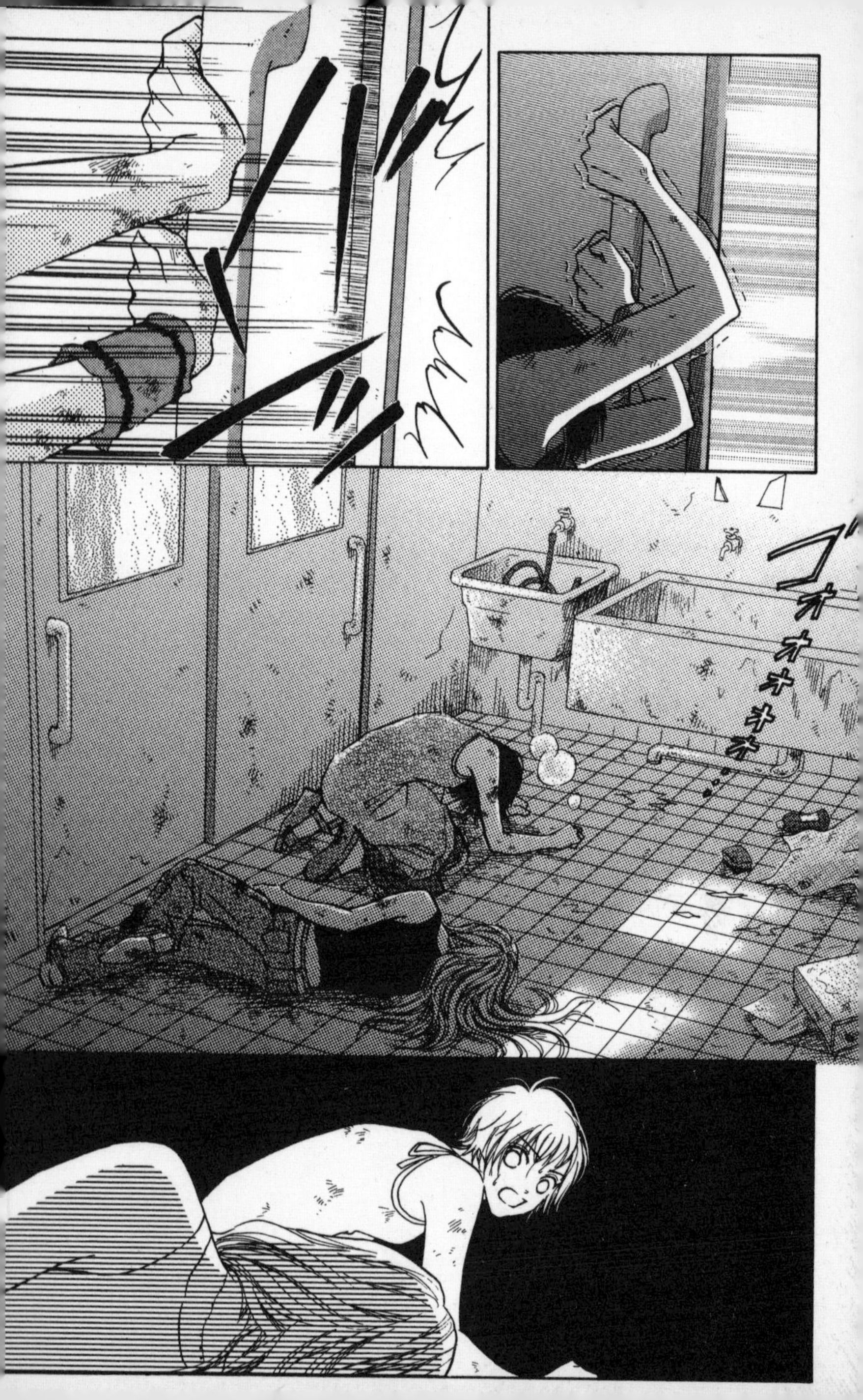
ゴォオオオオ…

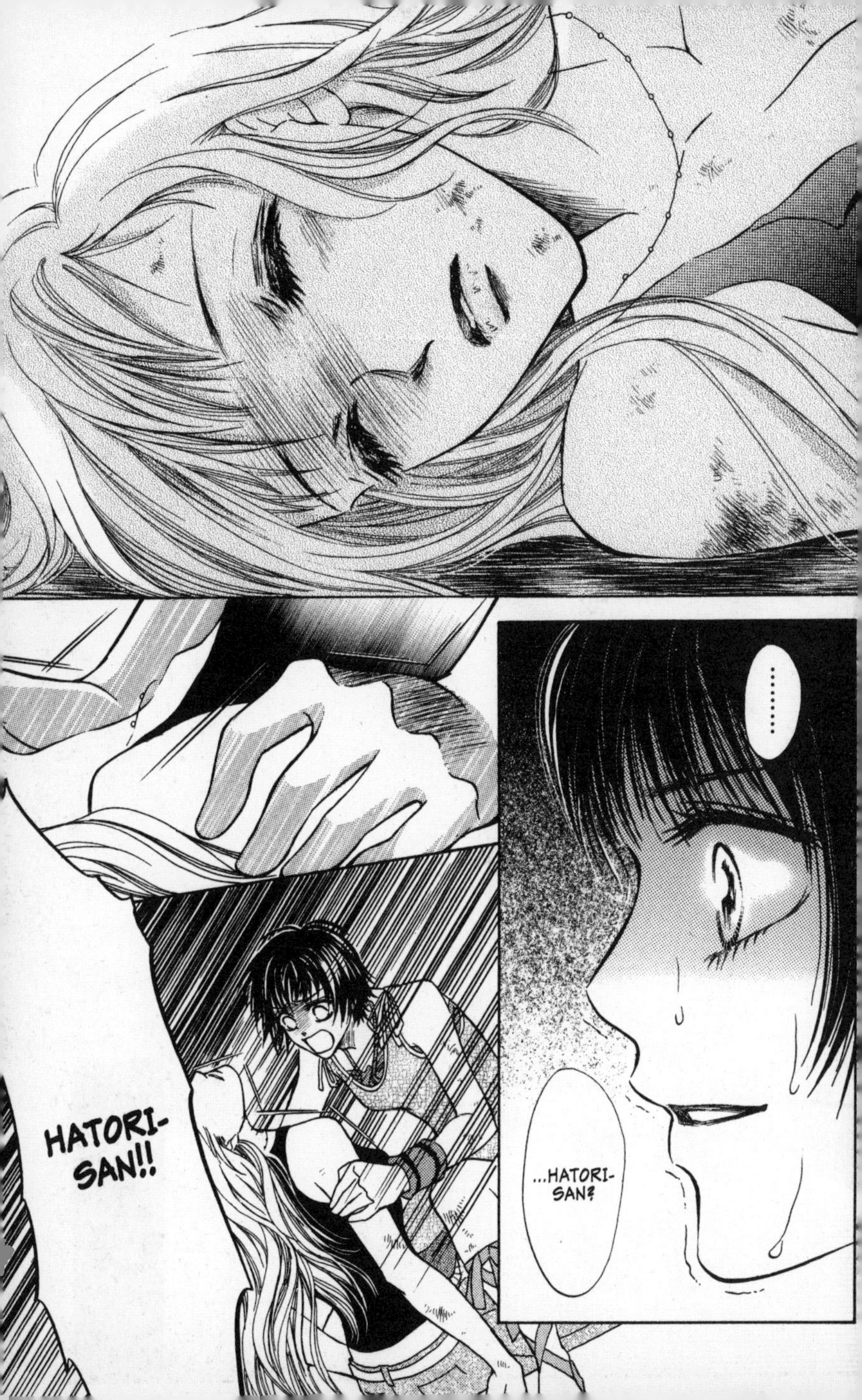
......
...HATORI-SAN?
HATORI-SAN!!

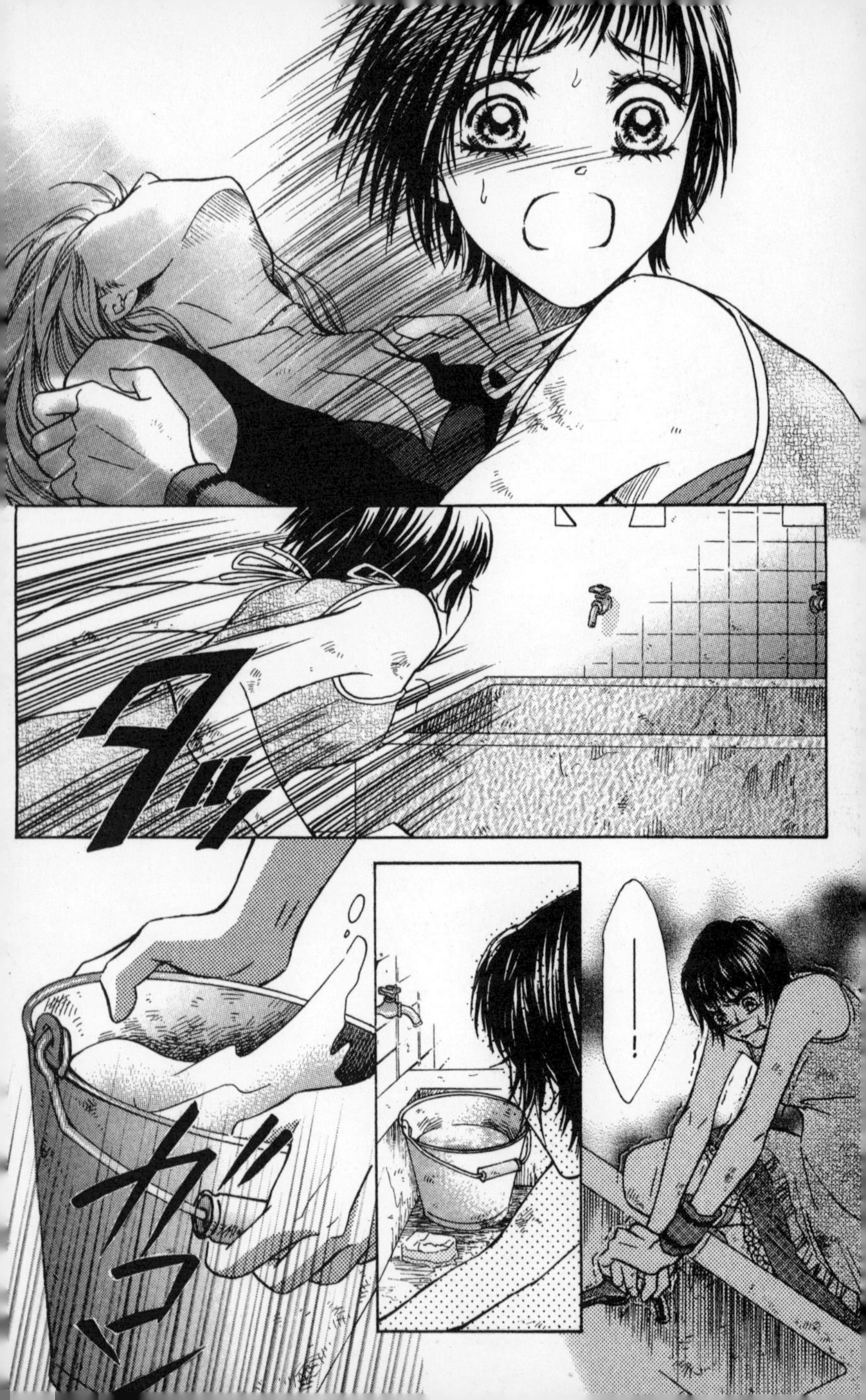
クッ
!
ガコン

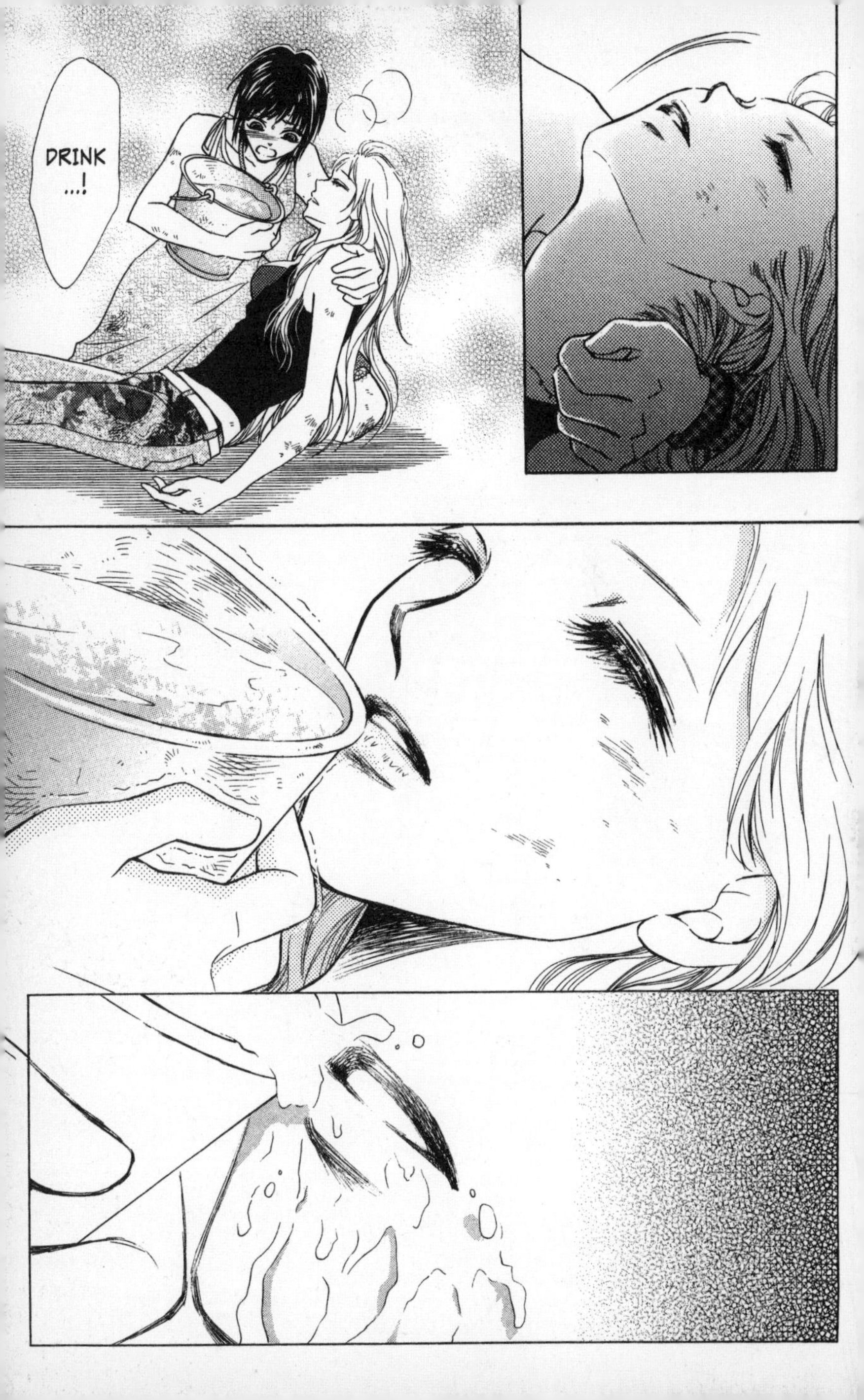
DRINK ...!

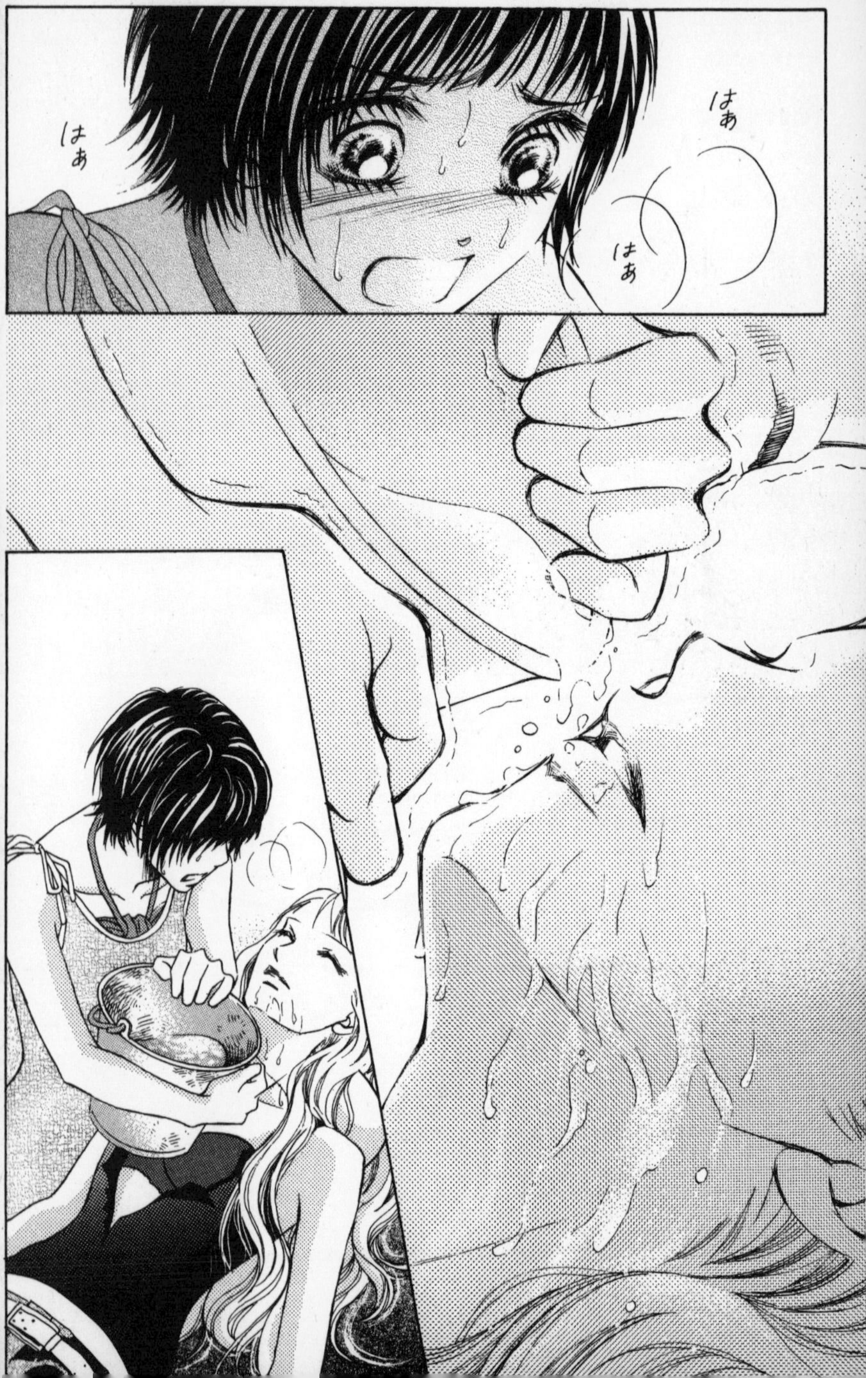
はぁ
はぁ
はぁ

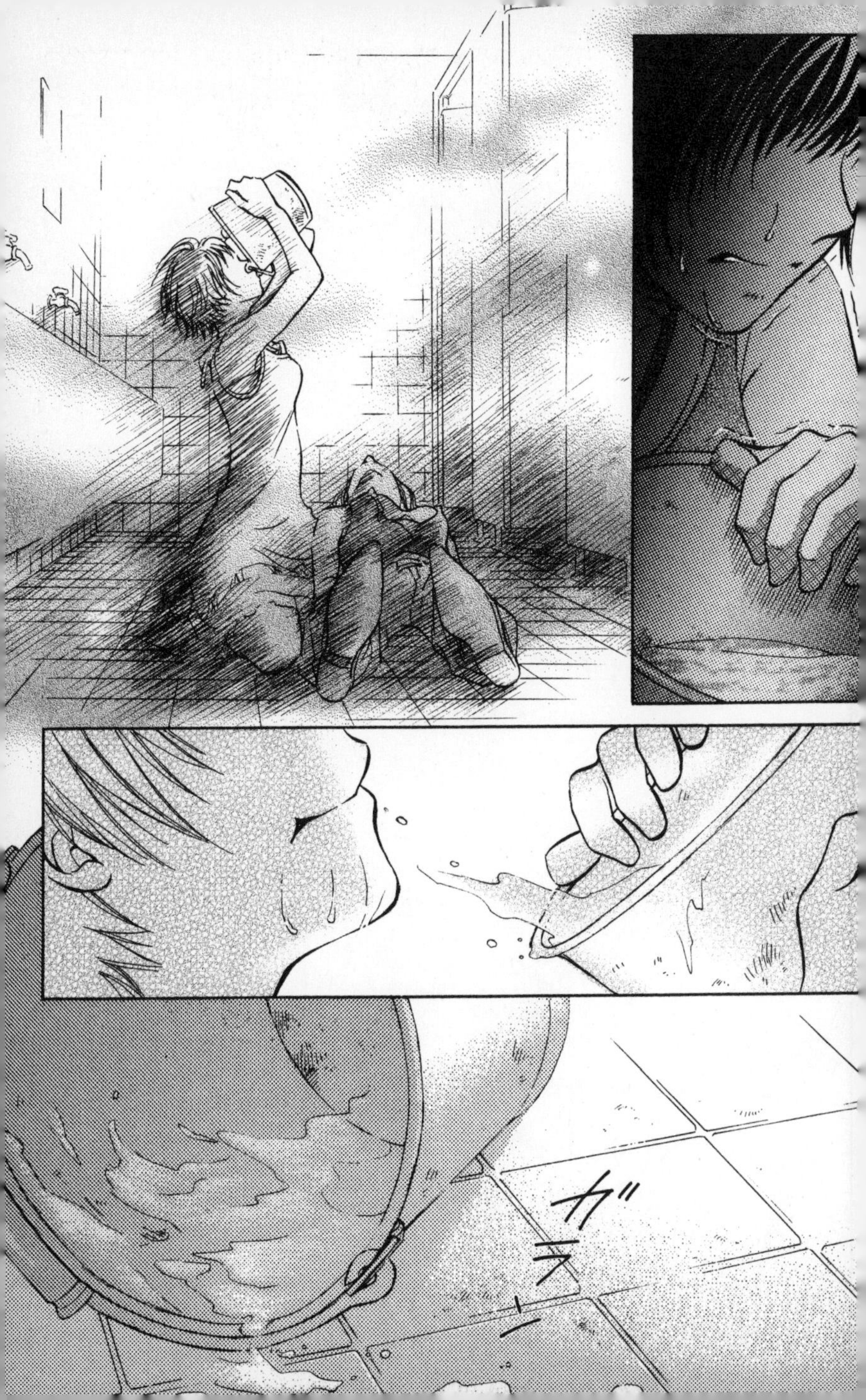
ガラン

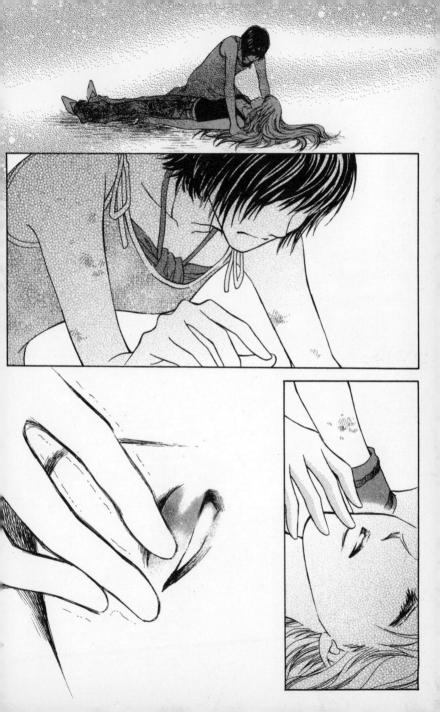

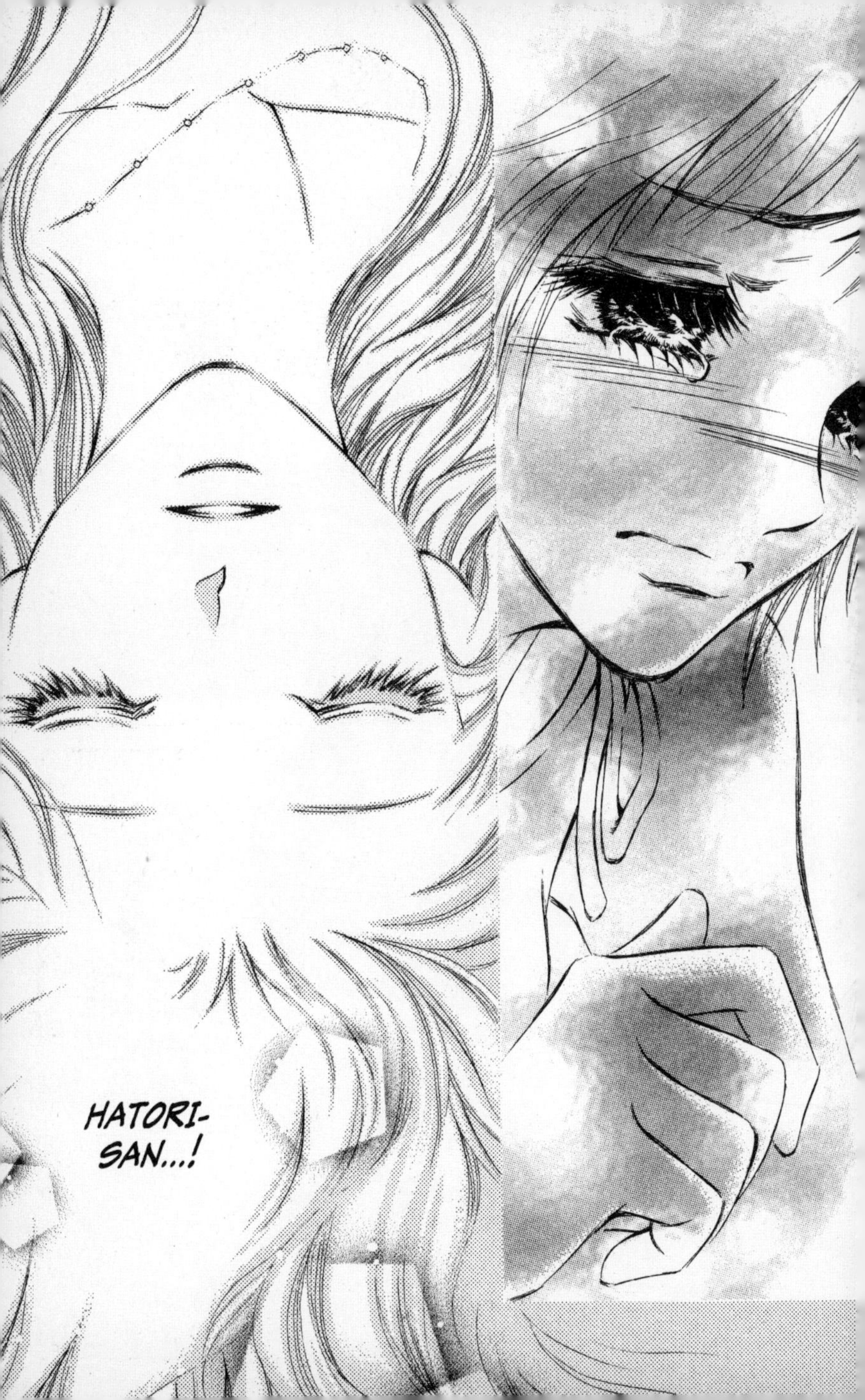
HATORI-SAN...!

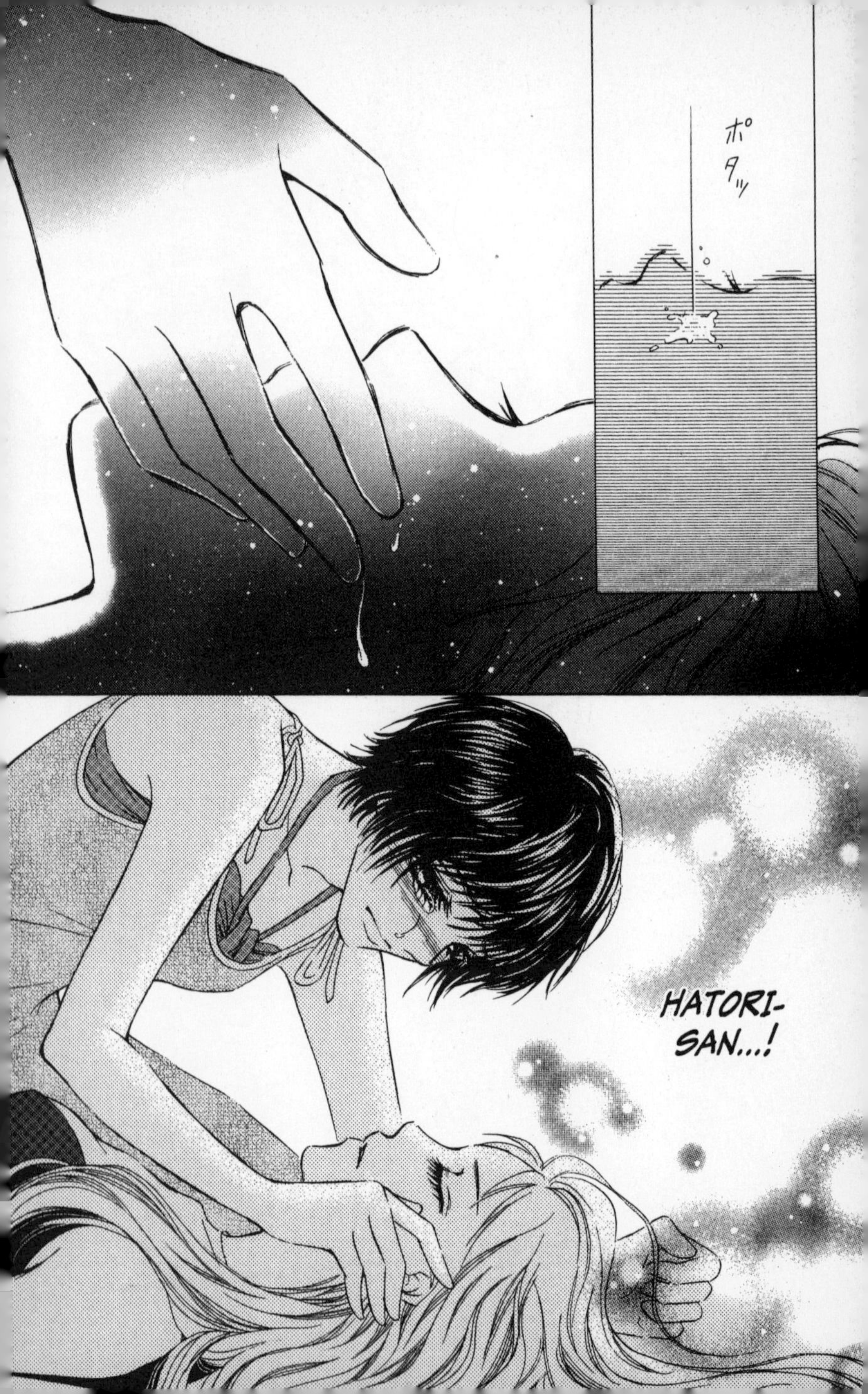
ポタッ
HATORI-
SAN...!

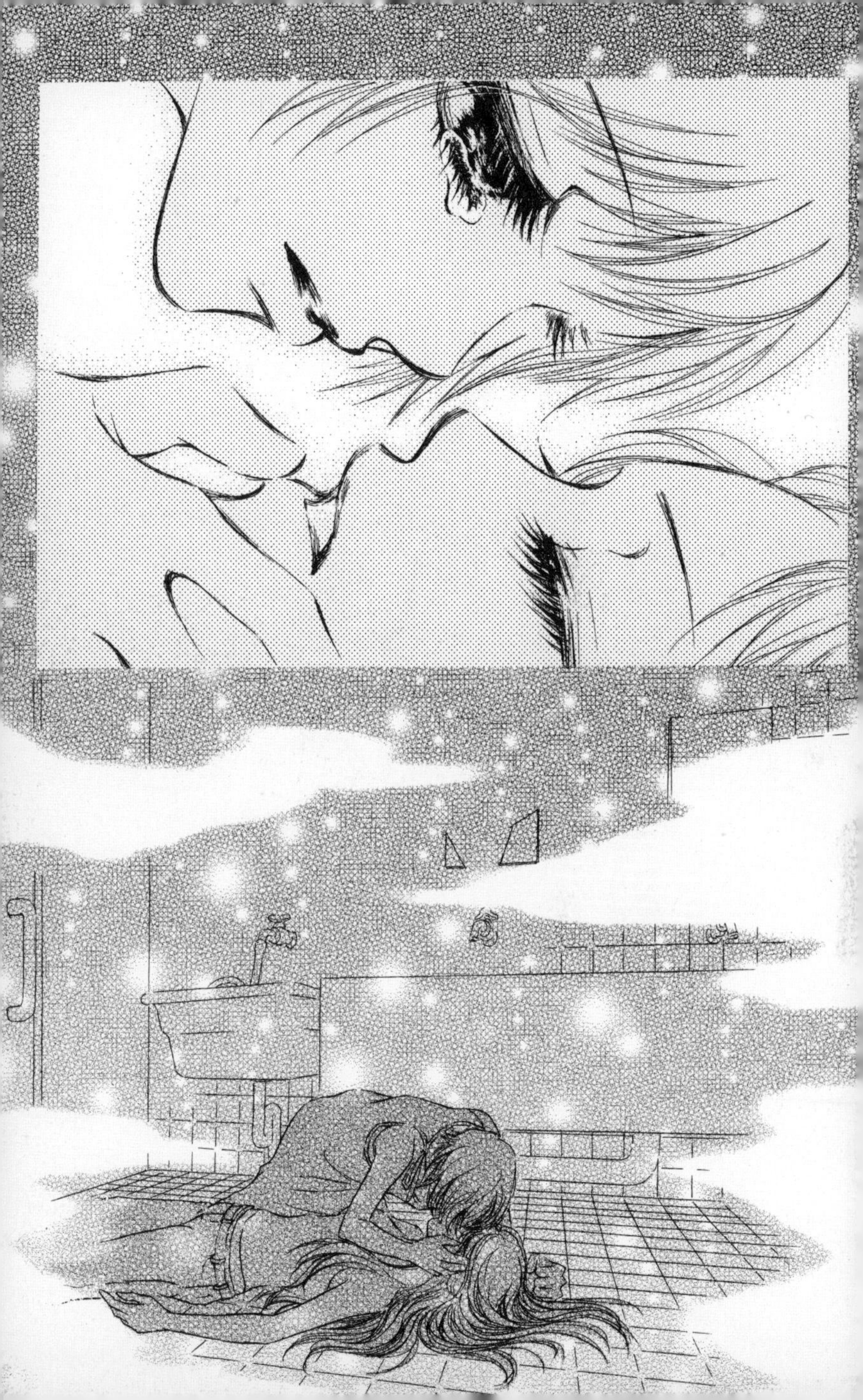

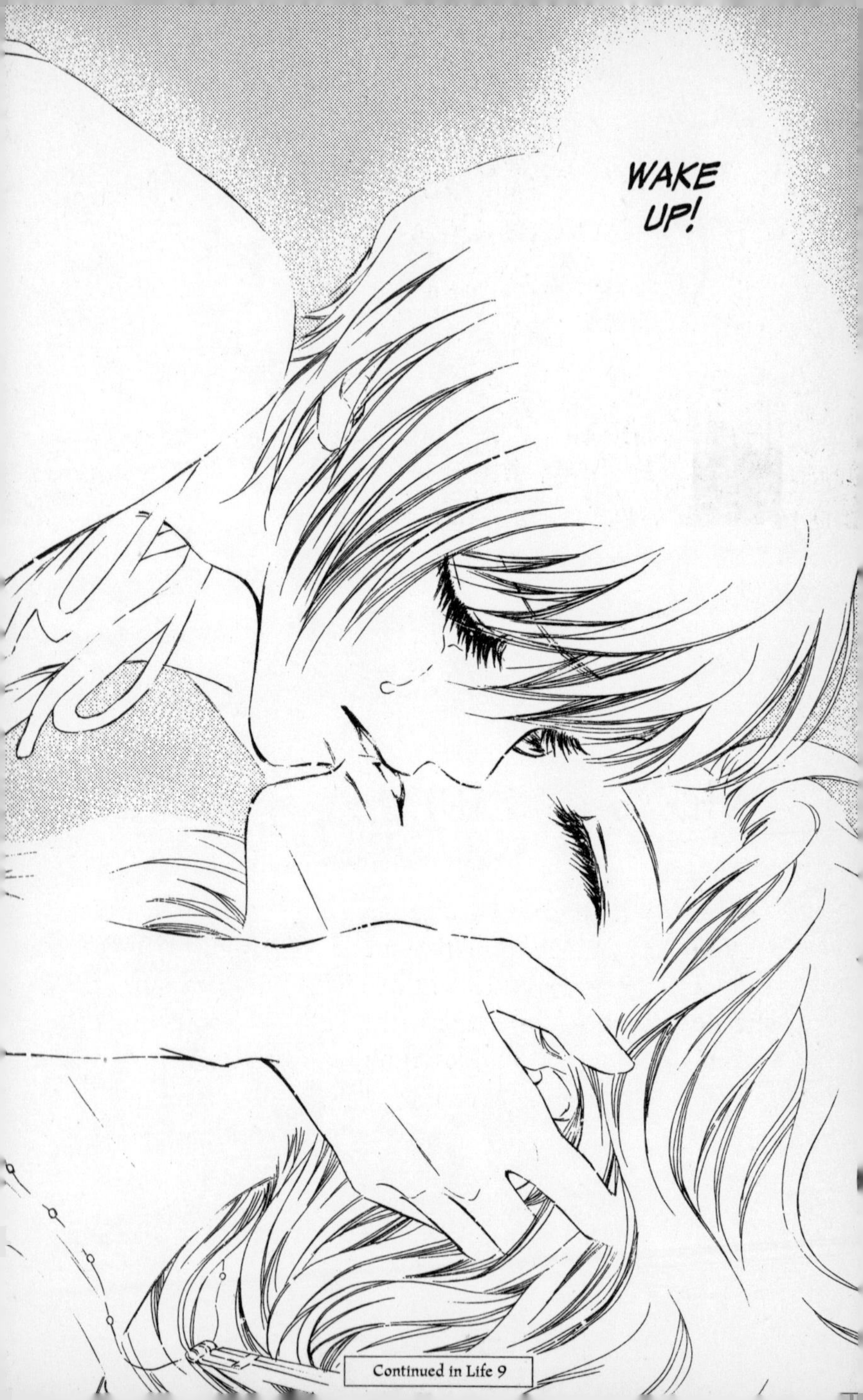
WAKE UP!

Continued in Life 9

What does LIFE have in store...

After the hospital incident, Ayumu has a little more sympathy at school, which makes things a lot more difficult for Manami to win everybody to her side. So she devises a scheme to cast herself once again as the victim...and she'll take down more than Ayumu with it.

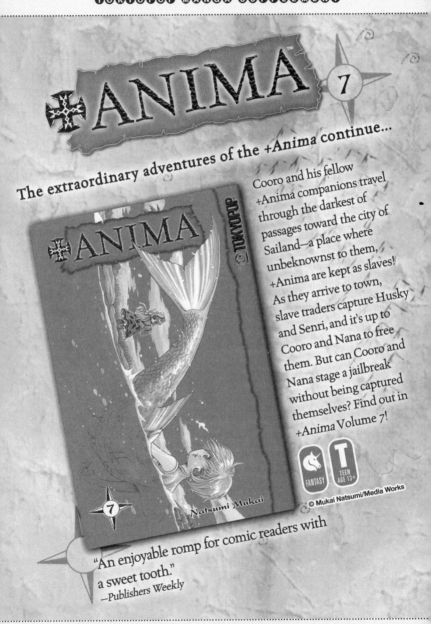

Fruits Basket

By Natsuki Takaya

Volume 19

Can Tohru free Kyo of his curse?

Tohru is conflicted as she realizes she might love Kyo more than she loves her mom. Then Shigure shows up to let her know that all the members of the Zodiac look down on Kyo. If she wants to save Kyo, she'll have to break his curse first!

Winner of the American Anime Award for Best Manga!

The #1 selling shojo manga in America!

ROMANCE

T
TEEN
AGE 13+

GAKUEN ALICE VOLUME TWO

Mikan is officially accepted into the mysterious Alice Academy, but things aren't exactly going smoothly...

Mikan is off to a rough start! Natsume still bullies her, her class ranking couldn't be lower, some of the teachers are outright hostile and she has been forbidden to contact anyone outside of the school. Will she be able to find others like her at the Academy, or will she be betrayed by the only people she still trusts?

The hit series from Japan CONTINUES!

FANTASY   T TEEN AGE 13+

© 2003 Tachibana Higuchi / HAKUSENSHA, Inc.

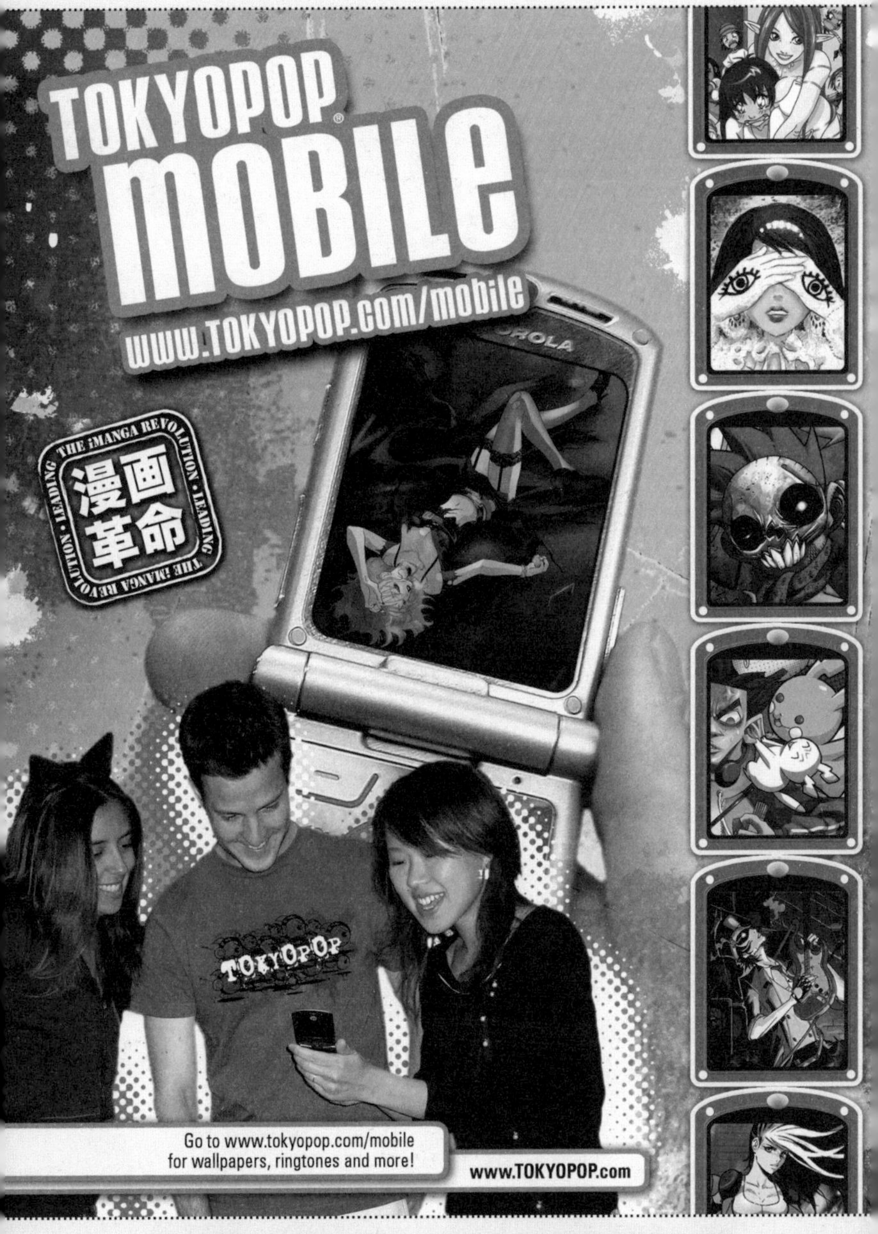
TOKYOPOP®
MOBILE
www.TOKYOPOP.com/mobile
THE iMANGA REVOLUTION • LEADING THE iMANGA REVOLUTION • LEADING
漫画
革命
TOKYOPOP
Go to www.tokyopop.com/mobile
for wallpapers, ringtones and more!
www.TOKYOPOP.com

STOP!

This is the back of the book.
You wouldn't want to spoil a great ending!

This book is printed "manga-style," in the authentic Japanese right-to-left format. Since none of the artwork has been flipped or altered, readers get to experience the story just as the creator intended. You've been asking for it, so TOKYOPOP® delivered: authentic, hot-off-the-press, and far more fun!

DIRECTIONS

If this is your first time reading manga-style, here's a quick guide to help you understand how it works.

It's easy... just start in the top right panel and follow the numbers. Have fun, and look for more 100% authentic manga from TOKYOPOP®!